BIG ITALY

ALSO BY TIMOTHY WILLIAMS

The Inspector Piero Trotti Novels
Converging Parallels
The Puppeteer
Persona Non Grata
Black August

The Anne Marie Laveaud Novels
Another Sun
The Honest Folk of Guadeloupe

BIG ITALY
TIMOTHY WILLIAMS

SOHO
CRIME

Published by
Soho Press, Inc.
853 Broadway
New York, NY 10003

Library of Congress Cataloging-in-Publication Data

Williams, Timothy.
Big Italy / Timothy Williams.

ISBN 978-1-61695-578-6
eISBN 978-1-61695-579-3
1. Police—Italy—Fiction. 2. Murder—Investigation—Fiction.
I. Title.
PR6073.I43295B54 2015
823'.914—dc23

Interior design by Janine Agro, Soho Press, Inc.

Printed in the United States of America

10 9 8 7 6 5 4 3 2 1

BIG ITALY

Glossary

ANTISOFISTICAZIONE: Nucleo Antisofisticazione, Italy's health and safety department

ARMA: Arma dei Carabinieri, a military corps with police duties

AVVOCATO: lawyer

BUONA SERA: good evening

CAMORRA: a Neapolitan criminal organization

CARABINIERI: Italian national police force

CASA CIRCONDARIALE DI CUSTODIA PREVENTIVA: remand prison

CASA DI RECLUSIONE: prison

CASERMA: station

CASSA DEL MEZZOGIORNO: a government-funded endeavor to stimulate economic growth in Southern Italy

CELERE: riot police

CHI L'HA VISTO: a television program dedicated to missing persons and unsolved mysteries

CHINO: Elisir di China, a hot drink

DEMOCRAZIA CRISTIANA: a Christian democratic political party, the successor to the Italian People's Party

DESTRA NAZIONALE: an Italian right-wing political party

DIRETTRICE: director (f.)

DONNAIOLO: womanizer

DOPOLAVORO: after-work recreational club

ESCHIMESE: a hooded anorak popular among left-wingers in 1970s Italy

FESTA PADRONALE: annual festival of saints

FIGLIO DELLA LUPA: the youngest sector of the Fascist party youth group (ages 6-8)

FOTOROMANZO: comic book

LA GIOCONDA: the *Mona Lisa*

I PROMESSI SPOSI: an Italian historical novel by Alessandro Manzoni, published in the 1820s

IN BOCCA CHIUSA NON ENTRÒ MAI MOSCA: a proverb directly translating to, "A fly never entered a closed mouth," implying that silence is often best

INGEGNERE: engineer

LANGHE: a hilly region in Piedmont

LASCIA O RADDOPPIA: an Italian game show, translating to *Leave It or Double It*, that aired from 1955–1959

LEGA: alliance/union, often short for Lega Nord, a regionalist party centered around the Po

LEGA LOMBARDA: a regionalist political party in Lombardy

LEGHISTI: belonging to a *lega* (see two above), especially Lega Nord

LOTTA CONTINUA: a non-terrorist extreme leftist group

LOTTIZZAZIONE: government-mandated allotment of funds

MANI PULITE: a national judicial investigation into Italian political corruption in the early 1990s

MATURITÀ: high school diploma

MEZZOGIORNO: Southern Italy

MINESTRA: soup; the same old stuff (idiom)

MINISTERO DELL' INTERNO: Department of Internal Affairs

MINISTERO DELLA GIUSTIZIA: Justice Department

'NDRANGHETA: an Italian criminal organization based in Calabria

OSPEDALE: hospital

OSTETRICA: maternity ward

PALAZZO DI GIUSTIZIA: courthouse

PARTITOCRAZIA: the hijacking of institutions by the party system

PENETRAZIONE MAFIOSA: pervasive mafia thinking

PIANO REGOLATORE: city planning

PIZZAIOLO: pizza chef

POLICLINICO: hospital

POLIZIA DI STATO: national police force

POLIZIA STRADALE: highway patrol

PROCURATORE: prosecutor

PRONTUARIO: short for *Prontuario farmaceutico*, or the Physicians' Drug Index

PSICHIATRIA: psychiatric ward

PUBBLICA SICUREZZA: Italian police force

PUBBLICO MINISTERO: public prosecutor

QUESTORE: chief inspector

QUESTURA: police headquarters

REPARTO OMICIDI: homicide division

REPUBBLICHINO: Republican

REPARTO RIANIMAZIONE: intensive care unit

SANGUE DI GIUDA: a sparkling red Italian wine

SANITÀ: health

SACRA CORONA UNITÀ: a criminal organization from the Puglia region in Southern Italy

SCUOLA MEDIA: middle school

SEZIONE FEMMINILE: women's branch

SEZIONE VIOLENZA INFANTILE: child abuse division

SEZIONE VIOLENZA SESSUALE: sexual assault division

SOCIOLOGIA: sociology

SOSTITUTO PROCURATORE: deputy prosecutor

STAZIONE CENTRALE: central station

TANGENTOPOLI: the network of corruption revealed by Mani Pulite, deriving from the Italian term *tangente*, which means "kickback"

TANGENZIALE: an expressway common to urban areas that allows vehicles to circumvent city traffic

TENENTE: lieutenant

TERZA MEDIA: the eighth grade

TORRE CIVICA: a tower equipped with bells (not to be confused with a bell tower, which has religious implications) that became symbolic of economic and military power in European cities

VU COMPRÀ: a term for immigrant street vendors, directly translating to, "Do you want to buy?" in a Neapolitan dialect

1: Clean Hands

Monday, 29 November 1993

SIGNORA SCOLA HAD left a message asking him to ring her, but an Elisir di China was what Trotti most needed now.

There had been a time when Trotti used to stay in the Questura working until all hours of the night. In those days, Agnese and Pioppi frequently dined without him and he would creep, tired and hungry, into a sleeping house. When Pioppi was a student at the liceo, months could go by without his ever seeing his daughter.

Now Commissario Piero Trotti rarely got home late.

In the last few years he had imposed a routine upon himself. He normally returned to the empty house in via Milano before eight o'clock.

A china before supper, he told himself, and then the walk home to burn off the extra calories. He knew he was putting on weight, but during the winter months Trotti enjoyed the feeling of warmth the hot toddy produced in him.

One of the rare pleasures of life.

He came out of the main entrance of the Questura and the burly policeman saluted briskly. "Buona sera, Signor Commissario." He wore a leather jacket and his beret was pulled down to his ear.

"I hope you're wearing tights under those trousers, agente."

"I'm from Bolzano." The man laughed. "Never been afraid of the cold."

"Salve!" Trotti gave him a wave. He pulled on the zipper of his English waxed jacket as he went down the steps into Strada Nuova.

It was dark and the overhead lamps cast their tinted light into the foggy street. Trotti turned right, pulling his scarf up to his chin and headed towards the Po.

His last winter in the Polizia di Stato.

After a lifetime in the Questura, Trotti could now enjoy those simple luxuries that he had systematically denied himself. Money in his wallet and no longer anybody to tell him what to do. Even Pioppi, now that she had a child of her own, had ceased to give orders to her father.

He softly whistled an air from *Andrea Chénier* to himself.

Although Strada Nuova was the center of the pedestrian zone, it was full of evening traffic. Rush hour and the municipal buses rumbled past, heavy with their load of passengers and misted glass. Passengers going home to minestra, Berlusconi and bed.

Trotti took the turning right and let the noise of the Strada Nuova fade behind him. Here the fog dulled every sound, dulled the fall of his shoes on the wet cobblestones.

Two hundred meters.

He could feel the damp fog working into his trousers and he longed for the dry cold of the hills.

He turned into Piazza Vittoria and along the empty, echoing porticoes. The door of the Bar Duomo was misted and twinkled with the light beyond. Trotti pushed the brass handle, to be met by the familiar smell of coffee, spirits, moist clothes and by the soft music of the radio.

"Buona sera, commissario," the barman said cheerfully, catching sight of Trotti through the crowd. "You're on time."

The barman stood in front of a serried row of bottles. Advertisements—Amaro Ramazzotti and playing cards from Treviso—had been carefully stuck to the tinted glass of a long mirror.

The mirror threw back Trotti's unsmiling image.

One or two coated backs moved aside and one or two heads nodded an evening salutation as Trotti went past, heading to a far table where nobody was sitting.

On the wall hung the price list in felt, with inserted white characters. Beneath it was a shelf and a vase of dried flowers. On the pink cloth of the table lay a discarded copy of the morning's *Repubblica*, stiffened by a wooden rod.

Trotti unfurled his scarf and unzipped his jacket before sitting down. He rubbed his hands, the warmth quickly returning. He picked up the paper. The reading glasses that Pioppi had scolded him into buying on his last visit to Bologna remained resolutely in his pocket while Trotti held the newspaper at a distance, trying to keep the print in focus.

A few minutes later, silent and discreet, the barman moved from behind the bar and transferred a saucer of cashew nuts and a glass of steaming Elisir di China from a steel tray on to the table. A slice of lemon had been clipped to the rim of the glass.

"The evening paper, commissario." The waiter slipped the sheets of *La Notte* into the metal clasp.

Trotti mumbled absentminded thanks as he scanned the front page of the paper.

The inquiries continued. Nearly two years of Mani Pulite and there were still more resignations in Milan.

The waiter turned on the wall light. "Anything else you need?"

"Milan." Trotti shook his head, speaking to himself. "Moral capital of the Republic."

"Times change, commissario." The waiter smiled philosophically, picked up an overflowing ashtray and went away with the crumpled *Repubblica*.

"Thank God soon I'll be retiring," Trotti muttered.

(In the 1970s, during the Years of Lead, when nothing was sure in Italy, Trotti had entertained a nostalgia for the certainties of his childhood, for the certainties arrogantly paraded by Mussolini and the Fascists. Then the adult Piero Trotti had longed for the distant, innocent time of his childhood when things were simple, when values were black and white. A time when you knew where you stood.

Of course, it was wishful thinking—but during the Years of Lead, with people being blown up on trains or outside factories, Trotti needed to believe in something.

Twenty years on, Tangentopoli and Mani Pulite had put paid to any idealism. Now there was nothing to believe in.

Nothing. Neither in the Fascist past, nor in the future of democracy. The politicians had taken the money and they had left nothing other than their cynicism and their debts. Nothing.)

"Mind if I sit down?"

Trotti glanced up. "You really have to?"

"Always so courteous, commissario."

Trotti returned his attention to the Milan newspaper. "I gave up being courteous years ago."

2: Bassi

THE MAN WAS a lot younger than Piero Trotti, in his mid-thirties. He wore a camel-hair coat and was removing matching leather gloves. He had slow, dark eyes, broad shoulders and a prominent Adam's apple. Black hair brushed forward to hide incipient baldness. His complexion was doughy; the result of a lack of sunlight and exercise.

Trotti continued reading the paper.

His name was Fabrizio Bassi and for ten years he had been a policeman—in Gorizia and then in the city—before leaving to set up his own detective agency.

"Another?" Bassi pointed at the half-empty glass of china in its steel frame.

Trotti looked up. "If you wish to talk, I'm sure there are many people who'd enjoy your company a lot more than me."

Bassi sucked in his cheeks. Despite the cold, his shirt collar was undone and the blue tie loose at his neck. He cultivated the appearance of a television detective. There was even an overlay of American to his flat, Lombard intonation. He liked to claim he was from Brooklyn. According to his identity card he was from Pieve del Cairo.

Trotti returned his attention to *La Notte*.

Leaning forward, Bassi asked, "Commissario, have you thought about my suggestion?"

On the Milan pages, there was an article about a teacher of a liceo classico who had been arrested for accepting a bribe. Two million lire in exchange for the maturità examination.

Trotti sipped the hot drink. "As I recall, you had your answer last week."

Bassi sat down on the edge of the chair opposite and placed a magazine on the tabletop. "There've been developments."

"Why do you keep bothering me?"

"It would be to your benefit."

"For nearly forty years I've had my colleagues imposed upon me from above. Why on earth do you think I should wish to work with you, Bassi?" A chilly smile. "Soon I'll be a free man, and can choose how to live my life as I please."

"I'm not asking you to marry me, commissario."

"I'm still married."

"You and I could work as a team."

"I can't help you, Signor Bassi."

"We can collaborate. Don't you see your name alone would mean so much? Your name alone would be a source of income for both of us."

"My name means a lot to me."

"We used to be friends, commissario."

Frowning, Trotti held up a finger. "You used to work under me."

"I worked with you. On the Biagi case. And later, when you sent me to Turin about the murdered train conductor. You used to say I was reliable. 'One of the best'—that's what you used to say, Commissario Trotti."

Trotti returned again to *La Notte*.

"You helped me, commissario, when I was thrown out of the Questura. When the Questore kicked me out."

"Please leave me alone. Please go."

"You're going to retire?"

"Button your coat and put your gloves on. Please, Signor Bassi. Take your magazine. Kindly leave me alone."

"You're going to leave this city that you love and that you've worked in for so many years? You're going to move into the hills and live among your animals?"

"You have an objection?"

In exasperation, Bassi started tapping the tabletop with the magazine. "We could make money."

Trotti lowered the newspaper. "I don't need money, Signor Bassi."

"Everybody needs money—particularly if you're living off a state pension."

"Then I'll have to sell freshly laid eggs."

For a few seconds the two men looked at each other in silence.

"Commissario, I need your help on the Turellini affair. It's important."

Trotti looked at the younger man. "Important for you."

"With your help, we could identify Turellini's murderer in next to no time. You'd be paid—you'd be generously paid. Turellini's family wants the killer identified and they don't mind paying good money."

Trotti set the paper down on the table without looking at Bassi.

"Good money you can buy the best hens with."

Trotti stood up. He had not finished his drink.

"Best goats and best hens and best goddamn pigs to sniff out the truffles up in your hills."

Trotti placed a five thousand lira note on the table.

"You'd better have a look at this, Trotti," Bassi said testily, snatching up the magazine and stuffing it into the pocket of Trotti's jacket. "Might find it interesting."

Piero Trotti pulled on the coat in silence. At the bar, several men turned to look at him. The barman nodded and gave a faint smile.

Brushing past the private detective, Commissario Trotti went out into the cold night and the fog of the city.

3: Magagna

"A SOUTH AMERICAN transvestite, for God's sake, a Peruvian, and I was getting a hard-on. In the sidings behind the Stazione Centrale."

"A transvestite almost got elected Miss Italia," Trotti said without taking his eyes from the colander of pasta and the steaming water that poured through the holes into the flat sink. "Anyway, I never told you to go to Milan, Magagna."

"Twenty years ago, Italians would go to Amsterdam or New York, and they'd say it could never happen here, people shooting up in the street. Not in Italy—good food, good wine, good women. And we're all Catholics. Who needs drugs?" Tenente Magagna was sitting on one of the upright kitchen chairs, his folded arms on the table.

"Who needs AIDS?"

"Heroin. Milan's one of the worst damn cities in the world, Trotti. Two thousand declared cases of HIV. Declared—that's not counting the addicts that are dropping off like flies at Porta Ticinese. You'd think the bastards'd have the sense to leave their veins alone. Dream on. No crack, no cocaine. It's heroin."

The kitchen window misted with rising steam.

"I wouldn't be surprised if the city of Milan subsidized the war in Beirut. Heroin, Trotti."

"You sound like a manifesto for the Lega Lombarda."

"Enough heroin to buy a Kalashnikov for every ayatollah."

"I didn't tell you to go to Milan, Magagna," Trotti said, concentrating on preparing the meal. "You were doing good work here."

"I should never have left Pescara." The younger man caught his breath. "Pescara—I sometimes wonder whether I'll ever get back there."

"You have a holiday due."

"Get back to living, commissario. Not for the holidays but forever. Take the wife and the boys."

"You think things are better in the South?"

"I should never have come to Lombardy." Magagna rapped the Formica table-top with his knuckles. "And to think I voted for the League at the last election."

"You're a Southerner." A pained sigh.

"Pescara's not part of the South."

Trotti briefly ran cold water on to the tight coils of spaghetti. "Milan's part of the South, Magagna. Italy's the South—ever since we kicked out the Austrians."

"You voted for the Lega, too, commissario?"

"I gave up voting years ago—and never noticed the difference."

Magagna shook his head. "Italians just can't enjoy themselves anymore. Money, drugs, sex—whatever happened to the old pleasures?" He got up from the chair and turned on the television.

"Like starving, Magagna?" Trotti went to the stove, gave the tomatoes a final stir before tipping the spaghetti into a glass dish.

"Your problem, commissario, is you're too . . ."

"My problem's I don't have any problems." Trotti winced. "I'm happy."

"Happy?"

"Another ten months and I retire."

"Happy? You'll be bored out of your wits. Are you going to live with your daughter?"

"Her husband's looking for a job in Milan."

"Must be mad."

"Worse places than Milan, Magagna."

"I can only think of Sarajevo." The large face clouded. "If I have to get out of Lombardy, it's for my boys."

"Come back here. You were happy here. And from next September I'll be out of your hair." Trotti nodded to a parcel on top of the old Zanussi refrigerator, next to the noisy clock. "There's a little present for Mino."

"If I didn't know you, I'd think you were human."

"How's Mino?"

"Eight years old and he thinks his parents were born yesterday."

"I've always thought you were born yesterday." Trotti took dishes from the oven. "And his little brother?"

Magagna smiled proudly. "An angel."

"There's a bottle of wine from the hills in that cupboard. Instead of telling me about your voluptuous transvestites, perhaps you could remove the cork."

"Wanted to whet your appetite." Magagna shook his head. "I swear to God, Trotti, I'd never've guessed it was a man. For heaven's sake, I saw the nipples."

"And nipples still get you excited?"

"You don't have a libido, commissario?"

Trotti frowned.

"And you're going to get excited over goats and chickens in the hills?"

"I'm a happy man."

"You could've fooled me."

"Peace of the senses, Magagna."

"You're a miserable old bastard. You've always been miserable, you've always complained. You've always been an old man."

"Every morning I wake up and I'm glad to be alive apart from the occasional toothache. I'm smiling as I make my coffee."

"The last time you smiled was during the Rome Olympics."

Trotti laughed. "One of the best, Magagna." Uncharacteristically, he slapped him on the shoulder. "I never understood why you wanted to leave this place, damn you."

"A wife, a child, commissario. Promotion—a man needs promotion to survive."

"I don't need any of that. I don't need transvestites. I don't need AIDS. I don't need being told what to do by younger men." He laughed. "And I don't need nipples."

"Not sure I approve of your peace of the senses."

"I've been like a mouse running after cheese. And now I discover there's no cheese. No cheese and no mousetrap."

"You'll die of boredom."

"I'll be free."

"You'll die of boredom in the hills, with just your animals to talk to," Magagna said. He had set the labelless bottle between his thick thighs and now the cork came out with a noisy pop. "I think I'll stick to Peruvian transvestites."

4: Sandro

"I WAS BORN in Acquanera but I went to school in Santa Maria. We used to see the American bombers on their way back from Milan."

"They didn't try hard enough."

"From the hills we could see Milan burning. Castellani was telling me over eighty percent of the buildings in Milan were hit by bombs or incendiaries. Didn't try hard enough? Consider yourself lucky you've never lived through a war, Magagna." Trotti made a gesture of irritation. "I lived in Santa Maria for eight years with my aunt and my cousins Anna Maria and Sandro. We were poor, but there were no bombs."

"That's where you intend to spend the evening of your life? In Santa Maria?"

"The afternoon of my life."

Magagna had turned on the old television set to catch the local news on RaiTre. The volume was low and the picture flickered, unwatched by the two men at the kitchen table.

"With Sandro," Trotti said. "Together we're doing the old place up. There's an architect he knows in Brescia. We should be able to make something really beautiful. An old house—the foundations are more than three hundred years old. On the edge of the town, in a grove of chestnut trees. It's where our grandparents used to live. And it's where I spent the happiest years of my life—despite the war."

"You'd be a lot happier on Lake Garda, commissario, at your villa."

"The Villa Ondina belongs to my wife."

"You're not divorced."

Trotti replied simply, "I want a place of my own."

"I thought you loved Garda."

"I've spent some glorious times on the lake." Trotti ran a hand across his chin. The wine had tinted the corners of his lips. "When she was a little girl, Pioppi always loved the Villa Ondina. Still does. Last summer she brought Francesca. I don't think I've ever seen Pioppi quite so happy."

"Why on earth go off into the hills of the OltrePò? Stay with your daughter—and with your granddaughter."

"I need a place to myself."

"Your daughter needs you."

"She has a husband and a family of her own. Why does Pioppi need me? I'd only get in the way." The rigidity in his face softened. "Pioppi's taken to being a mother like a duck to water. She doesn't need an old man getting between her feet. She has her own life to lead. She's radiant now."

"Pioppi always was lovely."

"Radiant—but that's why women are luckier than us, Magagna. What satisfaction do we men have? We have to work for it—power, wealth, fame, success. And once we've got what we want—the cheese in the mousetrap—it seems to crumble through our fingers." He added, his eyes on Magagna, "Pioppi's even overweight."

"You've always worried too much about your daughter."

"Perhaps."

"You don't have confidence in other people."

"I still worry about her."

"You worry about everything."

"Pioppi is a lovely girl." Trotti nodded proudly. "She has a good job in Bologna—but her real interest in life is her family. Her husband and her little girl. And soon there will be a new one."

"If I didn't know you, commissario, I'd think you were beginning to doubt your own immortality."

"You sound like my wife." Trotti raised the glass of Sangue di Giuda to a picture frame on top of the refrigerator, beside the small parcel.

The photograph was of a middle-aged woman holding a little girl and smiling with unrestrained delight into the camera.

"The woman I married—and now she's a grandmother."

"Self-doubt, Trotti?"

He turned fast. "What makes you say that?"

"I don't think self-doubt can be very good for you. It makes you human."

"Scarcely."

"Tell me about your granddaughter."

"Francesca?" Trotti put his glass down, stood up and took the photograph. "The reason I'm happy every morning as I prepare my coffee."

"Happy?" Magagna shook his head doubtfully. "Wait another ten months."

Trotti raised his hand and stroked the photograph with the tips of his fingers. Then he set it back on top of the refrigerator.

"Still see your wife?" Magagna asked.

"Sandro says he'll stay on in the clinic in Brescia for two more years. Then he'll come to Santa Maria."

"With his family?"

"Sandro never married."

"Why not?"

Trotti shook his head. "We were like brothers, Sandro and I. Slept in the same bed. He always accused me of farting but he never stopped. With the diet of those war years, it's no real wonder."

"I can see why he never married."

"Sandro's a couple of years older than me. In 1944 he went off to fight with the partisans. Nearly got hanged by the Fascists."

"Didn't you once tell me Sandro gave you his bicycle?"

Trotti dipped his head in admiration. "You've got a good memory, Magagna."

"Or perhaps you like to repeat the same things over and again." Magagna added, "And your cousin Anna Maria went and married a Dutchman, just to get away from pedaling in the hills."

"When on earth did I tell you that?"

"Many, many years ago." Magagna sighed.

"Sandro's done well for himself. Went back to study after the war and got his high school diploma. Goodness knows where he got the money from, but he went on to study medicine. Probably from Piet, the Dutch brother-in-law." He added, "Must be fifteen years since I last saw Piet."

"You could always go to Holland when you retire."

"In '56, my cousin Sandro set up his little clinic in Brescia."

"But he never got married?"

"Have some more wine, Magagna."

"I'm driving home in this fog."

"Some grappa, then?"

"Why did your cousin never marry, commissario?"

"Who knows?" Trotti sipped some more wine, running his tongue along his teeth. "It was Sandro who told me my brother Italo had been killed."

Magagna looked at his hands in silence. It was warm in the kitchen in via Milano and Magagna had undone his collar and tie. He lolled back on the upright chair, an arm looped over the back rest.

The television droned on, ignored.

"It's all so long ago."

"Sangue di Giuda makes you maudlin, commissario."

Trotti clicked his tongue in irritation. "Sandro's always had money. A nice car and a villa near Rimini. There was a time, twenty—twenty-five years ago, when he would take a different girl-friend there every week. He had a red Alfa-Romeo Spider coupé and for some reason, he was always with a blonde. He liked the Nordic type." Trotti made a gesture of impatience. "Sandro's so stubborn."

"At least you'll have someone to quarrel with in the hills."

"If you think I'm irascible, you haven't met Sandro. Stubborn—we're all stubborn in the hills. It was a hard life and without that stubbornness we'd never have survived. Sandro was always a lot more ambitious than me. I sometimes wonder if it's because of his pride he never found the right girl. Was looking for perfection—but I suppose it's not too late."

"They say if a man's not married by the time he's forty he's not going to marry at all."

"Sandro has a lot of qualities—qualities that are common to us mountain folk." Trotti glanced at the television. "He'd have made a good father."

After a short silence, Magagna asked, "You really think you can leave this city?"

"Why not?"

"You only pretend to dislike people."

"I dislike people?"

Magagna coughed politely.

The kitchen windows were misted. Occasionally there was the distant rumble of a bus along via Milano. The clock on the refrigerator ticked noisily. The parish news sheet had been tucked behind the alarm clock, forgotten there since Pioppi had visited her father in August and had persuaded him to take her to church.

"You know, I saw a private detective this evening. Like everybody else, he wants me to stay on in the city."

"Private detective?" Magagna raised an eyebrow.

"Fabrizio Bassi. Used to work in the Questura."

"After my time."

"And now he's set up his own agency here in the city—Fabrizio Bassi Investigations. He wants me to work on the Turellini affair."

"And you're going to?"

"I'm not paid to moonlight, Magagna."

"I hope you made your deontological position quite clear." Magagna paused. "Bassi—why did he leave the police?"

"He was thrown out and now he hopes I'm going to help him."

"Thrown out?"

Trotti raised his glass. "He thinks he and I could go into partnership once I've retired."

"Bassi? Wasn't Bassi the fellow who was having an affair with a politician's wife?"

"The only partnership I'm interested in is with my goats and hens in Santa Maria."

"You came out in support of this Bassi. I heard how you almost came to blows with some of your colleagues in the Questura. He'd been sleeping with the mayor's wife." Magagna smiled. "Good luck to him."

"You've got a good memory." Trotti shrugged.

"Why don't you want to work with him?"

"Magagna, I don't want to work with anybody."

5: Domenica Del Corriere

THERE WERE ALREADY several copies of *Vissuto* by the telephone, left there by the cleaning lady who believed Trotti might find solutions to his own inquiries.

(The cleaning woman had been Pioppi's idea. The first time Trotti's daughter came with the baby, Francesca, she was horrified by what she called the squalor. "You need a woman, Papa." Trotti said nothing, but he acquiesced when Pioppi found a home help for him, an old, kind woman who methodically went through the house twice a week. The woman rarely spoke and when she did, she grunted unintelligibly in a Veneto accent. She wore black and she was probably a lot younger than Trotti. She had cooked for him once or twice, but her cooking was unsatisfactory. A predilection for polenta that reminded him too much of his diet during the war years.)

When Magagna had left, Trotti bolted the door, stacked the plates in the sink and then heated some water in a saucepan as he washed the dishes.

(Pioppi had told him to buy a dishwasher.)

He made an herbal infusion of chamomile and waited for the water to cool.

It was nearly ten o'clock.

The television still flickered softly. Trotti glanced briefly at a Gina Lollobrigida film with Enrico Maria Salerno that he had seen thirty years ago at the cinema, then pulled the plug from the wall. The image vanished and Trotti sighed.

He got ready for bed. It was as he was hanging up his jacket, still damp with fog, that he remembered the magazine. It protruded from the side pocket.

Vissuto.

Trotti leafed through the copy of *Vissuto*. It was, Trotti realized, an updated version of *Domenica del Corriere*, which had been so popular in the fifties before the advent of television, in the years before Berlusconi. Now there were photographs instead of the old penciled sketches, but otherwise the articles were all very similar and had scarcely changed over the intervening years. Mothers in Naples, Genoa, Rome and Trieste complaining about the Camorra, the Mafia, the 'Ndrangheta, complaining about the drugs circulating in the schools, about the inadequacy of the hospitals. Mothers with cancer, dying so that their unborn babies could come healthy into the world. A mother committing suicide because her son had died in a car crash. Other mothers arrested for selling their daughters into slavery, for trading in human organs, for usury.

Then there were articles on mediums and clairvoyants and stigmata—after two thousand years, Trotti told himself, the Catholic church had been replaced by a new, secular obscurantism.

The only difference between the magazine and the *Domenica del Corriere* of Trotti's memory was the advertising for sexy phone calls, ribald jokes and soft-core titillation.

"Bassi," Trotti said under his breath.

The chamomile was still hot as he did the True or False quiz. Turning to page ninety-four for the answers, he discovered with glum satisfaction that all his answers were wrong. Did he really need to know if the Doges' boat was called *bucefalo*?

Trotti took honey from the cupboard and ladled two spoonfuls into the hot chamomile. Then he drank noisily.

(Agnese had always complained that he was a noisy eater.)

Trotti was smiling to himself when he saw the article. It was the main article and flipping through the pages with his left hand, he came to it last.

MISTER FBI SAYS, 'CHERCHEZ LA FEMME.'

6: Crime Passionnel

FROM OUR CORRESPONDENT *in Milan:*

Carlo Turellini, *fifty-four, a university professor and one of the most renowned obstetricians in Northern Italy, was murdered on Friday, 23 October 1992, while leaving his villa in Segrate on the edge of the metropolis. More than a year has passed since that morning, yet the death of Turellini remains a mystery. Official inquiries have so far failed to find an answer to the two questions the people of Milan continue to ask: Who murdered Carlo Turellini and why?*

*There is, however, somebody who has never ceased to trouble the turbid waters, to break through the thick curtain of silence surrounding the murder. Fabrizio Bassi is thirty-five years old. After a successful career in the Polizia di Stato, he left to become a private investigator (*see photograph, center*). His agency is named Fabrizio Bassi Investigations—or FBI.*

A name that speaks for itself.

*For over a year, Bassi has been following his line of investigation into the Turellini case. Yet several days ago he was forced to break off his inquiries because of an injunction from the Milan State magistrate. Fabrizio Bassi does not want his valuable work to be lost—and that is why he decided to speak to our journalist (*see photograph, top right*) about the mystery surrounding Turellini's untimely death.*

Let us consider that fateful day at the end of October, 1992.

At 7:52 in the morning, Dr. Turellini was leaving for work at the university and was going through the automatic gates of his villa, sitting at the wheel of his grey BMW, when the murderer burst out from behind a bush and, with a trembling hand, pulled three times at the trigger of an antiquated gun. Surprisingly, the assassin fired only two rounds from the 7.65-caliber pistol. The second round went into the door of the car—into the bottom of the door, proof indeed that the assassin was far from expert in his calling. The third and fatal bullet struck the doctor in the left temple.

Dr. Turellini was found a few minutes later, in the throes of death, his bleeding head propped against the seat headrest, his left foot on the ground, the car door open.

The details permit several interpretations.

The first is that Turellini opened the door to the car only after he had been shot in the head. The doctor had been sitting behind the wheel and did not notice anything amiss until it was too late.

Another possibility is that Turellini knew the man who appeared before the gate. Not suspecting anything, Turellini was in the act of getting out of the car to confer with him. The murderer did not give Turellini any time but took out his weapon and fired immediately.

A third possibility is that Turellini realized the danger he was in and tried to escape from the car but the clumsy killer managed to carry out his treacherous act. Turellini did not have time to react. Fatally wounded, his strength deserted him once he put his foot on the ground.

Professor Turellini did not die immediately. He was still alive when a workman found him slumped back in the BMW.

It is clear the assassin was not a skilled killer. The unfired round that the police found later was a 7.65, an old, rusting bullet that had not been carefully maintained. The 7.65 must have jammed and the killer had to eject it before placing another bullet in the barrel. The unused and damaged bullet fell to the ground.

Professional killers, it goes without saying, use high-quality equipment, not army surplus from the war in Spain.

Fabrizio Bassi, the "Rockford" of Lombardy, relates his entry into the affair: "I was entrusted with the inquiry three weeks after the murder, through the offices of Avvocato Regni, acting for the wife and the sister of the deceased."

Often in this sort of case, once Polizia and Carabinieri have decided it's not a Mafia killing, their inquiries lose much of their momentum—unless, of course, there's pressure on them from the press.

"My first job was to get the identity of the victim into sharp focus," says Mister FBI, who recently returned from a specialized detective course in Quantico, in the state of Virginia. "On the professional front, there was nothing of major importance about the man. A highly efficient doctor, respected by his patients and admired by his colleagues, even if there were many people jealous of his success and high profile."

Of course, a successful career for an obstetrician will inevitably cause jealousy among rivals. Associate lecturer in the ancient university on the Po (see photograph and article on p. 37), to which he commuted the forty-one kilometers three days a week in his luxurious German car, Turellini had also an extremely lucrative private practice on Lake Maggiore—the Clinica Cisalpina that he had created in 1979 with his associate, Dr. Quarenghi, the renowned specialist in clinical medicine. Clearly there were many who must have been envious of Turellini's success.

The one-man FBI continues, "As for his private life, it had been fairly chaotic in the past. He divorced his wife, Luciana Lucchi, ten years ago. The couple remained on good terms, largely for the sake of their only child, Carla, twenty. For the last couple of years, Turellini had been living with Mary Coddrington, now thirty-two, a stylish Englishwoman who works in a language school in Milan. There was talk of marriage."

Fabrizio Bassi smiles. "There had been other women in the professor's life—lots of other women. Most notable was a brief and fiery encounter with the beautiful, unbridled wife of a colleague. It's possible that this relationship had not entirely died out at the time of the professor's death."

Mister FBI pauses before continuing. "My two lines of inquiry have been into the professor's professional life and into his private one. In both cases, Turellini's world was peopled by doctors."

Let's first look into the professional line of inquiry.

"Turellini wanted a professorship at the university, but when he ran for it in 1991, he failed. He had long been a member of the Destra Nazionale and no doubt Carlo Turellini suspected the cards were stacked against him, for years a Socialist fief. At the time of his death he was looking into the offer that had been made to him to direct the new clinic at Sant'Eusebio. If he had become director of this private center, much larger than his own clinic on Lake Maggiore, Turellini would undoubtedly have been a thorn in the flesh for several colleagues and rivals who coveted the post. Was one of these rivals the person who ordered Turellini's death? We can't totally exclude this hypothesis."

The Rockford of Lombardy lights another American cigarette. "Let's turn to the other line of inquiry—le crime passionnel. Turellini once had—and perhaps continued to have—a turbulent relationship with the wife of an ex-colleague. A doctor of world-class renown who travels from one continent to another, giving lectures in universities and hospitals, a man who's close to several ministers of health, past and present. A man who quite clearly would not have readily accepted his wife's alleged infidelities.

"On several occasions, Turellini is believed to have received threatening phone calls during the night." Immediately following Turellini's death, the police sighted his mistress at the wheel of her cream Jaguar in the vicinity of Turellini's villa. Later that morning, she went to the Milan police and declared, "It was my husband who murdered Professor Turellini."

Bassi continues, "The inquiries, following the woman's accusation, were largely concerned with her husband. However he was able to supply a waterproof alibi, being four hundred and seventy-seven kilometers away in Rome for a medical congress on the day of the murder. Hundreds of witnesses can corroborate his presence in Rome."

Even if the assassin was not this man, there are people who believe that the cuckolded doctor may have paid a killer to carry out the murder.

"I can neither confirm nor refute," the private investigator says. "What's needed is concrete proof and for the time being there is only conjecture. However I have been able to ascertain that the pornographic videos allegedly in the boot of the BMW were no more than the fruit of a fertile imagination. If there'd been anything, I would have found out."

According to Signor Bassi, the inquiries have come to a standstill. The crime passionnel theory is the one that has earned the greatest support among police investigators.

Likewise, it is generally believed that the killer who could not shoot straight was recruited outside Milan and its hinterland, probably in the Mezzogiorno or Sicily where Turellini himself was born fifty-four years ago.

And if the killer were a woman disappointed in love?

Women tend to be less adept in dealing with firearms; this would explain why the first shot failed to go off.

"I don't think that's very likely, even if for a long time that was the main thrust of my inquiry," the private detective says. "I've been able to build up the recent past of the professor. Many years ago Carlo Turellini had lived through a tormented and tumultuous love affair. I believe at the time of his death he was leading a calm existence with his English lady friend. He worked a lot and frequently saw his twenty-year-old daughter, Carla, who is a student at the university Luigi Bocconi. Perhaps on occasion he met the woman in the Jaguar—but little else. Professor Turellini had become a tranquil and highly respected professional, working hard and leading a happy, domestic existence."

Mister FBI lights another American cigarette.

"Other women in his life? It's possible. A good detective must look everywhere. And as the French say, Cherchez la femme."

7: Radiator

TROTTI USED TO be ambitious.

Piero Trotti, the young man from the hills who had gone through technical school during the lean years of Reconstruction, was on the way to the top when he joined the Pubblica Sicurezza in 1954. He wanted the kind of success and recognition that had been denied to his own father. Older colleagues were seen as obstacles to his career, younger colleagues were seen as rivals.

Twenty-five years later, after having finally attained the rank of commissario and after his wife had left him, Trotti lost much of his desire to succeed. He had done well, slowly working his way up through the hierarchy and now for the first time he started asking himself questions about his life.

Asking questions after it was already too late for the answers to be useful.

It was because he had failed his own family that Trotti allowed himself to be swayed by justice—or rather, by his idea of justice.

"Justice," Trotti said to himself. He now snorted as he stepped into the lift, with its permanent smell of old cigarette smoke and the hammer and sickle scraped into the aluminum paint.

A vision of justice that allowed him for the first time in his life to question the values—and the authority—of the Questura. Of the Questura and beyond it, of the Italian Republic.

Piero Trotti, who had grown up in the hills, who had been taught to obey and to serve—the old Fascist slogans were still visible beneath the grime fifty years later on their farm walls—Piero Trotti, who as a child had been a uniformed Figlio della Lupa, who had worn a black shirt and a fez, who had carried a wooden rifle, who had never really questioned power or those who wielded it, finally discovered himself to be refractory.

The old arrogance of ambition was replaced by another, equally pernicious one—if he were to believe his colleagues and subalterns: the arrogance of knowing he was morally right.

The lift came to a halt and he stepped out.

The third floor of the Questura.

Surprised, the blonde woman looked up from her desk, gave a brief smile of her rubbery lipstick. She pointed down the corridor to the Questore's office. "He would like to speak to you." Her reverential tone left no doubt about whom she was speaking.

Without answering, Trotti went down the cold corridor to his own office.

(A provincial city on the edge of the Milanese hinterland but largely untouched by the problems of the big metropolis.)

Justice?

(A small, quiet city, a provincial university city that simply wanted to get on with its existence. Work, study, commerce, the pursuit of happiness. A city that now voted solidly for the Lega Lombarda. A provincial city with a pedestrian zone and a by-law forbidding the use of English on the shop fronts.)

Justice?

Like ambition before, justice was simply a motivation that Trotti had to give himself in order to get up every morning in the cold, when the thick fog lay across the damp and dreary plain of Lombardy.

A different kind of cheese in the mousetrap.

Trotti sat down, holding the telephone to his ear—the same telephone he had always had, with a ponderous dial that hid most of the grubby green plastic and an ancient sticker advertising Columbus cycle frames. The printed colors, like everything else, had faded with age.

"Signorina, could you put me through to Signora Scola, please, on 3030103."

The voice was censorious. "Commissario, the Questore wishes to speak to you." A hesitation. "He said it was very important."

"Then perhaps you could ask him to come through. At about ten o'clock. I have an appointment with Signora Scola at the hospital. I intend to be back here after that."

The radiator suddenly grumbled to itself and Trotti put the phone down.

Another ten months and he would be free. Free to go up into the hills, escape from the city. Escape from the younger, ambitious men.

8: Baobab

HER HAND TREMBLING, the woman raised a cigarette to the ill-applied lipstick of her mouth. She had long, thin fingers that were blemished with nicotine. The pale blue eyes watched Priscilla.

Priscilla sat on the floor, legs outstretched at a right angle.

Somebody had given the child a large book but she showed no interest in the grey elephants, the bright-eyed tigers, the luxuriant baobabs. The book had slipped from her hands on to the floor. Priscilla said nothing. Priscilla did nothing. She had the same pale blue eyes as her mother. Unlike her mother, Priscilla had long black lashes.

Somewhere in the building someone shouted.

Abruptly, Priscilla rolled on to her side, was still for a moment and then levering her weight on to her hands, she pushed her round bottom into the air. Priscilla tottered into a standing position. She went purposefully—more purposefully than the tottering legs—to the window.

Outside, in the grey light of the morning, fog eddied about the lower trunks of the blackened trees. A small quadrangle, hibernating during the damp winter. Scarcely visible through the fog were the pediatric wards and the opaque windows.

Priscilla looked out at the garden, then at her own reflection in the cold window pane. With a damp finger she traced a line on the glass. Abruptly she turned towards the sitting woman. "I want to go home."

"Not yet, tesoro." Her mother took the cigarette from her mouth. She spoke with the aspirant sounds of the Val Camonica.

Priscilla wore denim overalls and on her feet, miniature training shoes, unworn and stunningly white. Both mother and daughter wore thick jumpers. Priscilla's unwashed hand went from the damp window to her groin. "Mamma, I want to go home." The hand began to rub nervously. "Where's Papa?"

Signora Scola entered the room.

A necklace and matching earrings. A silk scarf. An elegant woman, late twenties or early thirties, in a woolen dress over aerobics tights. Under her arm she carried a box of toys, which she set down on the floor.

"Ouf!" Signora Scola smiled brightly at the mother, waved at the girl, sat down on a chair and pulled off her shoes. "Priscilla, I've brought you some toys." She slipped easily from the chair down on to the worn carpet.

Priscilla had gone to her mother's side.

Without waiting for the little girl's approval, Signora Scola began to rummage in the box. Conflicting desires on the small face. Priscilla's eyes went from the woman, sitting cross-legged on the floor, to the box of toys.

Signora Scola was engrossed in the toys. "I like playing. Don't you?"

The child slipped between her mother's legs.

Signora Scola looked up. She smiled, as if she had just thought of something agreeable. "Would you like to play with me, Priscilla?"

"I'm a little girl."

"I'm a grown-up but I like to play with toys. Don't you?" Signora Scola held out her hand beckoning to Priscilla who took the first hesitant step away from her mother, her leaning torso hindered by the reluctant feet. The left hand had returned to her groin.

"Please come and play with me. I don't like playing alone."

The child hovered, undecided, fascinated, tempted. Beneath the long lashes, Priscilla's blue eyes were intrigued by the deep box of toys. "Big people don't play with toys."

"Sometimes I like to think I'm a little girl too."

Diffidently Priscilla approached. She had slipped her thumb into her mouth. Twice she glanced back at her mother.

"I quite like nice toys," Priscilla remarked earnestly. Her left hand went from her groin as she pointed at the box.

"Just like me."

"You're grown up."

"I used to be a little girl. I've always liked playing with dolls. I still do, sometimes . . . when I have the time."

Again Priscilla turned to her mother.

The young woman from the Val Camonica nodded her encouragement. She did not smile nor did she take the smoldering cigarette from her mouth.

"I like dolls when you can brush their hair," Priscilla said breathlessly.

"Girl dolls, boy dolls." Signora Scola now held out both hands. "I've found some lovely dolls here—please play with me, Priscilla."

Oscar Luigi Scalfaro, president of the Italian Republic, looked down from the wall. His photograph and a crucifix decorated the pale green walls. There was an ancient poster of the group I Pooh. A couple of watercolors in bright pastel had been pinned to the lower wall. They did not mitigate the impersonal surroundings of the small room.

"I have a dolly at home. Don't I, Mamma?"

On the far wall was a long mirror. A television camera was bolted to the ceiling.

"Look, here's a little girl like you."

"She's not wearing clothes."

"She must be very cold, poor little mite."

"She's naughty."

"You're a naughty, silly dolly," Signora Scola acquiesced, turning back to address the pink plastic. "Go on like that and you will be very ill. You'll catch pneumonia. I think we'd better dress you."

Priscilla was now standing beside Signora Scola.

"Ah, Priscilla, my love." Turning slightly, Signora Scola's delicate features smiled down on the little girl. "You want to help me dress this silly little thing before she catches her death of cold?"

The box had once contained bananas from Somalia. It now contained various toys for both boys and girls: cars, cloth animals, plastic guns, wooden men. Rubber insects and creepy crawlies.

Signora Scola touched Priscilla's golden hair. "You're a pretty girl."

"I don't like those spiders." Priscilla brusquely pushed the woman's hand away and tumbled down beside the box. She was holding a black doll in her hand. "They're horrible."

"You want to help me dress this little girl?"

"You're very big." Accusatory eyes. "Big people don't play with dolls."

Signora Scola said, "I don't have any children."

"You have a daddy?"

"Yes."

"That's my mamma." Priscilla gestured to where the smoking woman sat in silence on the hard, upright chair. "Daddy's in the truck. He drives the truck. Sometimes he goes to the sea. Doesn't he, Mamma?"

"Yes, tesoro," the woman nodded; the young, thin face was pinched. "And I have a granny and an uncle. And perhaps I'll have a little sister soon." Priscilla had started to rummage. The black doll was discarded on the floor behind her. Priscilla had turned back to the banana box and now removed a snake—green, and of glaucous, lifelike rubber—from where it was entangled among the other toys. "I don't like this snake."

Signora Scola agreed. "I don't like snakes."

"A naughty snake."

"God likes snakes."

"This is a very naughty snake. A naughty and very bad snake."

"Why's he a bad snake, Priscilla?"

"He's a very bad snake."

"What's he done wrong?"

"Very bad."

Signora Scola nodded in agreement. She had light brown hair and dark brown eyes. Fine features and an olive complexion.

"Bad, bad."

"What's the snake done wrong?"

The grimy, little hand took hold of the rubber tail and angrily smashed the inert head against the carpet.

Violently.

"What's he done, Priscilla?"

Several times the child banged the green head and the yellow eyes and the forked, red tongue to the ground, Her strength was impressive. "I want him to die."

"He's been naughty, Priscilla?"

The little girl continued her merciless battering.

"Why is the snake naughty?"

Now with both hands and renewed vigor, Priscilla banged the snake against the floor, then against the banana carton, then against the wall. "I hate him, I hate him."

"What's he done wrong?"

Priscilla had started to cry hot tears of anger.

The mother stood up, a new, unlit cigarette held between her fingers. "Don't shout, tesoro."

Priscilla spoke from between gritted teeth. "I want him to die." Froth appeared at the corners of her mouth. "Die, die." Her voice grew louder and louder, her vehemence redoubled. "I hate him."

In a pique of rage, her round young face now quite red, her blonde hair disheveled, Priscilla threw the snake at Signora Scola. "I hate him, hate him, hate him."

Priscilla Ponti, three and a quarter years old, fell to the carpet, saliva forming a string at her mouth.

Behind her, the yellow eyes stared at the back of Priscilla's head and the forked tongue lolled mockingly.

9: Moka Sirs

"NOTHING FOR IT, I suppose," the Questore said, grinning as he closed the door behind him with his heel. The man from Friuli placed the tray on Trotti's desk. "If the mountain won't move, Muhammad must."

"Muhammad who?"

"I know your obsession with coffee, Piero. Let me assure you this stuff's the best—or at least your favorite, Moka Sirs." The man gestured to the two cups on the tray. "Three sugars."

Trotti noted with satisfaction that the Questore now favored more sensible coffee cups to the thin porcelain that he once preferred. "Very flattered, Signor Questore." Commissario Trotti's face broke into a tired smile. "But I'm not retiring for another ten months."

"Who said anything about retiring?" The Questore shook his head in amused disapproval. "Wouldn't be surprised if you outlived me in this wretched place." He frowned. "I'm no Greek and I'm not bearing any gifts, merely a cup of coffee. Cup of coffee and perhaps a chat."

The Questore slumped down on to one of the greasy canvas chairs. He was wearing a blue anorak that had both a zipper and leather buttons. There was a soft, woolen scarf around his neck, and beneath the outer clothes and a V-neck sweater, he wore a blue tie and a white shirt. "No heating in here, Trotti?"

"My radiator hasn't been working since Italy won the World Cup."

"Before my time." The Questore added, "You should ask for an electric fire."

"I'll be leaving soon."

"If you don't die of pneumonia first." The Questore nodded towards the tray. "Take your coffee."

Trotti did as he was told.

"Sweet enough?"

"Excellent, Signor Questore."

"You see, Piero, in time a man can learn anything. And with time, I've finally come up with a cup of coffee to meet your demanding standards."

"Just as I'm leaving the Questura."

The Questore raised his cup to his lips. Before drinking he said, "There are times when you can be extremely surly, Piero."

"The onset of old age."

"You were surly thirty years ago." The Questore did not appear amused. He hurriedly drank his coffee and then set the cup—taken, Trotti now saw, from the Dopolavoro in via Manfreddi—back on to the tray. He leaned back in the chair and crossed the legs of his thick, corduroy trousers. "You've just been at the hospital? At Pediatria?"

"Yes."

"With Signora Scola?"

Trotti nodded.

"A good woman."

Again he nodded.

"She has a lot of admiration for you, Piero."

"Strange."

"You sound tired." The Questore looked at him for a moment, then asked, "How would you like a holiday?"

"I'll be going down to see my daughter in a couple of weeks' time."

"A holiday abroad. How would you like that?"

"This is the golden handshake? You'd like me out of the Questura? Low profile—that's the problem. I've never known how to keep a low profile."

The Questore held up his hand, "Piero, Piero—you really must not let yourself get carried away. I honestly think I've never met a man like you to take offence. And bear grudges." He shook his head. "I assure you, there's really no reason for you to bear me any grudge. If you were in any way fair, you'd have to recognize that more than once I've defended you against my best interests."

"Never said anything to the contrary."

"You're worse than a Sicilian. You neither forgive nor forget."

"No grudges, Signor Questore. No grudges because within a very short time, I'll be out of your hair."

Unconsciously, the Questore put his manicured hand to his hair. There was no need. The hair was thick and lustrous. And artfully cut to make the Questore appear younger than his fifty years. Not a white strand, nor the slightest hint of thinning.

Perhaps the hair was the reason Trotti resented the man. Or at least the most important of many reasons that Commissario Trotti had accumulated over the last ten years.

"It is precisely about your retirement, Piero, that I came to see you."

"Very considerate."

"You've been doing some good work lately."

"Thank you, Signor Questore."

"I detect a note of irony in your thanks, Piero?"

"Only too pleased to learn I've been doing good work."

"Very good work. But then you've always been a man to work by himself."

"I'd like to think I've been doing good work for the last thirty-nine years or so."

"That's not what I meant. You take offence so easily, Piero. You've always been a star—you know that. Honest, motivated and efficient—despite this surly appearance you choose to put on."

Trotti did not speak.

"Several years ago, I decided to let Merenda run the Reparto Omicidi. Yet another decision you've held against me. Another grudge, but you know as well as I do that I would have much preferred you doing that. But I couldn't, Piero. Not because you're not up to it—I sometimes think that with your sly intelligence there are few tasks you're not capable of. It's just you're not a media man."

"Media man?" Trotti repeated flatly.

"Commissario Merenda belongs to a different generation. He's more than twenty years younger than you—and it shows. You know you can't work with Merenda—you're not a man to collaborate. Reparto Omicidi functions as a team. You like to do things in your own way—whatever you say, everybody knows you despise Merenda. There are lots of things you know that Merenda will never know, Piero." He held up his hand, whitened by the cold of the office. "But there's one thing he understands that you'll never understand."

"Only one?"

"Merenda understands that being a policeman at this end of the century in a country that has two presidents—Spadolini in Rome and Berlusconi in Milan—Merenda knows the importance of public relations."

"A media man."

"Precisely, Piero." The Questore frowned, worried lest Trotti were imitating him. "In these last eighteen months, since the Barnardi thing, you've been doing some very good work."

"Then I can walk out of the Questura in September with my head held high?"

The Questore paused for a second. "If you want to stay on, Piero Trotti, I think I've got just the job for you."

"No, no." Trotti was already shaking his head.

"Can you kindly hear me out before you make your decision?"

"No jobs, no nothing."

"Piero, you're the most infuriating of men."

"Precisely what my wife used to say. My wife and every wretched policeman who ever had to work with me."

"If you want it, Piero Trotti, there's a job waiting."

"The hills of the OltrePò, Signor Questore. The hills, my goats, my pigs and my chickens."

"You're the right man. The right man for the right job. You've already done good work with children . . ."

"Children?"

"Interpol, Piero? Does that mean anything to you?"

"What?"

"How would you like to be director of the regional child abuse section?"

"And my goats, Signor Questore?"

10: Interpol

"You've always been a family man. A good father and husband."

"My wife lives in America. We've been separated for the last fifteen years."

"In an occupation where most men end up burned-out and washed out—alcoholics or wearing tutus—you're notorious for your abstemiousness." A slow smile. "The only vice would appear to be your boiled sweets."

"And my grudges."

"If you say so, Piero." Their eyes met. "Point is, though, that should you decide to stay on with us, you could do some very useful work."

"You don't think I'm entitled to a rest after all these years?"

"You see, with the International Declaration of Children's Rights there's been a big move to control things which historically we've always dealt with at a purely national level. National or provincial."

Trotti was silent. He removed a packet of sweets from the drawer, offered one to the Questore who shook his head and took a cherry-red lozenge for himself.

"Like most other crime, crime against children has gone international."

"Child abuse?"

"Child abuse in its largest sense. Trafficking in children for various criminal purposes. Medical as well as purely vice. Children being stolen from their parents to be sold for adoption in a foreign country. Or being murdered for their vital organs."

Trotti popped the sweet into his mouth.

"We'll need to collaborate with our neighbors. As the frontiers between nations come down, there'll be more and more collaboration."

"You've just told me that collaborating's not my specialty."

"Your specialty," the Questore said, lowering his guard, "is that you're a decent human being."

"Don't jump to conclusions."

"And you like children."

"I'm an old man, Signor Questore. I've really got very little in common with children."

"And your granddaughter?" He gestured to a photograph on Trotti's cluttered desk. "You've nothing in common with Francesca?"

"I hope to spend time with her—once I've moved out of here."

"You've had a family of your own. And you care. Christ, Piero, I've always told you that you and I have much in common."

"Despite my grudges?"

"You care. That's why you've never gone further up the ladder. Nearly fifty before you got to be commissario. You're a professional, you're not a political animal. You've been treading water for fifteen years because you couldn't care less about promotion within the Polizia. You couldn't care because—Piero, you think we don't know you here in the Questura?"

"Why couldn't I care?"

"Because you don't need promotion."

"Then what do I need?"

"You care about people. Remember the Belloni thing? The headmistress?" The Questore lowered his voice. "For your sake, as well as everybody else's, I called you off the case—but you weren't having it. Not Piero Trotti, the grand old man of the Polizia di Stato. Your sense of loyalty."

"Signorina Belloni was my friend."

"Piero, that's why you and I have so much in common. Like you, I like to think I care about justice. And like me, I suspect you came to this job with high hopes, with the belief that you could change things."

"I came to this job because I was poor and ignorant and the war'd put paid to my hopes of going into the career of my choice."

"What career?"

"I joined the police force because, for an ignorant man from the hills, there wasn't much else I could do."

"You lie, Piero. To yourself as much as to anybody else. You put on your cynical front."

"No front, Signor Questore. Cynicism is a prerequisite for survival."

A dismissive movement of the Questore's hand. "This is the chance of a lifetime."

"Depends whose life you're talking about."

"Your heart is still young, Piero Trotti. I'm offering you a job that suits you—and you know it. You'll be protecting those who most need you."

"My goats?"

The Questore made another movement of irritation. "Children, Piero. The innocent. You're a good functionary of the state—of a corrupt state that doesn't deserve good functionaries. A state that's now crumbling down around our ears." He gestured to the window, the pebble dash wall and beyond it, Italy. "Or perhaps a new democracy that's just coming into being. The Second Republic. The younger generation—they're the hope. The only hope. And you must help them."

Trotti was shaking his head.

"Listen, Piero, I want you to think about it. With a man like you, we can set up a child protection center."

"In the hills?"

"Don't be facetious. A man like you and the logistic support of the university—we could establish something dynamic, something . . ." he paused. "Something European."

"There are a lot of younger men who can do this job."

The Questore held down his fingers as he counted, "Polizia, the Ospedale San Matteo, the university, the computer people. Bruni at Sociologia won't talk to me about anything else. Don't you see this city'd be ideal? We've already got the expertise. And with you staying on for what?—another two or three years—we could set up something really exciting."

"Younger men, Signor Questore."

"You set up a sezione violenza infantile and then we'll snatch this thing away from Milan."

"Milan?"

"Doesn't your daughter work with the UISL in Bologna? If ever she wanted to come north, we could find a place for her on the team. She's a bright woman."

"Milan?"

There was a gleam in the Questore's eye. "The Ministry will accept the regional headquarters for Lombardy in this city. We've got the Lega Lombarda giving us support. Not in Milan, but here. We've got the brainpower here, the manpower. And above all, we've got Commissario Trotti."

11: Lamborghini

"YOU HAD BETTER give me the number and I'll call you back in half an hour, Magagna. There's a couple here wanting to talk to me."

Trotti jotted down a telephone number with the Milan code as he placed the receiver back in its ancient cradle. Then he stood up, facing the two young people. "I don't see how I can help you."

"If you can't, commissario, then nobody can."

Trotti turned away and kicked the radiator contemptuously. "They could've changed the heating when they did this place up."

The couple watched him in silence as Trotti tugged at his scarf and returned to the chair behind the desk. He glanced at his watch and sat down. He had not removed his jacket.

"You knew Papa, commissario."

For a brief moment, Trotti was silent. He took a deep breath before speaking. "There are three reasons why I can't help you." Trotti leaned against the grubby canvas backrest. He held up a hand, thumb and two fingers extended.

"Of course you can help us, Signor Commissario." Like her brother, the girl was wearing a black anorak, a logo for Lamborghini on the chest. The bulky anorak and the sweater beneath it did not hide her youthful figure. Tight blue jeans over high boots. Black hair tumbled from beneath the woolen clasp of a ski cap. There was rouge on her cheeks—rouge, or perhaps the cold of the Questura.

Trotti raised one finger. "Because the Carabinieri are in charge, one."

"We need your help, commissario." She was pretty, in her early twenties, probably still at university. No wedding or engagement ring.

"The magistrate in charge of the dossier has sufficient confidence in the Arma not to feel the need to call in the Polizia di Stato. And you know what police rivalry can be like."

Cristina Pavesi glanced at her brother for reassurance. "That doesn't stop you and the Polizia from carrying out your own inquiry."

"Two." Trotti tugged a second finger. "Castel San Giovanni's not in this jurisdiction—it's not even in Lombardy. Emilia, not Lombardy. Without a judge's warrant, there's nothing I or anybody else in this building can do."

"We live here, commissario. Our home's here in the city. We live at Burrone."

"And thirdly," Trotti said, holding up his thumb, "last but not least . . ."

"What?"

He did not return her glance but turned to stare at the grey, monotonous sky. "Signorina, as much as I'd like to be of use . . ."

"You knew Papa, commissario. You know he wouldn't just disappear."

Trotti pulled vigorously at his thumb. "Thirdly, this is really not the sort of inquiry for someone like me." Trotti smiled blandly. "The Carabinieri are doing a good job—of that you can be sure."

"You'd be doing my brother and me a personal favor."

"The Carabinieri are quite competent."

"Cristina and I need you." Davide nodded.

"You've contacted the television. You don't need me."

"We can't leave any stone unturned." Cristina's hand took hold of her brother's. "We want our parents back. We know they're alive. They'd never have left us without so much as a word. We must get them back—that's why we went on television."

Her brother tilted his head to one side. "The Carabinieri have come up with nothing. Nothing except the car where they found it, left by the roadside. The Carabinieri seem to think my parents wanted to get away by themselves for a few days."

Cristina shook her head vehemently. "They've been gone twenty days. We want our parents back. Before it's too late."

"Where do you think they are, signorina?"

She took a deep breath. "No idea, commissario. Mamma and Papa are people who get on well with everybody. They don't have enemies—everybody likes them. If they'd intended to go anywhere, they'd've told us. Ours is a closely knit family."

"Your father was in local politics."

Davide said, "My father runs a *prêt à porter* shop—he's not a millionaire. We never went to private school in Switzerland. Cristina and I went to school here, in this city. Ours isn't a rich family. And Papa pays his taxes. There's never been a ransom note. He used to dabble in politics—mayor of Castel San Giovanni for several years." A shrug. "But he has no enemies. Everybody likes him. And everybody likes Mamma."

Cristina tapped the desk. "We love them." An exasperated and unhappy sigh. "Nearly three weeks since they disappeared. Into thin air."

"Three weeks since they vanished into thin air," Davide echoed. The voice had a rasping edge in discordance with the fresh, youthful complexion. "We've got to get them back."

Trotti glanced out of the window again. Light was breaking through the sky. The fog was lifting. It was nearly eleven o'clock and Trotti wondered whether the sun would appear.

"Cristina and I spoke to our lawyer." The boy's face was pinched by the cold of the small office. Davide Pavesi was good-looking, despite a weak chin. A lock of hair—the same hair as his sister's— fell into the dark eyes. "He thinks it was a good idea to go on national television."

"Your lawyer told you to come and see me?"

"My idea," Cristina mouthed silently and tapped her chest.

Trotti opened one of the drawers of his desk. "I'm not able to help you."

"We can't take no for an answer, Signor Commissario," Cristina retorted, folding her arms against the bulky jacket.

"I have other things to do." Again he looked at his watch.

"Put the other things aside."

Trotti now observed the girl while his hand fumbled around in the recesses of the drawer. "I don't like being told what to do." Trotti half rose in his seat. He tapped at his pockets.

"You can put the other things aside, commissario. For a few days."

Davide adopted a conciliatory tone. "My sister and I would never have come here unless we felt there was no alternative."

From the inside pocket of his jacket, Trotti took an old packet of sweets. "One of the pleasures of old age, signorina, is you no longer have to take orders from anybody." He offered a sweet from the packet of Kremliquirizia. "Not if you don't want to. Not even from a pretty young woman."

"Help us. Please."

"I've other things to do." Trotti smiled mirthlessly. "Anyway, if you were on national television, you don't need help."

"We need all the help we can get."

"It's been a pleasure meeting you and your brother."

"We met before," she answered coldly. "When you came to our house."

"Perhaps at another time. But not now. I understand how you feel. Your parents have vanished and you want to know whether they're still alive. But understand, even if it had been here in the city that Signor Pavesi and your mother disappeared, even if it had been within my jurisdiction, I don't think I could have helped you."

The voice was querulous. "Why not?"

Trotti did not reply.

"Why not, commissario?"

"I'm a dinosaur, signorina."

"Because you're losing your hair?"

"I belong to an earlier age."

She shook her head, and the dark hair danced along the collar of her anorak.

"I belong to the old school of policemen. The carrot-and-stick school. I'm the kind of flatfoot who thinks he can get to the truth by shouting, threatening and carrying a big stick."

"We want our parents back with us." Cristina added simply, "We don't care what methods you use."

"The big stick, signorina, doesn't go down very well anymore. In a few months I'm going to retire. After many years of having had things my own way. I'm the sort of policeman who gets used to kicking people in the head."

"So what?"

"Get this old man anywhere near a television camera or a microphone or a journalist's note pad and the entire Questura starts trembling. An earthquake worse than Belice."

"So far *Chi l'ha visto?* seems to have had no effect. Several phone calls from the South—but no real leads."

"Nice meeting you." Trotti stood up and held out his hand. "I sincerely wish you the best of luck in your search. Your father's a charming man."

"He was your friend, commissario."

Trotti nodded his head. "Very fond of him."

"He was your friend, Commissario Trotti, and when you needed him, Papa did several favors for you."

Trotti went to the door and opened it. "Signor Pavesi's probably taken your mother on a surprise honeymoon to Prague." He started tying a loose knot in his scarf.

"He did you several favors."

A moment's hesitation before Trotti replied. "I owe your father nothing, Signorina Pavesi." He faced the pretty young woman. He smiled at her but there was no amusement in his dark eyes. "Piero Trotti's a functionary of the Republic. He neither gives favors nor asks for them. I wish you both a pleasant day. Arrivederci."

12: Virginity

HE SMILED TO himself grimly, imagining Pioppi scolding him for not wearing his glasses.

Trotti always had difficulty remembering numbers. Now his cold fingers fumbled with the piece of paper that he held at arm's length. He had to dial three times before he got through to the Caserma San Siro.

"Magagna?"

"You're not in the Questura, commissario?"

"Phoning from the Bar Duomo. What was it you wanted to tell me?"

"You don't trust the telephones in the Questura?"

"It's not the telephones."

"What don't you trust?"

"At my age, Magagna, I don't trust anyone."

"A professional hazard?"

"You can only trust people as long as their interests coincide with yours."

"You don't have much faith in human nature."

"What was it you wanted, Magagna? I'm meeting an attractive young woman in a few minutes."

"Her interests coincide with yours?"

Trotti laughed. "She's not a transvestite, if that's what you mean."

"And now you're laughing?"

"First time since the Rome Olympics, Magagna."

"You still interested in the Turellini thing?"

Trotti hesitated, looking into the cracked mirror. "I never said I was interested in Turellini."

"Last night you said Bassi wanted your help."

"Well?" Trotti was standing by the old Bakelite telephone at the far end of the bar, beside the empty beer crates. It was the proprietor's personal phone, which he allowed Trotti to use. As a personal favor.

"You interested or not, commissario?"

"Depends on what you're going to tell me."

"Precisely nothing."

"That's why you asked me to phone you?"

"You read the article in *Vissuto*?"

"Over a cup of chamomile, Magagna. I fell asleep before I got to the end."

"Bassi's not making any friends here in Milan. Understandably, he's been trying to get his hands on the Turellini dossier from the Pubblico Ministero."

"Who's got it?"

"Both Polizia and Carabinieri were involved in the initial inquiries, under the direction of the Sostituto Procuratore."

"Who?"

"Abete." Magagna paused.

"Go on."

"Seems Abete's decided to shelve the dossier."

"Why?"

"It's over—Abete doesn't want anybody looking into it. Cold storage. Deep freeze."

"Meaning?"

"Meaning your guess is as good as mine."

Trotti lowered his voice. "According to *Vissuto*, Bassi received a court order."

"I made several phone calls earlier this morning—contacts in the Arma and at Giustizia. After twelve months the thing is still on Abete's desk in the Milan Palazzo di Giustizia. Apparently Abete's quite happy letting dust gather on the dossier."

"Why, Magagna?"

"I also spoke to Durano."

"Durano in via dei Mille? I didn't know you were friends."

"Durano's a useful contact in the Carabinieri."

"What does Durano say?"

"The Turellini thing's political."

"Why political?"

"Like everything else in Tangentopoli. As soon as there's a whiff of political corruption, the Pubblico Ministero starts back-pedalling. There's no alternative. For the last eighteen months, ever since the Mario Chiesa sting, the Mani Pulite pool of magistrates has been digging the dirt. And the dirt goes deep. They're still a long way from the bottom."

"There is no bottom."

"Precisely. The more dirt they find, the more the investigating judges are accused of undermining the fabric—the political fabric of our republic. That's why the PM's got to be careful about anything that's political. He can't afford to make mistakes—not now."

"After forty years of sitting on his hands."

"Not now that all politicians, on both left and right, are on the defensive. On the defensive and united against the Pubblico Ministero. That's why the Mani Pulite judges go for businessmen rather than politicians."

"Why?"

"Look at Olivetti and Montedison. Pretty clear that businessmen don't have the same clout—they're the weak link."

"Procuratore Abete's involved with the pool at Mani Pulite?"

"Not that I'm aware of."

"Then where's the problem?" Trotti snorted derisively. "The Turellini thing is a straightforward murder—probably a crime of passion. *Cherchez la femme*."

"What?"

"Look for the woman—it's French."

"Strange way of pronouncing French."

"Why would you think it's political, Magagna?"

"Abete's got the reputation of sticking at things. One of the younger judges—honest and ambitious. From Calabria and wants to show that they're not all Arabs down there. Used to be a young Communist."

A brief silence.

"Magagna, are you telling me Bassi and everyone else are off on the wrong track?"

"Wrong track, commissario?"

"Turellini's a political killing?"

"I'm just repeating what I've heard."

"Turellini was never involved in politics—or at least, not directly. He was too far out—Destra Nazionale. Not really the sort of person the Christian Democrats and the Socialists would want to get into bed with."

"Durano believes in Abete's integrity as a judge."

Over the line, Magagna's Abruzzi accent was accentuated and Trotti felt an unexpected sense of fondness for the man. Magagna, Pisanelli, Maiocchi—the good men whose company Trotti would miss after his retirement. An unwelcome tightening in his chest. "Thanks, Magagna."

"You're really not interested in Turellini?"

"I never said I was interested."

"A lot better that way, commissario." On the far end, Magagna chuckled noisily and Trotti could imagine him lounging in his chair, sitting back with his large feet on the desk, the telephone propped beneath his cheek and the premature stubble. Even in winter, Magagna wore sunglasses.

"A few more months and you can take your retirement, commissario. There's no need for you to make any more enemies." Magagna paused, then said, "Particularly not among the magistrates."

"Instant virginity."

"What?"

"The judges spend thirty years living off the rest of us and suddenly they decide they're the moral guardians of the republic."

"What republic?" Magagna's laughter surged from the Bakelite handset.

"See what you can do, Magagna."

"Do?" There was incredulity in the younger man's voice. "Do what?"

"I'd prefer it if you'd phone me in the evening. At my place after eight. Or better still, you can drop by—if you can endure my cooking. You liked the Sangue di Giuda."

"Assuming I don't have a wife and children at home waiting for me and assuming I enjoy crisscrossing Lombardy in my own car, paying for the petrol out of my own pocket, what exactly d'you want me to do, Commissario Trotti?"

"There's this veto on Bassi."

"I just told you why, Trotti."

"Bassi's been told by the Milan magistrates—most probably by Abete—to drop his inquiries. That's why Bassi went to *Vissuto* in the first place. There's money in the Turellini case for him. It's Turellini's family who want to know why the doctor was murdered. Bassi's trying to enlist my help because, as a private investigator, he's being shouldered out. He doesn't want the case to go cold on him before he gets paid."

"Why are you getting involved?"

"I never said I was getting involved."

Magagna asked, "You need the money?"

"You're in Milan, Magagna."

"You're not getting involved but you want me to help you?"

"You haven't got the Questore telling you to stick to rape victims and abused infants."

"Sounds like good advice."

"Approach Abete. See if you can find out why he's calling Bassi off. Turellini looks to me like a crime of passion. There's no reason for the PM to go slow—unless there's pressure from somewhere; I think the problem's there."

"Why bother, commissario?"

"Find out if it really is political, Magagna."

"Why don't you ask Bassi?"

"Bassi's a womanizer who's best sticking to divorce work—the kind of stuff he can understand. He wouldn't know how to solve a murder even if you gave him a confession in triplicate."

13: Bianca

IT HAD SUDDENLY turned into a beautiful day.

Magically, the dampness had vanished into the air; to the south the sun shone bravely in a sky now cloudless. Overhead, a jet plane flew northwards, taking its encapsulated passengers over the Alps to Switzerland, Germany and beyond, to a land as cold and pure as the perfect sky.

Trotti walked with his hands in his coat pockets; the sound of his footfalls on the cobbled street echoed off the closed buildings.

A Tuesday morning in late November, and the city was strangely quiet. He crossed Piazza Carmine. Ochre walls, brown blinds and the morning smells of coffee and baker's yeast. A fairytale city— except for the occasional car coming from behind and edging him towards the high, cold walls.

(The Lega Lombarda mayor wanted to abolish the pedestrian zone; he was allowing it to die away, ignored and unregretted. The Greens complained, of course, although they had done nothing to save the traffic-free zone or indeed anything else while they were sharing power with the Socialists.)

A woman was sluicing down the stone entrance to a building in via Tre Marie. Steam came from her mouth and from the head of the mop as she slapped it to the ground. Trotti could hear her singing. The song was in a Lombardy dialect that caused him to smile.

Old posters along the walls in the city center, advertising hearing aids, announcing the recent death of dear ones and inviting the people of the province to vote for the League. There was the helmeted silhouette of the Lombard warrior of Pontida, his sword held way above his head, in a defiant stance against the new Barbarossa—Rome and the perceived ills of the South.

Trotti popped a banana-flavored sweet into his mouth.

He deposited the wrapper into one of the green bins that the city used for collecting recyclable paper.

"Barbarossa," he muttered under his breath. Distant memories of primary school in the hills and the unsmiling, asthmatic war veteran who had tried to drum Fascist history into Trotti's bony head. In those days, before the Axis, Barbarossa was Adolf Hitler. Alberto da Giussano, the helmeted Lombard warrior, was Benito Mussolini.

He reached via Mascheroni and stopped in front of the marble plaque. It was screwed into the bricks of a somber building, a seventeenth-century palazzo. The wall had blackened with age.

MINISTERO DELLA GIUSTIZIA, CASA CIRCONDARIALE DI CUSTODIA PREVENTIVA.

Then, as an afterthought, on another plaque, this time without the insignia of the republic, the star and the laurels, SEZIONE FEMMINILE. Rain had run from the bronze letters, staining the plaque.

Trotti rang the bell and waited.

An old man cycled past. He wore a brown coat and a battered, flat cap. The bicycle was painted a fluorescent green. No mudguards above the thick, knobby tires. There was even an electronic speedometer attached to the flat handlebars.

It was time Trotti got the Ganna out of the garage, oiled it and pumped the tires. Time he started getting some exercise again.

Time he gave up sweets and the after-hours chino. And the Sangue di Giuda.

The door opened and the officer saluted cheerfully. "At least the fog's disappeared, commissario," the man remarked as he closed the wooden door. There followed a series of electronic clicks.

Trotti crossed the courtyard, past the statue of a naked goddess and into the main building. There was no particular smell or sound that revealed the repressive nature of the place.

The prison director was waiting for him.

Signora Bianca Poveri was smiling broadly and held out both her hands as Trotti entered the bright office. "You got my message, Piero?"

Her office was full of cut flowers, set in vases placed strategically around the room. They kissed. Or rather, he was about to kiss her right cheek when she turned her face, presenting the other cheek.

"Karma," she said, gesturing him to a seat. Bianca Poveri waited before sitting down opposite him on the far side of a wide desk. The inlaid surface was cluttered with piles of beige dossiers, newspapers and, incongruously, a doll in some regional costume. She moved a vase of carnations aside to get a better view of Trotti. "How are you, commissario? I thought you must have already gone into retirement." There was laughter in her voice. "I see you so rarely."

"How's Alcibiade?"

A slight hesitation, as if she were not expecting the question. "I scarcely get home before nine most evenings. Just time to eat and then bed. Head on the pillow and I'm out like a light." A sigh of her cashmere sweater. "With this job I don't get time to see my husband or my daughter."

"And Anna Giulia?"

"Thank heaven for the weekends. That's when we can be together. My greatest source of joy, commissario."

"She must be three years old."

"She'll be five in April." A proud smile.

"Nothing to stop you having another child. Anna Giulia will cease to be the center of attraction."

Bianca Poveri's countenance hardened. "I don't think so."

"There are times," Trotti grinned, "when you don't go out like a light."

Signora Poveri swiftly changed the subject, but not before Trotti noted her brief frown of displeasure. "And you, Piero Trotti? Isn't it about time you settled down?"

"I'm not divorced."

"Shame on you."

He shrugged. "I belong to a different generation."

"Divorce has been legal in this country for twenty years, Piero. You could easily find a companion. You're an attractive man—in your way."

He held up his hand.

"Although you must be a difficult person to live with." Bianca Poveri laughed to herself and then, turning her glance away, started rummaging among the piles of dossiers on her desk. "You got the message?" she asked as she shifted a pile from the table on to her lap and started going through it.

"You have something for me?"

"A letter, Piero. A letter from a friend of yours. Should be here somewhere."

"A friend," Trotti repeated absentmindedly, looking out through the window. The terracotta rooftops gave the city its fairy-tale appearance—everything neat, reassuring, cozy. His glance went from the sea of rooftops to the internal courtyard. A courtyard like any other in the city. Like any other in the city except for the high wire fence, topped with barbed wire and ungainly spotlights.

"Ah!"

Trotti returned his glance to Signora Poveri. She was a pretty woman beneath a harsh, brunette perm. She had married Alcibiade Poveri almost ten years earlier. At the time Poveri worked for a local publishing house, while the young Bianca was still a student in economics at the university. She had always been an ambitious girl and at the age of twenty-nine, thanks to a lot of hard work, she had become the youngest female prison director in Italy. Two months later she was pregnant. Her first posting should have been Sassari in Sardinia. Trotti had been instrumental in her being sent to her native city and the women's prison.

"I think you have an admirer, commissario," the direttrice said, handing him a dog-eared envelope.

Trotti Piero.

The envelope was grubby; the handwriting was that of someone who was unused to putting pen to paper.

Trotti smiled as he opened the envelope.

14: Eva

"HER NAME IS Eva. She's from Uruguay. She was a prostitute and she stayed at my place a couple of years ago before she was sent back to South America."

"Your friend's not in South America anymore."

"Eva Beatrix Camargo Mendez," Trotti said to himself as he turned the manila envelope over, looking for a sign of its place of origin. Just a smudge above the sealed rear flap.

"Where is she?"

"Trieste." Trotti smiled sadly. "She seems to think I can help her."

"You know what we women are like?" Bianca Poveri raised her shoulders. It was warm in her bureau. She wore an unbuttoned cashmere cardigan. A white blouse and a thin gold necklace at the pale, freckled skin of her neck. Matching earrings. A gold brooch with a cabalistic motif on the lapel of her blouse. "Acts of genuine kindness are so rare in men. When we meet them, we think we can go on asking for favors indefinitely."

"Eva cost me a fortune in new locks."

An amused laugh. "Locks were the only precaution you took?"

"After Eva had gone, I had to get everything changed in my house. I had no desire to see her friends come looking for her in via Milano."

She searched his face. "You enjoyed her company."

"A whore—with a son in Uruguay she hadn't seen in years. She talked about him incessantly."

"Prostitute with a golden heart?" Signora Poveri laughed. "I don't think I've ever met one. And in my line of business I meet enough whores. Whores, murderers, addicts, thieves. I've long believed the Merlin Act should be revoked, that prostitution should be legalized—if only to control the spread of AIDS. But I'm forgetting, you're a devout Catholic." She added, "And a married man."

"A black girl. Eva was only nineteen when she came to Italy—thought she was getting a dancing job. Instead she ended up in Milan, along with the transvestites and the addicts, trying to keep warm over an open fire, near the Stazione Garibaldi."

"Somehow those golden hearts don't go out to me," Bianca continued. "Perhaps it's something to do with my age and my gender. And I'm not a devout Catholic."

"A husband and a daughter who adore you, Bianca. What more do you want?" Trotti smiled. "Devout Catholic? Last time I went to church was when my daughter was here to visit me."

Bianca Poveri made an irritated movement of her hand. "You get involved with prostitutes, Piero?"

"They're human beings, too."

Bianca nodded wisely, "You'd be tempted to think otherwise if you worked here."

"Human beings."

"If you insist."

"The Questore's given me a directive from the European Community on prostitution. Sixty percent or more of the women who go into the trade are the victims of incest. This woman," Trotti tapped the letter, almost illegible in its blend of Italian and Milanese, "went back to Uruguay, courtesy of Alitalia and the Ministry of the Interior. Took her money with her. What's she doing back in Trieste?"

"What was she going to do in Uruguay?"

"She was returning to her son."

"After years of absence, you think her son remembered her?"

"Eva talked about nothing else."

"That's what women do. I see it all the time. It's a way of reassuring themselves they're normal, that they have feelings, that they aren't animals." She sighed. "Your Eva—she was in Milan, a foreign environment she couldn't understand. Her son was the one thing she could cling to, something belonging to a better past, and the promise of a better future."

"She could've gotten a job in Uruguay."

"A job—but not much money."

"A job, her son—and her dignity."

"You sound like the telenovelas, Piero. You watch too much Berlusconi."

"Because I think a mother should stay with her child?"

"These women carry their prison with them—they're like snails. Occasionally there's a whore who breaks out. Who finds her Prince Charming or who manages to buy herself a restaurant near Amalfi. But for most, the only exit is disease and death." Bianca shrugged. "Life isn't like *Dynasty*."

"I can see what you watch, Bianca."

"Eva got back to South America—and in all probability found a son who was nothing like her dreams." Bianca Poveri leaned forward and Trotti could smell her perfume—slightly musky, catching at the nostrils. "A bit like dying. You go through all the rigmarole, the pain and the fear."

"What's like dying?"

"Hope," Bianca said simply. "You tell yourself the worst'll soon be over. You hang on grimly to your rosary and you convince yourself you're leaving this world for something better and more beautiful. And . . ."

"And?"

Bianca Poveri clicked her fingers. "No pearly gates, no Saint Peter." She gestured to a vase of flowers on a filing cabinet. "No Saint Teresa waiting for you with white roses. No celestial *Dynasty*. Nothing. Death. You discover pretty fast you've been sold short."

Trotti frowned. "You don't believe in the afterlife?"

"Uruguay's a long way away from the bonfires of the Stazione Garibaldi. Home, where your Eva had her son. The one person she loved. And the only person who loved her. Of course, it was a dream, her own. But these women are always dreaming, always running from one failed dream to the next. Your Eva returns to the harrowing poverty of Uruguay. The poverty she'd hoped to escape in the first place."

"Spending the night in Milan or along the via Aurelia—that's not poverty?"

"Emotional—but not necessarily economic. That's the trouble with money, Piero. You know that better than I do. We all like to think we're above money, that we have values other than those of wealth. But once you've gotten used to a comfortable existence—it's hard to return to the bad old days."

"You're very materialistic for a young woman."

"Realistic."

"Then why don't these prostitutes get married?"

"Perhaps because they're more afraid of family life than of the via Aurelia."

Trotti bit at his lower lip. "I don't see what help I can give Eva."

"If you care to write her a note, I'll get it sent through the administrative hierarchy."

"What can I tell her?"

"I always credited you with a better understanding of female psychology than that, commissario."

"Trying to flatter me?"

"I deal with women every day and, unlike men, I don't allow my judgment to be influenced by a pretty nose or a pretty silhouette. Or by the sly promise of intimacy. Those bits of our anatomy that get men excited—they're just the equipment we need for bearing children."

"Glamorous equipment."

"The women here—they're all victims. Five, ten years ago when I was a feminist, Piero, I'd've said all women everywhere were victims. That was before I had a daughter of my own. Didn't take me long to realize a married woman gets a better deal for sex than the best-paid prostitute. These prisoners—they're in their cells long before ever turning up here. They come into the world as victims and they leave it as victims. Whores are not like you and me, Commissario Trotti. There are things that you and I believe in—things like affection and caring and warmth. We don't need Berlusconi's telenovelas to teach us how to feel, because our emotional equipment's already soundly in place, given to us by our parents, by people who care. At home and at school. You and I, when we were little, we mattered." She shook her head. "Whoring's merely the end result of everything that's gone on before. They've never been loved, and so they don't know how to do it."

"Eva loves her boy. She loves him as she loves herself. She wouldn't talk of anything else."

"Whores don't know what love is."

"Then why do they have sex?"

"Whatever love is, for the prostitute it's got nothing to do with the physical act in the back of a stuffy Fiat or behind the bushes off the highway. Whores can open their legs but not their hearts. What affection they have, they pour into animals or stuffed dolls or into people they don't have to live with. People like you, Piero."

"Like me?"

"You can't imagine how many dolls and little animals these women have—each cell is a menagerie." Bianca Poveri pointed to the letter. "That note's not really for you at all. It's for hers."

"What can I do to help her?"

"Your Eva realized long ago her son was beyond her." Bianca raised the silk shoulders of her blouse. "How old is he now? A grown man? What does her son need from a woman he's scarcely ever met? But you see, commissario, unlike her son, you've been good to her. In Italy, she dreamt of Uruguay. And back in Uruguay she spent her time dreaming of Commissario Trotti."

"I can't help her."

"Your Eva doesn't want help. She simply needs somebody to remind her she's a human being."

He shrugged. "Human being? I gave up being that years ago."

"Wrong again, commissario."

He put his head back and laughed.

"You're a good man—in your way."

"How on earth does Alcibiade put up with a wife wearing the trousers?"

Unexpectedly the face softened and a gentle grin made its way along her lips. "You think I wear the trousers in the Poveri home? You underestimate our little girl. Anna Giulia has both Alcibiade and me around her chubby finger. In the organization chart of the Casa Poveri, I come just after the tortoise, just before the yucca plant." The proud smile vanished. "You're going to take it, aren't you?"

"The letter?" Trotti frowned. "Of course I'm going to take it—though for the life of me, I don't see how I can help Eva."

"You're going to take the job?"

"Job?"

"Commissario Piero Trotti, it'd be a shame if you were to leave the Questura tomorrow."

"What job?"

"No point in being coy. There's been talk of a center for several months and I wasn't the only one to recommend you to the Questore, if that's what you think." Unblinking, she looked him in the eyes.

Perhaps his mouth had fallen open.

"And now you start quoting European Community statistics

to me. You know, you'd be making a lot of people happy, and not least me."

"You knew about the job?"

"I was asked if I wanted to head the team. I'd much rather work with you, Piero Trotti."

"My wife escaped to America to get away from me." There was a long silence. "I don't know many people who want to work with me. My daughter's now in Bologna."

Bianca Poveri asked fondly, "And Tenente Pisanelli?"

"Avoids me." Trotti shrugged. "Seems to think it's my fault he's not married."

"I'm too young for the job. No experience. Whereas you . . ."

"Yes?"

"Unlike me, commissario, you never lived through 1968. Or at least, you grew up at a different time, at a time when things were simpler. You have your solid values anchored in a simpler time. I'm a child of the sixties. All that stuff, Lotta Continua, feminism and throwing Molotov cocktails at the Celere—I grew up with it. That's why I'm still confused."

"You were too young for the Red Brigades."

"Perhaps it's my job—or perhaps it's having a child of my own. There are things I'm only beginning to understand now. I burned my eschimese with its politically correct cape several years ago. And, like everybody else, I've seen the dictatorship of the proletariat replaced by the more insidious dictatorship of Berlusconi."

"What are you trying to tell me?"

"My generation—we thought we could put things to rights with bombs and violence and P38s. We were arrogant—because life had always been easy for us. Your generation lived through the war. Your generation had gone hungry trying to survive. We thought our ideals were more important than life itself. But our ideals were bogus and we were arrogant because we didn't have any experience of the real world. There'd always been three meals a day."

"I saw my first corpse at the age of sixteen. A couple of partisans no older than me."

"The sixties generation—it's only now I'm beginning to understand. But you, Piero Trotti, you have experience. And you have wisdom. You understand other people—and you like women."

"My daughter nearly died. She stopped eating. And that—or so I'm told—was all my fault."

"These last few years, Piero, you've been marking time. With your experience, you could have done more. With your intelligence . . ."

"Yes?"

Signora Poveri breathed in. Her pinched nostrils turned white. "I've got the statistics here from Telefono Azzurro, the toll-free telephone." She took a blue brochure from a pile of books on her walnut desk. She ran her tongue along her lips before reading. "Over a hundred and fifty telephone calls a day in Italy from children complaining of abuse or violence in the home. There are probably five thousand cases of sexual exploitation in a year." She looked up at him. "You could do so much, Piero."

The phone rang softly, almost smothered beneath a pile of dossiers.

"With your experience and your decency, there's still so much you can do. For all the other Evas."

"I think I've done enough."

"Help them before it's too late. Help them before they've turned into snails with a prison on their backs." The young woman brushed away the hair from her ear with the receiver. "Women's prison," she said, speaking softly, her eyes turning downwards. Then she added, "Yes."

Trotti looked at her profile, almost girlish, softened by the oblique winter sunlight.

Bianca held out the receiver. "For you, commissario. You're wanted at Linate Airport—your plane's due in thirty-five minutes."

15: Linate

"AMSTERDAM?"

Two Air France pilots, both looking like Gérard Philippe, walked purposefully across the concourse. One wore a thin beige scarf, the other carried a leather case. Women's heads turned at their passage.

"I suppose so."

"Then it looks as if your cousin's going to be late." Bianca Poveri pointed to a nearby monitor screen. "And, as much as I'd like to stay, I've got to get back to the city."

"You've been very kind, Bianca. I'll wait here for my cousin."

"How will you get back?"

"A train. I'm surprised Anna Maria telegrammed me and not Sandro." Trotti raised his shoulders. "Perhaps Sandro's here too."

"What does your cousin look like?"

"Sandro?"

"Sandro's the doctor at Brescia, isn't he?"

"Distinguished and very bald." Trotti glanced around as if expecting his cousin to emerge from the milling crowd of travelers. "Don't worry about me. I'll wait for Anna Maria and we'll get a train into Milan."

"Your cousin should've contacted you earlier."

"Anna Maria? Very organized. More Dutch than the Dutch."

"When did you last see her?"

"Surprised Anna Maria didn't phone me. She always phones at Christmas. No idea what's got into her head. I haven't seen her in years . . . at least fourteen years." He glanced irritably at the flimsy blue paper of the telegram. "She hasn't even indicated a flight number. I can only suppose she's on the Amsterdam flight."

"Probably was in a hurry."

"A lot simpler to phone me." Trotti's face softened as he smiled at the young woman. "A coffee before you go, Bianca?"

Signora Poveri was going to refuse, but then changed her mind. She slipped her arm in his and together they moved through the crowd towards the long granite bar. He liked her musky perfume and was glad that he had given up smoking over twenty years ago.

Trotti bought a ticket from the woman sitting behind her isolated cash register. She did not look at him as she gave him his small change.

A couple of barmen, their white jackets crumpled and slightly stained by a long morning's work, served the customers. Efficiently and robotically.

In a small recess, another man was working the Cimbali coffee machine, nodding in concentration as he took the orders and set out the filled coffee cups in a single row. The cups were speedily whisked away by the two waiters. One waiter brought the sandwich and Trotti's brioche. The other waiter set their cups on to the polished granite of the bar and deftly spiked the receipt.

"A Stakhanov approach," Bianca said brightly, but Trotti did not appear to understand as he ladled two and a half spoonfuls of white sugar on to the dome of frothed cream.

Rows of liqueur bottles stood before a tinted mirror behind the perpetual motion of the waiters. Attached to the top shelf was the black and red shield of Milan AC.

"A coffee instead of a lunch." Amusement in Bianca's voice. "As good a way as any of keeping my weight down."

"There's a restaurant upstairs, if you want something to eat." Trotti could feel the warmth of her hand on his sleeve. "And you have a beautiful figure."

"Are you trying to flatter me, Commissario Trotti?"

"I wouldn't dare," Trotti said and he could feel strange muscles pulling at his smile.

Trotti liked Linate. It was more like a railway station than an airport. You got off the plane, stepped through the sliding glass doors and there waiting outside was the 73 tram, ready to run you down the viale Forlanini into the city center, to the Duomo, to the shops, clattering through the traffic jams.

"At least Anna Maria says Linate," he said.

"I wouldn't have run you to Malpensa, if that's what you think."

"Malpensa." He clicked his teeth.

"All part of Tangentopoli." The laugh was girlish and contagious. "You're not telling me with a surface as flat as the Po valley, they had to build Milan's bright shining new airport just beneath the Alps, almost into Switzerland."

"Everything's Tangentopoli," Trotti said simply. "Always has been, long before Mani Pulite. That's why we have the highest taxes in Europe."

"You're a cynic."

"A realist."

"I'm the realist, Piero."

"You're materialistic, Bianca."

"If you were a realist, Piero, you'd be a lot richer than you now are. And you wouldn't be retiring to some chicken coop in the hills." She tapped the back of his hand. "I feel guilty about leaving you here, commissario."

"Good of you to bring me into Milan."

"Nice to be with you. You're good company. Mellowing in your old age—like a good wine."

"Turning to vinegar."

"And it's about time you bought a car."

Trotti sounded offended. "I've got an Opel."

"That you bought the year Nuvolari was world champion."

"Before my time," he laughed. "Good cappuccino."

His young friend drank fast between bites at the prosciutto cotto sandwich. Dusty flour fell from the bread on to her coat.

"My cousin was always a great admirer of Nuvolari," Trotti mused, almost to himself. "That's why Anna Maria called her son Tazio. Tazio van Dijk. Well over forty now. Last time I saw him, he was in short trousers." He emptied another half-spoonful of sugar into the cup. "There was a time when Tazio was estranged from his mother. Anna Maria never liked the girl he married. A black girl from Dutch Guyana. They're divorced now."

"You're going to take it, aren't you?"

Trotti frowned. "Time doesn't stand still."

"You're going to take the job?"

"Job, Bianca?"

"Anyone ever tell you you're sly and devious?"

"Trying to flatter me?"

"It would be a shame if you were to leave the Questura tomorrow."

"I'm leaving in September." He turned his head towards her, noticing again the softness of her skin. She reminded him of his daughter.

"I wasn't the only one to recommend you to the Questore, if that's what you think." She looked at him unblinkingly in the eyes as she lowered the empty cup, with its blue insignia AEROPORTI DI MILANO. "Never understood why you loathe the poor man. Not his fault he can't speak your dialect."

Trotti cupped his hand around his chin.

"Piero, what on earth's that green thing on your tongue?"

"Rhubarb sweet."

"You even drink your coffee with a sweet in your mouth?" She looked unhappy. "Surprised you don't have diabetes, Commissario Trotti."

"It was you who recommended me to the Questore."

"You'd be making a lot of people happy, Piero—and not least me." She turned away and set the cup down on the bar. Taking a paper napkin from its steel holder, Bianca wiped her mouth. She did not wear lipstick. She looked small and fragile in her fur coat. "I was asked if I wanted to be on the team." She raised one shoulder. "I'm not a policeman and I'd much rather work with you."

"Nobody in their right mind would want to work with me."

"Certainly be a lot easier if you gave up those awful sweets of yours. Your breath smells of synthetic rhubarb."

"And coffee."

Bianca Poveri asked fondly, "Why does Tenente Pisanelli think it's your fault he's not married?"

"Pisa's working for Merenda and the *Reparto Omicidi*. Avoids me, and I don't think it's because of the rhubarb sweets."

"Perhaps he ought to thank you." Bianca nodded but her thoughts were elsewhere. "We could do some good work."

"You and Pisa?"

"You'll accept, commissario?"

"I'm not taking anything on—not now."

"Don't be silly. The best years of your life. You're looking marvelous."

"I'm an old man. A balding dinosaur."

"When your wife left you, you looked absolutely terrible."

"You didn't even know me then."

"You went around with a drawn face and harsh word for everybody. But you got over that—and now you look twenty years younger. And very happy. If only you could give up your sugar and take five kilos off your waist."

"Then I'll just have to retire as a happy, fat old man."

"You don't have ideals, commissario?"

"You can't feed your family on ideals. You were talking about hope, the rhetoric of hope. That's what I've always been fed with. Too long—and I can't go on believing. That's why I'm bored with Mani Pulite. That's why I don't care about the reforms. You can't reform people."

"You can care about people."

Trotti shook his head again. "When did you find out the Questore wanted to set up his children's section?"

Bianca smiled with satisfaction, then gestured to the Milan AC banner. THE DICTATORSHIP OF THE PROLETARIAT'S BEEN REPLACED BY THE MORE INSIDIOUS DICTATORSHIP OF SILVIO BERLUSCONI.

"Another coffee?"

She shook her head, not hiding her irritation. "The city needs you. You've been marking time, Piero Trotti."

"The city can get on well enough without Piero Trotti. It managed to get on without me for a thousand years, and unless it all crumbles away just like the Torre Civica, it'll survive another thousand without me. The cemetery's full of indispensable people. I think I've done my duty."

Suddenly the young woman burst out laughing.

"Well?"

"Piero Trotti, I will have another coffee."

"That's what makes you laugh, Bianca?"

"So determined to appear sour, so fed up. A grumpy bear. But of course it's all an act. You know, commissario, you're a big baby."

"That's not what Pisanelli says."

"Perhaps with my job, I'm going to end up like you, pretending I don't care. Trouble is, Piero Trotti," and she prodded his chest with a hard finger, "you can't fool me."

"Why try?"

"Because you like to fool yourself. You're a victim of your own myth. Your own private rhetoric. And you know what?"

"I soon will."

"You're going to take the job, Piero Trotti. Your goats and your chickens are just going to have to wait, I'm afraid. You're going to run the child abuse section."

16: Anna Maria

OVERHEAD, THE WHITE letters on the arrivals board fluttered and then the new times were announced.

Commissario Trotti stood alone at the elbow-high stand, drinking his fourth cup of coffee.

"Piero!"

He turned and recognized Anna Maria. He put the cup down and wiped his mouth with a paper napkin.

His cousin was wearing a coat and beneath it a black skirt and black stockings. She looked like one of the old women from his childhood in Acquanera, only stockier. She pushed her way through the crowd, a suitcase pulling her arm to the ground. A pillbox hat with a veil.

(Trotti was born in Acquanera but had gone to *scuola media* in Santa Maria, where he had lived with his aunt and her two children. Anna Maria was seven years older than Piero. She had loved him and looked after him like a scolding, solicitous sister.

It was with Anna Maria that he used to cycle down to Tarzi on Sandro's bicycle.)

"I've been looking for you everywhere." She spoke in dialect, the vowels oddly flattened by years of exile in the Low Countries. She pushed the black hat from her forehead. Her hair was as white as snow on the January hills above Tarzi. She kissed him hurriedly, smelling—it seemed to Trotti—of the same *eau de toilette* she had used as a girl.

Taking Anna Maria's bag, Trotti replied, "I've been waiting here for over an hour."

"You didn't get my telegram?"

"Anna Maria, why else would I be here? You forgot to put the flight number."

"I don't like planes."

"What flight were you on?"

"I managed to get on the Zurich plane and then change. I tried to phone you but you're never at home."

"There's an answering machine."

"What use is an answering machine?" Anna Maria said irritably, and added, "Why are you wearing that tie?"

Bickering had been part of Trotti's childhood. "Next time I'll come to the airport in plastron and bow tie."

"Always so frivolous."

"Not at all, Anna Maria."

"You could have worn a black tie. You know Sandro's dead."

"What?"

"A heart attack."

"Sandro's dead?"

She looked at him in stern surprise. "Piero, weren't you told?"

The noise of the airport, the smell of coffee and lemons and behind his cousin, the neon lighting of the arrival hall—suddenly Trotti felt weak. A band of metal across his head. His legs seemed to lose their support. "Sandro's dead?" He leaned against the table.

"Yesterday morning at the hospital."

"Why wasn't I told?" His mouth was dry. It was only now that he noticed Anna Maria's eyes were bloodshot behind her Count Cavour glasses. "Why wasn't I told?"

"They phoned me from Brescia at midnight. In his own clinic. They waited nearly fourteen hours before informing me. And now you tell me you weren't contacted."

"Sandro's dead?"

"Heart failure. Sandro was in intensive care for twenty-four hours."

Sandro was dead. Dead at sixty-eight.

Trotti gave a sigh and he could feel his eyes beginning to burn.

Sandro, climbing trees and catching frogs; Sandro, so young and cheerful on his bicycle; Sandro, the partisan bravely chanting "Bella Ciao," afraid of neither German nor Repubblichino. Sandro, who had gone off to Milan when peace had returned to the hills. Sandro, who had studied. Sandro, the handsome medical student with the glistening black hair, the pipe and the easy smile. Sandro, the ladies' man who had never married, who had never had children and who at twenty-nine had lost all the glistening black hair.

Trotti lowered Anna Maria's bag on to the airport floor and he took his cousin in his arms. There was a jerky movement and Anna Maria began to sob behind the round glasses.

Overhead, a speaker announced the delay of a British Airways flight to Manchester.

17: Autostrada

(PIERO TROTTI WAS nearly sixty-five years old and it was a beautiful day in December. He felt healthy and before long, he would be retiring to the hills far, far above the fog of the valley. To the hills where the sky was always a pure blue.)

They had left the airport and Trotti was surprised at the ease with which he had got on to the Venice autostrada. The morning fog had lifted and the afternoon traffic was fast.

It was rare that Trotti drove, but now with his cousin beside him he realized that he enjoyed driving more than he cared to admit. He rarely left the city and when he did, he normally took the train. He sat with his eyes on the truck in front, while the hired Fiat Panda ran smoothly along the newly resurfaced autostrada.

"You knew Sandro was ill, Piero?"

Trotti shook his head.

"You weren't in touch?"

"Not for some time." Trotti took his eyes off the truck and glanced at his cousin.

Anna Maria's skin was grey and wrinkled; she looked old. Not enough sun and too much Dutch coffee. She was a lot heavier than he remembered her.

Trotti said, "I've been busy lately."

"Not enough time to phone your cousin?" There was reproach in her voice and Trotti realized it was not necessarily directed at him.

"Sandro was supposed to contact me three weeks ago, but he never rang. The last time we spoke was over a month ago. It was about the house at Santa Maria."

"That's where you want to retire to, Piero?"

"You don't intend to leave Holland?"

"Don't worry about me." She laughed without feeling. Her round spectacles reflected the sky's light. "I told Sandro a long time ago I didn't need a share of it. Provided I can always stay at Santa Maria when I come back to Italy."

"Of course."

"Not very often, I should think. My three grandchildren are in Holland and they can't speak a word of Italian." She was still wearing the black pillbox hat with its strange veil. Anna Maria turned her broad face away to the countryside beyond the flashing parallels of the crash barrier. "It's all so different—all changed so much. This isn't how I remembered Lombardy."

"It's nicer in the hills—away from the pollution."

"I no longer belong here."

"How's Tazio?"

"Tazio?"

Earlier the fog along the autostrada must have been thick. Several damaged vehicles, Audis, Mercedes, Lancias, lay littered along the verge of the road, the densest highway in Italy. Orange ACI pickups, lights turning, cranes dipped, were removing the crumpled cars.

"My son doesn't write. As stubborn as Sandro. Doesn't even write to his own children."

The Panda went under the bridge of the restaurant on the edge of Bergamo Airport. Here, many, many years earlier, Piero Trotti had been kidnapped by a Sardinian. The place was no longer called Pavesini but Ciao, the red letters astride the road visible from a couple of kilometers away.

The old BP service station was now called IP and sold Q8 petrol.

Again he glanced at his cousin. She had fallen silent, preoccupied with her private thoughts.

With age, Anna Maria had grown to look like her brother Sandro, but harsher and broader. Trotti now found it hard to associate this Dutch woman with the girl he had known and admired and loved, with the lively young woman famous in Santa Maria for her bicycle and her appetite for polenta.

(The intense days of late childhood, when they had been together: Sandro, Anna Maria and Piero Trotti. Anna Maria always in charge, already a woman and waiting for her fiancé to return from Albania; Sandro eternally excited with a new idea, a new challenge to his sharp intelligence; and the younger cousin, Piero Trotti tagging along, glad to be sharing in their special, privileged world.

The fiancé had never returned and in 1947 Anna Maria had left with Piet van Dijk for a new life in Holland.)

Trotti turned his eyes back to the road and watched the truck ahead, labeled TRASLOCHI PETTERLE, SUZZAGA (MN). The driver was exceeding by at least ten kilometers the ninety-kilometer-per-hour limit of the white plaque. Beneath the ropes, the blue tarpaulin flapped angrily.

Sandro was dead.

Sandro, who had slept in the same bed as Trotti; Sandro, who had been grazed by a German bullet in the last weeks of the war and who had returned to the village with his arm heroically in a sling—Sandro was dead and Trotti felt strangely dispassionate. He should be grieving, but he told himself that would come later . . .

"I didn't know there was anything wrong with Sandro—I don't understand it. Last time I saw him he seemed well enough. Excited at the idea of getting the house done up. I think Sandro hated Brescia as much as I—"

"Of course they said heart attack." Anna Marla turned the broad, wrinkled face, the glasses perched on her nose. "I know Sandro committed suicide."

18: Canal

SANDRO'S VILLA WAS at the end of via Naviglio Grande, a three-story building that had been constructed by a local industrialist at the end of the previous century. Constructed in a garish Liberty style.

From the outside, it was ornate. Balconies and intricate stonework that looked like concrete. There was a small garden at the front, more gravel than grass, behind an iron fence.

After Bergamo, Anna Maria had scarcely spoken in the car.

It was now getting late and in the wan light of the winter afternoon a woman from the clinic was waiting by the front gate for Anna Maria. She had brought the key, but Anna Maria sent her away. Anna Maria had her own key that she removed from her inelegant handbag.

They entered the house.

It was a long time since Trotti had been there. In fact, it was a long time since he had been in Brescia. Now with the ring road, he avoided the city whenever returning home from Lake Garda. On those occasions he had needed to see Sandro, he had always gone directly to the clinic up in the hills overlooking Brescia.

Trotti wondered whether Anna Maria was offended by his cheerfulness, by his apparent indifference to the news of Sandro's death.

Trotti did not feel indifference. Simply he could not believe that Sandro was dead. Sandro had always been part of his world, a fact of life, like the sun and the rain, war and marriage, birth and death.

It had long been one of Trotti's more pleasant expectations that together he and Sandro were going to retire to Santa Maria. Each other's company and a lifetime of anecdotes to relate.

Trotti carried Anna Maria's heavy suitcase upstairs. She said she needed to wash. She busied herself settling into the empty villa.

The interior of the house had been recently redecorated in a style that was an amalgam of late Renaissance and European high technology. Digital barometers, sound-triggered lighting and dark Venetian furniture.

There were several photographs on the walls and on the shelves. Photographs of Sandro. Some had been placed in brass frames, others were set haphazardly beneath a broad sheet of glass. Trotti looked at the photographs. There were one or two pictures of close relatives, the rest were of people he did not recognize.

In his thirties, Sandro had bought a collection of wigs to hide his premature baldness. Later he had grown to accept his lack of hair.

There was only one photograph of Sandro and Trotti together.

It had been taken at Santa Maria, on the steps of the church. Trotti looked at the camera while his cousin, in white pleated trousers and two-tone shoes, threw his bald head back to laugh.

Pioppi, a little girl with black pigtails and a frown of concentration, sat on Sandro's lap.

Trotti found the villa depressing. It reminded him too much of Sandro and of Sandro's tastes. Trotti was wondering whether he had time before the funeral to go up to the Villa Ondina on the lake. Get a good night's sleep.

He allowed himself to slump on to a leather couch and he closed his eyes. Perhaps he dozed.

"You haven't asked me whether I'm hungry, Piero." Anna Maria looked at him reproachfully. She had bathed and changed from out of her black clothes into slacks and a sweater. "I didn't eat anything on the plane," she remarked as a proof of fortitude.

"You'd like to go and eat?"

"Why not?" His cousin' shrugged and for the first time since he had seen her at the airport, Anna Maria allowed herself a small smile. "Something light."

"A pizza, perhaps?"

She nodded. "Go and get ready, Piero. And you'd better take one of Sandro's shirts. You can't wear that awful thing."

At the airport Anna Maria had reminded him of the women in the hills; now she was like those aging actresses in the American films who choose to dress and behave as adolescents. The slacks were bright red. The sweater was a russet color. He did not know whether to admire her or to be irritated. She wore high heels and she had broad hips. She held the capacious handbag against her body.

Piero Trotti went upstairs.

He washed, and in Sandro's bedroom he discovered he had to clap to turn on the light.

Trotti tidied his hair with one of Sandro's brushes. A brush that was clogged with artificial hair.

19: Brewery

THEY LEFT THE villa at seven o'clock.

The air had turned very chill, and above the lights of Brescia the stars had come out in numbers.

Many, many years earlier, Trotti had eaten at the Birreria Wührer with his wife and daughter. They were coming back from the lake and were waiting for the evening train to Bari. Sandro, accompanied by a buxom German woman, had picked them up at the station ("The only Habsburg station in Lombardy," Sandro pronounced knowingly) in his red Spider and had taken them to the Birreria Wührer and the beer gardens beneath the steel cowled chimneys.

In those days, the air was heavy with the malt used in the brewing of beer. Now the air was cold with the penetrating damp of the plain and the smoke from the factories that had not yet closed with the recession.

Trotti and Anna Maria entered the wooden restaurant. There was no longer any malt in the air because the production of beer had been relocated south to Rome and Naples. Wührer beer, once the pride of Brescia, was now brewed in the South and could only be bought in cans.

They sat down and Anna Maria looked around her, at the wooden furnishings, old, bogus-Alpine in style, and at the empty tables and white tablecloths.

"How was he when you last saw him, Piero?"

"Sandro?"

She nodded. In the neon light of the birreria, the broad face appeared drawn.

"You know Sandro." Trotti shrugged. "Always cheerful, always the same."

"That didn't stop him from killing himself."

"You're joking."

She shook her head. "He phoned me a couple of weeks ago. I knew he had debts but I never thought . . ." The corners of her mouth turned downwards but she controlled her face as the waiter approached their table. They ordered pizza and beer.

"Debts?"

"He never mentioned anything to you, Piero?"

"Sandro always had money. Money and admiring women."

"That's what comes of growing up poor. You can never get enough. And I don't think I'm any different. Now that it's all over and done with, I realize it was to get away from the poverty of Santa Maria that I married a foreigner." She turned to look through the window. "And spent my life in exile."

Trotti followed her glance. Past the checkered curtain and the square window frame. Beyond the empty beer garden, now hidden by the dark, beyond the gate. On the far side of the road, he could make out the lights of the Pastori agricultural school. He turned back to look at her.

"What debts could Sandro have had?"

"He spent his money like a sailor."

"A villa here, the clinic and the cars. Everything was paid for years ago. When we spoke, Sandro and I, over the phone, it was about the house up in the hills in Santa Maria. His architect friend Alberto was going to restructure the place."

She shook her head.

"Sandro wanted a swimming pool but the mayor wouldn't give him building permission."

"You've been there lately, Piero?"

"Santa Maria? I went up for the festa padronale in August. Sandro was supposed to come, but in the end he phoned to say he couldn't get away from work. I went to look at the house."

"Sandro always put his work before everything else."

"The place is in fairly good shape, but there's at least a hundred million lire to be spent on it. That's what I told Sandro on the phone. He seemed to think I'd be able to do some of the work." Trotti smiled wryly. "We were going to share the cost of restoring. I've got some money put aside. And there's my pension."

"You don't prefer your house up on Lake Garda?"

"My wife's house," Trotti corrected her.

"And how is Agnese?"

"I'm not from Gardesana. It's a nice place, it's where I've spent many happy moments. Pioppi and I spent a fortnight at the Villa Ondina this summer and it was a joy to be with her and the little girl."

"Francesca?"

He nodded. "Like you, Anna Maria, I'm from Santa Maria. From the OltrePò. That's where I grew up—poor, stubborn and proud, And that's where I'm going to spend the last days of my life."

"Still poor, stubborn and proud."

"I've worked hard. I could have retired several years ago but I stayed on in the Questura for . . . for various reasons. Now I want to relax. I've been under pressure for far too long. I've seen too many things I need to forget. Even in my quiet, provincial city."

"Tell me about your wife, Piero."

"What I need is my livestock. And to go looking for mushrooms in the autumn. To drink good wine. And to taste chestnuts. It's time to smell wood smoke. Time that I forgot the city. Time I got back to nature."

"I have no desire to return to Santa Maria. Not now. I always hated the poverty." She shook her head. "It's nothing to do with me, Piero Trotti," she said, and the wrinkled face formed a weary smile.

"What, Anna Maria?"

"There's no house in Santa Maria."

"Of course there's a house in Santa Maria."

"Sold it."

Trotti could feel a coldness in his veins. "What?"

"To pay his debts. I'm afraid Sandro had to sell it. I thought he'd told you." She held her napkin to her lips as the waiter brought the pizzas and beer. "I now see he never consulted you."

20: Daughter

Wednesday, 1 December

TRAMPS, LONG-HAIRED AND apparently still young, sat on the steps of the Teatro Civico, huddling round a shared bottle of wine, while an African, probably from Senegal, watched a clockwork soldier crawl across the plastic sheet of his wares—matches, beads, counterfeit cassettes. The *vu comprà*'s black skin had turned grey with the cold.

Piazza della Loggia.

(Once Sandro had excitedly taken Trotti to see the Carlo Scarpa guardrail. Fascinated by architecture, Sandro could not understand Trotti's indifference before the memorial to the victims of the terrorist bomb.)

Trotti stepped into the telephone booth outside the COIN department store, and as he inserted the card into the slit, he saw that he had a credit for three thousand eight hundred lire.

"Pioppi, is that you?"

"Papa?"

"Pioppi, are you all right? And my little Francesca?"

"Where are you phoning from, Papa?"

"Brescia."

"Why Brescia?"

"I couldn't phone any earlier. How's Nando, Pioppi?"

"Nando's with me now."

"How's the pregnancy coming along?"

"What's wrong, Papa? Why are you in Brescia? You're going to the lake? I thought you were coming here for Christmas."

"I'll try. Perhaps I won't be retiring next year, after all."

"Papa, tell me what is wrong."

"I'd like to come to Bologna for Christmas but I don't want to impose."

"You never phone during the day, Papa. Why are you phoning now? Why don't you want to retire? What's happened? And whoever said anything about you being an imposition?"

"Sandro's dead."

"Who?"

"Your Zio Sandro. I'm in Brescia with Zia Anna Maria. She flew in from Holland yesterday. I picked her up at Linate and this afternoon we'll be driving up to Santa Maria. For the funeral tomorrow morning."

"Zio Sandro's dead?"

"I thought it best to tell you."

"How did he die?"

"His heart. He was in intensive care for nearly a day in his clinic. There was nothing the doctors could do."

"Zio Sandro was young."

"Nearly seventy."

"I'll catch the train first thing tomorrow morning."

"There's no need. You're pregnant, Pioppi, you must rest . . ."

"Have you told Mamma?"

"Agnese's got better things to worry about."

"Mamma's in California on holiday. I've got a number somewhere. I'll try to phone. Mamma's very fond of Sandro."

"Give your mother my best wishes."

"I'll catch the six o'clock train for Turin."

"That's absolutely stupid."

"I'll be in Voghera by tomorrow morning. What time's the funeral?"

"Why are you so stubborn, Pioppi? You're five months pregnant. You shouldn't tire yourself."

"You're my father. I want to be with you."

"It's really not necessary. And the little boy, Pioppi?"

"What little boy?"

"The baby—it's going to be a boy, I suppose."

"The baby's not due for another four months, Papa! I don't wish to know whether it's a boy or a girl. I'll see you tomorrow. I'll get a taxi from the station. Years since I last saw Zia Anna Maria. Just look after yourself, Papa. Ciao, amore."

"But Pioppi —"

"I love you, Papa. Ciao."

21: Phone

"PRONTO."

The telephone was taken off the hook on the second ring and he recognized Signora Magagna's soft voice immediately.

"Piero Trotti."

She did not try to suppress her squeal of joy, nor her Abruzzi accent. "Commissario, I'm so angry with you. You never come and see us. You never come and see the little boys."

"I'll be retiring soon."

"You've been saying that for the last ten years."

"For the last ten years I've been wanting to retire."

"It was good of you to send the present for Mino, but like me, like us all, he wants to see you. In flesh and blood."

"Soon, signora. Once I've retired."

"See you, commissario. It's time you got away from that awful Questura and you started visiting your real friends."

Trotti could not restrain a smile. "Your husband's there, signora?"

"He left this morning for Chiasso and he won't be back before late."

"Can you ask him to ring me, signora?"

"Signora? Don't call me signora, Commissario Trotti. You know there's always a plate of pasta and a bottle of wine waiting for you here. And there's a kilo of acacia honey we've been keeping for you for goodness knows how long."

Trotti laughed. "In September, Giovanna, I'll be free and then I swear I'll come and see you all in Sesto—unless you've already moved back to Pescara."

"Gabri told you, then? There's nothing I'd like more than to leave Milan."

Trotti heard her sigh, and he smiled into the mouthpiece imagining her sitting at the telephone in the neat apartment near the Rondò at San Giovanni. He had not been back in years and he had not seen Magagna's wife since the birth of the second boy. No doubt her waist had thickened, but she had kept her girlish voice and her infectious laugh.

"Do you have a pencil?"

"Just a second," Giovanna Magagna said, and he heard the click as she went to look for something to write with.

When she came back Trotti said, "It's about the Turellini dossier. Can you ask your husband to try and get a copy for me? We've already talked about it but I need to see it as soon as possible. Or sooner. If necessary, tell Magagna to get me a photocopy. It's urgent."

"Turellini—wasn't he the doctor they murdered at Segrate?"

"Tell Magagna to tell no one. It's a personal favor—I don't want anyone other than Magagna knowing I'm interested."

"Commissario, why don't you come here?"

"Perhaps I will."

"I'd love to see you." She added, "You're phoning from the Questura? Very noisy, isn't it?"

"I'm in Brescia."

"You want Gabri to ring you in the Questura?"

"Tell him to contact me on my home number. Tell him I've decided to go ahead with the inquiry."

"To go ahead?"

"For personal reasons. I want to get Turellini's murder sorted out before Christmas."

"Why don't you spend Christmas with us?"

"I'm staying with my daughter in Bologna but yours might not be a bad idea, Giovà," Trotti said.

Suddenly the line went dead and the blinking letters announced peremptorily that the credit had been used up.

Trotti smiled as he replaced the receiver. He abandoned the magnetic card in its red tray.

As he stepped out of the kiosk, Trotti glanced briefly at the huddled tramps. He noticed a syringe poking from a threadbare coat pocket.

22: Funeral

THE DRY COLD of the hills?

It had started to rain in Santa Maria. The clouds were coming up from the valley, encircling the pines, the fir trees and the gaunt power pylons and rapidly hiding the sun. The drizzle began to splatter down on the naked chestnut trees, onto the black umbrellas and the tombstones.

Piero Trotti stood beside his cousin. He held Anna Maria's arm. There were one or two people from the village whom Trotti recognized. There were also a couple of distant relatives who had hurriedly driven up from Milan. A few colleagues from the clinic in Brescia, including two pretty young women, probably nurses. There was nobody from Trotti's side of the family.

Anna Maria was wearing her black coat and the pillbox hat with its veil. She held a white handkerchief in her hand.

(The funeral arrangements, the transport from Brescia had all been organized by the vice director at Sandro's clinic, Riccardo Germani, a man with stooped shoulders and an ingratiating manner. He had seen to everything and Trotti was very grateful.)

Somebody had opened an umbrella for the priest.

Germani had arranged for the priest to be driven up from Tarzi. Trotti had never seen the ecclesiastic before. A plump man with slicked back hair and neat robes. He was from the South. He mumbled the prayers, as if embarrassed by death in general and by the death of Sandro in particular.

Trotti assumed that Anna Maria had not informed him that the cause of death was suicide.

The years that Trotti had spent with his two cousins had been hard. They had been the years of Fascism, of numbing poverty, of war and of sacrifice. They were in many ways the best years of Trotti's life. Years of innocence and hope. Innocence that was soon to be defiled and hope that slowly atrophied as Italy put poverty aside and finally found its place among the wealthy nations.

Days of innocence, and now Sandro was gone.

Suddenly the funeral was all over. The rain fell on the damp casket and the distant relatives threw their flowers, paid their last respects, crossed themselves beneath the drizzle and then headed towards the gate, the waiting cars and the Po valley.

Trotti dropped the flowers on to the grave, not knowing whether he was crying or whether the damp of his cheeks was simply the cold rain. Then the men began to shovel the hard dirt of the hills on to the casket. A harsh, scrabbling sound and Sandro was gone.

Germani was hovering at his side. He had intent blue eyes behind thick lenses.

"I'll need to see the death certificate, of course," Trotti told Germani as he turned away from the grave.

Santa Maria was emptier than Trotti remembered it. Many villagers had emigrated to the Po valley or to the mines in Belgium. The fields where people used to toil had grown into unkempt woodland.

Somebody had daubed *Viva S. Maria Ultras* on the low wall of the graveyard, exhorting the local football hooligans.

For a brief moment Trotti wondered how the village managed to find eleven players, let alone supporters.

Then he saw his daughter.

Pioppi was climbing out of a taxi at the cemetery gate. She wore a fur coat that could not hide the swell of her belly.

"Life goes on," Trotti said to himself.

Pioppi was holding a bunch of flowers. Pregnant and slightly overweight, she radiated beauty.

Behind her was Nando holding the sleeping, precious Francesca in his arms.

"Cheese in the mousetrap?"

Anna Maria turned her broad face towards him. "What are you mumbling, Piero Trotti?"

For the first time in a long, long time, Trotti felt there was indeed a purpose to his existence.

His eyes focused on his cousin. "What you need is a cup of coffee, Anna Maria." He smiled as he added, "I could do with a packet of rhubarb sweets."

23: Cyclamen

Friday, 3 December

TROTTI TRIED TO push the hammering away and rolled on to his side, but the banging continued and he opened an eye, squinted at his watch—an ancient present from Agnese.

Ten to four.

It was cold and Trotti wanted to burrow back beneath the warmth of the sheets but the banging would not go away.

Banging accompanied by the jabbing ring of the doorbell.

Trotti threw back the bedsheets. He could not find his slippers and the stone floor was cold. He slipped into his nightgown.

Ten to four, Friday morning.

A further burst of knocking and the bell was ringing with unbroken insistence.

"I'm coming," Trotti shouted irritably. He had no idea who the visitor was. It was now more than fifteen years since his wife used to come home at all hours of the night.

It briefly occurred to Trotti that it was stupid to risk your life when you were a grandfather, when you were only a few months from a well-deserved retirement in the hills of the OltrePò and when you could receive a bullet fired through the flimsy wood of the front door.

A friend of Eva's?

There was a service revolver somewhere in the house that he had brought home after Eva's sudden departure. Trotti did not bother searching for it. The experience of a professional policeman, the training from the police school in Padua were forgotten in a sleepy mist. "Who's there?" he asked, more annoyed than worried.

The ringing suddenly ceased and in the silence, he heard the voice, almost apologetic. "Pisanelli."

Trotti laughed as he pulled back the iron bolt and opened the door.

Tenente Pisanelli of the Polizia di Stato stood in the yellow circle of light of the doorstep. He had knocked over one of the pots of cyclamen by the balustrade.

"Who is it, Piero?"

Trotti spun round.

Anna Maria was in the hall, wearing a shapeless cotton night-gown and a bed cap from a different century. Concern had tautened the sleepy features of her face.

"A colleague." He gestured Anna Maria away, back to Pioppi's old bedroom.

Now that Pisanelli's hands had ceased their knocking, they were returned to the pockets of baggy trousers. Pisanelli was wearing his old suede jacket. With his bald head, with the long side hair hanging over his ears and down to his collar, he looked more like an unemployed mechanic than a lieutenant in the state police. He needed a shave.

"Felt like dropping by for a chat, commissario," Pisanelli said cheerfully, and ducking his head, slightly brushed past Trotti into the hall.

"You're carrying that Beretta of yours?" Trotti asked. He added, "I enjoy being woken up in the middle of the night."

"Then you'd better get dressed."

"Keep your voice down." Trotti gestured to the open door of Pioppi's bedroom. A myopic teddy bear stared down from where it perched on the top of the wardrobe. Its one glass eye was dusty. "There's somebody in there trying to sleep," Trotti said in a hoarse whisper. "Like most people in Italy at this time of night."

"I thought I'd have to wake up the entire city. The way you sleep, commissario, you must have a blameless conscience."

Despite the cold, Pisanelli was sweating. He ran the back of his hand along his forehead. "Which I find very hard to believe."

The two policemen went along the hall to the kitchen.

Trotti turned on the light. Plates and utensils were in the sink. The tap was dripping slightly. There was a smell of wine and chamomile and Anna Maria's eau de cologne. The clock faithfully continued its ticking on the top of the refrigerator.

"You'd better get dressed, commissario," Pisanelli said and unceremoniously slumped down on one of the chairs. He took out a packet of cigarettes.

"At four in the morning?"

"Perhaps I'm interrupting something." Pisanelli gestured towards the bedroom door.

"A seventy-two-year-old lady."

"Can you be fussy?"

"You're not going to smoke a cigarette here," Trotti said, but there was no anger in his voice. He noticed in the kitchen light that Pisanelli's thin hands were trembling as he fumbled with the packet of untipped Esportazione. "Want a coffee?"

"Not a bad idea, commissario. Go and get dressed before your feet drop off from frostbite. I'll make some coffee. Six sugars?" Pisanelli stuffed the cigarette into the corner of his mouth—the stubble was grey beneath his chin—and went to the sink. "We're in a hurry."

"We? I'm in no hurry."

"Get some clothes on fast, commissario." Pisanelli unscrewed the espresso machine. "A cold night to get murdered."

24: Corollary

LIKE DRIVING THROUGH watery anisette.

Trotti sat beside Pisanelli in silence. It was freezing in the old Citroën and Pisanelli concentrated on his driving, leaning forward over the steering wheel, trying to peer through the thick fog now whitened by the street lamps.

They went under the ring road, finally completed after twenty years, and took the turning for Melegnano. No sooner had the last lamp fallen behind them than the fog became an almost impenetrable pitch-black.

Pisanelli drove slowly, following the line of the ditch that separated the provincial road from the rice fields.

Occasionally a voice spoke over the two-way radio Pisanelli had installed in the car. A woman's voice, reassuringly metallic and timeless.

Trotti looked at the speedometer. The needle wavered at thirty-five kilometers per hour. Trotti huddled down into his waxed jacket; he felt dirty, and beneath a pair of trousers he was still wearing his pajamas. His feet were cold under the two pairs of unmatching socks. There was sleep in his eyes.

Too old to be driving across the Po valley in the middle of a December night. The taste of sweet coffee mixed with bile rising from his stomach.

They traveled without speaking for twenty minutes, only once overtaking another vehicle, a bundle of a man sitting astride a squat Vespa that was immediately engulfed into the fog behind them.

Through the darkness, suddenly strangely near and quite silent,

Trotti saw the revolving blue lamp; then the red taillights. Finally he saw the spotlight. It was directed downwards and it was only at the last moment that he caught sight of its uncertain rim on the cold, wet earth.

"Thanks for fetching me, Pisa."

Pisanelli did not reply. He pulled the aging Deux Chevaux on to the edge of the road, the front wheel only centimeters from the open ditch. Trotti had to wait for Pisanelli to get out before he could slide across the seat. He caught his sleeve on the stupid gear lever.

Polizia di Stato and a car of the Polizia Stradale. There was also another van, and in the flashing light Trotti read the inscription: ASSESSORATO ALL'ECOLOGIA/PROVINCIA DI MILANO.

The lamp on the police Campagnola was pointing down into the water of the stream. Two men in city shoes were leaning over the corpse. One looked up and recognizing Trotti, gave him a weary smile. "You got here fast, Rino."

Piero Trotti had seen his first corpse at the end of the war, and during his years in the Questura, Trotti had subsequently been required to deal with many dead bodies, some in an advanced state of decomposition. Each time the sight of death remained a shock. The sudden, abrupt end. The indignity. The complete futility of death—or perhaps worse, the implicit, unmentionable corollary: the futility of life.

A dead body was always a painful sight. When the dead body was a friend or an acquaintance, it was still more painful—a lot more painful. A face that he had once known, features that Trotti had once recognized, now frozen into terminal immobility. An end to the familiar intonation, an end to the mannerisms, the ticks, to the shared moments, to the shared passage through this life.

Trotti knew it was Bassi even though Pisanelli had not spoken a word.

He tried to force himself into adopting the well-worn professional approach. A matter of habit, but a habit that now deserted him. Before the reality of the pale face, the lolling tongue and the sightless eyes, the damp black hair no longer able to hide Bassi's incipient baldness, Trotti felt angry and ill.

(Despite the cold, Trotti could smell the stench of the polluted water.)

He crouched down and he noticed that Bassi was wearing his camel coat, that the tie was still undone at his neck. Even in death, Mister FBI had been faithful to his American models, only instead of the end coming in exotic Flatbush, Brooklyn, or beneath the Verazzano Bridge, Fabrizio Bassi had been dispatched, shot in the head and possibly drowned, in a foul-smelling tributary of the Lambro, between the dark rice fields and the Strada provinciale 22 to Melegnano.

The ambulance arrived, lit up by two revolving blue lights. An orange strip and a schematic snowdrop along the side. Two men jumped out from the rear.

Trotti turned back to Pisanelli, who was leaning against the bonnet of the Campagnola. "Pisa, give me one of your Esportazione."

25: Friend

"Why did you come looking for me, Pisa?"

"Thought you might be interested."

"Three years that I haven't worked on a murder case."

"Bassi was a friend of yours, wasn't he?" Pisanelli said sourly. He was driving with caution, following the irrigation ditch.

At regular intervals, they drove past a billboard advertising furs or parmesan cheese or Pirelli tires, standing in isolation like abandoned sentinels, caught in the yellow beams and then forgotten. It was still another half-hour before the sun rose to the east. Pisanelli added, "Poor bastard."

"Bassi was never my friend."

"He worked for you, commissario."

"You worked for me. Nobody's ever accused us of being friends."

"Thank you for those kind words."

"Bassi was kicked out of the Questura."

"You know why, commissario."

"Because it suited the Questore and all the Questore's Socialist friends."

"Socialists? I'm not sure I know that word."

"You should do, Pisa—they ruled this country for long enough."

"And now they've gone the way of the dinosaurs. Only to be replaced by new dinosaurs."

"I thought you voted for the Lega Lombarda."

"Of course I did. We've now got a bright new Lega mayor but it's really not too hard to see the Leghisti are just the same as the Socialists. The same or worse." Pisanelli suddenly grinned. "There was talk of bringing out a commemorative stamp to Bettino Craxi, our Socialist prime minister—only they were afraid people would spit on the wrong side of the stamp."

Trotti smiled perfunctorily.

"The Questore had Bassi thrown out of the police because Bassi was screwing the mayor's wife."

"The Questore was jealous?"

"A couple of weeks ago Bassi came looking for me."

"I know."

The radio continued softly emitting its metallic monologue, only now it was a man's voice.

"How do you know?"

"He told me."

Trotti turned and looked at Pisanelli. In the feeble light of the dashboard, he looked prematurely aged and weary; Pisanelli was gnawing at his lip.

"Bassi talked to you?"

"Yes, commissario."

"What did he tell you?"

"Seemed to think we were friends." Pisanelli shrugged and then fell silent.

"We?"

"Bassi for some strange reason believed you and I were friends."

For a moment, Trotti did not speak. He could feel Pisanelli's resentment and for once he did not know what to say. Or perhaps Trotti could not bring himself to say the words he should have said a long time ago.

"Thanks for coming to fetch me, Pisa—even if it meant destroying my cyclamen plant."

"I'll buy you another one."

"What made you come looking for me?"

Pisanelli pursed his lips.

"Why, Pisa?"

"Bassi wasn't very intelligent."

"Not if he thought you and I were friends."

"Not very sharp. And perhaps he wasn't particularly honest. He wasn't my cup of tea. A womanizer with a dick bigger than his brain."

"I wouldn't know. Both organs atrophied away many years ago." Trotti grimaced. "In my case."

"Too many boiled sweets."

"Why d'you come out to via Milano and pull me out of bed?"

"Away from your seventy-two-year-old girlfriend?"

"You're talking about my cousin."

"Incest?" Pisanelli grinned again and steam rose from his nostrils. "Best to keep it in the family." He continued to peer at the road.

Trotti sighed.

From time to time a truck went past in the opposite direction, trundling northwards to the metropolitan area of Milan, to the sprawling, sleeping hinterland.

Trotti had forgotten that his feet were cold, he had forgotten the taste of the cigarette and the bile rising in his throat. "What made you come for me? I thought you were angry with me."

"They treated Bassi like dirt. He'd done nothing wrong—other than getting into bed with the wrong woman. They kicked him out of the Polizia and he had to go into private investigation. Cheap divorce work that I wouldn't even give to my dog. And instead of finishing out his career in the Questura, warming his fat backside on a radiator like the rest of us, drinking instant coffee and grappa, he's now dead in a ditch."

"You didn't know he was dead."

"I knew it was Bassi—and I knew he'd seen you."

"Thanks," Trotti said simply. "I appreciate your thinking of me."

"You want me to drop you off in via Milano?" Pisanelli asked flatly. "You've got mud all over your pajamas."

"Are you hungry?"

Pisanelli shook his head without taking his eyes from the road.

"I thought you were angry with me, Pisanelli."

"What on earth for, Commissario Trotti?"

"Angry with me because you're not married."

Pisanelli hesitated, bit his lip and was about to speak when Trotti held up his hand. "Perhaps we should have a look at Bassi's bureau first."

"I'm thirty-nine years old and I'm still unmarried. A single man, commissario, with no wife and no children to go home to. I think I've got a lot to thank you for."

"Let's go to Bassi's place."

"I've got better things to do, commissario. Like sleeping."

Trotti started to laugh. "You shouldn't have got me out of bed, Pisa. Now let's go to Bassi's office." He slapped the younger man's shoulder. "Then I can treat you to breakfast. Care for a rhubarb sweet?"

26: Bureau

"YOU THINK BASSI'LL complain? He's dead."

They had reached the first suburbs of the city, the apartment blocks that had been built in the seventies before the piano regolatore began to slow down the sprawling concrete.

"You know where he lives, commissario?"

They were about a kilometer from the Visconti castle, in a well-kept quarter of the city. Trees, public gardens, sufficient parking space for the cars along the streets. "On the left, Pisa. You see that mini-supermarket? Turn left and then you go over the canal." Trotti's face was drawn. "You can park over there, next to the van."

Pisanelli brought the Citroën to a halt, turned off the engine but left the soft crackle of the radio. Together the two men got out into the cold morning and crossed the street, headed towards a four-story building.

Through the swirling cold fog drifted the smell of baking bread.

It was now seven o'clock and there were already people around. Men in winter coats were leaving home, climbing into their cars or walking briskly towards the nearby bus stop.

In this part of town there was no litter on the streets.

"Ten hours of sunlight," Trotti said. "I hate the winter."

"Why don't you retire to Argentina? I thought you had an uncle in Buenos Aires. You'd be happy there."

"And my pigs?"

They went through a small gate and approached the varnished front door of the building, via Nazioni Unite, 7. There was a camera above the nameplates.

FBI—Fabrizio Bassi Investigations was on the fourth floor.

"You're going to attract attention, commissario?"

Trotti did not answer but pressed one of the bells.

After a few moments, a small sheet of metal slid back and the peeping, black eye of a camera squinted at them. There was a red light and the squeaky sound of a woman's petulant voice.

"ENEL."

As if offended, the camera withdrew and the sheet of metal slid back into place. Another short silence while the two men looked at each other.

Pisanelli smiled. In the feeble light, his face seemed less tired.

Then a click and the front door was released.

"You never told me whether you're still carrying that Beretta?" Trotti asked as he pushed back the door and they entered the building. It smelt of polish and paint. A couple of bicycles leaned against the stairs.

From somewhere a voice was calling, "Who is it?"

"Electricity, signora. Reading the meters."

"At this time of the day?" the disapproving female voice replied and there came the angry snap of a door being closed.

They went up stairs of polished marble. The banisters were of iron with a wooden handrail.

"Nice place to have an office."

Trotti said, "Bassi lives here."

"You've been before, commissario?"

"At the time of his problems in the Questura, I came here."

"Why?"

"In eighty-eight or in eighty-nine. Time goes by so fast."

Pisanelli said, "Not for Bassi—not anymore."

They reached the top floor. Here the apartments were smaller than those on the lower floors because of the slope of the roof.

Pisanelli pointed to an old brass name plate on the left-hand door. FAMIGLIA BASSI. "I didn't know he was married."

"Divorced," Trotti said tersely and knocked noisily on the door. "Like most policemen."

"Or unmarried."

Trotti knocked again.

No sound.

They waited a minute before Trotti turned the handle.

"Don't you even have a warrant, commissario?" Pisanelli's breath was warm on Trotti's cheek.

The door did not budge. Trotti turned the handle in the opposite direction, leant slightly against the glazed wood and the door moved slowly, ponderously.

The two men entered the apartment.

Pisanelli held a small pistol in his right hand.

27: Pigsty

"YOU'VE GOT GLOVES?"

Pisanelli shook his head. "A Kleenex." His voice was strained and he seemed out of breath. His fingers were white around the butt of the Beretta.

Trotti took a pair of shabby leather gloves from his coat pocket. "Put these on before you turn on the switch."

Pisanelli did as he was told. The ring of overhead neon flickered and then came to life.

Trotti whistled softly.

"A pigsty," Pisanelli said. "Bassi was very messy or . . ."

"Somebody's made the mess for him." Trotti took a deep breath, looking at the disorder, at the scattered possessions.

The short hallway gave on to a larger room.

Diffidently the two policemen moved forward. Pisanelli kept his back to the wall.

Everything that could be opened, spilled or emptied had been opened, spilled and emptied. There were books and papers scattered across the floor. A divan had been tipped over backwards and a knife had been run along the bottom, slicing the jute protection.

"Unlike us," Trotti remarked, "Bassi's visitors knew what they were looking for."

"Unless of course it was Bassi himself who set to work. One of those evenings when they're showing the same Alberto Sordi film on every television channel."

Beyond the living room were a bedroom and a kitchen. Ripped

bedsheets trailed from the bed, spilled coffee in the sink, saucepans on the floor.

"The neighbors must've heard something."

"What the hell were Bassi's visitors looking for?" Trotti asked.

"If we knew that, we'd know why we're here."

The two policemen returned to the hall, walking carefully to avoid treading on the cassettes, books and papers. Old, yellowing copies of the *Provincia Padana*, dating back to the mid-eighties.

They entered the small study that Bassi had transformed into an office.

"Looking for a document or something. Something that could have been hidden between the sheets of a newspaper." Pisanelli slipped the Beretta into his hip pocket. He ran his hand nervously through his lank hair.

The damage was worse in the study. Filing cases had been prized open and the contents cast across the floor. One chair leg was snapped, but apart from that there were no signs of a struggle. "Doesn't look as if Bassi was murdered here," Pisanelli said. "Nothing broken, no signs of blood."

"Bassi wasn't necessarily here. If he'd been taken by force, there'd've been a fight. He was a big man. The neighbors would have heard."

"Bassi could have been drugged."

"Which would mean carrying him down four flights of stairs." Trotti raised his shoulders. "Eight families living here. Somebody would have seen something."

"Perhaps we ought to ask."

Neither the curtains nor the blinds were drawn. A grey light came through the window.

"We can't ask because we're not here."

Pisanelli pointed. The drawers were open but the locks were undamaged. "The drawers weren't locked or else these people had the key." Pisanelli stood beside Trotti. He was still breathing heavily.

"If you were a private detective, doing divorce work, wouldn't you keep everything under lock and key, Pisa?"

"Depends. Is this where his clients came?"

Trotti shrugged. "I don't imagine Bassi let many people in here."

"He had children?"

Trotti did not reply.

There were several posters in the living room, the Duomo in

Florence, and on the walls of the office were a couple of diplomas.
There was only one photograph.

It had fallen from the desk. The glass had divided into shards
that were still kept together by the plastic frame. Trotti crouched
down and looked at the picture. He pointed without letting his finger
touch the glass. "That's her."

"Who?"

A banner fluttered behind their heads. FESTA NELLA CITTÀ,
LUGLIO 1988.

Bassi was wearing a short-sleeved summer shirt. He appeared
to be young and healthy. He was looking at the woman who smiled
back at him quizzically. Together they were standing near an open
trestle table that was loaded down with watermelon.

Behind the couple, Trotti recognized the curved arches of the Ponte
Coperto, the bridge where fêtes were frequently held in summer.

A black and white photograph.

It was hard to tell whether the couple was together or whether the
photographer had unwittingly seized the moment of their meeting.

The woman was in her mid-twenties, broad and slightly fleshy
like a German or a Scandinavian. She was wearing a summer frock
that showed much cleavage to an ample chest. Delicate, intelligent
features.

Pisanelli bent over beside him. "The mayor's wife?"

"Signora Viscontini, the ex-mayor's wife."

"Bassi kept this photo in the office?"

"Perhaps it wasn't in the office before the spring cleaning," Trotti
said, turning to look at Pisanelli.

Pisanelli was no longer listening; a confident smile had split the
greying stubble of his face. He was pointing his finger.

Trotti's glance followed the line of Pisanelli's outstretched hand.

Outside, in the city, dawn was lighting up the sky and there was
enough daylight for Trotti to recognize the answering machine.

An answering machine placed on a shelf beneath the top surface
of the desk.

"Want to hear, commissario?"

Pisanelli was wearing only the right-hand glove. He deftly pulled
the machine out on its revolving support beneath the desk. He
pressed the replay button.

A click. A short silence, then an angry whir. A second click as
the answering tape began to play.

The Friuli accent. "I think you'd better give me that, don't you, Tenente Pisanelli?"

Together Pisanelli and Piero Trotti swung round in surprise.

Framed in the door, wearing a neat shirt and herringbone jacket, stood the Questore. He was smiling and his loden overcoat was held jauntily over one arm. The other hand was held out towards Pisanelli.

He wore a tartan tie.

28: Twin Udders

"THE ANSWER IS no."

Trotti looked at the Questore in silence, trying to retain his anger.

"Perhaps you'd care to sit down, Piero."

"I don't see what else there is to say."

"Why don't you go home then? Get shaved and get dressed." The Questore's smooth face broke into a friendly smile. "I believe you're wearing pajamas beneath that pair of trousers."

"Perhaps you'd care for my resignation?"

The Questore had moved to behind the large, empty desk in his office. He casually dropped his coat on to the glass surface. He did not take his eyes from Trotti, but leaning over, pressed a button and spoke into the telephone, without having to remove the hand set. "Giulia, could you bring me a pot of coffee?"

There was no reply.

"Damn lazy bitch's not in yet."

"You want my resignation, Signor Questore?"

"Just ten months away from a well-earned retirement? A bit melodramatic." He stood up straight, his hands on his hips and straightening his shoulders.

"On Tuesday you were asking me to stay on."

"Of course I'd like you to stay on, Piero." The Questore sat down. "And before you make any rash decisions, I'd like you to consider my proposal carefully."

The office was large and decorated in the same Italo-Californian style as the rest of the Questura. Modern and antiseptic. The air smelt of synthetic carpet.

"In Italy there are something like four thousand violent deaths a year. In our city, there are scarcely eight at most."

Beyond the window, in the grey fog of the early morning, the national flag hung limp over the buses in Strada Nuova.

Trotti could feel his anger slowly ebbing away. A kind of clinical coldness was creeping into his body, into his head and his reasoning. He had become a spectator. "You want me to stay on but you don't want me on this murder case?"

"You had no right to go to his place. I know you and Bassi were once friends."

"Bassi was a colleague."

"In your way, Piero Trotti, you're one of the best." A thin smile. "But I'm afraid I don't want you on this case."

"You haven't told me, Signor Questore, why you went to his office this morning."

"You're not part of the Reparto Omicidi and for reasons that really are nothing to do with me, you fail to collaborate with Merenda. Merenda's a good investigator."

Trotti took a sweet from his pocket. "Let me work with Merenda. Let me work with anybody you care to name, Signor Questore." His voice was calm, composed.

The Questore hesitated. His hand stroked the soft material of his loden overcoat.

"I should be quite happy to collaborate with Commissario Merenda. I am quite sure that . . ."

"Piero, for God's sake, why don't you just sit down? You're making me nervous."

Trotti lowered himself into one of the uncomfortable chairs.

"You know what I think of you, don't you, Piero?"

"Signor Questore, you don't know what I think of you."

A generous brushing aside of any hostility. "You're a good policeman."

A light knock on the door and a woman entered carrying a silver tray with a steaming pot of coffee and two cups taken from the dopolavoro.

"I thought you weren't there."

She wore a beige skirt and blue high heel shoes. The sweet perfume battled with the aroma of coffee. She placed the tray on the desktop, turned and went to the door.

"Thank you, Giulia."

Before closing it behind her the woman spoke almost inaudibly. "I should like to remind you I try to be diligent even if I am a lazy bitch."

The Questore blushed to the roots of his glossy hair.

Silently the door was closed.

With his hand, Trotti rubbed his lips. He frowned, "Why can't I work on Bassi's death?"

The Questore's eyes focused anew on Trotti. "Why do you want to?"

"At the end of my career you can allow me that."

"Since the death of the Ciuffi girl . . ."

"I do not care to discuss Brigadiere Ciuffi."

"I don't want you on murder. It's as simple as that."

"I identified the killer of the Belloni woman."

It was as if Trotti had hit a button. A smile spread across the Questore's complacent face. He ran a hand through the well-cut hair. "Precisely."

"Then why can't I work on this Bassi killing?"

"You identified Belloni's murderer—but you used your own, highly idiosyncratic methods. Against my express will. Against my orders, Piero Trotti. You identified the killer but in so doing, you managed to get another man killed."

"A drug dealer."

Suddenly exasperated, the Questore slammed his open palm against the desktop, causing the coffee cups to rattle. "It's not for you to play God. It's not for you to decide who gets killed and who doesn't."

"The man was a drug dealer, Signor Questore."

"He was a human being—and I was answerable to the public of this city when his charred remains were on the front of the *Provincia*." The man from Friuli caught his breath. "The answer's no, Piero. I don't like having you out in the streets. This isn't Los Angeles. It isn't Palermo or even Crotone. A small, middle-class town, getting on with its life beneath the twin udders of the university and the hospital. A city that used to vote Socialist and now—unfortunately—votes solidly for the Lega. Can't you understand, Piero, that you're a dinosaur?"

"Because I'm going bald?"

"Because you use the wrong methods."

"And that's why you want me to run the Child Abuse Unit?"

"The wrong methods on the street. But you're a good man, Piero."

"I'd like to believe you."

"A good man, because you care. Because you get involved. You've done some sterling work with Signora Scola and the others in the past eighteen months." The Questore gestured to the files against the far wall, next to a Piranesi-like print of the city's towers. "Glowing reports from the hospital, for heaven's sake. You're a gifted policeman—but when you get on to the front page of the paper, I need to know why." He took the coffeepot and started pouring into the cups. "You're answerable to me. And I have to carry the responsibility for your actions."

"Signor Questore, the answer's no."

"No coffee?"

Trotti was now standing up. "Your Child Abuse Unit—you know where you can put it." He turned on his heel and walked across the synthetic carpet. "Just as you know where you can put that Po water that you like to call coffee."

Trotti left the office.

"Get showered and shaved, Piero Trotti, and get changed into some decent clothes," the Questore called out after him. "We'll talk about it all once you've had a good rest."

29: Coffee

"AH, COMMISSARIO."

Trotti squinted against the light.

"I was looking for you," Pisanelli said cheerfully. He looked tired.

"What for?"

"What did the Questore say?"

"It's not important."

"I can drive you home, if you wish." Pisanelli ran a hand across his stubbly chin, repressing a smile. "You don't look your best in your muddy pajamas. Even with that fashionable English jacket."

Trotti shrugged and together the two men stepped through the metal detector and out on to the steps.

The man on duty gave a perfunctory salute. He was wearing a leather jacket and was stamping his feet to keep them warm.

They were standing, Trotti and Pisanelli, outside the entrance of the Questura. It was still too early for the sun to break through the morning fog. A couple of university janitors cycled past, smoking and chatting happily on their ancient bicycles.

Italia Felix, land of saints and heroes, poets and navigators.

"You found out what the Questore was doing at Bassi's place?"

Trotti said, "Take me home, Pisa. I need some coffee."

"You need some sleep."

"Time for that when I retire."

"When are you going to retire?"

"Probably this afternoon."

They went down the steps and around the side of the building to where Pisanelli had left his Citroën. The doors were not locked and Trotti climbed in beside Pisanelli. Pisanelli turned on the noisy engine, and taking the one-way street in the wrong direction, he turned into Strada Nuova. He drove the car over the cobbles, heading out of the city center, away from the white signs of the pedestrian zone.

"He lives opposite."

"Who?" Pisanelli turned, one hand on the wheel, two fingers on the lateral gear lever.

"The Questore lives in the via Nazioni Unite."

Pisanelli shook his head. "When have you known the Questore to do investigative work?"

"Perhaps he was afraid of finding me there."

"He's afraid of a lot of things." Pisanelli caught his breath. They had stopped at the Cinema Castello crossing, at the traffic lights, where the overhead red light was much larger than the amber or green. Like the eye of an angry giant. "The Questore's always been a good Craxi man. That's how he got where he is. But the Socialists are out of power. They don't even exist—and, God willing, Craxi should soon be in jail."

The lights changed and the Citroën moved forward.

"I don't see what that's got to do with the Questore finding us in via Nazioni Unite?"

"They wanted to print a stamp with Craxi. You know why they didn't?"

Trotti said flatly, "Too many people've been licking the back side long enough."

For a moment, Pisanelli seemed irked. Then he grinned buoyantly. "We live in a *partitocrazia*, commissario. You seem to forget that."

"D'you ever get the sense of déjà vu?"

"*Déjà vu comprà.*" Pisanelli smiled to himself. "The Socialists are a spent force. But the ties remain. There's something about Bassi that's seriously worrying the Questore. How on earth did he know so early in the morning Bassi'd been found dead? You don't believe he just happened to be making a courtesy call? And don't forget, commissario, it was the Questore who had Bassi thrown out of the Polizia."

"You're saying the Questore's involved with Bassi's death?" Pisanelli laughed.

"What's funny?"

"Remember what Indro Montanelli said in his newspaper in Milan? 'Vote for the Christian Democrats but be sure to hold your nose.' The Christian Democrats and the Socialists both ran this country ever since the early sixties—and together they had it sewn up, so that they could get on with the serious business of fleecing the entire nation."

"What's that got to do with the Questore?"

"You said yourself Bassi was a good policeman."

"Slow and unimaginative."

"A good policeman like the rest of us."

They had reached the bus stop opposite the Pizzeria Sans Souci in via Milano. Pisanelli pulled the car on to the edge of the pavement and the two men got out.

"You never lock your car?"

"Who'd want to steal anything French?"

They crossed the road, carefully avoiding the buses and cars that abruptly loomed out of the fog.

"You've got a player, commissario?"

They went up the stairs.

"What player?"

The potted cyclamen lay on its side, spilling dark earth on to the concrete.

"After all," Pisanelli said, producing the cassette from the pocket of his suede coat, "you might just understand what Bassi's message's all about."

30: Scola

"A POLITICIAN."

"Who?"

"The Questore."

"Piero, I've got little Priscilla in this afternoon. Do you think you could come again? You saw her on Tuesday morning, with the snake?"

"Signora Scola, I am very busy."

"For a moment I thought we were almost there. Not hard to see she's conflating the snake with something else. I think the mother would like to help. Sweet enough woman, but ignorant. If only she could stop smoking for a moment."

"Signora Scola, you catch me at a bad time."

The voice was slightly accusatory. "You weren't in the Questura yesterday."

"I was at a funeral."

"Oh, I'm sorry." A hesitation. "A friend?"

"My cousin."

He heard her catch her breath. "Ah." There was an awkward silence. "The Questore thinks . . ."

"The Questore's a bastard. A Socialist and a bastard."

"Piero, forget about the Questore. You'll soon be free. Free to worry about other things."

"The other day he was saying he wanted me to stay on."

She laughed and, hearing the amusement in her voice, Trotti allowed himself a wry smile. "I don't see what's so funny."

"Ever since I've known you, Piero, you've been complaining

about that man, saying he won't let you do your job, won't let you carry out your investigations."

"Our Questore from the Friuli doesn't like me rocking the boat."

"And now you say he wants you to stay on. Why?"

"Perhaps his boat's sinking."

He could imagine her, wearing her pale lipstick. The fine, intelligent features and the olive complexion, the exotically slanting eyes. "Piero, I really don't see why you let the Questore trouble you. Him or anybody else. You can get by without them—you've got your friends. Both inside and outside the Questura. And soon you'll be in your place in the OltrePò."

"My place in the OltrePò?" Trotti repeated. "I'm not quite so sure."

"Why not?"

"You know the Questore's setting up a child protection center."

There was a long silence. "What?"

(From the kitchen came the smell of coffee and toast. He could hear his cousin speaking with Pisanelli. They were both laughing, Pisanelli's voice deep, Anna Maria's voice high and rasping.)

"Council of Europe, Interpol—I don't know."

"Is this another of your jokes, Piero?"

"*Conseil d'Europe*," Trotti said in approximate French, recalling the logo on the sheaf of paper and the accompanying ring of twelve stars. "The Questore's scared."

"That's marvelous."

"Marvelous?"

(More laughter from the kitchen. It was pleasant to have visitors to the empty house.)

"Piero, isn't this what you've been working towards for the last two years?" A girlish giggle of delight. "A functioning child protection center—that's marvelous."

"Don't pin your hopes on me."

"With you in charge, Piero? Your pigs and chickens are going to have to wait."

"Last night Fabrizio Bassi was killed."

"Who?"

"A private detective. He used to work with me. A bullet in the head. They found his body this morning in a polluted tributary of the Lambro."

"And you want to work on the case?"

"The Questore won't let me."

"Why not?"

"Signora Scola, he doesn't want me anywhere near a murder."

"You said he needs you."

"That was Tuesday. And that was for the child protection sector."

"You tried to bargain with the Questore?"

"A deal's out of the question. I told him I'd run this child center if he'd let me come in on the murder. Assist Commissario Merenda, if I had to."

"I don't see why you want to get involved in another murder inquiry."

Trotti said nothing.

"So you're not going to take it? The child center—you're not going to take it?"

"I don't owe the Questore any favors."

"And me?" Over the telephone line Signora Scola gave a sigh of irritation. "You don't want to run the center, Piero?"

"I gave up wanting things a long time ago."

"I don't understand you. Child abuse, violence towards children—it's been your obsession these last eighteen months." She added more softly, "Remember—that's how we met. The Barnardi child?"

"I remember."

"You're being offered what you've always wanted. On a silver platter, Piero."

He shook his head slowly. He was sitting on his bed. For once it was neatly made. With Dutch precision. Anna Maria had pulled the white sheets tight and carefully turned down the edges. She had changed the pillow case, plumped the feathers.

"Getting what you wanted on a platter, Piero. What we wanted—both you and I."

Trotti was silent.

"Sometimes I think you're the most exasperating man I've ever met." She moved her mouth away from the handset. "Precisely what you always wanted. Why does this Bassi's death mean so much to you?"

"If I can't do what I want, then I won't do anything."

"I've never heard you mention Bassi."

"Bassi was a colleague. Not excessively intelligent and not particularly honest. But he worked for me, he came to see me a couple of times. Wanted my help on a murder in Milan. And now he's dead, assassinated in cold blood, a bullet in the head. I think I owe him something, don't you?"

"You owe the children something, Piero Trotti. Other people can carry out the murder inquiry. Perhaps as well as you. You've got no stomach for corpses—that's what you told me not so long ago. But the work we've been doing with all these children—that's something that only you could have brought about."

"Me? I scarcely ever see the children. It's you who's done it all."

"Without you, I'd never have got into the Pediatria, among all those balding, arrogant old men."

"Thanks."

"The interviewing room at San Matteo, the camera equipment. And the support from the university. The contacts—all that is thanks to you." She lowered her voice, bringing her mouth closer to the telephone, "You're the only policeman I've ever known to care about children. To understand children." She paused, "And to understand women."

Trotti looked up.

Anna Maria had entered the bedroom, carrying a steaming bowl of coffee on a tray—the steam had misted the Cavour glasses. She slid the tray on to the bedside table.

"Your breakfast, Rino. Three sugars in the coffee."

"You can make a new start whenever you want."

"Signora Scola, please don't talk to me again about a new start," Trotti said testily. "I'm not interested in any new start."

She caught her breath. "You say that because of that Ciuffi woman."

"Brigadiere Ciuffi's dead. So I don't know why you bring her up."

"You're going to turn down this . . . this . . . this marvelous opportunity?"

Trotti snorted. "Marvelous opportunity?"

"You don't want people to like you, do you, Piero Trotti?"

"People can do as they please."

"And if they do like you, you sulk. You're a proud and arrogant man."

"You're not the first person to mention that."

"You're being offered a beautiful job. But like a little boy, you're sulking. You want to hurt the Questore—and you don't give a damn about anybody else."

"Bassi worked for me."

"You're right, you don't care about children. Just your very private sense of honor. You live for yourself, you live in the past. You only think about your friends, about the wonderful Brigadiere Ciuffi. But Brigadiere Ciuffi's dead, Piero, and perhaps you ought to give a little more thought to the living." Again a slight hesitation. "And I hope your present girlfriend can make you better coffee than me."

31: Widow

SHE CAME TO the door of the apartment. Her nervous glance went from Trotti to Pisanelli. She set a hand to the two rows of necklace that hung from her neck and over the top of a blue lambswool jumper.

"Signora Turellini?" Trotti was expecting a younger woman. Doctors tended to marry pretty nurses half their age.

"My name is Lucchi," she said coldly.

"Polizia di Stato," Pisanelli announced, smiling while briefly showing his identification. "We'd like to talk to you."

"About my ex-husband." It was not a question. She nodded unhappily. There was something birdlike in the movement. She took a step backwards. "I suppose you'd better come in."

The floor was of highly polished parquet and the walls were decorated with various paintings, all in ornate ormolu frames. There was a smell of floor polish and dry flowers.

They followed her into a large living room that gave on to the street and the grey Milan sky.

"Please be seated."

The decorations reflected the taste and wealth acquired over generations of good living. Trotti observed Pisanelli admiring several of the paintings, many of which, despite their old-fashioned frames, were modern. In a style that meant nothing to Trotti. Greens, blues and lots of reds.

"Can I offer you something, gentlemen?"

"We're here on an official inquiry."

The same movement of the hand to her necklace. She was a

small woman with delicate features. Her small frame only added to the impression of a delicate bird, now aging. She must have been in her fifties.

"Some coffee, then?"

Pisanelli smiled and nodded.

The woman pulled at a long sash that hung by the window and immediately a Filipino majordomo appeared. He wore a white shirt, black trousers and a red and black striped waistcoat. "Coffee for these gentlemen please, Pablo," she said, without turning to look at the small man. "You can bring me a glass of acqua frizzante."

The butler bowed acknowledgement and silently left the room.

She sat down opposite the two men on a divan that was littered with silk cushions. "Perhaps you've finally identified my ex-husband's murderer?"

"Why did you hire Signor Bassi, signora?" Trotti asked.

She did not hide her surprise. There was a tightening of the lines around her mouth. Small lines that ran towards her thin lips.

"I suppose this is because of the article in *Vissuto*."

"Why did you hire him?"

"My lawyer hired him. Avoccato Regni knew the man. Regni seemed to think he was efficient."

"But at your request?"

She said nothing; she placed one hand on top of the other at the knee of her skirt. Freckles of skin cancer on the dry skin. She wore a long, pleated grey skirt that fell to beneath her knees.

"Surely an unnecessary expense." Trotti persisted.

"I discovered it was unnecessary when we—my sister-in-law and I—realized the incompetence of Signor Bassi."

"Incompetent in what way?"

"No need to tell you, gentlemen, I was quite furious about that terrible article in the magazine. I suppose that's why you're here. A muckraking journal, a magazine for concierges and superstitious peasants. Ever since the article appeared, the phone hasn't stopped ringing." She nodded towards a portable telephone on the low coffee table. "Which only goes to show you can never be sure of your friends' taste in literature. I prefer *I promessi sposi*." She hid a slight shudder.

"Why did you take on a private detective?"

"My ex-husband was murdered. It didn't take long to realize the police forces were more concerned about other things than discovering who shot poor Carlo." She added, "Since that article, I've discovered the forces of order aren't insensitive to bad press."

"He was no longer your husband. Why waste money?"

"He was the father of my daughter. Carla was very fond of him. And so was I."

"There was a will?"

"Of course."

Trotti paused. "Who inherited?"

"My husband and I had been divorced for a long time. It was very civilized. I neither needed nor wanted his money, if that's what you think. But my daughter—our daughter . . ."

"Then the inheritance . . ."

"Depends upon the outcome of the inquiry." A nodding of her small head. "You see, Carlo was a self-made man. He was from the South and he grew up poor. Like so many Southerners, there was something driving him. It was as if he had to prove himself. All the time. Perhaps that's why we broke up. He didn't know how to be happy with the present. I would say to him, *carpe diem*."

Trotti frowned.

"Seize the day—but it was no use. Carlo was always running, convinced he was getting to a brighter future. At the time I didn't realize he was running forward to get away from the past." She raised her shoulders. "That's why he invested so much."

"You saw your ex-husband just before his death?"

"He invested in his clinic and in his equipment. He wanted the best machinery. Like a little boy—but then, so many men are." She tilted her head as she appraised Commissario Trotti.

"There's good money tied up in the clinic on Lake Maggiore." She added, "The place is now being run by his lawyers."

"Then there aren't many liquid assets?"

She hesitated before shaking her head.

"None?"

"Not at the moment. You understand, Carlo's work was his investment."

Pisanelli was sitting forward, his arms on his knees. He nodded.

"I don't want it all to go to that woman."

"The Englishwoman? Signora Coddrington?"

"This isn't for me."

"Not for you?" Trotti repeated.

"It's for our daughter. For Carla. It was always understood

between Carlo and me that Carla should inherit her fair share."
Signora Lucchi shrugged. "He went off with another woman,
younger and prettier than me. He thought he didn't need me anymore. Perhaps he was right. I loved Carlo very dearly and when he
left there was a sudden emptiness. But at the same time, my life
became a lot easier." She smiled. "Are you married?"

"I haven't seen my wife in a long time."

"You live by yourself?"

"You get used to it after a time." Commissario Trotti shrugged.

"Then you know that living with another person isn't always a
bed of roses."

"My wife works in America for a big multinational company."

"Carlo and I'd been happy together. People used to say he'd married me because of my money. But that's not true. Carlo married
me for other reasons—not least because I'm from an old Northern
family and he was a poor Southerner . . . a Sicilian. And that, you
see, is why it's so important for me Carla should get her fair share
of Carlo's wealth."

"Why?"

"He needed money to reassure himself he wasn't a failure." She
laughed. "He needed money to reassure himself he'd come a long
way. Just as he needed a beautiful house, a luxurious car and he
needed to be surrounded by beautiful, admiring, young women."
She smiled sadly. "Unfortunately, I'm no longer young or beautiful.
And I ceased to admire Carlo Turellini a long, long time ago. Love
him, yes. But I could no longer admire him."

"It was for your daughter Carla's sake you decided to hire Signor
Bassi?"

She nodded. "Also party to the decision to employ a private
detective was Signorina Turellini, my sister-in-law."

"Did you see your ex-husband before his death?"

A wry smile moved the narrow lips. "You're trying to suggest I
was responsible for his murder?"

Pisanelli had cut his jaw while shaving in via Milano. He now
smiled at her, moving his body further forward. His suede jacket was
undone. He was wearing a woolen Canadian shirt with a checker-
board motif. It was a shirt that Trotti had lent him and it was a size
too big for Pisanelli. His face was friendly and very intent. "Please
answer my colleague's question, Signora Lucchi. Nobody's accusing
you or anybody else."

"Why is it so important? It's over a year since she killed him."

Trotti looked at her sharply. "She?" He could hear the flat, provincial accent in his voice.

"Of course she killed him. And that man Bassi was too incompetent to be able to prove it."

"Who killed your ex-husband?"

"We wanted that detective man to get the proof. The simpleton was not up to it. Just like the rest of you. I hope you're better at dealing with the Mafia than you are in your murder inquiries." She shook her head, an unhappy bird. "Polizia di Stato."

"Are you accusing the English teacher of murdering your ex-husband?"

"A stupid woman."

"If you're accusing the woman Dr. Turellini was living with at the time of his death, Signora Coddrington has an alibi. The maid gave evidence that she was still in bed at the time of the murder."

"You think I'm jealous of her?" She gave a brief cackle. "Mary Coddrington wouldn't know how to heat water. She wouldn't even know how to shit straight. Doubt if she knows how to use insecticide without poisoning herself. That's why my husband lived with her. I just told you."

"Told me what?"

"Carlo needed to be surrounded by young and beautiful and worshipping women. I didn't say intelligent women. Carlo Turellini hated intelligent women—that's why he never realized he needed me. He wanted to be surrounded by idiots, by pretty idiots."

"You think Signora Coddrington murdered him?"

"I've just told you she didn't."

"Who killed your ex-husband?"

"I would have thought it was obvious."

"Who?"

Signora Lucchi's thin chest heaved with indignation. "Signora Quarenghi," she said, sitting back, allowing her thin body to lean against the pillows.

The majordomo entered with two cups of coffee, a bottle of mineral water and a plate of biscuits.

32: Mistress

TROTTI DRANK THE sweet coffee as a sour-faced cat came into the room and jumped on to the armrest of Signora Lucchi's armchair.

"According to the magazine, Dr. Turellini once had an affair with the wife of a colleague."

"The wife of his best friend—best friend and associate at the Clinica Cisalpina." She laughed sardonically. "The wife of Dr. Quarenghi."

"Whom you accuse of murdering Dr. Turellini?"

The woman said, "Carlo had been living with the English-woman. With Signora Coddrington. I know he never loved her. He never loved any woman other than me. Sometimes he'd call me." She gestured to the telephone. "On several occasions Carlo would receive threatening phone calls during the night. And, of course, it was to me that he turned for support." A smile. "I was like a sister."

"Why do you say Signora Quarenghi murdered your husband?"

"Because she's crazy."

Trotti suppressed a gesture of irritation. "You have proof?"

"Because she's jealous. And because she couldn't have Carlo."

"And Signora Coddrington?"

"The Englishwoman's stupid—but at least she's not frigid."

"Signora Quarenghi's married."

"But there are no children, are there?" A triumphant glitter in the sharp eyes. "She'd always been buzzing around my husband. For years, like an aging dog in heat, except that she doesn't know what heat is. As frigid as an iceberg. She even pretended to be my

friend." Signora Lucchi took a sip of acqua frizzante. "As if I needed
her friendship!"

"Why should Signora Quarenghi wish to kill Carlo Turellini?"

"The police sighted that mad woman at the wheel of her car at
Segrate. The cream Jaguar—near Carlo's villa on the morning he
was murdered. Later that same morning she went to the police and
told them her husband had murdered my Carlo." The woman's voice
went very soft. "Don't think I'm naive. I knew all about Carlo's
affair with her a long time ago—twelve, fifteen years ago—long
before Carlo ever wanted the divorce. And long before she started
to grow old, before she finally went mad."

"Why would Signora Quarenghi want to kill your husband?"

She laughed.

"Why, signora?"

"It's so obvious."

The cat jumped to the floor as Signora Lucchi suddenly got up
and went to the window.

Seen from behind, in her lambswool sweater and her grey skirt,
Signora Lucchi had a youthful figure. Narrow hips and a small bust.
It occurred to Trotti that she must have been very beautiful in her
youth. She belonged to the old, moneyed class of Milan. Pure Milanese, more bourgeois than aristocratic, more refined than hedonistic.
And very rich; a spacious apartment in via Montenapoleone and in
all probability a villa on the Lakes or in the Langhe. A class that
was unafraid of using the Italian language as best it suited them.
The Italian language or anything else.

She turned to look at Trotti as if she had heard his thoughts.
Amusement hovered on her thin lips.

For a few moments Trotti and the rich woman stared at each
other in silence. Then she turned back to the window.

Signora Lucchi pulled at the lace curtain and looked down on to
the silent traffic and the crowds of affluent Japanese shoppers in via
Montenapoleone. The bright luxury shops that were impervious to
inflation, to economic crisis, to Mani Pulite.

(After the drive up in the swirling fog, Pisanelli had spent half
an hour trying to find a place to park the old Citroën. The inner
pedestrian zone of Milan was impenetrable. They had finally gone
into a private parking lot. The man at the exit had raised his shoulders with philosophical forbearance. "Thirty-three thousand cars to
four square kilometers." He looked like an out-of-work university

professor and possibly was. "What on earth d'you want to come to Milan for?" They had subsequently caught a yellow taxi. Pisanelli had insisted on asking for a receipt.)

Signora Luciana Lucchi turned back to face the two men. She placed her hands behind her back and leaned against the sill. "You don't behave like the other policemen."

"I really don't know how other policemen behave."

"You're from the Milan Questura?"

"Why would Signora Quarenghi want to kill Dr. Turellini?" Trotti placed the cup back on its thin saucer and slipped a licorice sweet into his mouth.

"Quite mad. She couldn't have him—and she was as jealous of that stupid English bitch as she was of me."

The cat was now rubbing itself against her narrow legs.

"Mad, completely mad."

"You believe Signora Quarenghi actually fired the gun?"

"Of course."

"Why?"

"The police, the Carabinieri—everybody knew it wasn't a professional killing. It was a killing carried out by someone who knew next to nothing about guns." She shrugged her frail shoulders. "I don't know much about guns but I was brought up in an environment where there were hunting rifles. I've been hunting with my brothers. Thank goodness, I've never killed anything. A horrid sport." She visibly shuddered. "With this Common Market and all its foolhardy legislation, one of the rare, good things is that the birds are coming back to Italy after all these years. This country, this city—I used to be so proud of being from Milan." Her face hardened. "If I were going to kill, I'd be sure to get something efficient. Not some rusting bit of matériel from the war in Libya. Something that would do permanent, irreparable damage to the person I was going to kill—and that wouldn't blow up in my face." The narrow features feigned incredulity. "One of the wretched bullets didn't even go off."

"Who would you like to kill, signora?"

"L'embarras du choix."

Trotti frowned.

Signora Luciana Lucchi returned to the seat. "I wouldn't have minded doing away with that Bassi man." Her laugh was surprisingly humorous. "And with my lawyer, too, for ever having engaged him."

"You didn't like him?"

"Out of his depth, and that's why I had to sack him. Quite amazingly, Signor Bassi has the reputation for being reliable. From the provinces. Not a Milanese." She paused, her glance lingering on Trotti. "I think he must've just got bogged down. He seemed enthusiastic enough but I suppose he wanted to be paid by us for as long as possible. I told him I wanted the Quarenghi woman arrested fast. If he'd tried harder, he could've gotten the evidence against her, the hysterical cow."

"That's what you paid him for?"

"What?"

"You wanted Bassi to prove Signora Quarenghi guilty?"

"She's guilty."

"That's why you paid him?"

She stared evenly at Trotti. "Of course."

"Bassi told you about the article in *Vissuto*?"

"Signor Bassi seemed a nice enough man at the time." She glanced appraisingly at Pisanelli. "But you can never tell." She turned back to Trotti. "Why this interest in my husband's death after so long? I don't think the article's going to change anything. You didn't want to arrest Quarenghi when you could have. You were afraid of her, afraid of her powerful husband."

"How can you be so sure Signora Quarenghi killed your ex-husband?"

"It's obvious."

"Is it not possible the killing was related to Dr. Turellini's business affairs? To the job he was offered as director at the Sant'Eusebio clinic?"

There was an uneasy silence. She turned away and again stared out on to the street.

"Please answer my question."

"This may surprise you. Particularly when it's coming from a woman who gave to her husband the best years of her life. Who gave her youth and her body, only to be tossed aside like a used and dirty tissue when Carlo Turellini had no further use for her. My ex-husband treated me shoddily—and I think I've forgiven him. A selfish man—but for all his failings, Carlo Turellini, for all his womanizing and his immaturity, was scrupulously honest."

"He had enemies."

"Carlo was a Sicilian. The Sicilians are more puritanical than our

Protestants from the Alps. You know what the Valdesi Protestants are like? Honest and rigorous in all their business dealings. To the point of being insufferable. Just like Carlo." She laughed. "That's what the Mafia was like thirty, forty years ago before it became an offshoot of the Americans—with cheap American values. And before the easy money of drugs turned Palermo into Beirut." She gave her birdlike nod. "As I said, Carlo Turellini was scrupulously honest."

"Except when it came to having affairs with women."

"Carlo was very attractive to women." She added softly, "As I imagine you must be."

Pisanelli glanced sharply at Trotti.

Trotti continued, "According to the article in *Vissuto* your ex-husband had many enemies."

"Perhaps people were jealous of him, perhaps people were envious of Carlo's success. And like most doctors, particularly parvenu ones, he wanted to go into politics."

"Destra Nazionale?"

She nodded. "My ex-husband was not a broad-minded man. Many years ago, when we were still together, Carlo was introduced into the political circles of the Democrazia Cristiana. Lots of his medical friends—particularly those from the Mezzogiorno—were doing well for themselves. After only three or four months, he got out of the DC. He'd wasted a lot of his money. But, as he told me, he'd retained his dignity as a human being and as an Italian." For a moment, her voice seemed to tremble. "It was around 1969, around the time of the first acts of terrorism. Piazza Fontana. Strange, really. Carlo was terrified by the idea of international communism." She laughed, truly amused. "Whereas a cousin of mine, who'd never known what it was like to travel in the metropolitana or on public transport, who'd had a chauffeur all his life, blew himself up at the foot of a pylon, dying for the cause of the downtrodden masses."

"The Years of Lead are over, thank God."

"Until we have democracy and decency in this country, there'll be violence and Mafia. They are simply the different faces of social injustice."

"I see you didn't share your husband's opinions."

"Carlo wasn't a corrupt man. A silly, maddening, childish man in many ways. But honest with others." She added, "And honest to his own ideals."

The cat suddenly leaped on to Pisanelli's lap.

The woman had taken a handkerchief from the pocket of her skirt.

Trotti held up his hand. "In your opinion, signora, why did Bassi go to *Vissuto*?"

"Because they had stopped him making inquiries."

"They?"

"You should know. You're the policemen." She held her head to one side. "What sort of policeman are you?"

"I often wonder."

"They stopped him, didn't they? And Bassi had got too accustomed to living off the money we were paying him."

"Who stopped his inquiries?" Pisanelli had started to stroke the long, white fur of the cat.

A sigh of annoyance. "I don't know. But Bassi was furious. He'd received an injunction. Somebody—the Pubblico Ministero—ordered him to cease his investigations. Signor Bassi dressed like something on one of those awful American series on ReteQuattro. I think he was afraid of having to go back to doing divorces. Liked to think of himself as an American detective."

"It was Bassi who told you this?"

"That he watched too much television?"

"Bassi told you he'd been ordered by the Pubblico Ministero to drop his inquiries?"

"I'd known for some time."

"Before the article in *Vissuto*?"

She agreed. "I haven't seen Bassi for over two months. I told my lawyer to deal with him."

Trotti and Pisanelli glanced at each other. "Then who told you about it?"

"It?"

"About Bassi being called off the inquiry?"

"Avoccato Regni phoned me. And of course Gennaro Maluccio . . ."

"Who?"

"The man from *Vissuto*." She gave them a thin smile, revealing perfect teeth. "The journalist. If you want, I can give you his phone number. His office is here in Milan. Near Piazzale Cadorna. I've got the information here somewhere . . ."

33: Tram

"Well, it's not her voice."

Trotti asked, "What voice?"

"The woman's voice on Bassi's answering machine. It's not Signora Lucchi who wanted to see him."

Pisanelli's anxiety was out of character. He lit another Esportazione and Trotti could see the stains of nicotine running along the index finger of his right hand.

"You smoke too much, Pisa."

"What do you want me to do?"

"I don't see what you're so anxious about."

"Nothing," Pisanelli replied glumly. "Apart from my career." He raised the shoulders of his suede jacket.

"You were happy enough to take the cassette."

"The Questore's a fool. He didn't realize there were two tapes. He didn't realize the one I gave him was Bassi's answering tape, not the tape with the phone message."

"No reason for slipping the tape with the message into your pocket."

A fleeting grin. "It seemed a good idea at the time."

The two men had entered a bar—the only one—in the via Montenapoleone where Pisanelli bought a packet of cigarettes for himself and a packet of kiwi-flavored sweets for Trotti. On the counter there were doughnuts and brioche, snowy with icing sugar, now turning stale within a Perspex pannier.

"We must act quickly if there's to be any hope of identifying Bassi's murderer."

"You think it's Bassi's murderer on the tape?"

"No idea, Pisa. But I'd like to know who it was. Whoever it was, she could've been trying to get him out of the apartment."

"Perhaps it was quite innocent."

"Perhaps," Trotti nodded. "But at least it's a line of inquiry."

"Why don't we just go home, commissario?"

"What for?"

"I don't see why it's all so important. Why do you care who killed Bassi? He's dead, isn't he? Bassi was nothing to you, commissario. He wasn't even a friend."

Trotti said nothing.

There was an untouched bottle of mineral water on the table before him. He nervously tapped a phone card against the rim of the empty tumbler.

"Why risk your retirement, commissario? And my career?"

"You should have thought about your career when you handed the second tape over to the Questore."

"Nice to be appreciated."

Trotti softened his voice. "If you want to go back to the city, Pisa, I'm not stopping you. Take your car. I'll get a train this evening. I'll continue asking my questions by myself. Perhaps Magagna'll be back."

"You got through?"

"Magagna's in Turin."

"You don't need me?"

"Magagna's wife calls him Gabri." Trotti smiled. "She says Gabri'll get back this evening. Go home, Pisanelli. I'll manage alone."

"There's no reason for your being here. The Questore . . ."

"I don't give a shit about the Questore."

"You spend your time saying you don't give a shit. But you're giving more than a shit over Bassi. It's not important."

"Perhaps I enjoy murder inquiries. They add spice to my kiwi sweets." Trotti placed a hand on Pisanelli's elbow. "I've no right to involve you in my private crusades."

"Private folly," Pisanelli said and suddenly he started to laugh. "Why on earth I like you, I just don't know."

"They used not to be this long."

"What?"

"Esportazione cigarettes. They used to be shorter."

Pisanelli shrugged. "Something to do with European Community Rules." He added, "Soon the Eurocrats'll have us all talking English and eating French food."

"The opposite would be a lot worse."

Pisanelli smiled wearily.

"You never used to smoke, Pisa."

"I never used to think I was going to end up middle-aged and bald and without a family."

A pause.

"I need you to help me."

"You always do, commissario."

"You work with Merenda—you haven't got the Questore monitoring you."

"I have now."

"I'd like to point out that I never asked you to like me, Pisa."

"Worse than liking you, Commissario Trotti. You ask me to sacrifice my career, my marriage and my life."

"You've never really wanted to get married, Pisanelli."

The younger man's face immediately clouded. "I think that's for me to decide." He tapped the cigarette ash into a tray advertising the Gazzetta dello Sport.

"Whatever happened to Anna?"

Pisanelli's brief cheerfulness had disappeared like water swirling down an open plug. His face now lengthened, grew more drawn. "She has her own life to lead."

"Anna Ermagni thought you were the most wonderful man she'd ever met." Trotti raised his voice in an imitative falsetto. *"Pierangelo understands women. Every time I look at Pisa, I go very weak."*

"You're a hard man, Trotti. You forget nothing and you forgive even less." Pisanelli raised his cold glance. "Sometimes I wonder whether you were jealous of Anna and me."

"Where's she now?"

"What's it to you?"

"Anna's my goddaughter."

"If you really cared about your goddaughter, you'd know where she is."

Trotti placed the telephone card in his wallet. He emptied the bottle of San Pellegrino into the glass and drank swiftly, feeling the bubbles dance into his tired face. "You're going home?"

Pisanelli shook his head.

"We try the other women? The Englishwoman and the mad Quarenghi?"

Pisanelli was silent. For a moment he looked like an old man in an outsized checkered shirt, slumped forward on to the table in the small café.

Outside the yellow ATM trams trundled past.

Milan, moral capital of the Republic. A dying Republic.

Finally, Pisanelli raised his head. "The *Vissuto* offices are nearby. Less than a kilometer to walk and I can see that you're not tired, commissario."

"I was born tired."

"You'll need all your energy for your goats, pigs and chickens in the OltrePò."

"Sandro sold it."

Pisanelli made no move to get up. He stubbed out the cigarette, squashing the yellowed end into the ash. "Who's Sandro and what did he sell?"

"The house in the hills. It's out of the question, now. My cousin was a secret gambler. In the last months of his life he'd apparently managed to squander the savings of a lifetime. Including the little place in Santa Maria."

"Then you'll retire to via Milano?"

"Doesn't look as if I've got much choice."

Brusquely Pisanelli stood up.

Trotti looked at him. "I'll retire to via Milano—unless . . ."

"Unless what, commissario?"

"I can get hold of enough money to buy the house back before it's too late."

Pisanelli ran a hand through the long hair at the sides of his head. "Let's go to the *Vissuto* offices."

"You don't want to go home?"

"Somebody's got to look after the old man."

34: Press

THE HIGH GREEN gate opened and they stepped into the courtyard. If on the outside the old building kept its traditional, wealthy appearance, on the inside everything was modern.

Tradition and modernity. The two faces of Milan.

Pisanelli followed Trotti through the revolving wooden doors and waited before a locked glass door.

The door was promptly buzzed open by a girl sitting behind a desk. She would have been pretty, but she appeared mildly distraught, harassed by two computers and a blinking light on the telephone console. A telephone receiver was jammed between her raised shoulder and her tilted head.

"The *Vissuto* offices?"

Across the top of the counter she pushed a book towards them. "Sign," she ordered peremptorily and they obeyed while she spoke softly into the telephone. She was talking about a consignment of something that had gotten lost at Codogno.

Trotti wrote the name of a distant uncle, now in Argentina. Pisanelli entered his habitual scrawl.

Without checking the signatures, the woman handed them identity tabs, telling them to clip them to their coats. With her thumb—her attention had returned to one of the computer screens—she gestured towards the lifts. "Third floor."

There were four lifts and three arrived simultaneously. They entered the first. It was a French lift and there were posters in aluminum frames. Each poster was an old cover of *Vissuto* magazine.

"You ever read it, commissario?"

Trotti shook his head.

"What do you read?"

"Directives from the Ministry of the Interior. And, whenever I get a free moment, the packets of Caramelle Elah."

The doors opened and they stepped out on the third floor, facing a very large, open-plan room.

There were many cubicles divided by shoulder-high glass walls. The ceiling was low, and the overhead neon light was much brighter than the December sky. The sound of people typing. Lots of computer screens and lots of young people, well dressed and well-fed, some in bowties, conferring in front of the screens. Jeans and expensive cardigans.

Nobody took any notice of the two shabby policemen.

A young woman was walking along the corridor. She wore black stockings and there was a felt pen stuck behind an ear.

Her T-shirt spoke of peace and love in English.

Pisanelli approached her and coughed politely. "Signora, we're looking for Gennaro Maluccio."

She stopped. Her look went from Trotti to Pisanelli. Neither man met with her approval. "You're policemen?"

Pisanelli briefly showed his ID card.

She was carrying a large folder beneath one arm. She placed it on the carpeted floor. "Enquire over there," she said, gesturing with an ink-stained hand towards a far cubicle. The dark eyes followed them attentively as they executed her directions.

They came to the cubicle.

Trotti turned back to look at the young woman. She gave a confirmatory nod, without moving.

Pisanelli knocked on the glass door.

A large man was sitting behind an archaic Olivetti typewriter. He was smoking a Toscanelli and ash had fallen on to his sweater.

Red eyes looked up, not hiding their irritation. The thick, grey hair on the man's head was greasy. His face was greasy. The desk before him was cluttered with books, sheets of typescript and dummy front covers. "Looking for someone?" His accent was thick Milanese.

"Polizia di Stato," Trotti said.

"Who else wears off-the-peg clothes?"

Pisanelli asked, "You're modelling for Gianni Versace?"

Trotti silenced Pisanelli with a gesture. "We're looking for a journalist. Gennaro Maluccio—the journalist who did the article on the Turellini murder."

"I know who Gennaro Maluccio is." He pushed himself away from the desk and looked at the two officers. "And you want to see him?"

"If it's possible."

"Gennaro Maluccio's freelance."

"What does that mean?"

"He's an investigative journalist and he normally brings his copy in at the end of the week. It means he's not on the staff of this magazine. He's paid for each of his articles individually."

"You know where we can find him?"

"You know Alessandria?"

"Of course."

"Nice town. It's where Umberto Eco's from, but I don't imagine you've ever heard of him. You know the prison?"

Pisanelli frowned. "Signor Maluccio's writing an article on Alessandria prison?"

"Quite possibly." The man removed the Toscanelli cigar from his mouth. The end was damp and chewed. Pieces of wet, black tobacco clung to his damp lips.

"Quite possibly?"

"All depends on the director of the prison. For all I know, Maluccio might be on a diet of bread and water." He laughed and the folds of his belly moved with delayed synchrony. "If you really want to see Maluccio, you'd better contact his lawyer first."

35: Cocaine

"GENNARO, WE BELIEVE you."

A telegram dictated by the heart and delivered by hand to Gennaro Maluccio in his cell within the confines of the forbidding prison of Alessandria.

Dictated by the heart but confirmed by cool analysis.

> *The absurdity of the crime for which our colleague is accused is quite blatant. And the manner in which his arrest was carried out is, to say the least, worrying. A roadblock in the center of peaceful Alessandria in the middle of a working day, carried out by functionaries of the Polizia di Stato who are in no way above suspicion.*
>
> *We believe that Gennaro Maluccio is the victim of a conspiracy carried out against him for reasons that we fail to understand. We await his complete pardon with anxiety. We know that he is innocent.*
>
> *Gennaro Maluccio, forty-two, a collaborator with this magazine for over six years and the father of two beautiful girls, was arrested on 29 November by the officers of the Alessandria Questura. An unexpected—and highly unusual—roadblock was set up in Corso Roma and a plastic bag containing pure cocaine was discovered beneath the dashboard of Signor Maluccio's Fiat Punto. He is now being held in the city prison, accused of the terrible*

*offence of drug dealing and association with orga-
nized crime.*

We know that Gennaro Maluccio is innocent.

*Gennaro Maluccio is no stranger to conflict with
the police. Several years ago he received six speeding
fines within a week. Yet Gennaro, a family man with
a beautiful wife and two daughters [Loredana, see if
we can use photo] is not the sort of person to risk his
and other people's lives on the highway.*

*Why this arrest? Why the quite arbitrary road-
block? Why the cocaine?*

*Until recently, cocaine was rare in Italy. It is a
drug more popular in America and northern Europe.
Because of the privileged links between Italian organized crime and the Middle East, historically heroine
is the major hard drug in this country.*

*Is somebody trying to warn Gennaro Maluccio—
and through him, the editors of* Vissuto?

*Gennaro Maluccio has never been afraid to deal
with the most delicate and the most dangerous
affairs. Readers will recall that it was* Vissuto *and
the reporting of Gennaro Maluccio that was responsible for the arrest of the serial killer, the "Monster of
Arezzo." More recently, Gennaro Maluccio carried
out an exemplary inquiry into the horrendous trade
in children between certain Third World countries
and the civilized, tranquil northern city of Cuneo.*

*What had Gennaro Maluccio been researching that
seems to have caused the ire of the Questura in Alessandria and most probably of high-ranking officials
within the Polizia and the Ministero dell'Interno?*

*For over a year, Gennaro Maluccio has been fol-
lowing the Turellini case through the meandering
inquiries of Polizia and Carabinieri. Two weeks ago,
Gennaro Maluccio submitted his most recent article
concerning Turellini's murder. Readers will recall
the fascinating interview with private detective Fabrizio Bassi in* Vissuto *no.? [Check and insert photo
of cover.] Fabrizio Bassi, director of Fabrizio Bassi
Investigations, thirteen months after the murder of*

the celebrated Milanese doctor [check specialty] was warned off further inquiries by a court order. Yet when Gennaro Maluccio approached the procuratore, he was told that there had never been a gag order from the Pubblico Ministero.

Contacted to comment, Fabrizio Bassi pulls at his American tie [use different photo, try second spread, Loredana] and speaking in his deep voice remarks, "There's a desire to suffocate the inquiry. And the desire comes from the top."

Meanwhile, Gennaro Maluccio's family continues to wait for him. His wife has moved into a hotel near the prison while the children have gone to Imperia to stay with their maternal grandmother.

Vissuto will spare no effort or expense in helping Gennaro Maluccio regain his liberty and his good name.

Yet again, the public is forced to observe that while many politicians remain free during the Mani Pulite inquiries, the State does not hesitate to throw humbler members of society into our overflowing prisons.

36: Journalist

TROTTI HANDED THE two sheets of typescript to Pisanelli, who was sitting on the other chair. Turning back to the journalist he asked, "What are you going to do?"

"Me?"

"This magazine."

The man laughed.

"What's *Vissuto* going to do about Gennaro Maluccio? You've decided he's not guilty?"

The journalist looked up from behind the cluttered desk, from behind the antiquated Olivetti, the bundles of paper and the various photographs. There was an opened can of Nastro Azzurro beer. "We journalists have many vices—but not cocaine."

"Why not?"

"Can't afford it."

"Maluccio could've been dealing."

"Unlikely." A ripple of amusement went through the pot belly beneath the sweater. "Too middle-class. Too upright and virtuous."

"A friend of yours?"

"Nobody likes the chief editor. I'm the cop on this floor. I don't wield the biggest truncheon—but I get in there first." Again the large man laughed. The eyes remained carefully watching Trotti. "I scrub an article and your family's eating Simmental corned beef until the end of the month." He placed the unlit cigar back in his mouth. "Why d'you want to know?"

"You believe Gennaro Maluccio's been framed?"

"What do you think?"

Trotti could feel himself getting angry. There was an intellectual arrogance about the journalist—Ambrogio Negri, according to the adhesive sticker on the side of the typewriter—that irked him. And the patronizing Milanese accent. "Let me ask the questions, Signor Negri."

A shrug of indifference. Negri was in his mid-fifties. His face was red, round and smooth. The eyes were bloodshot from too much cigar smoke, there were burst veins beneath the nose.

"You're Trotti, aren't you?"

"Commissario Trotti."

"And you don't even recognize me."

"I try to forget a lot of people."

"Because they remind you of yourself?"

"Because, like a journalist, I have to deal with a lot of people who are not particularly savory."

"I interviewed you five or six years ago about a murder case. In your city, Commissario Trotti—the once-upon-time capital of Lombardy. I came down with a photographer and you allowed yourself to be interviewed. I was working on another paper. You had more hair then." He added, "The article was scrubbed."

"And your children ate corned beef?"

"In a manner of speaking. At the time, Commissario Trotti, I rather admired you. I got the impression you were halfway honest."

"In your opinion, why was Gennaro Maluccio arrested?"

"Ask him."

"I'm asking you, Signor Negri."

"I'd've thought you were out of your jurisdiction here in Milan."

"Why would anybody wish to frame Gennaro Maluccio?"

"Commissario Trotti—the one policeman who's above everyday corruption. The man who believes in the State." A mocking laugh. "I forgot that you see yourself as the conscience of the Polizia di Stato."

"My conscience won't stop me from hitting you in the nose."

"You're almost as unfit as I am—all those boiled sweets, I imagine. And you must be at least ten years older. Don't try any roughhousing in here." He gestured conspiratorially beyond the glass partition to the people working at typewriters and screens beneath the white neon lights. "I'm the only alcoholic in here. The girls wouldn't like it. They're a crowd of maiden aunts. Feminists and maiden aunts—during the day at least." He settled back against the grimy headrest of his chair and unexpectedly roared with laughter.

"Is that funny?"

On recovering his composure Ambrogio Negri enquired, "You two flatfeet care for a beer? I hate drinking by myself."

Pisanelli had finished reading the article. He dropped it on to the desk. "Why don't you use a computer? It would correct some of your spelling mistakes."

"Computer? What's that?" Negri was leaning over sideways, opening a drawer in the desk. "A policeman that can read and write? There really is a shake-up going on in this wretched country. This isn't the end of the First Republic, this is the end of the *ancien régime*. Next you'll be telling me you can do joined-up letters." Negri regained his semi-erect position and tossed a chilled can of beer to each man. Pisanelli unceremoniously caught one. The other can of Nastro Azzurro fell to the floor beside Trotti.

"Who would want to make life difficult for Gennaro Maluccio?"

"I've had a chilled drawer installed. Eight cans of beer—which just about covers a working day. Twenty-five percent of my reserves to a couple of intellectual cops—I must be losing my grip." Negri looked at Pisanelli, "Maluccio's good at pursuing a story. Not much of a journalist. Has a lot of difficulty with punctuation. And he's got a—" The man hesitated for the word, "—a computer. Maluccio's got a computer. One of those flashy things that he carries around with him. Perhaps that's how he impresses people."

"How do you impress people?" Trotti asked, not hiding his annoyance.

"Gennaro Maluccio's style's lousy and normally requires a rewrite. But Gennaro Maluccio's stories are good." A gesture of his thumb. "Not like them. Old maids. They go out on a job and they start feeling sorry for some Calabrian bastard who's just eviscerated his wife. And when there's some reporting that requires a bit of balls, they all start getting period pains or one of their god-awful nephews needs to be taken to the dentist." He briefly glanced over his shoulder. "They all say I drink too much."

"Calumny."

"Pick up your beer, Trotti. Isn't it about time you retired?"

"Not always easy to frame somebody."

"You've tried?"

"You're tempting me."

Again the rippling of the belly as Negri laughed. "This isn't the first time Gennaro Maluccio's had trouble with your friends from the flatfeet factory. He manages to get the right information and that can irritate a lot of people. On a couple occasions we've had the Man on the phone telling us to remove an article."

"The Man?"

"The proprietor lives in Switzerland while we sweat blood and ink and pay our taxes." Negri opened his beer. The froth spurted out angrily, falling on to the desk and the typewriter. He raised the edge to his damp lips and drank. "Although why anybody should worry about an article in this shit magazine, I don't know. Violence and scandal for the ignorant masses, for the sort of people who can't read without moving their lips. The *Osservatore Romano* it isn't. A shitty magazine that gives the punters what they want. Violence, sex and alternative medicine. All in twelve-word sentences and seven-line paragraphs. A shitty reactionary rag—that normally ends up cut into four neat little quarters in the lavatories the length and breadth of our beloved peninsula."

"Who'd want him to shut up?"

"Gennaro Maluccio has a lot of enemies."

"Because of the articles concerning Turellini?"

"Ah," Negri said. Then there was silence.

Pisanelli was leaning forward. He had opened the beer and the stubble around his mouth was moist.

Trotti watched the journalist carefully. The Peroni remained at Trotti's feet.

"It's Turellini you're worried about, Trotti?"

"What do you think?"

"There are lots of things that I think. And there are lots of things that I don't necessarily put in an article."

"Listen, Negri, I know about power and I know about corruption. I also know a lot about the workings of the Polizia. It's possible somebody's trying to silence your man. Don't think I've any delusions about the force I work for. Don't think I've any delusions about the Ministry of the Interior. But I do know that if you need collusion from the police, you've got to have a lot of clout. Policemen are funny people. We're a funny lot."

"Evidently."

"We don't mind doing ourselves favors. But to get us to do favors for anybody else, you need a lot of friends. And that was before

Tangentopoli, that was before the public was made aware of what was going on in the Palazzo."

"Where does that place you, Trotti?"

"An old, old policeman."

"An old, balding policeman who enjoys pissing against the wind. One of the Northerners in the Polizia di State. A Northerner who has delusions of being honest."

"I'll be out of this job before long." Trotti allowed himself a thin smile. "Who ever said I was honest?"

"I'm sure you've got other failings too."

"I'll show you a few."

"Cops've never struck me as particularly nice people. You probably beat your wife and sleep with your daughter."

"My wife and daughter don't live with me."

"See what I mean, commissario?"

"Perhaps I'm curious, perhaps I just want to know about other people's lives."

Negri sat back and swilled noisily at the can of beer. Then he spoke. "Gennaro Maluccio wrote several articles last year. The beginning of 1992, just before the Chiesa affair and the start of Tangentopoli. Nothing particularly earth-shattering, but a few weeks later di Pietro and his pool of judges started making their arrests. Arresting the same people that Gennaro Maluccio had been talking to."

"The articles were published?"

Negri slowly nodded his head and Trotti wondered whether the man was wearing a wig.

"Maluccio was looking into racketeering. He was very Lega Lombarda at the time—it was before the Lega went the way of all political parties. He wanted to show the effects of l'Infiltrazione mafiosa in the North."

"And Turellini?"

"That was nearly two years ago. Before Craxi and Andreotti and all our other politicians became our public whipping boys." An amused shrug. "Now people are just getting sick of Tangentopoli. Sick because nobody's innocent. The difference between the politicians and the rest of us is a difference of quantity, not quality. A year ago l'Infiltrazione mafiosa would sell copies. Not any longer. Nobody's safe, everybody's got a skeleton in some cupboard. You, me, the cleaning woman, the pizzaiolo. Tangentopoli doesn't sell copies anymore."

"What sells copies now?"

"Murder. Murder and violence within the family. Murder that leaves the police stumped. Murder that can keep new copy coming in, week in, week out." Negri began to scratch his head and Trotti had the impression the scalp moved. "Remember last summer? Ten, twelve unrelated murders of women. The papers for a couple of weeks in August would scarcely talk about anything else. Nearly four thousand murders a year in Italy—and ten women are an infinitesimal percentage. Yet when people are fed up with Somalia and Bosnia, with Tangentopoli and more taxes, with the apparatchiks in the RAI, the corpse of some mutilated Czech whore in Torre del Lago's strangely reassuring. *Plus ça change.*"

"You think there's any connection between Turellini and Gennaro Maluccio's arrest?"

"I'm not paid to think."

"You didn't answer my question."

"You're the policeman, Trotti. If you want to know why Gennaro Maluccio's in jail, why don't you and your literary acolyte in the classy checkered shirt go to Alessandria and ask your friends in the Questura? Perhaps they'll want to tell you why they've thrown an innocent husband and father in jail."

37: Anna

IT WAS VERY warm in the lounge. Young people were arriving for their five o'clock lessons. A majority were girls, many of whom wore fur coats over Benetton sweaters and jeans. Others wore waxed jackets like Trotti's.

"Signora Coddrington is still teaching. She'll be with you in ten minutes. Why don't you wait for her? Perhaps you'd like some tea?"

They had sat down on the sofa. On the coffee table there were several magazines in English. The titles meant nothing to Trotti.

"Perhaps we ought to go home now, commissario."

"I need to see the Englishwoman."

Pisanelli sat forward, propping his arms on his knees. "Why do you think Bassi's death's connected with Turellini?"

"I've got no idea."

"Then what are we doing here?"

"I never said I knew what I was doing," Trotti said.

"I need to sleep."

"Then sleep."

"I prefer sleeping in my own bed."

"You've got a wife to go back to?" Trotti asked harshly and Pisanelli fell into an angry silence. He sat back and let his head loll. He loosely clasped a black volume that he had taken from the pocket of the suede jacket. He closed his eyes but it took time for the angry blush to disappear from beneath his stubble.

"Some tea and cake, gentlemen?" The woman spoke perfect Italian but Trotti knew she was foreign. Her skin was pale and she had large hips. She placed the tray on the coffee table. Trotti smiled and took a mug of tea. The woman nodded happily and went back to her desk, her typewriter and the telephone that never ceased ringing.

Above her, on the wall, was a color photograph of a woman in a long white robe and a tiara.

"Who's Elisabeth R.?" Trotti asked.

Pisanelli was sulking.

Trotti sipped the tea. It was the color of water—of the water he had once seen in the Po delta when a car was being craned out of the estuary. "Tea and milk?" He pulled a grimace. "This stuff tastes like the Po."

"Add ten spoonfuls of sugar." Pisanelli had opened his eyes. With his head propped against the coarse weave of the backrest, he was looking at the students from behind drooping lids.

"What's that book you're reading, Pisa?"

Several students had congregated around a service hatch where they ordered tea or coffee. Some people were talking in English and Trotti noticed that they used different gestures and different mannerisms. Keeping people at arm's length.

(In the last months of the war, there had been a few English pilots in Santa Maria trying to reach the Allied lines. Thin faces and an arrogant manner. One of them—on crashing, he had broken his jaw badly—had later gone on to become a prime minister somewhere in Africa.)

Like the Po, but very sweet with sugar. Trotti made a mental note to look out for tea-flavored sweets.

"You're an unpleasant man, commissario."

"Because you haven't got a wife?"

"I came to your house this morning because I thought I was doing you a favor."

"Thank you, tenente."

"I'm tired. I didn't sleep last night and instead of going home to bed, I called you. I've spent the day with you."

"You didn't have to bring me here." Trotti took a bite of the cake. A taste of ginger. "And if you haven't got a wife to go back to, it's because you don't want to."

"Because you don't want me to."

"Ever since I've known you, Pisanelli, you've been going to get married. How old are you now? Soon you'll be forty and if you're not married, it's because that's the way you've chosen to live your life. You could've married Anna Ermagni two years ago."

Pisanelli raised his head. "Don't mention her."

"She was in love with you. Why didn't you marry her?"

"It's got nothing to do with you."

"She wanted to get married."

"Anna's in Rome," Pisanelli said simply and letting his head drop back, closed his eyes. "She's studying to become an interpreter."

Trotti felt a twinge of sympathy for the younger man. Like everybody else, Pisanelli was getting old. "It's not too late, Pisa. Anna always said she wanted to have your children."

Pisanelli bit his lower lip without looking at Trotti. His hands played nervously with the pages of his book.

"Gentlemen, you're looking for me?"

38: Cortina D'Ampezzo

SHE CARRIED A pile of books.

She was in her mid-thirties. She did not have the strong, fiercely blonde hair of the Scandinavians but the hair of the English, the kind of mousy hair that, like whisky, is left to age beneath the Atlantic rain. She held out a narrow hand. "I'm Signora Coddrington. You're looking for me?"

They stood up—Trotti briskly, Pisanelli stumbling sleepily to his feet—and turning away she led them down a corridor that smelt of paint, and into a small classroom.

The Englishwoman had an attractive figure, long, strong legs. She wore a blue denim skirt and matching blue high-heeled shoes. She was broad but, strangely, had small hands and feet.

The room was well-lit.

There were posters on the walls showing scenes of England, with thatched cottages and swans on village ponds. There was one photograph that Trotti recognized as the Houses of Parliament in London.

Mary Coddrington gestured them to sit down on the classroom seats. She set down the pile of books that she was carrying and slid on to a desk.

(In the first months of Pioppi's pregnancy, Nando had suggested their taking a holiday together in England, Trotti had turned the invitation down. He preferred to spend his free time in the OltrePò. Or at the Villa Ondina on the lake.)

"I suppose it's about Carlo." Signora Coddrington ran the back of her hand across her forehead. It was a feminine gesture. Sitting less than a meter away from her, Trotti could smell her perfume.

She was pretty, of course, just as Signora Luciana Lucchi must have been pretty twenty years earlier. Turellini had been a powerful doctor and was able to surround himself with all the tangible signs of the good life, including beautiful women.

"I've got ten minutes before the next lesson—an Alitalia class of trainee stewards and hostesses." An amused laugh, engagingly spontaneous. "The beautiful hostesses all look longingly at the stewards and the gorgeous stewards all look longingly at each other." She giggled and Trotti enjoyed watching the movement of her mouth. "I suppose in this life, we can never get what we really want."

"You were happy with Dr. Turellini, signora?"

The laughter vanished from her eyes. "He's dead."

"You don't answer my question."

"Was I happy with Carlo?"

Trotti nodded, curious to know the answer. Pisanelli sat beside him like a dutiful schoolboy. Both men kept their eyes on the pleasant, even features of the teacher.

"We spent two very happy years together. I was twenty-nine when I met him and I was trying to get over . . . to get over a rather miserable experience. Carlo was gentle and I needed a lot of gentleness. I'd been rather badly bruised. I'm afraid and that's why I decided to leave London."

"Where did you meet him?"

She smiled at the walls, at the posters. "I met him here. Carlo was going to America and he needed a quick course in English." She paused. "I know this sounds silly, but it was love at first sight. He was twenty-four years older than me. And the first time we met—he took me to a Japanese restaurant—I realized he was the man I'd always been looking for." The white teeth nibbled nervously at the lower lip. "And I wasn't completely wrong about a man. For once."

"You moved in with him?"

"That's got nothing to do with you."

"He was living in his villa in Segrate and you moved in with him. That's right, isn't it?"

The door opened and an Asian man with glasses pushed his head through the gap. She smiled and said something in English. The head nodded and disappeared.

"Like me, Carlo had made a lot of mistakes. He needed female company—but often he went for the wrong sort of woman. In a way,

Carlo lived off conflict and he liked the company of domineering women. But that's not what he needed."

"What did Turellini need?"

"Me," the Englishwoman said simply.

"Why?"

"He needed understanding." She nodded. "Companionship. Complicity."

"That's what you gave him?"

"Carlo always gave me a lot more than I could ever give him." She added, "In a way, I knew it couldn't last."

Trotti wondered fleetingly whether she would cry. Instead she smiled, almost happily. "It was just when I'd persuaded him that we could have children, that he wasn't too old and that he wouldn't be making a mistake, that he'd be making me very happy—it was then Carlo had to get killed."

The door opened and closed again. Pisanelli got up and turned the key, and then stood with his back against the door.

"It was all planned. We were going to spend Christmas at Cortina d'Ampezzo and I was going to get pregnant." Her hand went to her belly. "It was then she had to kill him."

"Who?"

"She couldn't bear to see his happiness. That scheming, aristocratic woman couldn't bear to see I was able to give Carlo something that she was quite incapable of."

"Who?"

"She always said he'd married her for her money and perhaps she was right. She and that awful daughter—they hated me. Luciana Lucchi's a monster, her daughter's a monster and together they would rather have seen Carlo dead than see him happy with a woman half his age." Signora Coddrington raised her shoulders and looked Trotti squarely in the face. "The silly English girl and the Italian doctor. May and September, it was like some stupid fotoromanzo and we were happy. Both of us—we thought happiness had passed us by a long time ago. Yet this was the new deal. Better, more intense, more beautiful than anything either of us had ever expected. More beautiful than we deserved." The romantic Englishwoman momentarily lost her self-control. "That's why she had him murdered in cold blood. And only in this wretched, medieval country could the bitch still be walking free."

39: Motives

"Perhaps you're right, signora."

Somebody tapped lightly on the door, but the sound was muffled by Pisanelli, who was still leaning against it.

"Right in what way?"

"Signora Corr . . ." Trotti could not pronounce the foreign name. "Perhaps this is a medieval country. As you can see for yourself, it's only now we Italians are learning the meaning of democracy. But, even here, there are rules we have to obey."

"I never noticed." Her smile was amused. "What rules?"

"There'd appear to be no reason for Signora Lucchi's being in prison. Even in this medieval country, the police have to have proof."

"She murdered him," the Englishwoman stated.

"Why?"

"She was jealous."

"Signora Lucchi and her husband divorced more than ten years ago. If she was jealous, it must have been a long time ago. Between the time the Turellinis broke up and the time Carlo Turellini was living with you a lot of water had run under the bridge. You don't think she'd accepted the inevitable?"

"It was for her daughter. For Carla Turellini."

"What about her, signora?"

"The old woman was frightened Carla Turellini was going to be left out of the will."

"You just told me Signora Lucchi had a lot of money."

"Which didn't stop her from wanting more. For herself and for her daughter."

"You know about the will?"

"Carla was generously provided for. She made sure of that. She'd spent enough time buzzing round her father, trying to be his confidante, his secretary and his conscience. She even told him she was delighted to see him happy again." The Englishwoman nodded her head. "She told her father she'd nothing against our marriage."

"You were going to marry him?"

A distant smile. "Marry him, get pregnant and have his children."

There was more knocking at the door. The sound of muffled voices, both male and female.

"And you, signora?" Pisanelli asked. He looked tired and his eyes were bloodshot.

She moved her head. She propped her body with her hand against the desktop. Her chin now touched her shoulder. The position gave her an innocent, demure air. "What about me?"

"In the will?"

"It's yet to be applied."

"What do you get?"

"More than enough."

Pisanelli raised his eyebrows.

"The house in Segrate and a lot more." She shook her head. "Don't think for a minute I wanted Carlo dead." Her glance went back to Trotti. "Carlo was a lot older than me—but that's what I needed. Someone to look after me and someone I could care for." She breathed deeply. "And now I have nothing."

"Nothing?"

"Nothing but memories."

Trotti asked, "You're sure Turellini was killed by his ex-wife?"

"As sure as anyone can be."

"Carlo Turellini had enemies."

"Of course."

"Enemies within the medical world. People who were jealous of him."

"Carlo wanted the professorship at the university. He ran for it in 1991, but as you know, he failed. The cards were stacked against him. A lot of people didn't like him."

"He was interested in power?"

"He wasn't interested in politics. He'd dabbled a bit with the Destra Nazionale. Carlo was interested in his job. That's why he wanted to run the new university clinic."

"Why?"

"Everybody agreed Carlo was competent. Even his enemies. If he were to become director of the Sant'Eusebio, he would have been a thorn in the flesh for several colleagues and rivals who coveted the post."

"There were people who wanted him dead?"

"Dead?" She shook her head. "I don't think so. Out of the way, perhaps—but not dead."

The thumping was now imperious. Someone was shouting.

"Signora, did you meet Fabrizio Bassi?"

"Who?"

"A private detective—Fabrizio Bassi."

"You mean the man who never straightens his tie?" She smiled. "A couple of times. He was working for the Turellini woman, wasn't he? Why do you ask?"

"When did you last see him?"

Louder banging.

She raised her shoulders, "A year ago—perhaps even more." A shrug of exaggerated nonchalance.

More hammering outside. Trotti nodded and Pisanelli turned the key and opened the door.

It was already evening on a cold December night in Milan, yet Magagna was wearing his American sunglasses.

"Ciao, Pisa," he grinned happily. "You're with the old man?"

40: Magagna

"MY WIFE."

They sat in the car while the engine softly hummed, allowing the heater to warm the cold air. Occasionally a taxi hooted but Magagna ignored it. The right wheels of the Alfa were up on the curb and the taxi drivers had only to look more carefully at the registration plate.

"What about your wife?"

"She said you'd rung, commissario. Not often you come to Milan."

Pisanelli sat in the back. He started to light a cigarette but Magagna told him to put it out.

Pisanelli spoke in an aggrieved voice. "You smoke."

Magagna shook his head. "Not in the car."

Trotti asked, "When did you get back from Turin?"

Magagna seemed puzzled. "I was at Segrate."

"Your wife said you were in Turin." Trotti added, "She calls you Gabri."

"After Gabriele d'Annunzio," Magagna replied, emphasizing the Pescara accent that had almost disappeared beneath the Milan overlay.

"Did you find out about Turellini?"

"What exactly did you want to know, commissario?" Magagna had pushed the sunglasses up on to his forehead and he looked through the windshield as he rubbed his eyes with his balled hands.

Advertisements for the wax museum blinked in neon.

They were parked in the forecourt of the Stazione Centrale, between the Fascist façade and the station. Only the central escalators were now working, carrying people up to the main platforms. The rush hour was over and most commuters had already returned to the suburbs or the villages of the Milan hinterland.

"Very helpful."

"Nothing from the Palazzo di Giustizia." Magagna turned to face Trotti. "There are several floors that are virtually impenetrable to the rest of the human race. And since the bombs in Rome and Florence they've increased security."

"What about the judge? About Abete?"

"You want me to go into Abete's office with a spy camera? Force the locks on his filing cabinets? Is that what you want?"

Either Pisanelli was sulking or he had fallen asleep.

"I want to know why Bassi was warned off the Turellini case. And I want you to help me, Gabri."

"Nobody likes private detectives."

"Not everybody murders them." Trotti paused, catching his breath. "Pisa pulled me out of bed this morning and took me to where Bassi had been murdered."

The aviator sunglasses slipped from his forehead back on to Magagna's nose. "Murdered?"

"A bullet in the head and the body dumped in a tributary of the Lambro outside Melegnano. Where he was found by Milan Pollution Control unit."

"How did Pisa find out?" Magagna gestured to the back seat where Pisanelli had started to snore.

"Over the radio."

Magagna lowered his voice. "That's why you're getting Pisanelli to run you about Milan? Running you about when he works for Omicidi?"

Trotti shrugged. "He likes helping me, Gabri."

"Never seen him look so haggard. And he doesn't have a wife at home nagging him."

"Pisa seems to think I'm the reason he's not married."

"Why do you think I left the city to come to Milan? And please don't call me Gabri."

Trotti made a movement of irritation. "You've got nothing from Abete?"

"Tighter than a rat's arse."

"Why come looking for me in the English school?"

"You make me feel so loved, commissario. I could've gone straight home to Sesto, you know, to my wife and my children and instead I chose to come into the center of the city, just to be insulted by you."

"What were you doing at Segrate?"

"I spoke with Gamberi."

Trotti frowned and from behind the Alfa came a sudden, brief blare of a hooter as a yellow taxi pulled out. A screech of tires.

"Gamberi's been at Segrate for more than four years. There at the time of the murder. He got to Turellini's place some twenty minutes after the killing." Magagna grinned. "The Englishwoman's okay, isn't she? Nice solid chassis."

"Signora Coddrington?" Trotti said, pronouncing the name with difficulty. "You saw her, Magagna?"

"Not really. She didn't speak to me."

"You're a married man. Why do you need to look at other women?"

"You don't look at women?"

Trotti raised a shoulder. "I put my desires to sleep a long time ago."

"Yet you still eat those terrible sweets."

"I'm entitled to some pleasure in life."

Pisanelli grunted in the back seat. He was gently snoring through his nose.

On the other side of the road, opposite the station, the double arch of the McDonald's neon sign lit up its share of the Milan sky.

"I don't ask much of life—just sweets and giving Pisa a hard time."

"You and Pisa . . ." Magagna smiled. "You're like a married couple."

"Heaven forbid."

"You could do worse, Commissario Trotti."

"I haven't got the transvestite nipples that you get so excited over."

"Not doing enough to impress me," Magagna laughed. Then the smile vanished. "Gamberi considered her a potential suspect at one point."

"Who?"

"The Englishwoman." Magagna adjusted the sunglasses and

Trotti wondered how he could see anything through the dark lenses. "The Carabinieri and Abete now seem to favor money as a motive. Perhaps a disgruntled colleague or rival of Turellini's at the university."

"That's what Bassi thought. But Turellini led an active sex life. There were a lot of women."

"Gamberi maintains the sexual thing doesn't hold water."

"*Cherchez la femme.*"

"The dialect of the OltrePò? Your poor chickens."

"*Look for the woman.* It's French."

"What woman?" Magagna shook his head. "There are three possible suspects—but none had any reason to kill him."

"Who told you?"

"You don't think Gamberi and his pals are pissed off at seeing their hard work gathering dust in Abete's office?"

"What did Gamberi tell you?"

"Three women, commissario. The Englishwoman you've just seen. She had no reason. There's proof she'd been trying to have a child. She'd even been on several cures. Endometriosis, I think it's called. Something to do with the walls of the uterus. Signora Coddrington was already thirty years old. She was desperate to have a baby. You don't kill off the potential father when you need to get pregnant." Magagna tapped his thumb. "Too big a drop in the sperm count."

Trotti popped a sweet into his mouth.

"As for the ex-wife . . ."

"Signora Lucchi."

"Both she and the daughter were accounted for in the will. Perhaps Lucchi was frightened there could be a change in the will. But at the time of the divorce, there was a written agreement over what she and her daughter Carla would get."

"I went to see Signora Lucchi this afternoon. She's rich—one of those bourgeois families living in a big apartment on the via Montenapoleone. She accused Quarenghi."

"The doctor's wife." Magagna pulled at his index finger. "Signora Quarenghi's unbalanced. She had once been attractive, according to Gamberi."

"Signora Quarenghi was seen near the scene of the crime within half an hour of the murder."

"That's true," Magagna nodded. "It's also true she made

accusations against her husband. But Dr. Quarenghi was in Rome at a congress at the time of the murder."

"He could've paid someone to shoot Turellini."

"Precisely the direction the Carabinieri inquiry took. According to Gamberi, although they were associates at the clinic, there was no love lost between the two men—Signora Quarenghi had been Turellini's lover. And Quarenghi, as a Socialist and as a close collaborator at the Ministry of Health, was in a position where his wife had to be above all suspicion."

"Why don't the Carabinieri think it was Signora Quarenghi?"

"The Carabinieri don't exclude anybody. They just don't favor the crime of passion thing. There's no motive."

"Signora Quarenghi was jealous," Trotti said. "Turellini had been receiving phone calls in the middle of the night. That's the sort of thing a jealous and unhinged woman might do."

"She was taken to the barracks at Segrate and agreed to have the paraffin test. Negative. She hadn't used a firearm that morning."

"Perhaps there's another woman."

"Perhaps," Magagna said, "but that's not the line of inquiry the Carabinieri favored."

"It's the line of inquiry Bassi favored. And now he's dead."

"Bassi had spoken to the Carabinieri. He'd spoken to Gamberi—but, unlike Bassi, Gamberi had been into the house at Segrate."

"So?"

"There's more of a case against Signora Coddrington than Turellini's other women."

"What case?"

Magagna lowered his voice. "The sheets on Signora Coddrington's bed."

"What about them?"

"She'd been teaching at her language school the previous evening. She'd got home late and tired. In her statement she said she'd gone straight to bed and was already asleep when Carlo Turellini joined her in bed."

"So?"

"The sheets had been thrown back and ruffled. But they were not creased. They were clean sheets and Gamberi knew nobody'd slept on them. Neither the Englishwoman nor Turellini."

Trotti shrugged.

"That's not all. According to various neighbors, the relationship had been going through very bad times. She'd been heard screaming and threatening Turellini. Reliable witnesses, Trotti—friends and even the maid."

"She told me she loved him."

"Your delectable Signora Coddrington was lying."

41: Cavour

"WHERE ON EARTH have you been?"

It was past nine o'clock. Trotti smiled sheepishly at his cousin, and behind him he heard the noise of the Citroën as Pisanelli turned back into the via Milano.

"I was in Milan." He brushed past her and he noticed immediately the sweet smell of perfumed cleaning liquid.

"I made food," Anna Maria said, more an accusation than a statement. Closing the front door behind Trotti she followed him into the kitchen. "That was an hour ago."

Fifty years earlier in the hills, it had always been Anna Maria who ran the small house. She had slipped naturally into the maternal role when her own mother, Trotti's aunt, had been taken mysteriously ill and confined to bed.

"Hardly anything in the cupboards."

"I don't get time to go shopping."

"You've got a cleaning woman," Anna Maria said testily.

"She doesn't cook." Trotti hung up his coat on the back of the door and went into the bathroom to wash his hands and face.

Everything was unexpectedly neat. There was a new flannel by the hand basin and it smelt of lavender.

His face looked back at him in the mirror.

A balding dinosaur?

He smiled quizzically and ran a comb—it had been cleaned and placed in the cabinet—through his hair. His hair might be thinning, but it was still black. Or at least was black on top.

He returned to the kitchen, pleasantly warm, and turned on the television.

"I never allow the television during meal times in my house."

He went through the different channels but returned to RaiTre and the end of a local news bulletin. Despite the end of lottizzazione, the control of television by the political parties, he still found the news boring.

"You could at least turn the volume down, Pierino."

He slumped into his old armchair, setting his feet on the stool. His cousin lit the gas and soon water was boiling on the stove.

The pile of magazines by the television looked neater and thinner. The parish magazine next to the clock had disappeared. The clock had been removed from the top of the refrigerator and was now on the mantelpiece, along with the freshly dusted photographs of Pioppi and the little Francesca, Agnese and the little Francesca, the little Francesca alone.

"What's that?"

"What?" Anna Maria set the plate of melon and ham on the tablecloth.

It was his photograph. A brown and white photograph of Piero Trotti in his first uniform. Trotti looking foolishly young and innocent.

The photograph was slightly crinkled and there was a white border and the edges were serrated, like a postage stamp.

"Where did you get that awful photo from?"

"It's mine," Anna Maria replied simply. "I've been carrying it around in my handbag for years."

"What on earth for?"

She shook her head, dismissing the silliness of the question. "I had a nice long chat with your friend Signora Scola."

Trotti looked at the television screen and frowned.

"I went to the shops and got something to eat. I never realized Italy had become so expensive."

"You should have gone to the hypermarket."

"Perhaps you'd care to grace the table with your presence."

The same words, the same intonation as fifty years earlier. Anna Maria had not changed. Holland, marriage, children. The estrangement from her own son. The loss of Piet and now of her brother Sandro had not really changed the young, authoritarian woman who had once regimented Trotti's existence during the years of war. He could feel the resurgence of old resentments. Resentments because he, likewise, had not changed. Not really.

He rose from the armchair, switched off the television and sat down at the table.

"You could've bought a remote control, of course."

Trotti started eating.

"Don't worry about me," Anna Maria said. She sat, arms folded in front of her. "I wasn't going to wait for you. I have to eat at regular hours. With age and with my ulcers, I'm becoming a creature of habit."

"You always were."

The old, broad face, the wrinkles deepened by the shadows of the overhead lamp, came forward, an invitation to greater intimacy. "She's married, isn't she?"

"Who?"

"She sounded nice. She clearly likes you a lot, Pierino." A raised eyebrow. "But do you think with a woman . . ." The question hung unfinished in the short space between them.

"What are you suggesting?"

"I'm not suggesting anything." The stiffness of her back suddenly matched Anna Maria's moral rectitude. "But you've been living by yourself many years, Rino."

"Happily."

"I really think it's about time you thought of your future."

"A future at my age?"

"Don't be silly."

"My future's my grandchildren."

"There are a lot of women who'd be happy to share their lives with you." Anna Maria hesitated. "And don't talk to me about your goats and your chickens because you know you won't be retiring to the hills. How you and Sandro could ever entertain such an idea's quite beyond me." She shook her head unhappily. "You have good memories of those years?"

"We were young, Anna Maria."

"Young? Underfed, with bones pushing under the skin. All those years I suffered from boils. And you remember how you cut your leg and it never healed?"

"We were happy."

"No, Pierino, you don't belong in the hills. You belong here among your friends."

"A policeman doesn't have friends. Too many favors and I know too much about people."

"I really do wish you'd stop feeling sorry for yourself. You're like an old man."

Trotti laughed and melon juice ran from the corner of his lips.

"I thought Pioppi was marvelous. Such a beautiful girl. So glad to see she's put on weight at last. You remember how thin she used to be?"

Like the solicitous mother she had once been for him, Anna Maria took away the plate of melon rind and produced a warmed dish into which she ladled risotto. The steam rose and it seemed to soften the old face behind the austere Cavour glasses. Perhaps, for a moment, she reminded Trotti of the young Anna Maria of fifty years before.

"She really seems to like you, Piero."

"Pioppi?"

"Sounds like a very nice woman and Signora Scola had such a lot of good things to say about you. What a pity she's married."

42: Mirror

PRISCILLA SAT ON the floor. She had been given a large book but she showed no interest in the grey elephants, the bright-eyed tigers, the luxuriant baobabs.

Signora Scola raised her head.

She had been looking through the box of toys and several dolls and trains lay on the carpet beside her. She now looked towards the large mirror and gave a little wave.

Trotti wondered how she had seen him enter the cubicle.

He sat down at the desk. There were several stools but they were all uncomfortable. He took the only chair. It was low and he had to sit forward in order to see what was happening in the adjacent room.

Overhead the camera gave its black and white picture on to the monitor screen.

From where he was sitting, Trotti could see Priscilla's mother. She sat by the window, nervously smoking, her eyes going from her daughter to the garden of the hospital, dark and enclosed by the gloomy architecture of the pediatric wing.

"I'm playing with this doll. You know, she's got lovely blonde hair." Signora Scola had found a plastic comb.

Priscilla took no notice. Priscilla said nothing. Priscilla did nothing.

The radiator creaked noisily and somewhere in the building someone shouted.

Trotti placed an anisette sweet in his mouth.

"I don't like snakes," Priscilla announced suddenly, not looking at Signora Scola.

"Neither do I." Signora Scola nodded her head in friendly agreement. "They do naughty things and they're not nice. She paused. "Have you seen this lovely doll? She has long black lashes, just like you."

The child began to show interest.

"Perhaps you'd like to help me dress her. She's a bit silly and she's put her clothes on all wrong. A big girl and she can't even dress properly. Have you ever seen such a thing?"

Through the speaker Trotti heard Signora Scola's cheerful laughter.

(*"Sounds like a nice woman and Signora Scola had such a lot of good things to say about you."*)

He was smiling as the door of the cubicle was abruptly opened.

Turning in surprise, Trotti removed his headphones.

"Ah, Piero," Commissario Merenda said as he entered, "I was hoping you might be here."

43: Merenda

"CIAO, MERENDA."

He held out his hand and smiled.

They rarely spoke to each other. An implicit rivalry kept them apart, reduced their intercourse to brief nods and hurried smiles. No doubt Trotti envied Merenda his youth and his success.

Perhaps Merenda resented Trotti's reputation as the grand old man of the Questura.

Of course, in many ways the two men were similar. In a Polizia di Stato that was a creation of Fascism and subsequently the victim of nearly forty years of a crippled democracy, both Merenda and Trotti had the reputation for implacable, almost aggressive probity.

And they were both Northerners.

(*"You know you can't work with Merenda—you're not a man to collaborate. Reparto Omicidi functions as a team. You like to do things in your own way—whatever you say, everybody knows you despise Merenda."*)

"How are you, Piero?" Merenda's glance went from Trotti's face to the room beyond the one-way mirror. "I see you're still working with children."

Trotti shrugged. "Signora Scola asked me to come down this morning."

"There are even rumors you're staying on beyond your retirement age."

"Rumors?"

Merenda smiled cautiously. He was a tall man in his late thirties who was courteous with everyone but had no close friends within the Questura. No one ever got invited back to his place in San Martino Sicomario where he lived with his family. It was generally believed that his wife was French and a former model.

Merenda kept his own company. He had grown up in the Camargue, where his parents went to grow rice. He had returned to Italy in the early seventies. Apart from the guttural, French R in his speech, there was no regional accent. He had not picked up the slow, drawling baritone of provincial Lombardy.

"For the children's sake." Merenda gestured to where Signora Scola and the little Priscilla were now playing. "I think it would be a marvelous idea. You're the right man, Piero, and it'll be our loss when you go."

"Thanks."

"I hear you were at Melegnano yesterday morning."

Trotti said nothing.

Merenda continued, "They found Bassi's corpse and I'm now running the inquiry. I want to get this out of the way fast."

"So the Questore told me."

"Thing is, with a private detective like Bassi, there are so many leads you can never be sure you're following the right one."

"I'm not sure that as a private detective Bassi had all that much work."

"At four in the morning, how did you find out he'd been killed?" Merenda smiled. He had a wide smile and regular teeth. He was one of those men who appeared unshaven at any time of the day, a shadow of darkness across his cheeks and chin.

"I have my contacts."

"You're not part of Reparto Omicidi, Piero."

"I think I know that."

"Then why bother with a murder?" A mocking tone had entered Merenda's voice. "You're not happy dealing with molested children?"

"I'll be a lot happier when I've left here."

"So you really are going to retire?"

"After a lifetime in the Polizia, I'm beginning to feel I could do with a change."

"You haven't answered my question."

"Yes, Merenda, I am going to retire. In September. I will get out of the Questore's hair. He has always accused me of practicing a cult of the personality."

Merenda's grin widened. "Nicolae Ceauşescu?"

"That sort of thing."

"I know how you feel."

"He accuses you, too, Merenda?"

"When it suits him." The younger man had lowered himself on to one of the high stools, half-sitting, half-standing with his legs unbending and his hands in his pockets. Merenda was well-dressed. His shoes, Trotti noticed, were thick-soled Timberlands, much like the ludicrously expensive pair Pioppi had bought him for his birthday.

"You surprise me."

"What were you doing at Melegnano at four in the morning?"

"I told you. I have my contacts."

"No need to tell you that Tenente Pisanelli's with the Reparto Omicidi and for murder inquiries comes under my command."

"How is Pisanelli? You know, I hardly ever get to see him. I heard he was getting married."

"Being arch, Piero?"

"I don't think Pisa's ever forgiven me. Seems to believe I came between him and my goddaughter. They were engaged and then something happened." Trotti clicked his tongue, "I haven't heard from Anna Ermagni for over a year. Sweet little thing. Always said she wanted to be an interpreter at the FAO in Rome."

Merenda held up his hand. "Piero, Spare me."

Trotti smiled.

"You seem to think it's my fault you're not in Reparto Omicidi."

"At my age, I've learned not to think anything. Start thinking and you get ulcers—or even worse."

"You're devious, Piero."

"That's not what our Questore from Friuli thinks. He tells me I share his innocence. The innocence of an outsider. That's why I never managed to get further. Too innocent of Power Politics."

"Devious and intelligent."

"You flatter me."

"Not at all. The grand old man and they've shunted you over to the hospital to watch abused children through a dark glass. I think I can understand your rancor."

"Why bother? There's no need for you to have come here, Merenda. You have a nice office on the third floor of the Questura. Unless I'm mistaken, you have my old office, now nicely renovated."

"You neither forget nor forgive." Merenda smiled and then started to laugh. "Perhaps it's your grudges that made you the best officer in this city."

"And now I work with children. The Questore's even hoping we can set up a national center."

"I wouldn't worry yourself too much over the Questore, Piero. In many ways he's a spent force."

Trotti was astounded but he hid his astonishment.

Merenda had arrived in the city a year after the Questore from Friuli. It was well-known that Merenda was one of the Questore's appointments. Merenda was perhaps not a Socialist, but he was perceived as the Questore's man. Between the two of them there was a symbiosis that many, not least Piero Trotti, resented. Neither of them really understood this small university city of the Po valley. They were outsiders yet they wielded enormous power.

"You see, Piero, I want you aboard."

"Aboard what?"

"I would have offered you a cup of coffee and we could have talked about Bassi like professionals. Like civilized people. But I know your high standards in coffee—or indeed in everything else. You have your bars that you frequent and a tasteless coffee would have been just another thorn in your heavy crown."

"I didn't know you had a sense of humor."

"I surprise you?"

"I thought you were French."

The flash of bright teeth. "You were with Pisanelli yesterday and I don't give a damn what he does in his spare time—provided it isn't against the law. To be honest, Piero, I don't really care what you do."

"What I do? You think I'm a necrophiliac or a pedophile?"

"I want you in on this Bassi thing. You knew Bassi because he worked for you before he was kicked out of the Questura."

"You want me in on the Reparto Omicidi inquiry, Merenda?"

"Of course, Piero."

"I don't think the Questore's going to be thrilled. He believes my methods are out of the dark ages."

"I've always had a soft spot for the Inquisition." Merenda shook his head. "Perhaps you'll make an effort for me."

"Low-profile?"

"I want results. I want this Bassi thing tidied up fast and you're the natural choice for my team. You always have been."

"Thank you."

"You knew Bassi, and prior to his death he'd been seeing you."

"You know a lot of things."

Merenda held out his hand. "Welcome aboard, Piero."

"The Questore's not going to be happy, Merenda."

"The Questore can go fuck himself."

In the small observation room the two men shook hands. Trotti appreciated Merenda's firm grip.

44: Venezuela

IT WAS TEN past ten.

"You have a very flexible timetable, Piero."

With the renovation of the Questura, they had installed a modernistic clock above the desk. "I was with Signora Scola at the hospital," Trotti said as he stepped out of the lift.

"The Questore's got a new job for us."

"For you and me, Maiocchi?"

Commissario Maiocchi grinned blandly. An unlit pipe was held between his teeth.

Neither man acknowledged the blonde secretary at the desk as they headed towards Trotti's small office.

"I can't wait to leave this place," Trotti said as much to himself as to his companion. They walked along the carpetless corridor. "I had to take a day off for a funeral. But that won't stop me from going down to Bologna at Christmas to see my granddaughter."

"How is Pioppi?"

Trotti gave Commissario Maiocchi a sharp glance. "You ever meet her?"

Maiocchi shook his head.

"Pioppi and Nando've got a lovely place on the Piazza Maggiore." They went into the office.

"Are you going anywhere at Christmas, Maiocchi?"

The battered filing cabinets, the greasy canvas armchairs and the teak desk that for some reason the cleaning lady had decided to tidy that morning. The sticky, sweet wrappings had disappeared, the wastepaper bin had been emptied.

"It's cold in here, Piero."

"Young man like you—the cold's good for you. Just don't take your coat off."

Maiocchi removed the pipe to laugh. "You ought to get a heater."

"I'll be out of here soon."

"For your pigs and truffles in the hills?"

"Perhaps," Trotti replied, unamused. He did not remove his jacket—it was bulky but it kept out the chill of the office. Another present from Pioppi, but one he appreciated. "Are you going anywhere at Christmas?"

Maiocchi ran a hand through his long hair. In his baggy trousers, he looked more like a student than a policeman. Yet there were rings under his eyes. A cracked vein beneath the skin of his nose. Telltale signs of drink. "Italy has the lowest divorce rate among advanced countries—less than eight percent—and I have to end up divorced."

"You should've given up your job here."

"It's not my job Elena didn't like, Piero. It's me." He shook his head. "She never liked me. Even before we were married. Things just got worse after the marriage. But I swear to God I miss the girls."

"You see them?"

"Not since the divorce."

"They're here in the city?"

Maiocchi said, "In Genoa with their mother."

"Then go and see them, for heaven's sake. Girls need a father."

"My wife's found somebody else. He's very good with the children, apparently. The girls don't need me." Maiocchi added, "What I most hate is going home to an empty house in the evening."

"Love is passing. Solitude is forever."

"Television and then bed—not much of a life. Sometimes I take something to help me sleep—but work's better than alcohol. My job's my home now."

"Your job's your family."

Maiocchi had slumped down into a canvas chair. His cheeks were sunken and he looked thinner than Trotti remembered him. "I don't have a family. Not anymore."

Trotti said, "Your daughters need you."

"You get on with your daughter, Piero?"

"I never gave enough time to either my wife or my daughter. I lived for my job—until it was too late."

"Too late?"

"About twelve years ago, Pioppi stopped eating and I didn't realize a thing until I saw her in the hospital. Her black hair billowing out on the pillow, the light from the table lighting up her pale face. Against the white sheets she looked like a dried-up locust."

"And now?"

"She'd been trying to tell me something—and I hadn't taken the slightest bit of notice."

"How's Pioppi now?"

"I like to think she's forgiven me." Trotti thought for a moment. "But Pioppi no longer needs me. She needed me in those days—but not now. She has a husband and a family of her own."

"You see her?"

"I saw her a couple of days ago—she came up for the funeral of her uncle. Five months pregnant and looking marvelous—looking just like her mother when Agnese was expecting."

A strange silence fell between the two men, each for an instant lost in private nostalgia.

It was Maiocchi who spoke. "Women—they're not like us, are they?"

"Thank God."

"You could always marry again, Piero."

"So could you, Maiocchi. And we could both commit suicide."

"I write to the girls but they never reply."

Trotti leaned forward on the desk. "What job's the Questore got for us?"

Slowly Maiocchi marshalled his thoughts. "He's asked me to look for Pavesi."

"Who?"

"He believes it'd be good if you'd help."

"The Questore wants me on everything except Bassi's murder."

"You know, the Questore speaks very well of you, Piero. There are times when he can behave decently."

"I never noticed." A dismissive gesture. "Pavesi? You mean the shopkeeper?"

Maiocchi nodded.

"For heaven's sake, it's out of our jurisdiction, Maiocchi. That's what I told the girl and her brother when they came to see me. Not in this province or even in Lombardy."

"They live in the city, at Burrone."

"Let the Carabinieri do it. Or Piacenza."

Maiocchi shook his head.

"Why does the Questore want me involved? Normally he doesn't like letting me loose on anybody over the age of thirteen."

Maiocchi grinned. "How's Signora Scola?"

Trotti shrugged. "What can we do that hasn't already been done by the Carabinieri?"

"Perhaps they're in Venezuela."

"Who?"

"The Questore wants us to find Pavesi and his wife—even if it means you and me flying to Caracas."

45: Terrone

"COCAINE? THE QUESTORE must be mad."

"It's coming through Venezuela. The stuff's grown in Medellin or in that other place in Colombia."

"Castel San Giovanni—not Palermo." Trotti shook his head in incredulity.

"Medellin and Cali."

"You're not going to tell me the drug cartels have set up shop in some sleepy village on the via Emilia."

"Pavesi's wife's from Calabria."

"So what?"

"She has close relatives who are now in prison. Has an uncle who's a big fish in the Calabrian Ndrangheta."

"That doesn't make Pavesi a drug dealer. Or even a courier. He's a shopkeeper. Off-the-peg clothes—nothing pretentious. He doesn't sell fur coats. Just earns enough for him and his family to survive." Trotti shrugged his shoulders. "He's got a franchise from one of those companies in the Veneto that like to give themselves an American name."

"That's not what Customs believes."

Trotti crunched noisily at the rhubarb sweet. "With Mani Pulite, everybody's suddenly doing overtime. Everybody's suddenly trying to justify their pay."

"What do you know about Margarita, Piero?"

"If the Questore's so keen on our involvement in the Pavesi case, why on earth didn't he tell me, Maiocchi? When I last saw him, he was telling me to stay off Bassi's murder." Trotti shook his head. "He wants me out of the way."

"You don't want to go to Caracas?"

"I'm happy where I am. I don't even like going up to Milan."

"Margarita's in the Caribbean."

"The only place I want to go is out of here."

"There are goats and chickens in Venezuela," Maiocchi volunteered. His smile disappeared. "A big community of Italians in Venezuela. And not all of them are criminals in hiding."

"So what?"

"Somebody saw *Chi l'ha visto* on TV."

"They have that in Venezuela?"

"Satellite TV," Maiocchi nodded. "A program on Pavesi. And a few days later the same person bumped into Pavesi on the street. In a place called Porlamar."

"A lot of people look like Pavesi. A lot of people look like me and you."

"Really?" For a moment Commissario Maiocchi seemed genuinely distressed.

"Go on."

"The person informed the embassy in Caracas and the embassy informed Customs."

"Then Customs can set up their own inquiry. And they can send their own people."

"You're right, Piero, but the Questore wants you and me to go. Because if it's Pavesi, we'll have the extradition papers."

"You go, Maiocchi, if you're so keen to get away. A few weeks in the tropics might do you some good. But leave your pipe here."

"You come with me, Piero."

Trotti crunched the sweet noisily. "I'm planning to spend Christmas with my daughter and my granddaughter."

"You know Pavesi. You'd be able to recognize him."

"Who told you I knew him?"

"You used to be friends."

"That's what the daughter said." Trotti shook his head, "Pavesi and I were never friends. He used to live near us in via Milano. I saw him once or twice and perhaps we went for a meal together. But we had nothing in common."

"That's not what the Questore thinks."

"You know what the Questore thinks?"

"Pavesi went into politics."

"He tried to. Back in the late seventies he was a city councilor. You could see he was attracted by power. In those days, he was a liberal or something. One of the small parties. When he went to Castel San Giovanni he became a good Craxi man."

"You didn't like him, Piero?"

"I don't like anybody."

"I think I'm beginning to notice."

"I don't like anybody. Why else do you think my daughter got anorexia . . ." Trotti stopped speaking, his mouth still open.

"Anorexia?"

Trotti frowned unhappily. "Don't use that word."

Maiocchi stood up. "Why didn't you like Pavesi?"

Trotti shrugged. "There was little to like or dislike. I found him insignificant—other than I always felt his interest in me was driven by ulterior motives."

"A criminal?"

"Anybody can be a criminal in the right circumstances. But if you want to go in for money and power, you don't set up a clothes shop in some provincial backwater." Trotti suddenly banged his hand against the teak surface of his desk. "I know nothing about drugs. Why don't they send Gabbiani? Or why don't they send that Sicilian."

"Sciacca?"

"Why not send him? He comes from Palermo."

"Precisely—and you've probably noticed that he never goes out of the Questura unless he's accompanied. And wearing a bulletproof jacket."

"Then he needs a holiday."

"Sciacca's hiding. That's why he's here, that's why he left his wife and his children in the South. So that he could go underground. He was with Judge Falcone's pool and he's already escaped one attempt on his life." Maiocchi had pulled a penknife from his jacket pocket and was cleaning the bowl of his pipe. The black ashes he tapped into a bin beside the cold radiator.

"You're not going to smoke that thing in my office?"

"Wouldn't dream of it, Piero. I enjoy the smell of synthetic rhubarb too much." Maiocchi returned the pipe to between his lips. "Sciacca's got balls. A small terrone but with balls."

"There's a danger in Venezuela?"

"Of course."

"And the Questore thinks that with only a few months to go before I retire, I'm going to risk my life for some sordid drip."

"Why do you dislike him?"

"The Questore? Guess."

"What have you got against Pavesi?"

"Nothing. Nothing at all."

"You're not a good liar, Piero."

"Why should I lie?"

"Pavesi used to be your friend."

"He tried to use me."

"How?"

Trotti shook his head. "It doesn't matter. And anyway, it was a long time ago; just after the time Pioppi got her degree. He tried to make use of me—of my position. For political reasons."

"He'd done you a favor?"

Trotti looked at his watch "I've got to go. I want to see the Quarenghi woman."

Maiocchi repeated the question. "Pavesi did you a favor, Piero?"

"I don't accept favors. You know that."

"Never?"

"I learned a long time ago that when somebody does you a favor in Italy, you spend the rest of your life paying it back a hundredfold. I don't want to pay that kind of interest." He shook his head. "Mafia thinking, Southern thinking. Perhaps I'm a racist—but it's too late for me to change my mind now."

46: Pretext

"Ah, commissario."

The two men turned. Trotti squinted against the light.

"I was looking for you," Signora Scola said and gave a forced smile. She had put on a scarf and a pair of sunglasses. "Actually, I left my car here and I was about to go home for an early lunch. Perhaps you'd care to run me home."

"Bit early for an early lunch, isn't it?"

"I've got a headache. That woman's cigarettes. I can't get her to understand she should stop smoking. For Priscilla's sake as much as her own." Signora Scola slipped her arm through Trotti's. "Please take me home, commissario. I couldn't drive with this migraine."

"Perhaps you're eating too much salt, signora." Maiocchi smiled openly, his pipe clenched between regular teeth.

She returned the smile. "Salt?"

"Blood pressure, signora. Or you should take up a pipe. It's as good a way as any to relax." He tapped the bowl of his pipe knowingly. Maiocchi turned back to Trotti. "When you get back, perhaps you could drop by in my office, Piero."

"Why?"

"Various reasons. Not least, I've got some coffee."

"Mafia thinking, young man." Trotti placed his hand on Maiocchi's sleeve, "Penetrazione mafiosa. You can't buy Piero Trotti with favors."

"Moka Sirs coffee."

"Of course, there are exceptions."

With Signora Scola holding on to his arm, Trotti went through the metal detector. The policewoman on duty was talking to a foreigner, possibly an Albanian or a Yugoslav, and she failed to salute as Trotti and the young woman stepped out into Strada Nuova.

The fog had lifted and the sun had come out. The sky was now quite clear.

Trotti breathed deeply, taking in the morning air and the odor of Signora Scola's fur coat.

"I was hoping you'd stay this morning for little Priscilla."

Trotti said flatly, "I was called away by Merenda."

"I thought I was almost there."

"There?"

"You don't seem particularly interested in Priscilla's case."

"Forgive me, signora. There are other things on my mind at the moment. And now the Questore wants me to go to Venezuela."

"I told you he liked you."

"He wants me out of the way."

She pulled at his arm. "Can you run me home, commissario?"

"I'm seeing somebody, I'm afraid."

"You can't take me home first?"

"Somebody I've got to interview."

"I'll leave my car here."

"A long interview."

"I'm going to try again with Priscilla. Tomorrow morning I can drive out to the hospital in a taxi."

Trotti looked up at the ancient clock above the entrance to the university. It was nearly eleven.

The industrious northern city quietly went about its business. In Strada Nuova or along Corso Cavour there were no signs of the profound changes Italy was going through. The end of the First Republic. The biggest political upheaval since the Allies—with bombs and guns and the blood of young men—had overthrown the lost years of Fascist folly and bombast.

With Signora Scola holding his arm, Trotti walked along Strada Nuova. It was good to be out of the Questura and Trotti was acutely sensitive to the smells emanating from the shops; from the chemists and from the cake shop. And the perfume of a young woman who passed by him.

The things he would miss in retirement.

"I don't have my car," Trotti said.

"Then if you wish—and if you don't mind my accompanying

you—I can wait for you while you interview this person. You can run me home later. I'm in no hurry."

He stopped walking. He came to a halt in the middle of the pavement. He moved away slightly to look at her. "Signora Scola," he said, a smile pulling at the corner of his mouth, "I have the impression you always get your way."

"Call me Simona."

"You always have your own way?"

"Always." Glumly she shrugged the collar of her ample fur coat without returning his smile. "Except when it's really important."

Her car was in the Piazza Leonardo. An old Fiat Seicento, it was parked near one of the medieval towers. The Fiat was at least twenty-five years old and apparently in excellent condition.

"Can you drive, Piero?"

"Only if you've got a headache."

With a weary smile she handed over the key. "I've got a headache."

Trotti opened the passenger door for her. He then opened the driver's seat door and climbed in beside her. The car was ludicrously small and their shoulders were touching.

Sitting beside him wrapped up in her fur coat, Signora Scola was almost as tall as Trotti. "Where are you going?" she asked. She did not look at him.

"To interview Signora Quarenghi."

"I really don't understand you." She was peering through the misted windshield, staring at the corrugated metal billboards at the tower's base. "It was you, Piero, who called me in to help with the Barnardi child. You wanted me in the Questura working for you."

"Of course I wanted you."

"It was you who was so interested in the setting up of a team. But now that it looks as if you've finally created something viable, you no longer care."

"Of course I care."

"The Questore's offering you what you always wanted, Piero."

"I think it's time for me to retire gracefully. Don't you?"

"You show no interest at all in Priscilla."

"I've been busy."

"You were interested in earlier cases."

"You've done good work, signora."

"You were genuinely interested. That was before."

"I'm busy."

"Now I never see you." Her face softened. "Priscilla's a lovely child and she needs help. Your help, Piero, just as much as mine." She turned to face him. "The help of a man."

47: Abuse

"THE BEST COME from Alba in Piemonte. They're worth their weight in gold."

"How much, Piero?"

"Nearly five million lire for a kilo."

"That's why you're going to keep pigs?"

"And like gold you've got to know where to look. Even with the best pig, you can spend your time looking and end up finding absolutely nothing."

"Why don't you grow your own truffles?"

"The life cycle is twelve years at least. I can start now and be a rich man in my coffin."

Signora Scola clicked her tongue angrily. "I really don't understand why you talk about death all the time." She had not removed her sunglasses and she had to raise her voice over the noise of the straining Fiat engine. "There's nothing wrong with you, Piero. You look wonderful for your age."

"A balding dinosaur."

"You've been watching too many American films. A bit of exercise and perhaps a change in wardrobe—you'd look very good. You just need a woman to look after you."

"Change in wardrobe? My daughter bought this coat for me. It cost a fortune."

Signora Scola turned away. They had reached the edge of the city. The sun was shining out of a blue sky, on to the brown flatness of the rice fields. "You look marvelous and there are a lot of women who'd like to spend time with you." She added, still staring out of the car window, "You never told me about that woman at your house."

"Two kinds of truffle. What we normally eat is tuber borchii which is a lot less expensive than tuber magnatum. There's a difference in price but it's not always possible to identify the difference just by taste. There are researchers in the university who've been working on a fast genetic identification for some time. Precisely what Anti Sofisticazione need."

"You didn't answer my question, Piero."

"Restaurants charge exorbitant prices for tuber borchii. And there are people gullible enough to pay. It's like baccalà. North Sea cod, food of the poor. And now Italians think it's five-star food and are willing to pay absurd prices." Trotti smiled to himself. "What's really needed's a way of identifying the mycorrhizae before you spend twelve years growing them. At the moment, you've got to wait ten years."

"Who was the woman, Piero?"

"Woman?"

"When I phoned the other day?"

"You mean my cousin?"

Signora Scola gave a cold, unbelieving laugh. "I really don't understand you, Piero."

He took his eyes from the road. "Did I ever ask you to understand me?"

"There was a time when you were desperate for my help. Now you don't care."

Piero Trotti frowned. "I don't understand why you say that."

"It was you that called me in on your child abuse undertaking. And now you don't care—either about the children or about me. I thought we were friends."

"There never was any child abuse undertaking. The rape of a fourteen year old. Later a couple of other cases turned up. So I called in the help of the professionals. People like you."

"You're not even interested in Priscilla, are you?"

"I know you're doing good work, Signora Scola. I have a lot of faith in you."

Beyond the fields they could see the new extension to the university, rising like a modern cathedral from above the leafless plane trees.

Trotti spoke softly—as softly as the whining motor allowed. "Tell me about Priscilla."

"Not much to say."

"Then tell me."

A quick, uncertain look at Trotti.

"Please, Simona." His hand touched her elbow.

"One day the mother went out and when she got back into the house, the poor child was screaming. There was blood round the anus."

"Why did the mother go out, leaving the child unattended?"

"The grandmother was there." Signora Scola added, "They live in an old building where there are two or three different families under the same roof—or at least around the inner courtyard. The hospital thinks the brother-in-law'd been touching Priscilla even before that. But there's no proof. No proof—other than the child hates to be anywhere near him. He's a truck driver—like the husband—and sometimes he sleeps next door. In the grandmother's part of the house."

"There are other possible molesters?"

"They live in Esine."

"Where?"

"It's a small village in the Val Camonica. Province of Brescia. About twenty kilometers north of Lake Iseo, with virtually everybody working in the steel industry. A lot of family businesses, but, like everybody else, they've been hit by the recession. A lot of the time the father and the uncle are out of work."

"There are other possible molesters?"

"Hard to say. Initially the mother didn't want to lodge any complaint at all—which implies she knew what was going on. But the people at the hospital in Lovere contacted the Carabinieri." Signora Scola caught her breath. "The mother had come home and found the child covered in feces and blood. She managed to get the brother-in-law to drive her, Priscilla and the grandmother to the hospital. Of course, he's not really the brother-in-law because the woman isn't married." Again she breathed deeply. "There's even some doubt whether her boyfriend is Priscilla's real father."

"What do the doctors think?"

"Priscilla was in a terrible state—a torn rectum, gaping sphincter."

"The grandmother had heard nothing?"

Signora Scola shook her head solemnly. "Once inside the hospital, Priscilla didn't stop screaming for hours."

"No semen on the child's bed?"

Signora Scola did not reply.

Trotti repeated his question. "Didn't the rapist leave anything? Even fingerprints?"

"The mother cleaned everything. And burned the bedsheets. By the time the Carabinieri were called in—it was the doctor at Lovere who lodged the complaint—the mother had managed to get back to Esine."

"Why?"

"Your guess is as good as mine, Piero."

"You think you can get the child to tell you the truth?"

"Brescia's sent the little girl to San Matteo. Both mother and daughter are staying at the hospital. Problem is, there's nowhere for them to sleep. There's a small room in Pediatria but it's not adequate, little better than a cubbyhole." She tapped his arm lightly. "Piero, there are a lot of people who know about the work we've been doing."

"What makes you think Priscilla will tell you who touched her?"

"It's happened before. You saw that with the Alda child."

"Alda was a lot older."

"Eventually it has to come out."

"Then why hasn't Priscilla told her mother?"

"I don't think Priscilla really trusts her mother."

"Why not?"

"The hospital at Lovere started the official inquiry. Not the mother."

"The mother brought her child to the hospital."

"Not much choice. The poor thing was bleeding badly. But the mother didn't want to press charges. Children are sensitive. They're sensitive to affection, they know whether they're being protected or not. Perhaps Priscilla can feel her mother is trying to protect somebody else."

"Why would the mother want to save the brother-in-law's skin?"

"It seems incredible—but then I've never had a child of my own."

"Why not, Simona?"

"I find it hard to understand how a mother can put anything above the interests of her child."

"Time you had a child of your own." Trotti took his hand from the steering wheel and fleetingly touched her arm. "Your husband would be only too delighted."

Signora Scola took a deep breath. "You really should accept the Questore's offer."

"A trip to Venezuela?"

"If you took on the child abuse center the Questore's trying to start up, Piero, there's just so much we could do." She held her hand up preemptively. "I know, I know. You must worry about your pigs and your truffles."

Trotti hushed her, putting a finger to his smiling lips. "Don't mention truffles to anybody."

"But perhaps you could do both."

"I don't want to work for the Questore."

He turned left and the car came to a halt outside an iron gate that opened on to a small estate of expensive, low houses hidden among the plane and cypress trees.

"Why not?"

"It's not with a child abuse center and with Piero Trotti that the Questore's going to buy himself a clean slate now that the Socialists are out of power."

"You don't care about the children?"

"I don't care about the Questore."

"And the little Priscilla? You don't care about her?"

"Time I started thinking about myself."

"You don't care about me, Piero?"

"I don't want to stay on in the Questura. It's as simple as that, Simona."

48: Quarenghi

"COMMISSARIO TROTTI OF the Polizia di Stato."

A young maid answered the door. She was black and spoke with a French accent. "The signora's expecting you." She beckoned Trotti and Signora Scola to follow her and took them into the house. The maid was very small and the tight waist of her blue work-blouse accentuated her ample hips. The shining skin of her calves was marked with dark blemishes.

Signora Quarenghi was waiting in the large lounge.

The maid said something in French and then vanished.

Signora Quarenghi stood up and held out her hand. "I was expecting you." A hint of dramatic resignation in her voice. She wore a short skirt.

"Commissario Trotti," Trotti said and gesturing to Signora Scola, added, "My assistant."

"Very attractive young women in the Polizia di Stato nowadays."

"We like to keep up with the times."

"Of course, of course." The eyes watched Simona Scola coldly. "A commissario—well, that does make a change."

Signora Quarenghi was in her early forties. She had no doubt once been an attractive woman, with blue eyes and blonde hair, but the hair had lost its texture and her eyes appeared tired. Her skin had aged, as if from too much exposure to the sun. There were lines around her large mouth. Lipstick had been applied haphazardly and scarcely followed its natural ridges. There was blonde hair along the upper lip.

"I won't waste your time, signora."

"I've already wasted enough time in these last thirteen months. I really don't see how a new inquiry is going to change anything. Carlo's dead and, anyway, you know who's guilty."

"Guilty?"

"You know as well as I do who murdered poor Carlo."

Trotti gave her a bland smile. "I've absolutely no idea who murdered Carlo Turellini."

She was not wearing a brassiere. She had put on a powder-blue sweater over a flat chest. The nipples pushed against the woolen weave. Beneath the short skirt, the tights had a bright harlequin pattern of greens and reds. Narrow hips that managed to give her a boyish look. A loose blue scarf was tied at the neck in an attempt to hide the premature wrinkling. Several rings on her fingers and large plastic earrings. "Then you are wasting my time. Goodness knows why you never arrested her."

"Her?"

"That awful Englishwoman."

Commissario Trotti smiled. "Would you mind if we sat down?"

With a broad gesture, she invited Trotti and Signora Scola to use the vast Chesterfield.

The room was large, decorated in Spanish hacienda style. The furniture was of black wood and there were various ornaments to suggest that the proprietor raised cattle—rough-hewn yokes and wheels with wooden spokes.

A cellular telephone lay on the piano, near a pile of telephone directories. In a far corner stood a beige computer with its satellite printers and matching accessories.

The room would have been somber but for the daylight coming through the large French windows. Beyond the windows was a garden with a hedge of cypress trees. The hedge gave on to the flat rice fields.

"Signora Quarenghi, do you know Signor Bassi?"

"Bassi?" She shook her head. "It's not about Carlo you've come to see me?"

"Do you know Fabrizio Bassi?"

"I know some Bassis—but not in this city."

"A private detective. I believe you spoke to him."

"Ah!" She smiled with recollection. "You mean that strange man who left his tie undone."

Trotti nodded.

"Like some character on television. Or Umberto Bossi of the Lega Lombarda. Yes, I met him." An amused curving of her lips. "A friend of yours?"

"Fabrizio Bassi was a private detective who used to be a policeman."

"Why do you mention him? He was, you say. He's dead?"

"Bassi was making an inquiry into Carlo Turellini's death."

"That's what he said."

"When did you meet him?"

"Is he dead?"

"Please answer the question."

Another cold glance at Signora Scola as the woman tried to recollect. "It must have been some time after Carlo's death. He came to see me." She raised her thin shoulders. "I'm afraid I got the impression he was somebody in from the fields. A nice man—but not terribly intelligent. Bit of a peasant."

"He asked you a few questions?"

"You all do."

"What sort of questions?"

"The same questions that everybody else asks."

"When did you last see Fabrizio Bassi?"

She thought for a moment before replying. "I saw him twice. The first time soon after Carlo's death. Then he came back six, seven months later. The second time I let him in and he told me he was working for the old woman."

"What old woman?"

"Carlo's ex-wife." A movement of her hand. "The man was sitting where you're sitting now and he asked all sorts of stupid questions about me and Carlo, about me and my husband. Worse than the police and all the time he was playing a little recorder to get my answers on tape."

"You never saw him again?"

"Like the police, he wanted to know why I was in the vicinity of Carlo's place at Segrate when Carlo was murdered . . ."

"Why were you in the vicinity of Carlo Turellini's place when he was shot?"

"I see you're no more imaginative than all the others."

"Kindly answer my question."

Signora Quarenghi lowered herself into the leather armchair opposite. Beside the chair was a potted rubber plant. The woman sat with her back to the French windows and her face in the shade. Girlishly she brought her legs up beneath her thighs. "I had a pre-monition."

"Premonition?"

"That's what I told the police. I may be a stupid woman—a lot of people tell me so, not least my dear, dear husband—but I believe in premonitions. I dreamt Carlo was going to be murdered—and I tried to help him."

"Too late."

She nodded. She placed a thin hand on her thigh. There was an ashtray on the arm of the chair.

"Why did you accuse your husband of Dr. Turellini's murder?"

"At the time . . ."

"Yes?"

"At the time, I thought . . ." She stopped.

"What did you think?"

"I was having problems with my husband. Paolo's not always a very understanding man. You see, he is quite a bit older than me. He's an intellectual and he's not really interested in anything he can't measure—measure or weigh."

"Why did you accuse him?"

"I was being silly. It was a mistake. I realize that now."

"Where is Dr. Quarenghi at the moment?"

"In Rome," she said, raising the shoulders of her V-necked sweater. "He has an apartment there. I haven't seen Paolo for a cou-ple of weeks. He often has to go to the ministry for weeks on end."

"You don't have any children?"

She shook her head, and then looked carefully at Signora Scola who was sitting beside Trotti taking notes on a pad. Signora Scola did not return the glance.

"Why did you accuse your husband, Signora Quarenghi?"

"Paolo knew about me and Carlo. Of course, the affair had been over for some time. By then Carlo had found someone younger and more beautiful and more stupid—a foreigner. But you can't imagine how jealous my husband is. He found a letter—that was the evening I had the terrible dream."

"A letter Turellini had written?"

"I'd written."

"Why would your husband want to kill Turellini? The two men were friends."

"They used to be friends."

"They were colleagues."

"That was before." Again her glance turned to Signora Scola. "Doctors can be as jealous as women, you know."

"Why kill Carlo Turellini?"

"My husband killed nobody."

"You said he'd killed Turellini."

"On the day of Carlo's death, my husband was in Rome." She shrugged her acquiescence. "Carlo had been having an affair with me. That was something my husband could not bring himself to accept."

Trotti coughed. "I imagine Dr. Quarenghi, living alone in Rome, must have ample time to have his own affairs."

The woman said flatly, "I hope so for his sake."

"Why?"

"It would be something other than his work." Signora Quarenghi shrugged. "My husband's a jealous man. But don't think he's some passionate Latin lover." She laughed to herself and it was then, as her face caught the light from the window that Trotti noticed there was a nervous tic agitating her eyebrow. "His job, his house, his car, his dog, his young wife. They're symbols of his success. And he doesn't want anyone touching them. Because if you do . . ."

Signora Scola raised her head. "Yes?"

"You touch them at your own risk." She met Trotti's glance. "At your own very considerable risk."

49: Paolo

"CARLO TURELLINI WAS murdered early in the morning of Friday, October twenty-third while leaving the garage of his villa in Segrate."

Signora Quarenghi nodded.

"The previous evening, your husband found a note you had written to Carlo Turellini and there was a quarrel?"

"No."

"No what?"

"There was a letter—it's true. A stupid letter I wrote to Carlo."

"And your husband found it?"

"My husband was in Rome."

Simona Scola held her pen motionless above the note pad and watched the other woman in silence.

"About a week before Carlo's death. A letter I'd sent him."

"To Turellini?"

She nodded again. "Somebody—goodness knows who—made a photocopy and sent it to my husband at the Ministry in Rome."

"And your husband was furious?"

"I wasn't with him."

"Then how did you know about the letter?"

"I didn't—at least, not until much later."

"But you had a premonition?"

"I think I was still in love with Carlo. He was with the English-woman but I still loved him."

"And, on the basis of a premonition, you accused your husband of murdering Carlo Turellini?"

She started to fumble with a packet of Muratti cigarettes that lay on the black piano near the directories. "I was acting strangely."

"When did you see your husband?"

"I spent the day at the barracks in Segrate. The day Carlo was murdered. They tested me because they seemed to think I could have murdered Carlo."

"And your husband?"

"He came up from Rome on the Pendolino to take me home."

"There was a quarrel?"

"No quarrel." A thin laugh. "My husband isn't like that. He doesn't have to shout or raise his voice to impose his will."

"Your husband was very angry?"

"I had accused him of murdering my lover. What do you think, Signor Commissario? Paolo's always considered me as a personal possession."

"In this instance, his own wife was being seduced by a close friend."

"You understand perfectly, commissario. Only Carlo didn't seduce me. He screwed me, he penetrated me, we made love for nights on end." She nodded as she placed a cigarette in her mouth. "Paolo Quarenghi gave up sharing the same bed with me a long, long time ago. He had better things to do."

"You had a premonition your husband intended to do something rash?"

"I told you my husband was in Rome."

"If your husband was in Rome, how could you be afraid of his reactions?"

"I was acting strangely. Perhaps . . ." She shook her head, as if trying to dismiss an idea. "I knew it was over between Carlo and me. That's what frightened me. I knew he was with the Englishwoman— but I couldn't take it seriously. A stupid, ignorant Englishwoman."

"She wanted to have his child."

She looked at Trotti and she could have been a little girl. She spoke very softly. "The realization I was going to be alone again."

"Why were you afraid of your husband?"

Signora Quarenghi's hand went to the blue scarf. "Paolo Quarenghi's not a violent man. He's never raised his hand to me, if that's what you think."

"You had reason to believe he could be violent if he was angered?"

"Nothing like that." A thin smile. "We hardly quarrel anymore. My husband has other interests in his life."

"You didn't quarrel over the letter?"

"Paolo simply becomes very distant. It's as if I were the maid from Mauritius. He speaks to me only to give me orders or because he needs something. Sometimes he disappears from the house. The rest of the time he sits in front of his computer and does his homework."

"It might be a good idea if I spoke with Dr. Quarenghi."

"My husband's in Rome."

"Then when he returns."

"Paolo is a very busy man. He works for the Ministry of Health. This entire affair has understandably irritated him considerably." There was another movement of the nervous eye. She lit the cigarette with a large lighter in the form of a conquistador. "All my stupid fault, of course. I should never have made my silly accusations. I suppose I just can't have been thinking clearly."

"You take medication, Signora?"

"Not really."

"Either you take medication or you don't."

"I used to."

"But not now?"

She put the cigarette to her lips and inhaled, her eyes on Trotti.

"No sleeping pills?"

"Just the occasional one."

There was silence.

Outside a wind was causing the plane trees to sway gently.

Trotti wanted to get away. To get out. Signora Quarenghi made him feel uncomfortable.

She spoke again. "I wanted to have a child, you see."

Signora Scola looked up.

"I often felt that with a child, perhaps . . ."

"Yes?"

"Perhaps my husband and I would have been closer. You understand, Dr. Quarenghi and I aren't very close. Perhaps children would have drawn us together."

"What has stopped you?"

"I am forty-six, you see."

"That's not too late." Signora Scola spoke softly.

"I was taking sleeping pills. There wasn't really much else I could do, was there?"

"Do?"

"Sleep—I needed to sleep. Because as long as I was sleeping, I didn't think about anything else. And most of the time I was here by myself. With just the maid for company. While Paolo's in Rome to earn money for both of us." Her wan smile went from Trotti to Signora Scola. "Paolo was very angry I made those silly accusations. I wanted to have a child and then I discovered that Carlo wanted to have children with that awful Englishwoman." She added softly, "I thought I was in love with Carlo Turellini." She tapped her chest. "On my own again. I'm a woman—and I need to be desired, I need to be wanted."

Trotti asked, "Why an affair with another man?"

Simona Scola asked, "Why didn't you adopt?"

Signora Quarenghi did not answer either question.

"If you really wanted a child," Trotti said, "why did you have an affair with another man?"

"My husband was living most of the time in Rome."

"You could have joined him."

She shook her head. "He doesn't care for children. And he doesn't want me in his bed."

"So you had an affair with Turellini?"

The eyes suddenly blazed behind the cigarette smoke. "I wasn't having an affair."

"You wrote letters," Trotti said. "According to various people, there was a liaison between you and Turellini."

"A liaison? Of course there was a liaison. We were screwing, we were making love. We were friends. Carlo was good. He was good because he was like a little boy." She started to laugh but she could not control the movement of her eye. "But there was no affair. There was no future. You think I didn't realize that? I knew about the Englishwoman. I knew all about her. And I wasn't jealous." Her voice grew louder. "And I really don't appreciate your making these insinuations. You're in my house and it is not for you to insult me under my roof."

Trotti held up a calming hand. "Nobody's making any insinuations. We're simply trying to get to the truth."

"It doesn't matter." Like a deflated puppet, she fell back into her seat, the cigarette forgotten between her fingers. "Carlo's dead, isn't he? And I'm still here."

"Even unnatural death matters, signora. If it didn't, I'd be out of a job."

"You haven't done a very good job so far."

"We'd've done an even worse job if we'd believed your accusations against your own husband."

She shrugged. "Perhaps my judgment was unsound."

"Perhaps?"

She had grown calm, like a child curled up against the dark, leather armchair. The Muratti smouldered between her pale fingers. "My husband wouldn't murder anyone."

"And now you accuse Mary Coddrington." Trotti raised his eyebrows. "How do you expect us to place more importance on this accusation than on your earlier one?"

"She murdered him." Signora Quarenghi inhaled deeply then folded her arms against her chest. She snorted smoke through her nostrils.

"Why do you say that?"

"It's obvious."

"There was no motive. Carlo Turellini and this Englishwoman were living together. She was going to have his baby. She was happy."

"The bitch."

"Harsh language, Signora Quarenghi."

"Carlo didn't love her."

"That doesn't mean Signora Coddrington murdered Carlo Turellini."

"Of course she murdered him."

"She had everything she wanted. A house, a job, security and the prospect of a child on the way. Why murder him?"

Suddenly, unexpectedly the woman sitting in the armchair started shouting. "She murdered him. She murdered him. Because she hated him. She didn't like him. She wanted his money. But she didn't want Carlo. She couldn't stand Carlo."

The voice had risen louder and louder.

Signora Scola glanced unhappily at Trotti.

Signora Quarenghi now stood up. She was gesticulating and there were traces of froth at the corner of her lips. "She couldn't love him as I loved him. Of course she knew Carlo loved me. It was to spite me. Don't you understand? Of course she wasn't pregnant. That was just another of her clever little tricks."

The Muratti cigarette had fallen to the floor.

"The English cow was jealous and it was to spite me that she killed him. To spite me, the stupid, scheming little bitch."

The maid had reappeared. She carried a tray, a glass of water and a medicine bottle.

"To spite me, and now my dear sweet Carlo's dead." Then Signora Quarenghi started to sob.

50: Methuselah

SHE HAD PUT the sunglasses back into place. "I don't believe her."

Trotti raised an eyebrow as he turned to look at Signora Scola.

Her headache, if indeed there ever was one, had now disappeared. She was driving, leaning, forward slightly and holding the small wheel of the Fiat Seicento between her beige gloves. "Signora Quarenghi's lying."

Trotti asked, "How do you know?"

"You couldn't see it was an act—the frothing at the mouth?"

"I appreciate your feminine intuition." Trotti smiled and touched the sleeve of her coat. "My problem is I always work with men."

"You used to work with the Ciuffi woman before she got herself killed."

"What makes you think Signora Quarenghi was lying to me?"

"Like all men, Piero, you only see what you want to see."

"All my fault. My daughter got me to buy a pair of glasses but I hate to wear them."

She took her eyes from the road. They were invisible behind the sunglasses. "You see, you do have a sense of humor." The corners of her lips moved upwards in a tentative smile. "Despite your advanced age and thinning hair."

Trotti liked the way the soft skin of Signora Scola's cheeks formed slight ridges of amusement. Wrapped in the large fur coat, she seemed almost fragile.

"Very rudimentary sense of humor at best. A peasant from the hills beyond the Po."

"Quarenghi was playing with you."

"Why?"

"I don't know, Piero."

They were returning to the city and the wintry sun glinted on the lead plates of the cathedral roof. Beside the dome there was the emptiness where for over a thousand years the Civic Tower had once stood, between Duomo and Broletto. Like a tooth that had been removed—you grew to accept the change but you could not forget the loss and the disfigurement.

"You think Signora Quarenghi killed Turellini?"

"That's not what the Carabinieri think. The paraffin test was negative—she hadn't fired any gun that morning." Signora Scola smiled. From where Trotti was sitting beside her, he saw the wrinkling at the corner of her eyes behind the dark lenses.

"What d'you think, Simona?"

"I'm not a policeman."

"Then how do you know she was lying?"

"Because I'm a woman. And like all women, I use the same tricks to get what I want."

"There's no difference between you and Signora Quarenghi?"

"A difference of motives."

"What are her motives?"

"I don't know that, Piero."

"What are yours?"

Signora Scola bit her lip, then, "You shouldn't ask me."

"Why not?"

"You may not care for the answer."

"What's the answer?"

She hesitated before answering. "We're all the same. Women all want the same things."

Trotti turned away and looked at the rice fields that were slowly being replaced by the spreading expansion of the university and its satellites—new housing, new shops, new services.

"We women can be quite ruthless."

"I have a wife and a daughter," he said. "I learned about female ruthlessness a long time ago."

"Why do you always have to talk about your wife, Piero Trotti?"

He shrugged as if he had not heard her question. "A woman has three lines of attack to get what she wants."

"Only three?"

"Her favorite method's flattery. It works wonders—even with the worst misogynist."

"You're a misogynist?"

"I don't hate women in particular, if that's what you mean. My wife once told me I hate everybody." He smiled. "You haven't told me your motives."

"What are the lines of attack women use?"

Trotti held up a finger. "The most efficient is flattery. A woman will tell you you're a wonderful, wonderful man and her voice promises so much pleasure. The voice in the Garden of Eden."

"You've been there?"

"For a very short time—just before my marriage."

"You really are a misogynist."

"If flattery doesn't work, the woman then resorts to blackmail."

"Blackmail?"

"And if blackmail doesn't work, she retreats to the third and last ditch of war. That's when the pots and pans start to fly."

"Breaks diplomatic ties and recalls all her ambassadors?"

"But the strange thing is, Signora Scola . . ."

She kept her eyes on the road. "A minute ago you called me Simona." She was smiling.

"A man can give in to a woman's charm, a man can give in to her blackmail, he can even run up a white flag of truce when she brings out the heavy artillery—it doesn't make any difference."

"We always get what we want?"

"Of course you get what you want."

"Then we're nice to you?"

"Nice? A woman can never stop herself from despising a man who's given in to her, to her silly, feminine whims."

Simona Scola, thirty-two years old, with a degree in child psychology (110 marks, cum laude), beautiful, elegant and with a very wealthy husband, put her head back and laughed, almost taking the car into the back of a municipal bus.

"You said you knew nothing about women."

"I know nothing about women."

"And where does that place Signora Quarenghi, Piero?"

"Now tell me what your motives are, Simona."

"You'll find out in time."

"Precisely what frightens me."

"That woman was acting, Piero. You could see that."

"What were her motives?"

"Acting because she wanted something from you."

"What did Signora Quarenghi want from me?"

"You tell me."

"To be left alone, I suppose." Trotti shrugged. "I don't know."

"Worse than her brother. More devious and even less honest . . . if that's possible."

Trotti ran a hand through his hair. "Her brother?"

Again Simona Scola laughed, and if Trotti had been listening to her laugh he would have found it pretty. Like clear water running through the pines of the Penice on a summer's day.

"Her brother?"

"Methuselah of the Questura—and you don't even know Signora Quarenghi's maiden name is Viscontini? You don't even recognize our Socialist mayor's sister? Why else do you think a man like Quarenghi married her? An unattractive neurotic like her. Unattractive and flat-chested."

51: Utet

"YOU'LL HAVE SOMETHING to eat with us, won't you Piero?"

They went under the bridge of the Genoa-Milan railway line and came to the traffic lights where the traffic converged at the feet of the statue. Minerva, goddess of learning, deity of the university city, stood proud and erect, immune to the noise and pollution of the angry cars, the delivery vans, the articulated trucks coming in from the city bypass.

"I need to get back to the Questura."

It was as if she had not heard him. Simona Scola took the car nimbly around the statue—Minerva as arrogant and immutable as the Socialists before Mani Pulite—and headed down viale della Libertà, with its long line of trees and six-story apartment blocks. A street that was built in the years following the Second World War and the ravages of Allied bombardment, when the architects abandoned the pebbles from the Po and the red, Roman brick of the city for massive granite façades and concrete.

She found a parking space opposite the Communist bookshop and was out of the car before Trotti, opening the door for him and almost forcibly hauling him from the low seat.

"I should be getting back to the Questura, Signora. I need to see Maiocchi."

She silenced him with a finger to his lips. She then took his arm in hers and together they crossed the pavement and went into an apartment building.

The iron and glass doors swung open and as they went up the

highly polished steps a concierge put his head out of a small window to acknowledge their passage.

"A nice part of town to live in," Trotti remarked.

"My husband's family bought the place in nineteen sixty-two," Signora Scola replied simply.

They did not take the lift but went up two flights of steps. With the young, lithe woman beside him, Trotti felt old and overweight. He was soon out of breath.

Reaching the second floor, Signora Scola rang the bell of a polished walnut door. Almost immediately various heavy-duty bolts were pulled back and the door was opened by a maid.

"Ah, Enza," Signora Scola said. "I've brought a colleague home for lunch. Could you set another place—if that's not too much trouble?"

The maid nodded and Trotti followed Signora Scola into the house.

A smell of cooking, of olive oil and garlic.

The maid took Trotti's waxed jacket and his shabby scarf.

"Come on through." Signora Scola removed her gloves and sun-glasses. She beckoned him into a bright living room.

There were paintings on the wall and various photographs. Photographs of the city, of the Duomo, of the covered bridge, of San Teodoro and San Michele.

There was also a large portrait of Signora Scola in student robes and the peaked academic cap, set above a mock fireplace.

More photographs on the piano and on the bookshelves.

Lots of bookshelves.

Heavy Garzanti and UTET encyclopedias and dictionaries in various languages, but the books gave the appearance of not having been disturbed in a long time.

The furnishings, expensive and somewhat old-fashioned, were comfortable and indeed elegant, but there was a lumpiness that dated them as late fifties or early sixties.

"Perhaps you'd care to wash your hands, Piero?"

She took him to a bright and spacious bathroom. He could feel the touch of her body against his. "Clean towel by the sink."

Left to himself, he washed his hands and face and ran a comb through his hair.

The bar of French soap was new and unused.

("You'll find out in time," she had said in the car.)

In the tinted mirror, his eyes appeared tired and bloodshot. They stared back at him noncommittally.

"Ready to eat?"

The table was placed by the window and the midday light flooded on to the spotless tablecloth, the cutlery and fine china plates. Packets of grissini and freshly cut white bread.

The table had been set for two.

A dish of celery was in the middle of the table and the slices of parma ham had already been served.

Two places facing each other across the dazzling breadth of the tablecloth.

"Piero, do sit down."

"And your husband, signora?"

"This morning you were calling me Simona. You make me feel like a schoolmistress when you call me Signora. An old schoolmistress."

Trotti smiled sheepishly. "I thought we were having lunch with your husband."

She had kicked of her shoes and her feet were small against the grey wool of the carpet. She moved towards him. He admired the movement of her girlish hips beneath the neat skirt. Simona Scola took hold of his forearm. "Before we eat," she said.

"What?"

She was a lot smaller without her shoes. "You want to meet Massimo?"

She crossed the room, pulling him like a child in need of guidance. She opened the far door.

Trotti allowed himself to be guided by the young woman into the adjacent room. It was a lot less bright. The blinds had been drawn and the only source of light came from a bedside lamp.

"Massimo, I'd like to introduce Commissario Trotti."

Ingegnere Scola sat in a chair. The head rest had tilted backwards. The man's head was to one side and he appeared to be sleeping with his mouth open.

She pulled Trotti forward.

Massimo Scola was in pajamas. A blanket covered the lower part of his body and beneath the blanket, his slippers came together at an unusual angle.

"He's sleeping."

Trotti recognised the smell of medicated soap.

"Massimo's been paraplegic ever since the skiing accident," Signora Scola said brightly. "Best not to bother him now. He's already eaten."

52: Thermal

A LIGHT KNOCK on the door and then, without waiting for permission, he entered Trotti's small office. His glance went from Trotti to Maiocchi and back to Trotti. "Commissario Trotti?" A hopeful smile.

He had to be wearing thermal underwear, Trotti decided, as the man held out his right hand. Beneath the other arm, he carried a briefcase of crocodile leather. "I'm Regni."

"Do I know you?" Trotti queried, slightly puzzled.

"Avoccato Regni." A smile that revealed bright teeth. "I represent Signora Lucchi. I understand you spoke to her yesterday."

Trotti was surprised by Regni's youth. He must have been thirty-five years old at most. Long blond hair, even features and fashionable tortoiseshell glasses with blue-tinted lenses. He had a short mustache, slightly darker in shade than his elegantly cut hair.

Despite the cold weather, the lawyer wore no coat and his jacket was undone. A navy blue tie and a well-pressed Oxford shirt of a paler blue. He was dressed for a mild day in autumn, not for the rigors of the Po valley in the middle of a long cold winter.

Just looking at him, Trotti felt cold and pulled his jacket tighter to his chilled body.

"I was hoping I could speak with you, commissario." He tilted his head slightly towards Maiocchi. "Alone, if that's possible."

It was past three o'clock and a fog was fast coming up from the river, engulfing the provincial city outside the window. "If you wish to speak with me alone, perhaps you should first ask Commissario Maiocchi. There's been a rather unpleasant murder—"

"You work for the Reparto Omicidi?" the lawyer asked. Before Trotti could reply, he continued, "You don't mind if I sit down?"

"Best if I leave you," Maiocchi said, addressing Trotti. Maiocchi was now standing behind Avoccato Regni who had lowered himself into one of the greasy canvas armchairs. Regni could not see Maiocchi as Maiocchi raised a hand to his ear—the Italian gesture signifying male sterility and homosexuality.

Grinning, the empty coffee cup in one hand and an unlit pipe in the other, Maiocchi left Trotti's office, quietly closing the door behind him with his foot.

"You must forgive my barging in on you like this, Trotti."

"Commissario Trotti."

"It was Signora Lucchi's sincerest desire I contact you as soon as possible."

"Signora Lucchi?"

"You were with her yesterday."

"You know my name?"

"You went to her apartment in via Montenapoleone in Milan."

"I don't recall Signora Lucchi's ever having asked me for my name."

A glint of the glasses as the man held his head to one side, "You are Commissario Trotti?"

"Of course."

Satisfied, the man sat back in the armchair, folding his hands over the briefcase. He appeared immune to the damp chill of the unheated office. He seemed similarly immune to Trotti's rising irritation. "Bassi told me all about you, commissario."

"Why should Bassi feel the need to tell you anything about me?"

"You'll soon be retiring, I believe."

Trotti bit his lip. "Next year."

"And you have a state pension?"

"I've been a policeman for a few years."

"Well that's good."

"I fail to see how my private finances can possibly be of interest to you, Avoccato Regni."

"Precisely what Bassi told me." There was another movement of his head and it was only then that Trotti understood Maiocchi's suggestion of homosexuality. Despite the brash approach, there was something delicate, even feminine, about Avoccato Regni.

Trotti also noticed that the nails were well manicured. "I fail to understand."

Regni raised his hands—the gesture of a priest or of a talk show host on Berlusconi. "Not really all that much to understand. After all, you don't work for Reparto Omicidi. Even if you did, there could be no justification for your carrying out inquiries in Milan. At least, not without proper authorisation."

Trotti looked at his watch. "I'm a busy man."

An ingratiating smile. "I certainly won't keep you any longer than is absolutely necessary. I studied in America. I know all about doing business." He added in English, "*Time is money.*"

Trotti frowned gloomily.

"To come to the point . . .I think we could do business."

"I don't even know you."

"Signora Lucchi says you're a charming man." Regni pursued blandly. "I've good reason to believe you are."

"What precisely is it you want?"

"You were in Milan yesterday. For an inquiry which does not officially concern you."

"You know very little about police procedure, Avoccato Regni. You don't know who I work for." Trotti went to stand up. "Perhaps it would be a good idea if you left this office now."

A placating hand. "It is not my intention to quarrel with you, Trotti."

"Most people call me Commissario Trotti out of common courtesy."

"Of course."

"It is not my intention to waste time."

"Then we can see eye to eye, can't we?" A priest, a talk show host or, perhaps worse, a patronizing schoolmistress.

"What makes you think I want to see eye to eye with you, Avoccato?"

"Bassi told me Commissario Trotti could be prickly."

"If you choose, Avoccato Regni, Commissario Trotti can be violent."

"Bassi also said you were scrupulously honest and that's why he wanted you helping him in his enquiry. Your honesty, Trotti . . ."

"What about it?"

"Signora Lucchi's willing to pay good money for your honesty."

"My honesty's not for sale." Piero Trotti snorted faint amusement. "If it were, it wouldn't be honesty."

"Of course, of course."

Trotti waited.

The lawyer gathered his thoughts. He sat back and looked around the small office, as if noticing it for the first time—the greasy armchairs, the piles of dusty beige folders, the teak topped desk and the ancient telephone with its faded Columbus sticker.

"Signora Lucchi wants you to work for her, commissario. She wants you to carry on where the poor Bassi left off."

"Left off?"

"You name your price."

"Where Bassi left off?"

"You know, Signora Lucchi was very upset to hear Bassi had met with a tragic accident."

53: Fountain Pen

"I HAVE POWER of attorney for Signora Lucchi." Regni took a checkbook from his jacket pocket. "What sort of sum do you feel would be reasonable?"

"How did Signora Lucchi hear about Bassi's murder?"

The lawyer smiled sweetly. "I told her."

"Where did you find out?"

"Don't forget, Commissario Trotti, it was I who engaged Fabrizio Bassi in the first place. My client was understandably very upset about the death of Dr. Turellini. Even if they were no longer man and wife. Signora Lucchi wanted the killer brought to justice, and that's why she asked me to hire someone. Someone who'd be willing to work fast, efficiently and discreetly."

"You didn't answer my question."

"Question?" the lawyer repeated, raising his eyebrows in mock astonishment.

"How did you find out about Bassi's murder? I'm not aware of the papers mentioning anything."

"I would be most remiss in my responsibility as Signora Lucchi's lawyer if I didn't keep some kind of tabs on people she chooses to employ."

Trotti frowned. "You'd seen him?"

"Who?"

"Had you been in touch with Bassi recently, Avvocato Regni?"

He nodded. "Very recently."

"When?"

The hands came together on top of the briefcase. "Am I right in assuming you're willing to accept Signora Lucchi's proposition of employment?"

A shrug. "I can give no engagements, Avoccato, without first having some idea of the details of the proposition."

The young face stiffened. "It's not Bassi's demise which concerns my client. This should be quite clear from the start."

"If I'm to take up the inquiry where Bassi left off, I might just worry about ending up in a polluted stream with a bullet lodged in my brains."

"Then you accept her proposition?"

"Tell me how you discovered Bassi had been killed."

"Why?"

"Do you want me to work for you or not?"

The lawyer took a deep breath. "The Turellini inquiry's been going on for over a year. The various police forces of our Republic seem to be at a complete loss. And the poor Bassi until very recently was getting nowhere. Understandably, I needed to know whether it was worth my client's while to continue paying the private detective a retainer. Thirteen months's a long time for somebody to pay out good money and get very little in return."

"When and where did you see Bassi for the last time?"

Regni frowned and then suddenly laughed. "You talk to me as if you think I were in some way responsible for the poor man's murder."

Insincere laughter and it grated on Trotti's nerves. "Perish the thought."

A moment of silence as the two men looked at each other carefully.

Regni was the first to lower his glance. He ran a hand through his hair. "The day before yesterday. I was driving back from Genoa and he called me in my car, asking me to speak to him. At about eight o'clock."

"What did he want?"

"To see me."

"What did he want to tell you?"

"That he now knew who'd murdered Dr. Turellini."

"And he told you?"

"Not over the telephone. Signor Bassi believed his telephone was being monitored. He wanted to speak to me in person."

"You saw him?"

"No."

"Why not?"

"I came off the autostrada. There'd been an accident in the fog. A car had gone through the red lights at Zinasco. Two or three people were badly injured and with all the ambulances and the police, the traffic had slowed down to a snail's pace for eight kilometers. I got to Bassi's place at nine thirty—half an hour late and he'd already gone."

"Bit strange."

"Not really."

"Why not? After over a year, you weren't thrilled at the idea the murder was going to be cleared up?"

"Cleared up?" Regni lowered his hand in a gesture of moderation. "It wasn't the first time Bassi had found the murderer of Carlo Turellini. He was on a retainer. The golden goose and he needed a few ersatz eggs. For the occasional omelette." Regni laughed again. "That was the whole point of the *Vissuto* operation. Or so I believe. As I understand it, there wasn't—never had been—any word from the Pubblico Ministero telling Bassi to lay off the Turellini case."

"Then why the article?"

"Just another figment of Signor Bassi's fertile imagination, just another way to stay on my client's books for a few more months."

"That's not the impression I got," Trotti replied simply. "Bassi came to see me a couple of times. The last time he seemed very keen to sort out the case. He offered me money."

"Not his money."

"You're suggesting Bassi wasn't honest?" Trotti asked.

"Who is?"

Trotti made a gesture of irritation.

"Who's honest in this country? Tangentopoli, Commissario Trotti—it didn't just come about. It wasn't just the politicians sewing things up among themselves to their own advantage. It wasn't some evil Mafia living on the edge of society and preying off it. An ulcer on the surface of the Republic?" He shook his head. "The disease will remain. Tangentopoli'll remain because it's in us. We are Tangentopoli, Trotti, and Tangentopoli is Italy."

"Bassi was dishonest?"

Regni hesitated before answering. "Neither honest nor dishonest. Signor Bassi—God rest his poor soul—was only too pleased to be earning good money. I assume the inquiry into Turellini's death was more exciting than his normal run of divorce work. And it let him live out his fantasies of being a private detective like the Rockfords and the Colombos of those American films he loved so much."

"He was keeping the case going as long as possible?"

"You understand fast, Commissario Trotti."

"Meaning Bassi was neither efficient nor particularly honest?"

"In a manner of speaking."

"Then why on earth, Avoccato Regni, did you employ him in the first place? I observe you know so much about Commissario Trotti. You know all about me, including the arrangements for my pension. Didn't you carry out the same market research before handing over Signora Lucchi's money to a rather dumb private eye?"

The man did not reply. He uncapped a fountain pen that he had taken from his jacket pocket and he opened the checkbook.

"Did Bassi say anything about where he was going, Avvocato Regni?"

"I beg your pardon."

"You spoke to him over your car phone, didn't you?"

Regni nodded.

"You were one of the last people he ever spoke to. Was there anything else Bassi told you?"

"Not that I can recall." He shook his well-cut hair. "Nothing— except that I was surprised he insisted on my driving to his place."

"Why?"

"He had a car and he knew I wanted to get back to Milan. We could've met earlier in a bar on the autostrada. That way I wouldn't have been held up at Zinasco."

"Why on the autostrada?"

"I was driving back from Genoa. And he told me he'd just left Alessandria."

"Alessandria?"

"Said he'd been seeing someone in the prison there."

54: Piemonte

"She'd said she'd ring for me."

"Who?"

"Bianca Poveri."

"Do I know Bianca Poveri?"

"She runs the women's prison."

"Well, that's good. Ring about what?"

"I need to see Gennaro Maluccio in Alessandria." Trotti turned, showing a quizzical smile. "You're still angry with me, Pisa?"

"Why should I be angry?"

"A lot of people are. Apparently they find me difficult and demanding?"

"You, Commissario Trotti?"

Trotti acquiesced by raising his shoulders.

Pisanelli drove the Citroën. He had shampooed his hair and shaved. Perhaps he had even slept. He looked less tired, but that could be an illusion. There was little light within the car. The grey of dusk was fast turning into night.

"At least you're no longer risking your career prospects."

"That's what you tell me, commissario."

"I'm in on the Bassi inquiry. You saw Merenda, didn't you?"

"It's not Merenda who pays my salary at the end of the month."

"I sometimes wonder what you need a salary for."

"I've got into this habit of eating and sleeping and paying my rent."

"At the end of the month, what can you possibly spend your salary on?"

"Does that concern you?"

"Not on your car and certainly not on your clothes. And you don't have a wife and family to maintain."

"Thanks to you."

"Don't forget to get a receipt for the petrol."

Pisanelli tapped the inside pocket of his suede jacket. "Got it here."

The fog was getting darker, thicker and colder.

They had driven through Zinasco where there had been another accident—due, no doubt, to faulty traffic lights—and got on to the Milan-Genoa autostrada. Pisanelli kept close to the car in front, exploiting the aerodynamic drag. They were traveling at ninety kilometers per hour and Trotti had to shout over the straining engine of the Deux Chevaux.

"You don't have to drive so fast."

"I want to get back to the city before midnight."

"Saturday night, Pisa? What were you expecting to do on Saturday night?"

"Spend some time on myself."

"Time enough for that when you retire."

Pisanelli shook his head in wonderment. "Wasn't there talk of your retiring?"

"Stay on the autostrada until you get to the Tortona exit."

Pisanelli nodded glumly and his long hair moved against the collar of his suede coat.

Trotti looked out of the window.

Piemonte.

Trotti had grown up in Santa Maria. It was not in Lombardy but Piemonte, a few kilometers over the boundary into the province of Alessandria. Yet Trotti rarely felt at home in Piemonte. Turin was as much a foreign city for him as Bologna or Bari where he had served several years.

For some reason Trotti saw the Piemontesi as different. He was aware of an atavistic hostility in his blood. Perhaps it was because his own father, an uncommunicative man who had died young from war wounds, came from the Bassa, from the lower Po valley. Even in Mantua, such a distant Lombard city, with a different, awkward and ugly dialect, Trotti felt more at ease than in the city of Alessandria where the people were much more like his friends and family in the OltrePò.

Pisanelli spoke and Trotti came out of his reverie. "Three kilometers to the Turin-Piacenza exit."

Trotti asked, "What did Merenda tell you, Pisa?"

"Said you were now with us on the Bassi thing."

"He knew you were with me yesterday in Milan."

"Yesterday in Milan was a day off."

"And you're not working tomorrow. It's a good life, Pisa." Trotti nestled down lower in the flimsy bucket seat. "Like everybody else, Merenda's scared."

A draft worked its way inside the French car and the heating failed to reach his feet. Perhaps he ought to take Pioppi's advice and buy thermal underwear. Like Avoccato Regni. "He knows the Questore's on his way out. Merenda knows the Socialists are going to be flushed out. Out of government and out of the Questura. Why else d'you think he comes looking for me at the hospital. Why else, after all these years, does Merenda suddenly decide he wants to talk to Commissario Trotti? Commissario Trotti, persona non grata?"

"Perhaps he thinks you're a good detective."

"Merenda could have thought of that five or six years ago when he got me chucked out of my office."

"Chucked you out but you insisted on keeping your awful furniture. You could've had a fax, a phone and something to replace those terrible armchairs."

Trotti clicked his tongue. "Merenda needs me."

"Needs you?"

"Needs me on the Bassi case more than he needs the Questore's approval."

"And you're doing him a favor?"

"I don't do favors, Pisa."

"Never?"

He rubbed his cold chin. "Or if I do, I do them for my friends."

"What friends?"

"Precisely."

Pisanelli sniffed.

"Merenda's interests and mine happen to coincide over Bassi. It's no more complicated than that."

Pisanelli braked sharply as the rear lights of the car in front came on.

The fog was thickening along the autostrada.

"I wish you didn't drive so fast, Pisa."

"Scared of dying?"

"I've been paying into my pension scheme long enough."

Pisanelli laughed as he allowed the car in front to pull away. "I still don't understand why you care so much about Bassi's death. You never liked him, commissario. A womanizer and a fool."

"Perhaps it's a habit I've gotten into."

"Habit?"

"Perhaps I don't like people I'm associated with getting murdered."

"You were interested in the Turellini thing before Bassi got killed. That's why I came out to via Milano—I knew you were getting involved in the Turellini inquiry."

"Bassi came to see me. He offered me money to help him." Trotti added, "And now Signora Lucchi wants to pay me."

"What for?"

"Her lawyer was in my office and he pulled out a fat pen and an even fatter checkbook. Signora Lucchi wants me to continue where poor Fabrizio Bassi left off."

"Where did Bassi leave off, commissario?"

"In a ditch off the Provinciale 22 to Melegnano, a bullet in the head. That's where we found him on a cold winter's morning. Remember?"

55: Santa Corona Unita

HIS NAME WAS Ugo Rubino, he was from Taranto and he was serving a life sentence for murder.

Rubino had scarcely spoken since entering the office, just a few mumbled words of presentation to Trotti and Pisanelli. He had not smiled, nor had he held their glance for more than a fraction of a second. Dressed in drab clothes, he was a small, narrow-shouldered man with a swarthy complexion.

He had, however, nodded when the director proposed a shot of grappa with his coffee.

Gennaro Maluccio spoke. "I've got to protect myself." The journalist held a cup between his narrow hands. "There was a killing in this place only three weeks ago." A pause. "Another killing."

"A high percentage of the prisoners are from Puglia." The director—a small Neapolitan in a three-piece suit and a very large orange tie—nodded unhappily from behind his desk. "Santa Corona Unita."

"Nobody's safe, Trotti."

"Twenty years ago I used to live in Bari. At the time, everybody maintained there was no organized crime in Puglia. They said Bari was the Milan of the South—honest and hard-working, the moral capital of the South." Trotti allowed himself a wry smile. "At the time, a lot of people were being killed. While a lot of other people were making a fortune from the Cassa del Mezzogiorno. I was glad enough to get back north to Lombardy."

"It appears," the director remarked, "the Santa Corona Unita followed you."

They were in the director's office. It was nearly six o'clock and the temperature had dropped sharply. Despite the concealed heaters, Trotti felt cold. Outside, snow had started to fall in the prison courtyard and he could see the flakes swirling in the beams of light that swiveled in relentless, revolving arcs.

Casa di reclusione, Alessandria.

The director finished his coffee in a hurried gulp, then coughed politely. "You can ask Signor Maluccio your questions, Commissario Trotti." A gesture. "Please go ahead."

Trotti turned back to the journalist.

Gennaro Maluccio appeared tired, more tired than in the photographs Trotti had seen at the *Vissuto* offices. The pale skin appeared puffy. Yet the eyes were bright and they had never left Trotti's face.

Maluccio was wearing a red Milan AC tracksuit over a T-shirt, running shoes and white socks. "I was expecting the worst when I came here," he said.

"I can understand that."

"The other inmates have been very considerate towards me. At least, so far." One hand played nervously with the zip of the tracksuit. "They seem to think I'm from a different planet."

"Perhaps you are."

"Nothing but kindness which I have tried to repay in my own way." Gennaro Maluccio looked sideways at Ugo Rubino sitting on the same sofa.

Rubino's dark eyes remained on the synthetic carpet.

"A lot of people here can neither read nor write. I was astonished. I was equally astonished by their gentleness towards me. If I can be of use to my fellow inmates in taking down letters they wish to send home, I'm only too happy."

"There are classes in literacy," the director said, addressing Trotti. "It's just not always easy in getting teachers. The prison service isn't a high priority in Rome, I need not remind you."

Gennaro Maluccio continued. "I'm willing to talk to you, Trotti, although I don't see what good it can do. Bassi's told me about you and if the devil himself can get me out of here, I'm willing to do business with him." A pause. "With you."

Trotti lowered his head in a gesture of acknowledgement.

"I have to insist on the presence of Signor Rubino."

"I understand."

"I'm not a stool pigeon, as Signor Rubino can witness. I certainly don't wish to end up with a homemade knife stuck between my shoulder blades. Signor Rubino's my guarantee of good faith before the other prisoners."

"We're most grateful to Signor Rubino," Trotti said.

"In return for Signor Rubino's presence here, the director's generously agreed to resolve a couple of minor grievances that've been detrimental to the interests of my fellow prisoners." He added, "Grievances of a purely logistic nature."

The director from Naples coughed, gave a small smile and glanced at Ugo Rubino.

In his ill-fitting clothes, with his gnarled hands and his prematurely wrinkled skin, his taciturn manner and his motionless features, Ugo Rubino could have been a shepherd from Sardinia. In fact, Ugo Rubino had been born in Bari Vecchia and was believed to have murdered three people, including his half-brother, found dead in a well amidst the dusty vineyards of Noicàttero, his palate perforated and his brains blown out. A palate perforated by a gun inside the mouth. The Santa Corona Unita disposing of someone who had spoken out of turn.

In bocca chiusa non entrò mai mosca.

The director coughed again simultaneously pulling at his unfashionable tie. "Commissario, kindly proceed with your questions."

It was Gennaro Maluccio who spoke. "I'm not a criminal, although nearly everybody seems determined to consider me as such." He grimaced, "Everybody knows the cocaine found in my car was put there to incriminate me."

"By whom?"

"Your colleagues here in Alessandria. By the flatfeet of the Polizia di Stato." Jerkily he ran the fastener of the zip up and down the tracksuit. "I want to get back to my wife and children."

"Of course."

"My imprisonment's even harder on them. The little girls." He caught his breath. "And I need to get back to my job."

Trotti nodded.

"I'm not a criminal, Trotti. I'm a freelance journalist and while I'm here, I'm not earning money. There's no insurance for this sort of thing, you know." He paused. "No insurance for wrongful arrest."

The director stood up—he was very small, one meter sixty-eight at most—and took the coffeepot from the table. He offered more coffee to everybody.

Pisanelli, sitting in a far corner and apparently reading a book, accepted. He also accepted a shot of grappa.

There were lithographs on the wall and a couple of photographs on the desk, one of Turin, another of Alessandria, yet the place, with its government furniture, grey cabinets and ugly carpeting, was soulless.

Unlike in the office of Bianca Poveri, there were no cut flowers.

It was getting a lot colder.

"More coffee, commissario?"

Changing his mind, Trotti held out his coffee cup and like Pisanelli, he took a few drops of grappa.

"I'd like you to tell me about Fabrizio Bassi, Signor Maluccio," Trotti said. "You've spoken to him?"

"Not for several days. Why not speak to him rather than to me? I scarcely know him."

Trotti gestured with his free hand.

A frown. "Where is he?"

"Bassi's dead."

Gennaro Maluccio's face visibly paled. "You're joking."

"Not at all."

"But I spoke to him—two days ago, I spoke to Bassi. He came here to see me."

"What did you speak to Bassi about, Signor Maluccio?"

"Dead? How can he be dead?"

"Fabrizio Bassi was murdered in the hours following his visit to you, here in Alessandria."

"That's not possible."

"He went home and later that same evening Bassi was murdered. Somebody shot him in the head and the body was left in a tributary of the Lambro at Melegnano."

Maluccio's nostrils were pinched and very pale. "Who'd want to murder Bassi?"

"I was hoping," Trotti replied, "you could answer that question for me."

Gennaro Maluccio seemed to be having difficulty in breathing. "Why me?"

"You were among the last people to speak to him."

"I scarcely knew him. We'd met just a couple of times."

"When did you first meet?"

"When I wrote the article." Gennaro Maluccio, his face now

very pale, raised his hands in a movement of bewilderment. "Bassi contacted me, said he wanted to get the Turellini murder into the magazine. He thought I could help him—and, for once, an article of mine wasn't spiked."

"And the second time? Why did Bassi come to see you here on Thursday?"

"He wanted to ask me questions."

"What sort of questions?"

Gennaro Maluccio shrugged. "He knew I'd been arrested on a drugs charge. He wanted to know whether there was a connection between my arrest for drug dealing and the article on him in *Vissuto*."

"What did you tell him?"

"What I've already told everybody else."

"What?"

"That I've got absolutely no idea."

"Somebody's setting you up?"

"You've got a fast mind, Trotti."

Trotti brushed away the sarcasm. "Who'd want you out of the way?"

"This isn't the first time the police have tried to denigrate me. You're supposed to be honest—Bassi told me about Commissario Trotti. I find that fairly hard to believe. I know the Polizia di Stato well enough. I know its way of thinking."

"You needn't worry about me."

"I worry about everybody in your business."

"Most of the time I'm dealing with molested children. And, as you know," Trotti smiled at the director, "I'm going to retire within ten months."

"Then why come here?"

"Perhaps you and I can be of mutual assistance."

"What I need's a good lawyer, not a policeman. A lawyer who's willing to take on the Alessandria Questura—the entire police force."

"I don't believe you're guilty of dealing in cocaine, Signor Maluccio."

"Who does?"

Trotti continued, "Bassi came asking me for help and four days later he's found dead."

"Bassi told me you didn't like him."

"I don't like anybody."

"Then why bother about him? And why bother about me?"

"I don't like people being murdered."

"Go and live in Greenland. And change jobs."

"Before I retire to the OltrePò, I want to know who killed Fabrizio Bassi."

"Is it important?"

"Bassi worked for me in 1998."

"So what?" Gennaro Maluccio sounded aggrieved.

"Later he was thrown out of the police on bogus charges. Signor Maluccio, I didn't particularly like or dislike Fabrizio Bassi." Trotti raised a hand. "That doesn't stop me from feeling responsible."

"Responsible?"

Trotti finished his cup of coffee. It wasn't bad and he liked the tang on the edge of his tongue that the brown sugar and the grappa gave.

"Why do you expect me to help you, Trotti?"

Beyond the windows, large, white snowflakes swirled and danced towards the earth. Trotti could see the snow settling on the far walls of the floodlit courtyard.

"I should've stopped them throwing Bassi out of the Questura. Before he ever set up his FBI agency."

"Bassi didn't work for you anymore. You weren't responsible for him."

"The Questore was being manipulated by the mayor in our city. The mayor wanted Bassi out of the way and the Questore had Bassi kicked out of the Questura simply because he'd been having an affair with the mayor's wife."

"Bassi was old enough to know what he was doing."

"The Questore and the ex-mayor are both Socialists."

"Responsible, Trotti?"

"Policemen are like everybody else."

"You surprise me."

"We're not necessarily worse."

"Policemen like power. It's your drug—the power your job gives you over other people's lives."

"I didn't enter the PS because I wanted power."

"I'd like to believe you."

"I'm from the hills." Trotti gestured to where he imagined the Apennines to be. "An ignorant peasant. The police was a job that accepted any healthy young man. And it offered promotion." He added softly, "I never went to school beyond the terza media. Until I went to night school at the age of twenty-five."

"A check on the twenty-seventh of each month. A check and a good pension."

"A job for a poor and ignorant peasant like me."

"When peasants get a little power, they're worse than everybody else."

"Long before I went to Bari and the South, I knew what it was like to work an unforgiving land for subsistence."

Ugo Rubino momentarily raised his eyes. Small, cold, bloodshot, Mediterranean eyes.

"I've never voted for the Lega Lombarda," Trotti said. "Unlike the leghisti, I haven't forgotten what it's like to go hungry."

"A caring policeman?"

"I also know that when you're poor you don't have many choices. Perhaps if I had been able to choose, I wouldn't have ever joined the Polizia di Stato. Perhaps I'd share your hostility, Signor Maluccio. And perhaps I wouldn't be here."

56: Motta

GENNARO MALUCCIO NOW appeared more relaxed. Blood had returned to his face and the thin hands had ceased to play with the zip of his tracksuit. "I don't believe I can be connected with his death."

"I never said you were."

"Then what did you say, Trotti?"

"There was something you said."

"What about it?"

"Bassi left you and subsequently spoke with Signora Lucchi's lawyer. Over the phone Bassi claimed to the lawyer he knew who'd killed Turellini."

"And Bassi told the lawyer?"

"No." Trotti shook his head. "I believe something you said to him enabled Bassi to identify the killer. Or at least, enabled Bassi to believe he'd identified the killer."

"And that's why he got killed?"

Trotti gestured with both hands. "Strange he should get killed just as he'd solved a year-old murder."

"Perhaps the lawyer killed him."

"I don't think so." Trotti grinned. "I don't think Avvocato Regni would've killed Bassi."

"Why not?"

"No motive."

"Perhaps the lawyer was involved in Turellini's death."

Again Trotti gestured. "And just supposing Avvocato Regni did murder Bassi, he certainly wouldn't have then told me about the phone call."

"Which means I wasn't the last person to speak to Bassi?"

"You're one of the last people to have seen him alive." Trotti glanced briefly through the window, thinking of Fabrizio Bassi, now a corpse at San Matteo morgue. "I don't know who else Bassi saw. We think it was from his apartment Bassi phoned Avoccato Regni—but that's something we'll check with the SIP. Fabrizio Bassi left you and this prison just after six. He spoke to the lawyer a couple of hours later. He was murdered some time during the next four hours. I don't even know whether Bassi returned to his apartment in the city or whether he was taken directly to where they shot him."

Maluccio seemed to shiver. "Where was Bassi murdered?"

"Probably at Melegnano where the body was found. We'll only know for sure after the autopsy."

Pisanelli spoke. He had looked up from what he was reading and now said softly, "Bassi's apartment was broken into, Signor Maluccio. Somebody was looking for something—and most probably found it."

"Looking for what?"

"A letter, a note, a fax—we don't know."

Maluccio frowned.

"Something that could be hidden between the sheets of a newspaper. Or behind a photograph."

"He never mentioned anything to me."

"He appeared scared?"

"Not particularly."

Pisanelli continued. "We found an answering machine in Bassi's place and on it there was a new tape with just one message. An untimed message, unfortunately. A message Bassi never got to hear."

"What message?"

Pisanelli glanced at Trotti who nodded. "A woman's voice."

"Saying?"

"Saying she was expecting Bassi for twenty-three hours—eleven o'clock—at the agreed place."

"That's all?" Gennaro Maluccio sounded faintly amused.

"That's all." Pisanelli nodded.

"Whose voice?"

"No idea." Pisanelli leaned forward. "Various people were hoping to see Bassi. We believe they wanted to see Bassi because of you."

"A good-looking man like Bassi? I imagine there were women

who were interested in him. Why d'you think the woman wanting to see him had anything to do with me?"

"Because Bassi had visited you here."

Gennaro Maluccio shook his head. "I find that hard to swallow."

Trotti made a movement of irritation. "It's possible, probable even, there's some connection between Bassi's death and your being put in prison on a trumped-up charge. That's what Bassi thought. So try and help us, Signor Maluccio. Help us find that connection, help us find out why Bassi was killed."

Snowflakes now fell against the window, deforming the swirling beams of the prison searchlights.

"Helping us is your best way of getting out of here."

The journalist looked carefully at Trotti. "Why?"

"You want to get out of here?"

The journalist snorted. "I've been framed and you know that, Trotti. I've been framed by the Polizia di Stato and you really expect me to believe Commissario Trotti's willing to take on his colleagues? Take on his powerful colleagues just for my sake? For the sake of an insignificant journalist? You may be senile, Trotti, but you're no Don Quixote."

Pisanelli asked, "What exactly did you tell Bassi, Signor Maluccio?"

Both men were probably of the same age, but Pisanelli, now nearly forty and almost bald, looked badly overworked. He needed rest and there was unreasonable irritation in his voice as he repeated the question. "What did you tell him, Signor Maluccio?"

Maluccio did not answer.

"What did you talk to Bassi about?"

A moment's hesitation, as the journalist caught his breath. His glance flickered between Trotti and Pisanelli. "It was during the daily visiting hours—half an hour for each prisoner per day—and the visitor has to make a demand in writing at least two days in advance. I was glad to get out of the cell. No bigger than this room and it sleeps six grown men."

Pisanelli said, "What did Bassi talk to you about?"

"The cocaine."

"Bassi thought it was a setup?"

"Of course," the journalist retorted. "He believed there was a connection with my article on him."

Pisanelli asked, "What was the connection?"

"I told you—I don't know."

A sigh escaped from Trotti as he sat back in his chair. He had found a long-forgotten English toffee in his jacket pocket and was now playing with the wrapper.

Pisanelli continued. "How long did you and Bassi talk for?"

"Ten, fifteen minutes."

"What sort of questions did he ask you?"

"He wanted to know what had brought me to Alessandria in the first place. I told him I was doing an article on an apparition of the Virgin Mary to a couple of schoolgirls." An apologetic smile for Trotti. "Just the kind of thing that gets into *Vissuto*. Anything that'll sell the magazine to its ignorant and superstitious readership. The sort of thing to stop my daughters from going hungry."

"Simmental corned beef?"

Maluccio's smile disappeared as he turned back towards Pisanelli. "I got the impression Bassi was trying to reassure himself."

"In what way?"

"He wanted to know whether I'd been to Alessandria before. He wanted to know whether I knew anybody here in the Polizia di Stato. It was as if he believed my arrest was his fault and he was trying to find reasons to let himself off the hook."

"And it was about . . ." Gennaro Maluccio stopped, his mouth open.

"What?"

The journalist shook his head.

"You've remembered something, Signor Maluccio?"

"*Cherchez la femme.*"

"What?"

"Of course, Bassi couldn't speak French. Pig ignorant—like most policemen. *Cherchez la femme* was the section editor's idea."

"A fat man with a liking for beer?" Trotti asked.

"You've been to the Milan offices, I see." Maluccio smiled while his eyes remained on Pisanelli. "*Cherchez la femme*—a crime of passion. It's what Bassi thought when he was first called into the inquiry. But Bassi told me he'd finally given up believing the Turellini killing had anything to do with a jealous woman."

Pisanelli asked, "When you saw Bassi on Thursday, you had time to talk about the Turellini case?"

Another hesitant pause.

"Please answer my question."

"I'd done Bassi a favor. It was because of the Turellini affair he wanted to get into the magazine. He felt he was being hindered, somebody was stopping him from getting to the truth. He was determined to get Turellini's death back into the spotlight after a year of marking time. He said they'd put the case on hold at the Palazzo di Giustizia. Bassi wanted to embarrass people into action. That's why he went to see the celebrated Commissario Trotti." Maluccio made a gesture of mock admiration.

"For all the good it did him," Trotti remarked.

"Yes."

Trotti frowned. "Yes what?"

"Yes. To answer your question. There was something Bassi told me."

Pisanelli asked, "What?"

"When he'd first been called in on the inquiry, Bassi was told by the lawyer—"

"Avoccato Regni."

"He was told by Regni that the madwoman had probably killed Turellini out of jealousy."

"Madwoman? You mean Signora Quarenghi?"

"Signora Quarenghi." Maluccio nodded. "It's also what the Carabinieri at Segrate believed."

"Why?"

"Bassi told me she was unbalanced. The kind of woman who'd never come to terms with being childless. When she'd found out Turellini was trying to have a child with the English teacher, she killed out of blind jealousy." Maluccio's glance went from Pisanelli to Trotti. "This Quarenghi woman had turned up at Segrate soon after the murder. Turned up in her cream-colored Jaguar. Insisted upon talking to the Carabinieri. That's when she started making accusations about her husband."

"Her husband was in Rome at the time."

"Precisely."

Trotti and Pisanelli glanced briefly at each other. Trotti now sat forward, resting his arms on his thighs. He asked, "You mentioned Signora Quarenghi to Bassi?"

"Bassi talked about her to me."

"But there was something about her that you told Bassi?"

"Not really." Gennaro Maluccio bit his lip. His hand had returned to the zip, fiddling nervously with the metal runner.

"Not really. You told him something about Signora Quarenghi
or not?"

The convicted murderer had not moved. Ugo Rubino sat beside
the journalist, his face a mask, his lids almost closed and his hands
loosely clasped between his knees. Like a laborer waiting for work
in a dusty piazza of Puglia. Only the beret and the acrid cigarette
were missing.

"Not really?" Trotti repeated mockingly. "You mentioned
Signora Quarenghi, didn't you?"

"I don't know her. Never had any reason to meet her. It's not as
if she's had visions of the Virgin Mary or there were stigmata on
her hands and feet."

"You said something about her to Bassi, didn't you?"

Gennaro Maluccio bit his lip nervously.

"Well?"

"I'm a journalist," Maluccio said, "and I get to hear various
things. That's all."

"That's all what?"

The hand along the zip was moving faster upwards and downwards. Despite the cold, Gennaro Maluccio was now sweating in
his tracksuit. He turned slightly on his chair, revealing the sponsor's
logo—Motta, red letters on a white synthetic background.

"Well?"

Maluccio glanced sideways at the other prisoner; Ugo Rubino
simply continued to study the worn carpet.

"What had you heard, Signor Maluccio, about Signora Quarenghi?"

"I happened to mention . . ."

"Yes?"

"I told Bassi what I'd heard from a couple of sources."

"Please continue."

"Her husband . . ."

"Whose husband?"

"I told Bassi I'd heard Quarenghi was under inquiry. Several
weeks ago I heard the rumor. An inquiry coming from Milan, an
inquiry under the direction of Abete."

"Judge Abete?"

"Bassi seemed to think the Turellini dossier had been shelved by
Abete. That's why I told him . . ."

"Told him what?"

"Abete was working on something."

"Something to do with Quarenghi?"

"Something to do with Quarenghi's job in Rome—to do with pharmaceuticals."

Trotti had forgotten all about the cold in the prison director's office. Like the journalist, he was sweating in his waxed English jacket.

57: Hybrid

HE POPPED A sweet into his mouth. "What do you think, Pisanelli?"

"It's Saturday and I'm cold and I want to get home. That's what I think, commissario."

"Very interesting."

"I also wish the bastard in the Volvo behind us would keep out of my exhaust pipe. Must've been snowing heavily in the hills because he's got chains on his wheels."

"Let him pass."

Pisanelli laughed without conviction. "Gets any closer and we'll be producing a hybrid of a Volvo and a Citroën."

"Tell me what you think."

"About what?"

"A connection between Bassi's visit to the journalist and his ending up dead a few hours later?"

Pisanelli shrugged.

"And the doctor?" Trotti asked, irked by Pisanelli's silence. "You think Dr. Quarenghi's got anything to do with Bassi's being killed?"

"How d'you expect me to know?"

"You have an opinion."

"Too tired to have an opinion."

"What makes you so tired, Pisanelli? You're half my age."

Pisanelli said nothing.

"You ever heard anything about an inquiry into Quarenghi's job at the Ministry?"

"Rome," Pisanelli said mournfully. "A different planet."

"What's wrong with you?"

"I'm tired, commissario."

"You were good, Pisa. You were good with that journalist—you asked the right questions without alienating him. I'm grateful. When you put your mind to it, you're one of the best investigators I've ever worked with."

"Pleased to hear it."

"Now tell me why you're sulking."

"It's Saturday night, commissario, and I want to get home." Pisanelli drove carefully, a lot slower than on the trip down to Alessandria, sitting forward in his seat, peering into the feeble yellow beams that the French car cast on to the treacherous road ahead.

They had left the autostrada and were heading towards Zinasco. It was still snowing and towards the middle of the road, between the lanes, were the beginnings of white drifts. It was cold inside the car but Trotti felt strangely pleased. Perhaps it was because he had always liked snow—anything was better than fog. Or perhaps it was because he believed—he did not quite know why—that soon he would know who had murdered Fabrizio Bassi. Then he could leave for Bologna. For Pioppi and the little Francesca.

Francesca. For Christmas he'd buy his granddaughter a teddy like Pioppi's old teddy bear at home in via Milano, but with two good eyes.

"You don't feel we're getting somewhere?"

"Goodness knows why you care so much about Bassi," Pisanelli retorted, without taking his eyes off the road.

"An old man's pride," Trotti responded.

A sound of irritation. "Even if he was kicked out of the force because he was screwing around, that was his own fault. Bassi was a married man. He had no reason to get involved with another woman."

"You sound like a priest."

"Nothing justifies adultery."

"I can see you've never been married."

"Thanks to you, I'm not likely to be."

Trotti pretended not to have heard. "Bassi was single. His wife had left him a long time ago. Left him and taken the children."

"Viscontini's wife was committing adultery."

"Perhaps the mayor's wife was unhappy," Trotti remarked.

"Signora Viscontini could have gotten a divorce." Pisanelli briefly took his eyes from the road to appraise Trotti in the light of an oncoming car.

"There was never any talk of her wanting to leave her husband."

"You ever cheated on your wife?" Pisanelli asked with a sudden earnestness.

"I think tomorrow we'll have to talk to her, Pisa."

"You'll have to talk to her."

"She's the key to something."

"Key to what?"

"No idea but I'm sure you'll want to accompany me."

"Tomorrow morning's Sunday and I'm going to stay in bed." Trotti made a dismissive gesture. "You know her?"

"I recognized the photo of Signora Viscontini at Bassi's place, if that's what you mean."

"You met her?"

"Not personally. Not my type. I don't go for blondes."

"What do you go for?"

"Thanks to you, commissario, I don't get either the time or the opportunity." Pisanelli shook his head and his long hair danced along the collar of the suede jacket. "Even when her husband was mayor—before the Lega Lombarda ever took over the town hall— Signora Viscontini stayed out of the limelight."

"You knew she was Quarenghi's sister-in-law?"

"So what?"

"It doesn't occur to you that there's a coincidence there?"

"What coincidence?"

"Bassi had been having an affair with Signora Viscontini."

Pisanelli again raised his shoulders.

"At the same time, the mad Quarenghi woman—Signora Viscontini's own sister-in-law, her husband's sister—was possibly the very murderer Bassi was called in to track down?"

"That's a coincidence?"

"Of course."

"With such a marvelous coincidence, why did it take Bassi more than a year to identify the murderer?"

"Assuming Bassi did identify the murderer. Which doesn't necessarily mean Signora Quarenghi killed Turellini." The heavy zip of his jacket was cold against Trotti's chin. "But the coincidence seems more than odd."

"I don't see any coincidence. Anyway, Signora Quarenghi didn't fire a gun the day Turellini was murdered."

"Pisa, there may be a different coincidence. It's precisely because Bassi took more than a year to get to the truth that he was allowed to live."

"You're suggesting Avvocato Regni hired him so that he wouldn't find the murderer?"

"I don't know what I'm suggesting."

"You don't hire somebody to find a murderer and then expect him to do nothing."

Trotti clicked the sweet noisily against his teeth. "It was precisely when Bassi finally did do something that he got himself killed."

"You think Avvocato Regni killed Bassi?"

"Just another coincidence," Trotti said. "Fabrizio Bassi gets killed when he's found out who killed Turellini."

"It wasn't the first time Bassi thought he'd identified the murderer."

Trotti laughed. "Perhaps at last Bassi'd got it right."

"He didn't tell Regni who the murderer was."

"We've only got Regni's word for that."

In the distance it was possible to distinguish the overhead lights of Zinasco. They had been repaired since the afternoon's accident and were now working, beaming their alternating reds and greens through the falling snow.

"Saturday night, commissario," Pisanelli said wearily. "Why d'you bother?"

"What you need, Pisa, is a good rest. You look terrible."

"Then perhaps you should stop bullying me into helping you."

"You enjoy it."

"An old man's pride, Commissario Trotti? It's your old man's pride that makes you so obsessive about Bassi?"

"I've always been obsessive. Or so people tell me."

"You didn't always give a shit about Bassi."

"He came to see me."

"A lot of people have been to see you over the years. That's never sent you scurrying across the Po valley in the middle of a snowstorm."

"Bassi came to see me because he trusted me."

"I really don't see what's so special about Bassi."

"Bassi was once a cop."

"The Pavesi couple came to see you about their parents who've disappeared. You told them to get lost."

"Not the same thing."

"You'd been a friend of their father's. More of a friend than you'd ever been of Bassi's."

"The father's a shit. A loser, a sycophant and a shit."

"You refused to help his daughter."

"Nice girl with big tits, Pisa? Is that what you mean?"

"Why not help the girl look for her parents? The Pavesis are rich."

"Bassi used to work for me."

Pisanelli laughed cynically. "Fabrizio Bassi was a fool and you know it, commissario. An idiot who watched more American rubbish on television than was good for him."

"Bassi was a cop—not a loser with political pretensions."

"Let's just suppose Bassi was thrown out of the PS simply because of the Questore's intervention." The aggressive tone had disappeared from Pisanelli's voice. "You know as well as I do Fabrizio Bassi wasn't exactly the ideal functionary of the state. Never had the reputation of being particularly honest. Or diligent. Not of course that that makes him any different from the rest of us." A snort of cold amusement. "But in addition, Bassi was a womanizer and a fool. Divorce work was about all he was capable of doing without shooting off his big toe. Or his oversized prick."

"He'd worked for me."

"And when he came to see you he offered you money for your help."

"So what?"

Pisanelli went on. "You didn't like him, commissario. Like most other people in the Questura, you despised the man. Bassi's womanizing and his big prick were just part of the problem. Just part of the problem." Pisanelli hesitated before adding, "Wasn't there talk of his having an affair with Brigadiere Ciuffi—with your good friend Ornella Ciuffi?"

"Absurd idea."

"You say you don't have friends but there are a few people you like."

"And there are many, many people I don't like."

"It was always quite apparent you couldn't stand Bassi. At the time I thought it was because of Ornella Ciuffi."

"If all the people I disliked got murdered, the Questura'd be a pretty empty place."

"Italy'd be a pretty empty place."

"For your information, Brigadiere Ciuffi was killed long before Bassi left the Questura."

Pisanelli again glanced hurriedly at Trotti. "As I understand it, Bassi told you there was good money to be earned with the Turellini enquiry."

"He wanted me to collaborate with him on a permanent basis. I replied I'd be happy enough with my state pension."

"What you replied to Bassi was before you ever found out about your cousin's death."

Trotti laughed.

"Signora Lucchi has a lot of money, commissario."

"So what?"

"Money that could be useful."

"I don't need her money."

"Money that'd let you buy back the place in Santa Maria."

"What are you trying to get at?" Trotti laughed awkwardly. "I told you Avvocato Regni offered me money. He even pulled out a fat checkbook."

"Hope you accepted, commissario."

Trotti said nothing. He could feel blood rising to his face and he was glad the darkness hid him from Pisanelli's eyes. "You're joking, Pisa."

"You accepted?"

"What do you think?"

"Gave up thinking a long time ago."

"But you didn't give up asking foolish questions." Trotti could not suppress the tremble in his voice which seemed high-pitched and out of character. "I'd like to remind you it was you, Pisanelli, who pulled me out of my warm bed at four o'clock on Friday morning because Bassi'd got himself killed."

"Sure."

"Now you're surprised I continue with the inquiry?" His voice was getting more shrill. "Or perhaps you don't understand me."

"I understand you, commissario."

"For the last few years, I've been shunted off to dealing with molested children. Persona non grata, Pisa. But molested children are not what I trained for. That's not what I've got experience in.

That's not what I am good at—despite what the Questore may say.
Despite what that shit Merenda'd like to think. I'm a detective,
Tenente Pisanelli. I've done some useful work in my time. Now that
I'm about to leave the Questura for good, I . . ."

"You know if you really needed money for your place in the
OltrePò there are always ways of getting it." Pisanelli glanced at
Trotti but his companion had fallen silent and was now biting his
lip as he stared at the approaching traffic lights.

"Ever thought of marrying some rich widow, commissario?"

58: Angel of Death

"I still think it's the Englishwoman," Pisanelli said respectfully.

Trotti did not answer.

"Signora Coddrington, commissario. It's her voice on the tape. I recognized it."

Piero Trotti continued to look out of the window as Zinasco fell behind, engulfed in the night. The wipers battled noisily with the large flakes of snow that now struck the windshield.

"I told you that after meeting her in her school."

Trotti clicked the sweet against his teeth.

"I told you it was her voice as soon as we left her English school in Milan."

Trotti made more clicking noises before speaking. His voice had recovered its normal pitch but there was no affability. "Why should Signora Coddrington phone Bassi?"

"No idea."

A signpost, caught briefly in the yellow beams, announced a distance of three kilometers to Carbonara.

"You're right, commissario. I do need a rest."

Another silence before Trotti unexpectedly tapped Pisanelli's arm. "That looked like a book of anatomy you were reading in the prison director's office."

A smile fluttered across Pisanelli's weary features. "Two possibilities, commissario. Either Bassi's death was connected with Turellini's or it wasn't." He held up his thumb. "Let's assume it was. Now what do we know about Turellini?"

"That he was murdered. Just over a year ago in the suburbs of Milan."

"According to Bassi, there were two possible lines of enquiry. Either Turellini was murdered for business reasons and his business was essentially among doctors. Or it was a crime of passion. As always, either sex or money."

"*Cherchez la femme.*"

Suddenly and surprisingly, Pisanelli laughed very loudly.

"I don't see what's funny."

"The Questore's hoping to set up his regional child abuse center. He wants it to be a European thing, in direct contact with Interpol in Lyons." Pisanelli had difficulty in speaking between his laughter. "I suppose he'll be wanting you to do the liaison work with the French."

"You see, I can speak French."

"So I notice."

"*Tartufòn, c'est si bon.*"

Against his will, Trotti too started to laugh. He was still laughing after they had been over the railway line and there was a sudden jolt of the Citroën.

"Careful!"

His head was pulled backwards, then forwards.

"What's that, Pisa, for God's sake?"

"He's turned off his lights!"

A sudden, horrid sense of fear.

"The dangerous bastard."

Fear of a kind that Trotti had almost forgotten about. The fear of his imminent demise and the adrenaline coursing, unannounced and uncalled for, through his whole system as again the car was rammed from the rear and Pisanelli seemed to lose control of the steering.

"The Volvo!"

"What's he doing?"

"Trying to kill us, heaven help us!"

"Pisa, pull on to the shoulder."

Pisanelli did not reply but, anyway, there was no shoulder. Trotti knew the road well and, although he could scarcely see through the snow, he knew that there was no stabilized edge, just a few centimeters of snow and then darkness.

A dip, a ditch.

They were less than eight kilometers from the Po but here the road ran along a dike, built to hold back the flooding. Flooding that came three or four times in a century.

A third, violent shove and he saw the Volvo now edging level. No traffic in the opposite direction. Looking past Pisanelli, gripping the overhead strap, Trotti thought he could make out a faceless silhouette.

"Stop, Pisanelli. The bastard's going to send us over the edge."

Trotti remembered that beyond the road and below it there were ranks of plane trees. Trees for the cellulose factories that had been closed down years ago.

Five, ten meters beneath the Citroën, to both left and right.

Perhaps Trotti or perhaps somebody else was shouting. Shouting in uncontrolled, uncontrollable fear.

A few months short of retirement and a good life behind him, wife, daughter and now grandchildren, and he was afraid of dying.

Afraid of dying when Sandro was already dead.

As terrified as the young boy hearing the bombers over Santa Maria on their way to Milan.

Angels of death.

"Where's your damn Beretta, Pisa?"

A fourth, a fifth violent ramming and this time Pisanelli lost all traction on the icy surface. The rear of the car skidded to the right as the back wheel hit the edge and Trotti felt himself being thrown sideways, being thrown upwards and he was thinking about the little boy in Pioppi's belly, the boy who would never know his grandfather, who would never know just how much Piero Trotti had loved him.

59: LAB COAT

"COMMISSARIO?"

He was wearing an anorak and he had shaved; he looked plumper than when Trotti had last seen him in Milan.

"Commissario?"

If Magagna had not been wearing his American sunglasses, Trotti would have had difficulty in recognizing him.

"Well?"

He had been sitting on a steel chair. He now stood up and emptied the contents of his pockets on to the bed. "I bought you these." Half a dozen packets of boiled sweets.

"A rich man."

"One of the advantages of working for the Polizia di Stato—easy money and good prospects."

Trotti smiled, then he winced in pain as they shook hands.

"Unwrap one of those sweets for me."

"What flavor?"

"After all these years you've forgotten rhubarb's my favorite?"

Magagna took one of the packets, removed the wrapping and placed the sweet in Trotti's mouth. "Looks as if you've been in a fight."

"I walked into a door."

"Coming back from Piemonte?"

"You can't be too careful."

"This is why you shouldn't go to Alessandria." Magagna was from Pescara and considered anywhere else as insignificant. The smile vanished. "Who did it, commissario?"

Trotti's shoulder ached and, as he moved his head, there was a sharp pain in the back of his neck. "Trying to remember."

"They clearly didn't like you."

Trotti clicked the sweet against his teeth and it was then he realized there was a chip in the enamel of what used to be one of his good front teeth. "How did you know I was here?"

"The Polizia Stradale see a Volvo with no lights pulling out into the middle of the road? The sort of thing that goes unremarked?"

"They got the number?"

"It was the snow that saved you. Instead of falling, the Citroën slid down the embankment. Backwards. And hit a tree. If it'd turned over, you'd be dead." Magagna added, amused, "There were medical books scattered all over the snow."

Trotti frowned, not understanding. "What's the time now?"

"I was driving back from Monza. After all these years, I felt you were worth the detour."

"What's the time?"

"Unconscious for over forty minutes. And then under light sedation." The other man looked at his watch. "Half-past midnight."

"Christ—and Pisanelli?"

The white door opened and a nurse entered. A middle-aged woman with grey hair and a harsh, narrow face. She wore a silver crucifix in the lapel of her spotless laboratory coat.

"You're not supposed to have visitors." She placed her hand on the back of Magagna's chair. "With blood coming from my mouth and what looks like diabetes, I'd make sure I was getting some rest instead of getting excited." She spoke in a flat monotone.

"Polizia di Stato," Magagna said lamely and fumbled with his card.

The lips pulled tight, as if activated by a pursestring. She turned on her heel and left the room in offended silence.

"And Pisanelli?"

60: Pendolino

Sunday, 6 December

HE POURED HONEY into the herbal tea and sipped slowly while his eyes scanned the parish magazine that Anna Maria had left on the table. The clock, carefully dusted and now set on top of the mantelpiece, ticked noisily. The bedroom door was open. He could hear the sound of Anna Maria's breathing and he envied her restful sleep.

From time to time a car went past in via Milano, the sound dulled by the snow; no car stopped.

The phone woke him. He must have dozed off, his head lolling forward. He sat up with a jerk and winced with the pain in his shoulder. Trotti looked at the clock. Four o'clock, Sunday, December the sixth.

The chamomile was cold.

"Zio?"

"Yes."

"Is that you, Zio Piero?"

Trotti ran a hand through his hair. "Who's speaking?"

"How are you, Zio? Are you all right?"

His goddaughter. "Anna?"

"You're all right, aren't you?"

"I was sleeping."

"Is Pierangelo with you?"

"Pierangelo?"

"I didn't want to phone you so late, Zio, but a friend just called me from Stradella saying she'd heard about an accident on the radio. It's not true, is it?"

"I was in an accident," Trotti said rubbing his shoulder.

"My friend thought she heard Pierangelo's name. How is he?" she asked and Trotti could hear Anna Ermagni catch her breath on the far end of the line.

"You phoning from Rome, Anna?"

"Zio, please answer me. How's Pierangelo? You must tell me the truth."

"Pisanelli was with me. We were in his car and were hit from behind. At about eight o'clock. The car went off the road and slid down the embankment. There was a lot of snow."

"Where's Pi?"

"At San Matteo."

"He's not dead?"

Trotti gave a little laugh. "Of course not, Anna."

She began to sob. "Oh, it's all my fault."

"Don't be silly. How on earth can it be your fault?"

"Pi's going to be all right?"

"Pisanelli? Of course he's going to be all right."

"You were beside him? Were you sitting beside him, Zio? Are you all right? You're not hurt, are you?"

"It'll take more than a Volvo to kill Piero Trotti."

"Tell me about Pierangelo?"

"I dislocated my shoulder—nothing very serious. But I was wearing my safety belt as the car went over."

"Went over?"

"The car went over the edge of the road and down into the trees."

"That stupid French car—it hasn't even got a proper roof. I was always telling him to get a proper car. But he's just like you, Zio. Pi's so stubborn."

"The Citroën stayed on its wheels."

"What's wrong with him? You've seen him? You must tell me, Zio."

"Pisanelli's still in intensive care, Anna. He banged his head badly and when I left—"

"Yes."

"I left San Matteo after midnight and he still hadn't regained consciousness."

"Oh, my God!"

"But there's nothing to worry about."

"I'll phone the hospital. Give me the number. Never get an

answer out of Enquiries. Give me the number, Zio. I'll phone San Matteo now."

"Wait until the morning."

"How d'you expect me to wait until morning? It's already morning. Please, Zio, for God's sake. Just give me the number."

"I saw the doctor. I was with Magagna—you remember him? Magagna and I saw the specialist. There's no danger. The doctor says the X-rays are all right."

"Pierangelo's unconscious, Zio! How can he be all right?" Her voice was lost in a wave of uncontrollable sobbing. "Oh, God."

"Pisa's going to pull through, don't worry. There are no broken bones. No blood or wounds—he just must've whiplashed his head as the car fell. But you know Pisa—"

"I'll catch the Pendolino now. I haven't got any money but I've just got to come up. I can't stay here." More sobs. "It's all my fault. I should never have left him. I should never have come to Rome in the first place."

"If you want, I can put you up here, Anna. Don't worry about the ticket, I can pay for that. I'll pick you up at the station. Just ring—my cousin's here from Holland. She'll take the call if I'm not here and someone'll pick you up. But you really mustn't say it's your fault."

"I should've stayed with him."

"You're in Rome, Anna. You're studying."

"Pierangelo's more important than my studies, Zio. Don't you understand? Pierangelo is everything—Pierangelo's my life."

"You still love him, Anna?"

"That's a stupid question. The most stupid question I've ever heard. How can you be so ridiculous? Of course I love him," Anna Ermagni said. "I've always loved him. Ever since that first time— when I was a little girl. That first time when you and Magagna found me at the bus station. Pi was my knight in white armor—always has been. That's why I wanted him to get out of the police. I was always telling Pi I wanted him to go back to his medical studies. A real job. To get a job that wouldn't destroy him. That wouldn't destroy us."

Trotti could hear her crying. He bit his lip.

"With a father and a godfather in the police, Piero Trotti, I know just how that job can destroy a family. That's something I couldn't accept for Pi and me. I told him to change jobs."

61: Sacristan

THE SOUND OF women's voices.

He was coming out of a dream and the voices were talking to him, but when Trotti opened his eyes he was alone. He could no longer recall the dream but he recognized the voices.

He also noticed the ice hanging from the upper edges of the window. The shutters were not completely closed; beyond them, above the plain of Lombardy, the sky was a blue vault.

Trotti climbed out of bed. His body ached. Carefully he put on a dressing gown and went into the kitchen.

He had to lean against the back of a chair. "Buongiorno."

They turned and smiled hesitantly, like two girls caught by the sacristan while gossiping in church.

"I thought I smelled coffee."

"You've got a nice bruise, Piero," Anna Maria remarked, regaining her habitual severity.

"A nice bruise that hurts."

"Which only serves you right for gallivanting across the north of Italy on a Saturday night when most civilized men are at home with their families."

"Nobody's ever accused me of being civilized. And my family is in Amer—my family's in Bologna."

Simona Scola had been drinking coffee. She stood up from the table—there was a notebook and a rag doll on the Formica top—and came towards him, both amusement and concern on her face.

"How are you, Signora Scola?"

She came closer and Trotti held out his arm, thinking she wished to shake hands. She ignored the gesture and brushed her fingers against his forehead. "You hit your head, Piero?"

Trotti shrugged. He could smell her perfume, he could see his reflection in the bright, dark eyes. Intelligent eyes. "I lost consciousness. It's my shoulder that hurts." He stepped sideways away from the touch of her hand and sat down at the table. "Any news from the hospital?"

His cousin gave him a perfunctory kiss—a Dutch habit, no doubt. "Your man Magagna rang half an hour ago. Said he'd be picking up a young woman at Centrale. He said he'd drive her down. He also asked if you could ring him back in Milan."

"And Tenente Pisanelli?"

"No developments," Anna Maria said in a firm voice, implying that Pisanelli's problems were all Trotti's fault. She rose from the table. She seemed to have now given up wearing slacks, opting instead for the shapeless, somber clothes of an old woman from the hills. "Would you care for some coffee?"

Trotti nodded, noticing at the same time a conspiratorial glance passing between the two women.

"I was expecting the worst." There was a forced joviality in Simona Scola's tone. "I heard about the accident on the radio this morning but I didn't realize it was you until your cousin told me."

"All his own fault. But then even as a little boy Piero Trotti was stubborn."

"Really, Piero, apart from that nasty bruise, you look fine. In fact, for once you don't even look tired."

"Thanks to the dislocated shoulder. And the three stitches in my arm."

"I was going to the hospital. I dropped by thinking you might want a lift."

"A lift?"

"I'm seeing the little Priscilla this afternoon." She added, "For the last time. I realize you may have other things to do. Anna Maria told me you'd be spending the day in bed."

"Not much chance of that."

"Priscilla's mother's insisting on going home to the Val Camonica. Fed up with the cramped room in Pediatria. She says there's nothing wrong with her daughter and she wants to get back to Esine." Today Signora Scola was wearing a red woolen dress that showed off her flat belly and the narrowness of her hips. She folded her arms beneath the swell of her small breasts. She gestured with the outstretched fingers of her right hand. "Your Commissario Maiocchi said he'd help me this afternoon."

"Maiocchi?" Trotti placed three lumps of sugar into the bowl of coffee.

"A nice man," she said warmly.

"Don't see how he can help you," Trotti said, wondering whether it was jealousy altering the naturalness of his voice. "There are times when I wonder if Maiocchi can help himself."

"He's been very kind. On a couple of occasions I've come looking for you in the Questura and he's managed to locate you. Not always so easy." She nodded towards the clock. "I'm seeing Commissario Maiocchi at two. You want to see your Tenente Pisanelli but I was hoping perhaps you could come down to Pediatria and have a look in."

"You need both Maiocchi and me?"

Signora Scola tapped the inert body of the rag doll on the table as she let out a sigh. "One last attempt before Priscilla returns to Esine and the maniac the mother's trying to protect."

62: Pediatria

THE LITTLE GIRL, her upper lip wet with running mucus, opened the door and hurried to the middle of the room where she flopped down onto the floor.

She gazed thoughtfully at the box of toys.

Signora Scola, cross-legged with the rag doll on her lap, raised her head. "Ciao, tesoro."

Priscilla's hair had been brushed back into two short bunches, held in place with Mickey Mouse clips.

"You want to play with me today, tesoro?" Signora Scola held up the doll. "I'm playing with a little Priscilla."

Less reticent than in the past, Priscilla edged forward on her small behind and began to rummage distractedly through the box's contents of animals, balls, skipping ropes, puppets. Her attention, however, was held by the rag doll in Simona Scola's lap.

After a while, she asked, "That's Priscilla?"

"You want her?" Signora Scola was caressing the woolen hair. The rag doll had the same color hair as Priscilla, brushed back the same way into bunches. Like Priscilla, the rag doll wore denim overalls and a thick sweater.

"It's hard," Priscilla said and shook her head.

(Trotti, sitting behind the observation mirror, while beside him the tape recorder slowly uncoiled from one bobbin to the other, was surprised by the maturity of the child's voice.)

"Done a pipi again?"

"Who?"

Priscilla slid towards the woman and took the doll from her lap. "She's naughty, isn't she?"

"Sometimes my Priscilla's naughty."

"She's yours?"

"You can have her, tesoro."

"She's a very silly Priscilla," the child said, and taking the doll from Signora Scola's hands, began to sing softly. A strange nursery rhyme in an incomprehensible dialect.

Signora Scola looked with lingering regret at the doll.

(Like a mother on her child's first day at school, Trotti thought. He smiled privately as he adjusted the headphones against his ears.)

Signora Scola sorted through the banana box. In consolation she pulled out a moth-eaten Topo Gigio.

"It's hard, isn't it?" Signora Scola agreed, and by the movement of her shoulders Trotti could see she was addressing the mother.

The woman was sitting on a straight-backed chair. She nodded without removing a cigarette from her mouth.

"D'you remember when your little girl was hurt?"

"Yes."

"You got back to the house, didn't you, Mamma?"

"I remember?"

"You went upstairs and your little girl was crying?"

The cigarette moved with her lips. "Yes."

"Was the little Priscilla crying because she was unhappy?"

"She was crying a lot."

"Was your little Priscilla hurt?"

"I think so. There was a lot of blood."

"Where was your little girl hurt?" Signora Scola was rubbing noses with Topo Gigio. The cloth animal in front of her mouth deformed her voice.

"In her bottom."

"There was blood, Mamma?"

"A lot of blood."

"Where?"

"In Priscilla's bottom. There was some blood in her crack, too."

"The poor sweetie. You must've been terribly worried for her."

"Of course," the mother said, finally bringing emotion to her voice. "Priscilla's my precious angel."

"With all that blood in her bottom, what on earth did you think? Who on earth could've done that to your little tesoro?"

The mother inhaled deeply before shaking her head.

Priscilla had found a comb in the banana box. The comb was made of blue plastic and several teeth were missing. It was grubby. With the last three teeth, Priscilla had started to comb the rag doll's hair.

"You rang for the ambulance, Mamma?"

"Immediately."

For a moment Priscilla stopped to look at her mother.

"I was out of my wits."

"You think someone very naughty tried to hurt your girl?"

Again a deep inhalation of a cigarette. "Perhaps."

"If someone hurt your little Priscilla, would you be angry?"

"I'd be very angry."

"Would you be cross with your Priscilla?"

"Of course not. How could I be angry with my daughter?"

"D'you think we must try to find this naughty person?"

Suddenly, Priscilla ceased all movement, her hand and the blue comb held above the yellow halo of the doll's hair.

Neither Signora Scola nor the mother spoke as the little girl dropped her hands to the carpet and pushed her backside into the air. Priscilla got on to her feet. In a determined pace, going almost faster than her legs would carry her, she hurried to the small sink.

There was a large crucifix.

She stood on tiptoe to look at herself in the mirror.

Then the little girl hurried over to where Signora Scola was sitting. She went behind Signora Scola, while above Trotti's head the same movement was projected on to the small television screen.

With a clenched fist the child pushed against the woman's back. Trotti could see that the child was smiling.

Signora Scola asked, "What do you think, Mamma?"

Priscilla's mother had stubbed out the cigarette. "I love my daughter."

"I think we should catch this bad person who does naughty things to Priscilla's bottom?"

The mother was silent.

"Perhaps a policeman could catch him?"

"Perhaps."

"Perhaps a very strong and very brave and very kind policeman could help us, Mamma?"

"Perhaps."

"Shall I call a policeman?"

"You think he could help?"

"There's a very nice policeman I know. A policeman who likes children."

"Call him if you think it can help."

"You won't go away?" Without waiting for an answer, Signora Scola picked up a toy telephone. Putting the yellow receiver to her ear, she spoke. "Pronto, pronto. 113? Is that the Carabinieri. Ah, better still, it's the police. Pronto." She gave a little laugh, "Yes, it's Simona speaking. Could you please help us?" She nodded, speaking into the mouthpiece. "I'm with Priscilla's mamma and we think there's a naughty man who does some very silly things to little girls' bottoms and we really do need a strong policeman because this man is so naughty and we're afraid he might get angry. What we want's a very kind and a very good and a very, very big"—she was nodding as she reiterated the words—"a very big policeman. Do you think you can help us?"

A scratching sound and the little girl looked up. She had returned to her place beside the banana box and resumed her job of combing the doll's hair.

"Very big and brave? Oh, that's lovely. But there's another thing . . . Does he like little girls?"

More scratching.

"He likes girls and he has three daughters at home that he takes to the lake and they paddle in the water? Oh, that's excellent. He has a little girl who plays with dolls? Marvelous, marvelous. Well, could you please send us this nice and brave policeman? We need him here because there's a very bad man who does naughty things to good little girls and we must stop him as soon as possible."

Scratch.

"Precisely. We must stop him before he ever does it again. We must put him in prison because he càn make a little girl bleed. It's not fair. I know this lovely girl who's her mummy's angel but she's very unhappy. This bad man hurts girls' bottoms and their cracks and that's not what bottoms are for. Of course," Signora Scola nodded, "bottoms are for cacca, cracks are for pipi." A brief giggle. "This is a very silly man because he does other things and he's naughty because he can hurt Mamma's tesoro."

Priscilla seemed to have temporarily lost interest in the telephone conversation just as she had lost interest in the rag doll, her alter ego. She was staring vaguely at the far wall. From time to time she rubbed the legs of her denim trousers.

Signora Scola hung up, placing the bulbous receiver back in its cradle.

Priscilla came out of her reverie. She started to undress another doll, a pink plastic princess, in order to use the stiff tutu and the satinette body sock.

"You can play with me if you want," she said magnanimously.

Signora Scola played.

Priscilla played and after a while her forehead touched Simona Scola's.

The mother smoked.

There was a loud knock on the door.

Signora Scola lightly got to her feet, glanced for an instant at the long mirror and went to the door.

"My goodness!" She opened the door very slightly before letting the man into the room. "You're a very big policeman, aren't you? I can see you're strong. And I can see you're very brave."

Heaven knows where Maiocchi had found the uniform.

He stood, framed in the door, his long hair tucked beneath the flat cap of an agente and hanging from the white webbing at his waist was a service pistol in its holster.

"Do you like children, Signor Agente?"

63: Dinosaur

TROTTI RECOGNIZED FULVIO Bruni from *Sociologia*. He was wearing a turtleneck sweater and he entered the observation room with his eternal cigarette held between gnarled fingers. He was accompanied by the Questore.

"Ciao!"

Trotti nodded perfunctorily, his attention on what was happening on the far side of the mirror.

"Are you the strongest policeman in the world?"

"No, of course not. I'm just very strong."

"Very strong?"

"Very, very strong." Maiocchi's face broke into a smile. "Hello young lady." Bending down, he touched her forehead. "What's your name?"

Priscilla looked at him in awed silence.

The mother spoke from where she was sitting, "Tell the nice policeman your name, stella."

"Priscilla," the girl blurted. It was only now that Trotti noticed she had difficulty in pronouncing the R.

"Priscilla? Isn't that a nice name?"

For a moment Priscilla returned Maiocchi's glance. Then she hurried to the protection of her mother's side.

Simona Scola said, "I rang for a strong policeman. Have you come to help us?"

"I was told there was a little girl who needed some help."

"Do you like children?"

"I like children. I have three lovely daughters at home." He gave a warm laugh.

"You're strong, Signor Agente?"

"Of course," Maiocchi replied, slightly taken aback, slightly offended.

"I bet you can't lift that." Signora Scola gestured to the box of toys.

In peevish silence, Commissario Maiocchi picked up the box of toys and balanced it on the flat of his hand.

Priscilla stared at him, her mouth agape, the lines of mucus going from her nose to her mouth.

"You're very strong."

"I eat broccoli and spinach."

"I'll make a mental note of that," Simona Scola said. "Are you afraid of bad men?"

He tapped the handcuffs hanging from his belt. "I'm afraid of nobody, signora. I'm a policeman."

"Do you like bad men?"

"It's my job to put them in prison." Maiocchi now folded his arms complacently against a broad chest.

"What do you do when you catch a bad man? I bet you don't get angry."

"I get very angry. I'm famous for getting angry."

"Why do you get angry?"

"Grown-ups must look after little children. Little children are a very special gift from God."

"Do you shout at bad men, Signor Agente?"

Maiocchi nodded and winked simultaneously.

"You shout very loud?"

Again he nodded. "It's the only language these people understand."

"Shout something, Signor Agente. Shout, 'Go away, nasty man.'"

Maiocchi shouted and Trotti did not get sufficient time to remove the earphones from where they were sticking against his ears. Captured by the hidden microphone, Maiocchi's voice was loud and peculiarly unpleasant.

"Shout louder!"

Maiocchi did as he was told.

There followed a strange silence—silence except for the continued ringing in Trotti's ears.

"You like girls?"

"Of course I do. I have three lovely girls at home."

"Would you like to help a lovely little girl I know?"

"No problem."

"You see, she's a super little girl but," Signora Scola's voice took on a husky tone, "we think a nasty man's been hurting her bottom."

Maiocchi flared his nostrils.

"Perhaps, Signor Agente, you could help the poor little mite. This naughty man does silly things to her."

"Some grown-ups are very naughty. That's why I have to put them in prison."

"What'll you do if you catch this naughty man?"

Maiocchi took a notebook from his pocket. "I'll shout at him, Signora. Standard procedure, you understand."

"That's all?"

"I'll shout at him and then I'll put him in prison." A pause. "Then the Pubblico Ministero will throw the key away. Standard procedure, signora."

"You're not afraid of him?"

A deprecating laugh. "Signora, just give me his address and I'll pick him up now. His days of doing silly things to little girls are over. He's going to spend the next one hundred and six years in prison."

"You're going to catch him?"

"Trouble with you, signora, is that you have too little faith in the Polizia di Stato." Maiocchi played menacingly with the handcuffs.

Signora Scola replied, "I once knew a very nice policeman. He pretended to be gruff and horrible but I knew he loved children. And he loved chickens and goats. He loved animals and women and children. Do you know him? He even looked for truffles in the hills."

"An old, balding dinosaur, signora. Diabetic from eating too many boiled sweets. What we need here is a dynamic policeman of the new generation." Maiocchi made a gesture of irritation. "Give me the name, signora."

"You need the name of the bad man who does naughty things to little girls?"

"Of course I need the name. Can't go around arresting every Pinco Pallino."

Priscilla had started to shake her head, burrowing into her mother's shallow chest.

"I need to know the name," Maiocchi said softly.

"No, no, no." Priscilla was now hiding her face, nuzzling into her mother.

"Signor Agente, the little girl doesn't know."

"Oh dear. Does anyone else know? I really must put that bad man in prison before he does more nasty things. But I can't do anything without a name."

"Nobody else knows." Signora Scola raised her hands. Trotti could hear the calm desperation in her voice. "You know, Signor Agente, there are some very bad men who do bad things to little girls' bottoms. And then they tell the little girls they must say nothing."

"Really?"

"They tell the little girls they must keep the secret. Or else . . ."

"Or else what?"

"These silly men try to frighten little girls."

"They are naughty men."

"I'm just wondering if someone very naughty indeed's told my super little Priscilla to keep a secret."

"A secret about her bottom?" Maiocchi appeared genuinely shocked.

"Just wondering, Signor Agente, if you could bend down—I know you're very big and strong but this is important. Now perhaps if you could put your ear close to this little girl's mouth—that's right, put your ear to her mouth. Perhaps she could whisper the name of the horrid, bad man. You see, it would be a secret. And me and Mamma, we'll turn around and we'll pretend we're not here. I want to talk to Mamma about some clothes she was going to buy for Priscilla. But if you could listen to Priscilla, it could be a special little secret just between you and her."

"I certainly can try."

"A secret between you and her and nobody else need ever know."

Maiocchi gave a brisk salute and Signora Scola turned away, going over to where the mother sat smoking.

Trotti watched as Priscilla looked carefully at Maiocchi. Still holding the handcuffs—they were old issue, not the more recent American model—Maiocchi brought his face towards her running nose and her small mouth.

In the end he had to get down on his hands and knees.

Signora Scola had briefly gestured towards the mirror before going to talk to the girl's mother by the window.

Both the mother and Signora Scola turned their backs on the little girl and Commissario Maiocchi, red-faced and looking quite ridiculous on all fours.

Priscilla pulled at the handcuffs before approaching Maiocchi's ear.

The little Priscilla began to speak and her strange, pathetic words were picked up by the recording machine beside Trotti.

She spoke breathlessly and then she laughed.

Maiocchi laughed and kissed her on the forehead.

Trotti recognized the word *Nonna* as Priscilla began to gabble away, touching Maiocchi's face and pulling at his ear whenever his attention appeared to lag, talking to him about her grandmother and what the old woman in Esine did whenever Priscilla was a naughty girl.

Priscilla spoke without interruption for over five minutes.

At the end she was laughing happily. She liked the handcuffs.

64: Umberto Giordano

"ABSOLUTELY AMAZING, PIERO. All my congratulations."

The hospital porter was whistling "Come un bel dì di maggio" from Andrea Chénier. Trotti wondered whether it had become the theme for a program with the RAI or Berlusconi's Fininvest.

"Bel dì di maggio?" There was dirty snow beneath his feet and the fine days of May seemed a long way off.

A cold Sunday morning in December and the city was empty. Trotti glanced at his watch. "I'm afraid I can spare you very little time."

"The time to drink a decent coffee? And stock up on those awful boiled sweets, Piero."

"I need to get back to Tenente Pisanelli."

The Questore nodded understandingly. "I gather the situation's static."

"I'm meeting his fiancée in a couple of hours. Anna Ermagni's coming up from Rome."

"Excellent, excellent."

They went through the main entrance of the hospital and crossed the road to the Bar Goliardico. The Questore pushed open the glass door for Signora Scola and Trotti.

An advertisement for Moka Sirs coffee on the wall clock above the bar. The pin-table and the telephone appeared abandoned.

For a brief moment, the smell of coffee and lemons reminded Trotti of Brigadiere Ciuffi. He had been back only once since her death. Six years that he had been trying to forget all about Ornella and it now suddenly occurred to him that if Ciuffi were still alive, she would be Simona Scola's age.

Alive, married and with children.

They sat down at a window-side table. The Questore ordered drinks.

"I was very worried, Piero, you were thinking of dropping the SVS."

"The what?"

"You and Signora Scola—quite frankly it's marvelous." An approving look that went from Trotti to the attractive young woman sitting beside him. "No need to tell you how much I appreciate your coming in to see the little girl so soon after the accident."

"No accident." Trotti gestured. "Pisanelli's Citroën was pushed off the road and whoever's responsible was trying to kill us. I only hope . . ."

Simona Scola said, "The mother was insisting on taking little Priscilla back to Esine in Brescia province, Signor Questore. Without a formal complaint, there wasn't much we could do. And the hospital wanted back the room she was staying in. The mother agreed to one last try."

The Questore addressed Trotti. "You mustn't worry about Pisanelli." He spoke as if he held the key to life and death.

"I was surprised how willing the mother was to collaborate this morning." Signora Scola's hand touched Trotti's. "Until now, she's been behaving like an ostrich, refusing to admit there was any problem."

"A young, healthy man, Pisanelli. Just a temporary thing. The doctors aren't particularly worried. He's going to pull through, Piero. Of that I'm quite sure. Your theory it was an attempt on your life . . ."

The waiter brought the drinks. A coffee for the Questore, thick hot chocolate for Simona Scola and a cappuccino for Trotti, who had almost forgotten how good the coffee was in the Bar Goliardico. The waiter also set a basket of croissants on the tablecloth.

Outside the buses rumbled past the Policlinico.

"SVS, Signor Questore?"

"Sezione Violenza Sessuale. Of course, Signora Scola will have a full-time contract as a police ancillary worker." He rubbed his hands. "Excellent work."

Looking at the Questore, Trotti realized that he had never really scrutinized the man's face before. The regular features were as they had always been—the mustache, the cold grey eyes, the arched eyebrows, the closely shaven skin—but now they seemed to form a different total.

For the first time, Trotti was aware of an underlying weakness. The receding chin, the nervous muscular movement at one corner of the man's lips.

"At the moment I'm concerned about Pisanelli."

"I'm concerned about everybody who works for me, believe me. But the doctors are optimistic." The Questore raised the coffee to his lips. The cold eyes remained on Trotti. "The SVS is what I want and I want you to run it. You postpone your retirement for a couple of years, Piero, and we can make something of it. Something that'll go beyond this province, beyond Lombardy—and perhaps beyond Italy. I'm convinced you're about the only man in the Polizia di Stato capable of doing it. The only man in a world of phallocrats who knows how to deal with women and children."

("Pisanelli's a pig-headed phallocrat, you mean." Ciuffi had spat the words out. "A balding, ineffectual, greasy phallocrat."

"Pisa?"

Brigadiere Ciuffi looked carefully at Trotti before answering. The young eyes were tinted with blood. Ornella Ciuffi had not been getting enough sleep. "Pisanelli," she had said. "And all the other men in this wretched Questura.")

"Signor Questore, I think I've already made my position clear."

"You *think* you've made your position clear. But, Piero, we've just seen the little girl. You must realize how important all this work is. She needs you. And all the little Priscillas like her."

Signora Scola said, "Little girls and little boys." She had not touched her steaming chocolate.

Maiocchi entered the Bar Goliardico. He had changed into corduroy trousers and jacket. His pipe was set jauntily between his lips. He now sat down beside Simona Scola, who looked up at him and smiled.

"Gelli's running the mother and daughter to the station."

Trotti nodded his thanks. Turning back to the Questore, he said, "I have no intention of postponing my retirement."

"Piero, Piero. You're a father yourself. A father and a grandfather. You don't think all children deserve the care and the protection that your daughter and granddaughter can take for granted?"

"There are people other than me who can run your Sezione Violenza Sessuale."

"Three-year-olds, two-year-olds and even younger—their minute genitalia having to accommodate the sexual organ of grown men. That doesn't shock you? It doesn't incite you?"

Signora Scola interrupted. "Not their genitalia, Signor Questore. When a man molests a little girl, it's the rectal passage that has to accommodate the organ."

An awkward hush fell across the table.

"At that early age, a penis will rip a little body apart. Whereas the anal sphincter is more flexible."

The Questore coughed. "Of course, Piero, you could have all the people you want. I'm sure Maiocchi here would be only too glad . . ."

"These last few days, many people have been asking me to accept your generous proposition. The answer, I'm afraid, is no."

"Consider everything carefully. While you're in Venezuela with Maiocchi, discuss it." He glanced at his hands. "I'm sure Signora Scola could accompany you to Caracas. That's something that shouldn't be too difficult to arrange."

"At this moment, a collaborator and a close friend of mine is in a coma. A friend for whom I feel personally responsible." Trotti gestured towards the hospital. He took a ten thousand lira note from the pocket of his jacket and stood up. "Now, please forgive me. I'd rather be with Pisanelli."

The Questore's face, the regular, even features, had blanched. He gestured Trotti to sit down.

Trotti did not move.

"There's nothing you can do for Pisanelli now."

"Sitting here drinking coffee's not helping him."

"Moka Sirs, Piero? Your favorite? Kindly be seated."

Trotti returned the smile, but without warmth. "You wish me to stay?" He slowly lowered himself back on to the chair. "Perhaps I could ask you a question?"

"Of course."

"Signor Questore, perhaps you can tell me what you were looking for in Bassi's office on Friday. At seven o'clock in the morning. At a time when news of Bassi's murder hadn't yet been divulged."

The Questore from Friuli was now frowning, although the remnants of a smile lingered on the anaemic lips. "This isn't the place to pull out our dirty washing, Piero. If you have any doubts, there's nothing to stop you accompanying me now to the Questura and I'm sure that—"

"Very strange, isn't it, that Bassi was murdered after returning from the prison in Alessandria? And that two days later, somebody tried to kill Pisanelli and me on our way back from the same prison? From the same prison where, like Bassi, we'd been talking to a journalist."

He laughed with embarrassment. "Sounds to me, Piero, you're making a strange amalgam of things."

Commissario Piero Trotti suddenly allowed himself to lose control of his temper. "My friend Pierangelo Pisanelli would like to know why unpleasant things happen when people start asking questions about Dr. Quarenghi's work at the Ministry of Health."

The Questore frowned.

"The same Dr. Quarenghi whose brother-in-law is our ex-mayor. Quarenghi's the brother-in-law of Sindaco Viscontini. And—unless I'm mistaken—you've done several favors in the past for our ex-mayor."

"Piero, Piero . . ." the Questore said wearily, still smiling.

"Quarenghi and Viscontini—both good Socialists." Trotti stood up. He took Simona Scola by the arm of her fur coat. "Socialists like yourself, Signor Questore."

65: Tangenziale

"DON'T ASSUME FOR one minute children tell you everything." She pulled at the collar of her coat. "They always hold back on the worst part."

"We'll take the car."

Surprise in her voice. "You're not going to see Tenente Pisanelli?"

"Not yet," Trotti replied tersely. "Sitting and holding his hand while he's in a coma isn't going to help him."

"You'd be surprised."

"Then Anna can hold his hand."

"Anna?"

"His girlfriend's coming up from Rome on the Pendolino."

"There are times when you can be very unfeeling, Piero."

"You surprise me."

"An act, of course."

They re-entered the hospital grounds. The shoulder of her coat touched Trotti's.

"All an act. Like the Ciuffi woman. You choose to pretend you've forgotten about her." A snort of amusement. "Any woman can see that's not the truth."

"There's somebody I've got to see."

No clouds and the sky was clear. The air remained cold, and underfoot the snow was turning to ice. It was nearly four o'clock.

"And you'd like to use my car, Piero?"

"I'd like you to come with me." He added, "I'd appreciate that a lot, Simona."

"You always call me Simona when you want something."

"That's a good sign. There are times when I think I'm past wanting anything. I would like you to come with me."

"For my car?"

"For your feminine intuition." He smiled wryly. Then, on an impulse, added, "As for Brigadiere Ciuffi, I never give her a second thought. Not now."

"She's dead, Piero. She's been dead a long time."

"I don't want Pisanelli to die like her."

"Then perhaps you should go and hold his hand." A sidelong glance. "And, just for once, show that you care about other people. About their feelings."

They found the Fiat Seicento, parked between the expensive cars of the doctors from Pediatria and the neighboring wards of Ostetrica and Psichiatria.

She unlocked the doors. "I'm not happy about leaving little Priscilla."

"You got what you wanted, didn't you?"

"My God, Piero. Sometimes you sound just like the ignorant policeman you pretend to be."

"Thanks."

"The whole point of an abuse section is to protect the child. To protect the children. That's what it's all about."

"I'll drive."

"No, Piero."

They got into the low seats, Signora Scola sitting behind the steering wheel. "We now have Priscilla's words on tape and, with a bit of luck, the grandmother's going to be taken out of her life. But that's not what we're fighting for. At least, that's not what I'm fighting for."

"Take the Vigevano road."

"A child molester—it's not as simple as catching a murderer or a thief, Piero. Is that little girl going to be able to return to the semblance of a normal life? Is she going to forget the pain of what happened? Is she going to forget the terrible shame?"

"She seems resilient enough."

"What happens to these kids—it's going to influence the rest of their lives. That's what's important, Piero."

"Turn left once we get out of the main gate and take the direction for Vigevano." Trotti gestured. "I know, Simona. Abused women carry their prison with them—they're like snails."

She was about to put the key in the ignition but her hand stopped in mid-action and Signora Scola turned and looked coldly at Trotti. She had put on her sunglasses. "You're laughing at me?"

"About snails?"

Trotti could not see her eyes behind the dark lenses. "A friend of mine says that."

"A woman friend?"

"It's her theory about prostitutes and all the other women who end up in prison. Snails carrying a prison on their backs. Carrying it through life."

Simona Scola bit her lip. "What do you expect? Children are supposed to be happy. Childhood's a time of innocence—the moment when you can play and laugh before you take flight on your own wings. The age of innocence; and, instead, some adult's making use of you. Making use of your fragile body in the vilest and cheapest way. You who deserve everything—your anal sphincter's being dilated in pain and humiliation for the sake of someone else's easy pleasure, physical gratification."

"And you end up a whore?"

"Not necessarily." She seemed to blush behind the glasses.

"You end up like some Mother Teresa of Calcutta?"

She turned on the engine that came to life as happily as the day the Seicento had left the factory in Mirafiori. "You end up trying to cope with the lack of self-esteem that dogs you for the rest of your life."

"You never told me why you got involved in this work, Simona."

She retorted hotly, "You never told me why you did."

"That's easy," Trotti replied. "The Questore and his friends don't want Commissario Trotti poking his peasant's nose where it's not wanted. A nose that is not, never has been a Socialist nose. So they send me where I'm out of the way—and where they can earn points for political correctness."

"That's not what you told me eighteen months ago when you asked me to collaborate."

"That was eighteen months ago, Simona. I needed your help with the Barnardi child."

"Very flattering, I'm sure."

Signora Scola's face was like a mask behind the dark glasses as she took the car slowly through the gates of the hospital and over the Milan-Genoa rail bridge.

There was hardly any traffic. It could have been a day of summer except for the iced snow and the gaunt leafless trees. And the subzero temperature within the car.

"Un bel dì di maggio."

"Thanks," Trotti said softly.

She glanced at him. "For what, commissario?"

"For Priscilla, for everything—I appreciate it, Simona."

"You appreciate my work?"

"I'm having more and more difficulty with the whole idea of a sexual abuse center."

"You're the right person for the job."

"It's not easy for a man."

Her eyes were on the Iveco van ahead. "What?"

"A little thing like Priscilla."

Signora Scola sighed.

"Priscilla's innocence worries me."

"Worries you, Piero?"

"It's not as if she's a woman. Just a little girl—and as you say, she deserves our protection. A little bundle of hope and promise. She deserves our protection because eventually she'll be a mother herself and will have children of her own. Children to whom she must bring all her affection."

Signora Scola smiled. Her gloved hand touched his. "Piero, you must stay on. Even if it means satisfying the Questore. But he's right. You're not a phallocrat. You care about women and children because you care about justice. You really must take on this Sezione Violenza Sessuale. For all the other Priscillas."

"I want to believe that only a maniac—only a sick person can do what was done to that child—to that child who could have been my daughter. Or my little granddaughter, Francesca."

"A sick old woman. With luck, the Carabinieri will have a case against her. You can understand why the mother tried to protect her. In all probability, the grandmother had done exactly the same thing to the mother when she was a little girl. Thanks to you, the caserma in Lovere should be able to send the nonna away."

"I hope you're right."

She shook her head, "Of course I'm right." They were heading for the Tangenziale.

"There are times, Simona . . ."

"Yes?"

"There are times when I can't help wondering whether we're not all maniacs. Times when I wonder whether there isn't a demon in us all."

"In who?"

"A demon in all of us. Not just the maniacs—but in us all. The reliable men, the good men. And just occasionally that demon will break loose. Not, I hope, with an innocent little girl. But the older I get—and I hope, the wiser, the more I'm aware of the demons. Lingering, waiting in the belly. Waiting for our moment of weakness."

66: Charlemagne

THE CHAPEL STOOD on a small hill. It was about ten kilometers upstream from the city, overlooking the river and the regional park. The trees that followed the gentle curve of the river fifteen meters below were bare and gaunt. The slow-running river was shallow.

Legend had it that it was here Charlemagne had crossed the Po and set up camp.

Legend also had it that on crossing the river his officers had erected the small Roman chapel within a day.

What was certain was that the residents' association of Podere CarloMagno had paid a local architect to renovate the chapel. It now had a new roof and the brick walls had been painted a deep carmine. The sundial on the wall gave a sharp shadow beneath a Latin motto: VOL OMNIBUS LUCET.

Signora Scola parked the car facing the chapel and together they climbed out of the Seicento.

"I've never been here before." A wind blew across the plain, and her light brown hair, escaping from the collar of her coat, was flung backwards. She had removed her sunglasses and her eyes were watering with the cold.

"The place was derelict for years."

There had been a large farmhouse, dating back to the Austrians, surrounded by two rows of stables. The previous year the whole complex had been completely renovated and refurbished. The old farmyard was divided into separate gardens that were now individually fenced. Pushing bravely through the thin snow were saplings that would soon grow into plane trees. A series of garages had been built underground for the four-wheel drives and the children's bicycles.

A couple of children, in bright woolen caps and gloves, were playing in the shallow snow. One had a toy rifle, the other a Red Indian headdress.

"The only way the residents could get permission to rebuild the place was by promising to restore the chapel. And now everybody's happy. Fifteen luxury apartments in the middle of a national park and the mayor can boast of a chapel that's been restored after centuries of dereliction."

"You're cynical, Piero."

"I'd rather see this place inhabited than being left to rot."

"I'm not sure I believe you. You hate everything that's modern."

Trotti took her by the arm and following the newly paved surface of a path led her to a gate.

A dog barked playfully at the children, undecided in his allegiance to redskin or cowboy.

There were several names. Trotti rung the button beside the nameplate announcing Famiglia Viscontini.

"Somebody's expecting you?"

Before Trotti could answer, there was a buzz and the heavy wooden door opened. They entered the building, glad to be out of the wind.

It was suddenly dark.

It was now Signora Scola who guided Trotti. "Trouble with you, Piero, is that your eyesight's going."

"I'm a sixty-five year old man," he retorted.

"Sixty-four."

A door was opened on the first landing.

"Signora Viscontini?"

Her features were scarcely visible. The lighting on the landing was poor and her silhouette was back-lit by the large windows of the apartment behind her. "Yes?"

"Commissario Trotti."

"Ah," Signora Viscontini said. "Then you'd better come in." She spoke well. If Trotti had not been told that she was from Zagreb, he would have taken her for a local woman.

67: Donnaiolo

SHE SMILED TENTATIVELY. "Police?"

"I'm Commissario Trotti and this lady is a close collaborator. Your husband's not at home?"

"Signor Viscontini's in Portugal."

"Why?"

"For a conference of European Socialists." Again she smiled. She had led them into a large room that looked out onto the Po. At a distance of a couple of hundred meters, the waters seemed almost white. "You wanted to speak to him?"

Trotti glanced at the vast photographs on the wall. A picture of Pietro Nenni. Another of Bettino Craxi. "Probably better we're alone." Trotti showed her his identification. "I believe you knew Signor Fabrizio Bassi."

There was a spontaneous movement of her hand that Trotti noticed, although the woman tried to repress her reaction.

It was warm in the house and she was wearing fashionable trousers and a V-necked sweater that revealed the very white skin of her neck. She wore grey socks that were rolled over at her ankles. She was young, less than thirty, and her features were delicate. Yet the frame was large, like that of a sturdy peasant woman.

Trotti noticed that her fingernails were carefully painted.

She spoke flatly. "Yes, I know Signor Bassi."

"You know he's dead?"

"Yes," she said after a moment.

"How?"

"From the radio."

"I'd like to know when you last saw him."

She sat back in her chair. "Why?"

Signora Viscontini had not offered them drinks. She now looked quizzically at Trotti and Signora Scola sitting beside each other on the settee.

"Signor Bassi was murdered. A bullet through his brain. We would like to know who killed him. And why."

"You think I killed him?" It was in her question that Trotti could hear the foreign intonation. She had mastered the Italian language almost to perfection—but in the question, the intonation was foreign, different. There were some accents that Trotti liked. Despite his general disapproval of those French people he had met, he liked the way they transformed Italian. There was something both attractive and flattering in the way they changed the rolled r. He even liked the slow, amusing Anglo-Saxon deformation of the Americans.

Although scarcely perceptible, Signora Viscontini's Slavonic accent was unpleasant. It gave the impression of arrogance. An irrational impression, of course, but Trotti found that because of it he felt little sympathy for the young woman sitting opposite him. At the same time, he could admit that she was beautiful. Delicate, fragile features and a sturdy body. Trotti had no difficulty in understanding how Bassi had been attracted to her. Undoubtedly, Bassi had been attracted by anything that wore a skirt—or so at least the rumor went in the Questura. Bassi the womanizer. "Il donnaiolo di Brooklyn," as colleagues used to call him.

"Signora Viscontini, I'm a policeman. I'm not paid to think. I'm paid to discover the truth."

"You think by accusing me of Fabrizio's death you'll discover the truth?" Her eyes looked steadily at him.

"I believe you had an affair with him."

"That's none of your business."

"Anything that can help me find out who murdered Bassi is my business." Realizing that he had allowed a certain harshness to enter his voice, Trotti was about to ask another question, this time more mildly, when Signora Scola spoke.

She had produced the notebook. She sat with her coat unbuttoned and now she balanced the notebook on the knees of her red dress. She smiled at Signora Viscontini, a smile of feminine collusion. "Nobody's accusing you of anything. That's not how the police work." She threw a sidelong glance at Trotti. "We'd simply like to find out why Signor Bassi was murdered. We believe you can help us."

"I don't know why he was murdered."

"Of course not. But you knew him, didn't you?"

The woman nodded.

"It was common knowledge . . ." Signora Scola lowered her voice, as if afraid to reveal a secret to the walls and the framed political posters of the large, bright room. "Common knowledge you were seen with Signor Bassi."

"A long time ago."

"Three years ago, I believe."

Signora Viscontini looked at Trotti. "There was nothing in it. My husband was often away and I felt very homesick. Homesick for my country."

"For Yugoslavia?"

"For Croatia. I'm from Zagreb. It was in my city that I met my husband. Luigi came with a delegation of the Italian Socialist Party. I was working as an interpreter—and we got married in a couple of weeks. Love at first sight." A smile. "His first wife had died and his children no longer live in this city. They're in Rome and Luigi was very lonely. It's not easy being a mayor. Politics in your country—it was something I was not used to." Another smile of the pale lips. "In my country—before independence—at the time of the communists, a mayor didn't have enemies. He was a member of the party and everyone respected him. But this is not Yugoslavia. This is Italy."

"You're happily married?"

"A happy marriage, believe me." The broad face confirmed the honesty of her assertion. "Unfortunately, my husband's a very busy man. Oh, I know now there's a lot of talk about the Socialists. There's a lot of talk about Bettino Craxi and all his friends in Milan. Tangentopoli, Mani Pulite—and perhaps it's true. This is Italy. But Luigi's not like that. A good man and a very honest man. Yet . . ." She made a gesture with her hand.

Trotti noticed there were two gold bracelets around the strong wrist. "Yet what, signora?"

"I was often very lonely. A young girl—I wasn't even twenty-four years old. I had money, of course, and I had a car. But I come from a big family and I like having people around me."

"And you met Bassi?"

"I realize now I embarrassed my husband."

Signora Scola asked, "You don't have children?"

The other woman shook her head. "Luigi's not interested in children. Not now. He has two sons living in Rome."

"You wouldn't like to have children?"

"No." She smiled blandly. "Not yet."

"Your husband's a lot older than you. You're not in a hurry?"

"Children?" She folded her arms. "We'll see."

"Signora Viscontini, where did you meet Fabrizio Bassi?"

She thought for a moment and she stroked her chin with the back of her hand. "I suppose I first met him in the foreigners' bureau at the Questura. I had to go there because I didn't have Italian citizenship." She shrugged. "Now, of course, I have a passport."

"And that's where you met Bassi?"

"I met him, yes. But the first time we ever really spoke—it was funny really. It was during a political rally. A Socialist rally. There were policemen. They came to protect the various speakers."

"And Bassi decided to protect you?"

"I was sitting in the front row. An open-air meeting in Piazza Vittoria and they were testing the sound system. He came over. Fabrizio came and talked to me. You know, a lot of people were very unkind to me in those early days. They said I'd only married Luigi to escape from the Communists. They couldn't understand what attracted Luigi and me. And so I appreciated Fabrizio's kindness."

"You often met Bassi after that?"

She nodded. "Fabrizio was a kind person."

"And through his kindness, he lost his job with the Questura."

"A private detective agency—that'd always been his goal. He wasn't kicked out—please don't think that. Fabrizio left the police of his own accord. He was very happy."

68: Knowledge

"Was he in love with you?"

"Who?"

"Was Fabrizio Bassi in love with you, Signora Visconti?"

She took a deep breath. "I don't know."

"There was an affair?"

"What do you mean by that, commissario?"

"Did you and he make love?"

She shook her head with disbelief. "Commissario, I'm a married woman."

"Plenty of married women have affairs."

"But not me."

"Of course not."

"I won't deny I spent time with Fabrizio."

"A happily married woman?"

"I spent time with him because I was lonely, because my husband was often busy and I rarely saw Luigi from one convention to another. I know now it was a mistake."

"In what way?"

"Fabrizio was kind. And by being with him, I suppose I was trying to make my husband jealous."

Signora Scola asked, "Did it work?"

"There are people who say Luigi was very angry. I didn't want to make him angry. I suppose I wanted to embarrass him. I wanted him to take notice of the young wife he'd forgotten all about. If I had married him, it was because I wanted to be with him."

"You managed to embarrass him?"

"There are still people who say my husband was instrumental in Fabrizio's leaving the police force."

"Your husband is a friend of the Questore," Trotti said flatly.

"My husband has many friends. And even more acquaintances. I can't tell you whom he likes and whom he simply meets with for political reasons."

"You know the Questore, Signora Viscontini?"

"Of course." She shrugged her shoulders. "The Questore's a Socialist. He's been to this house on several occasions."

"Do you think it's possible there was a deliberate attempt to have Fabrizio Bassi leave the force?"

"As I understand it, the Polizia di Stato's part of the Ministry of the Interior. And, as such, policemen are civil servants, employed and paid by Rome. You should know that better than I, commissario. I really can't see how anybody at a local level could influence the career of a civil servant."

"You didn't answer my question."

"I thought I already had."

"You're forgetting—perhaps because you're still new to the Byzantine workings of this Italian state of ours—you're forgetting, Signora Viscontini, that in our democracy, the ultimate power lies in the hands of the parties. Not in the hands of the people. This is a partitocrazia—and for nearly a decade, we've had two parties running this country for us. For us and without us. Two parties, including the Italian Socialist Party. Your husband's party. In other countries, not in Yugoslavia or in Italy, but in the old democracies—in countries where power belongs not just to the strong but to everybody—civil servants do not brandish their political allegiances. In those countries, the civil servant merely executes the wishes of the democratically elected government."

The young woman glanced at Simona Scola. "I'm afraid I don't understand what you're saying, commissario."

"Perhaps I should speak a bit slower."

"Speak a bit more clearly. With clearer ideas."

Trotti asked, "In your opinion, was there pressure at a political level for the removal of Fabrizio Bassi?"

"Fabrizio Bassi was not sent to Sicily or Calabria or the Adige. There was no pressure in this city that had him posted elsewhere. At least, that's what he told me."

"Then why did he leave the police?"

"I think I've told you."

"Then tell me again."

"Is this so important?"

"Why did Fabrizio Bassi leave the Polizia di Stato?"

"To set up his agency."

"You're quite sure?"

"Fabrizio was aware he'd be losing all the advantages for his pension. He knew that. But working in the passport office or having to accompany politicians and hang around in the cold or sit and wait in a car while they ate their official lunches—that was something he was fed up with. Fabrizio wanted excitement."

"That's not what he told his colleagues."

"I can only tell you what he told me."

"He told you the truth?"

"I hope so." The young woman made a gesture of amused irritation. "There were times when he liked to embellish, just like a little boy. He once told me he'd studied investigation in America—but I knew it wasn't true. That doesn't make Fabrizio a liar. Fabrizio was a good man. Naive, possibly. And perhaps he was influenced by all those television programs. He really wanted to be a private detective, just like the characters he saw on television. And perhaps . . ."

"Yes?"

Signora Viscontini took a deep breath.

"And perhaps what, signora?"

"Fabrizio Bassi was in love with me."

"So?"

"He'd come out of a messy divorce and he needed female company. For him, being with a woman meant showing off. He had this very strong need to impress people. In his way, Fabrizio wasn't very bright. I'm not saying he was stupid. Just that he had difficulty in understanding other people."

"Most men do, signora," Simona Scola remarked. She was writing in her notebook.

"Fabrizio could never really understand there was no need to wow or dazzle people. His goodness was sufficient. It was his goodness that I liked about him."

"And that's why he set up his detective agency? He wanted to dazzle you?"

"Yes." She raised one of her legs and tucked it under her thigh.

"He wanted to impress me. He wanted to impress everybody. And I suppose he wanted to impress himself."

"You still love him?" Trotti asked.

"You want me to collaborate—and then you ask stupid questions."

"Your voice was on the answering machine."

"What?" Color seemed to drain from the broad face.

"There was a message on the tape. A message from you."

"Not possible."

"Possible or not, signora, I can assure you it's your voice."

"I haven't spoken to Fabrizio Bassi for months."

"The affair's over?"

"There never was any affair." She caught her breath. "He liked me more than he should. And perhaps I was childish. Childish and flattered because I was lonely and I enjoyed Fabrizio's company. But there wasn't any affair." Blood was now returning to her features. The pale blue eyes went from Trotti to Signora Scola. "I suppose I used him. Perhaps it was because of me that he left the police. But I would never have harmed him. I would never harm Fabrizio."

"Why not? You no longer needed him."

"Why not? Because when I felt alone and abandoned in a foreign country, he was a good friend to me." She shrugged. "He wanted something that I couldn't give him and I told him that. But Fabrizio Bassi will always remain one of my best Italian friends."

69: Cousins

"YOU HAVEN'T ANSWERED my question."

"You ask so many."

"A professional hazard."

"Which question, commissario?"

"When did you last see Fabrizio Bassi?"

She sat back in the chair, one leg still tucked beneath her thigh. The other leg rocked gently, the woolen sock grazing the carpet. "See him? It must be several months now. July, August. I saw him once at the Lido on the river. I was with friends and he came over to talk to me."

"You never saw him since?"

"I spoke to him."

"When?"

She gestured to a portable phone. "From time to time he would ring me."

"What about?"

"The same sort of thing."

"What sort of thing?"

"He seemed to believe there was some kind of future for us."

"What sort of future?"

"He felt I was too young for my husband. He believed I was unhappy in my marriage."

"Of course you're not?"

"Who's happy?"

"A good question, signora."

"Even when you're happy, are you really aware of it? We spend our lives chasing after various goals."

"Cheese in the mousetrap?"

She frowned her incomprehension. "I grew up very poor. I come from a happy family, very united. Yet as soon as I was aware of what was happening in my country—I used to listen to the Italian radio and Radio Free Europe, that was how I learned your language—I knew I'd have to escape."

"And you escaped?"

"I now have everything I ever dreamed of." She gave a disarming smile that went from Trotti to Signora Scola. "The strange part is, I can't tell you whether I'm happier than before. I can tell you that I miss my family. I miss my sisters and my cousins."

"Why did Fabrizio Bassi think you were unhappy?"

"Perhaps he was more unhappy than I."

"In what way?"

"I've achieved much of what I desired. You asked me a moment ago whether I wanted children. It's true—I wasn't totally honest. I'm a woman and I'd like to have children. But that'll come. I can wait a bit more. I can wait for Luigi to calm down, to cease his running backwards and forwards in the name of the party. I thought when he lost the mayoralty, he'd spend more time at home. I was wrong about that. If, as everyone says, there are going to be elections in the spring, then for my sake and for the sake of my family, I hope the Socialists take a beating. Then we can start living the life of a normal couple."

"How are you happier than Bassi?"

"I'm dissatisfied precisely because I've achieved what I always wanted. Fabrizio was dissatisfied because he must have known he would never achieve his aims."

"That's why there was no affair between you? His dissatisfaction?"

"There's that." She lifted a shoulder in begrudging acquiescence. "Plus the fact I didn't love him."

"Then why did he contact you?"

"Because he still hoped."

"You told him there was no hope?"

"I told him that a long, long time ago."

"Yet he still phoned you?"

There was a Gioconda smile on her face, both melancholy and complacent. "He thought I could help him."

"In what way?"

"He kept telling me he was going to be rich."

"Richer than a Socialist, signora?"

She ignored the jibe. Although it was Trotti who asked the questions, the young woman spoke to Signora Scola. "The Turellini affair. He told me about it. He said there was a lot of money to be made if he could identify the killer."

"And what did you say?"

"Very little." She glanced at Trotti. "Please understand. I liked Fabrizio. He brought a warmth into my life. There's so much about him that reminds me of my cousin Jani. The same dark, good looks. D'you understand? There was nothing sexual. For me, Fabrizio was just like a cousin."

"What exactly did he say about Turellini?"

"He knew who the murderer was."

"Really?"

"He always knew it was a woman."

"When did he tell you this?"

"Nearly every time we spoke together."

"And who was the murderer?"

She laughed, suddenly gay. "My sister-in-law, of course."

"Signora Quarenghi?"

"Precisely."

"You'd spoken to him recently?"

"Fabrizio?" She nodded. "It must've been about two weeks ago. I'd told him not to ring anymore. I told him he was only hurting himself. But he insisted." She paused. "Somehow Fabrizio always knew when my husband wasn't here. I even wondered whether he was watching me."

"What did Bassi say the last time you spoke to him?"

"He mentioned you, commissario. He said Commissario Trotti wanted to work with him. I believe you're retiring quite soon."

Simona Scola smiled. "Very soon."

"What I don't understand, signora," Trotti said, "is why Bassi acted the way he did—if he knew your husband's sister had murdered Turellini."

"A murder of jealousy."

"Precisely." Trotti nodded. "Why didn't he inform the police?"

"No proof."

"What proof did he need?"

"He seemed to think I could help him. And I think he was worried for me. Or at least that's what he said."

"Worried in what way?"

She smiled. "Fabrizio saw himself as my knight in shining armor—although how he expected me to share that poky little apartment of his, he never did say."

"What knight in shining armor?"

"My sister-in-law's mad. And so, in his opinion, is my husband. It was to protect me from them that Fabrizio phoned me."

"When did this start?"

"When did he start getting obsessed with my sister-in-law?" Again she stroked the soft, pale skin of her chin. "About a year ago."

"A year?"

"A year ago." The young woman nodded. The Gioconda smile remained. "With time, he grew gradually more obsessed. And the more obsessive he became, the more I tried to avoid him."

"Why?"

"Fabrizio thought everything depended upon getting my sister-in-law arrested. Get her arrested and he'd be rich. And then, if he were rich, he seemed to think I'd leave Luigi to go and live with him." The girl from Croatia smiled, but she could not hide the sadness around her eyes.

Trotti stood up and looked through the window. Late afternoon on a Sunday. The trees along the Po were becoming indistinguishable in the gathering dusk.

70: Coma

THEY WENT TOWARDS the large lifts. Almost immediately, the steel doors drew apart and, as they stepped inside, Magagna hit one of the buttons. The lift moved swiftly upwards.

"Pisa's going to be all right?"

It was very hot inside the hospital.

"I'd hate to be in one of these things during an earthquake," Magagna said.

Trotti rummaged in his pocket for a sweet. "How's Pisa, Magagna?"

Magagna looked at Signora Scola who was carrying a bunch of flowers. "You know what doctors are like."

"What are they like?"

A movement of Magagna's head and Trotti noticed the first signs of a double chin. Too much food and not enough exercise. "You needn't worry about the girl—they've given her a bed so that she can be with Pisa." Magagna smiled, "Italy," he said, as if the word alone were a joke. "Go to Naples or Bari and you're lucky if they don't let you die on a mattress in a corridor. But because this is a university hospital where the professors are often politicians, they not only have enough beds for the sick, they even have beds for the relatives." He gestured. "Anybody'd think we were in America."

"All the pharmaceutical firms sponsor the university," Signora Scola said.

"What do the doctors say, Magagna?"

Magagna looked at Trotti with his lively smile. He nodded and was about to say something when the illuminated roundel in the panel indicated they had reached the fifth floor.

The doors slid open. Magagna stepped aside to allow Trotti out of the lift.

Simona Scola held Trotti's arm.

"I don't know whether you'll be able to go in. At least not immediately."

"I can wait."

Magagna shrugged. "Deep coma and there's not much Pisanelli's going to tell you."

"Deep coma? What does that mean?"

"Ask the doctor."

"I can't find any doctor."

Typical of Riparto Rianimazione.

There was a long corridor. Evening had fallen—it was now past six o'clock and the place was lit by harsh neon. The sound of their footfalls echoed off the spotless walls.

There was a smell of perfumed detergent. Trotti had found a banana-flavored sweet and placed it in his mouth.

"Anna's with him now. They wouldn't let me in—there's a God-awful nurse who must've been a Swiss guard in an earlier incarnation."

"Anna?"

"I picked her up at the Stazione Centrale, as you asked me to." Magagna grinned. "She recognized me before I recognized her—I hadn't seen her since she'd gone back to the South with her parents. At least ten years ago. Pretty girl. She's filled out a lot since then." Magagna said admiringly, "Pisanelli's got good taste."

"What do you mean by deep coma?"

"I saw one of the doctors about twenty minutes ago—they all look so young, for heaven's sake. They're unwilling to give any prognosis. They just say it can go either way."

"Deep coma, Magagna?" Trotti repeated and he could sense a tightening of Simona Scola's fingers on his arm.

Magagna held his hands down in front of him, like a contrite child. "Either way, commissario. There's nothing wrong with his body apart from a few bruises. Whiplash. At some point when the French car was sliding over, there must've been a sudden deceleration of the body. You were lucky. Goodness knows why—it seems unfair."

"Who said life's fair?"

"The doctor was telling me it's like pilots when they use the ejector seat. The body can't always cope with sudden, excessive acceleration. Or, in Pisa's case, deceleration."

"Deep coma?"

"I'm not a doctor."

"So I see."

"Pisanelli's been here all day. You've had ample time to consult a real doctor."

Trotti replied tersely, "I've been busy."

"Now you're no longer busy?"

"For Christ's sake, Magagna, who can tell me about the coma?"

Signora Scola spoke from behind the bunch of flowers. "The difference between sleep and coma is that somebody can be woken from sleep. In a coma, the brain's activity as a whole is suppressed."

"Meaning?"

"You can cough or sneeze in your sleep. They're spontaneous reflexes which are unaffected by sleep. But not when you're in a coma."

Although the temperature in the corridor of Riparto Rianimazione was high—outside it had started to snow again—Trotti felt cold.

"What are the chances of Pisa's pulling through?"

"When there's continuous bleeding in the brain or if the body continues to absorb poison, a coma can go deeper. Which means the brain's slowing down. Which means the brain's less and less able to carry out its functions. Such as breathing."

"Pisa's going to stop breathing?"

Signora Scola said, "I don't know anything about Pisa's situation. But there are a lot of people who pull out of a coma without any side effects."

"Is he going to pull out?"

"I studied it a bit for my degree. Epilepsy's a brief form of coma—and nobody really knows what causes it. But that's why you've got to have intensive care."

They had come to a door and Magagna gestured with his thumb.

"The deeper the coma, the more attention that's needed to prevent the patient from choking to death. From choking on his own saliva. Or mucus."

Magagna had folded his arms. "They won't let us in."

Trotti turned the handle. The door was locked. Glancing at

Magagna, he knocked, not softly, at the painted surface. "I should've come earlier. I didn't realize . . ."

Trotti felt slightly giddy. The sickly fragrance of the sweet cleaning liquid that could not completely mask the underlying hint of ether. Even the perfume of the flowers made him feel uncomfortable. The neon lighting hurt his eyes.

He knocked again. It was as if his knuckles suddenly unlocked the door. It was opened by an unsmiling nurse.

Perhaps she was a nun. She did not wear a coif but Trotti noticed the discreet cross attached to her lapel.

Behind her was the bed, bathed in a subdued light. Both the head and the feet of the bed had been raised.

Anna was there. She was sitting in an armchair. Her eyes were closed; she appeared to have fallen asleep.

The woman asked crossly, "Commissario Trotti?" She looked tired, with lines under her eyes.

Beyond her stood a couple of monitors. A dancing spot, like a ball in a strange video game. The feeble guarantee of Pierangelo Pisanelli's survival.

"How is he?"

"Commissario Trotti?" A harsh face, red, blotchy skin. "You're wanted."

"Wanted?"

"An urgent call just a couple of minutes ago from the Questura. There's a car coming for you now. Should be downstairs any minute." For a moment, the weary face softened. "You mustn't worry, commissario," the woman said softly as she closed the door. "Trust in the Lord."

71: Esselunga

"THERE SEEMS TO be a blackout on the radio, commissario."

The driver took the car fast over the cobbles through the back streets, heading towards the Questura.

"Who told you I was at the hospital?"

"Commissario Merenda."

"On a Sunday evening?"

The speeding car crossed the Ghislieri piazza, almost hitting a student on her bicycle. Then going past the Carabinieri barracks, the revolving light reverberating off the cold walls, the car braked slightly. The driver accelerated into Corso Carlo Alberto and turned right into Strada Nuova.

For a moment, Trotti thought it was a road accident. There were cars parked haphazardly in front of the Questura. Doors hanging open and the revolving lights, out of phase, were swirling to different rhythms.

Trotti and Magagna jumped out of the car before the driver had brought it to a halt.

Up the granite stairs.

The man on door duty was trying to hold back a small crowd of journalists. Another man, in dark civilian clothes, was helping him. Recognizing Trotti, he stood back, making way for Trotti and Magagna to step through the metal detector.

Inside the Questura people were running up and down the stairs. No one took any notice of them. The lift door was open. Together Trotti and Magagna stepped into the small cubicle with its permanent smell of old cigarette smoke and the hammer and sickle scraped into the aluminum paint.

Surprisingly, the third floor seemed empty.

Nobody was at the desk.

Trotti headed towards his office just as Merenda stepped out of the Questore's bureau. "Where in God's name were you?"

It was, Trotti realized, the first time he had ever seen Merenda ruffled.

Merenda beckoned vigorously and they entered the office.

The first person Trotti recognized was the Questore's personal secretary. She was impeccably dressed. It could have been nine o'clock on a Tuesday morning. The woman was wearing the same beige skirt and blue high heel shoes.

She rarely, if ever, spoke to Trotti, but he knew that her first name was Giulia.

Giulia saw him and she stepped aside. As she did so, Trotti saw that she was crying. Mascara ran down her powdered cheeks in two dirty rivulets.

Maserati from Scientifica, his plump face pale, nodded.

"Ciao, Piero." He also stepped back.

Trotti and Magagna approached the vast desk. Somebody must have ripped off the bag—a recycled plastic bag with the logo of *Esselunga*. For some reason, Trotti recalled an article in the newspaper, announcing the merger of the Esselunga chain with the biggest supermarket in England.

The expensive loden coat lay on the desktop.

"Must've been dead for ten minutes. His secretary found him."

String, tightly knotted just above the Adam's apple, encircled the Questore's swollen neck.

The body had been pulled back against the armchair and now the bulging eyes stared up at the Italo-Californian chandelier.

Behind Trotti, Maserati remarked flatly, "Classic example of cyanosis and petechial hemorrhaging."

"Not even a suicide note," Merenda was saying in Trotti's ear. "Self-inflicted death from asphyxia."

72: Giuda

"A HUMAN LIFE," Trotti raised the glass of Sangue di Giuda. The kitchen light bulb was refracted in the dark wine.

"You don't seem particularly upset."

"I'm not going to cry crocodile tears, Magagna."

The clock on the mantelpiece ticked noisily. It was past ten and Trotti knew he had drunk too much.

Anna Maria said nothing. She sat with her hands folded on the table, her eyes fixed on Trotti, her lips pressed together, as if she had just taken a vow of eternal silence.

"He killed Pisanelli."

"Pisanelli's not dead," Magagna retorted.

"He tried to kill me and Pisanelli's going to die. Trouble is, the Questore killed the wrong man." In one swallow, Trotti emptied the glass. He smacked his lips noisily.

"Why kill you, commissario?"

"Because with time I would get to the truth."

"What truth?"

"I don't know." He shook his head. "I haven't gotten there."

"You can't accuse the Questore like that."

"He committed suicide, Magagna. The act of a desperate man. The act of somebody who sees there's no alternative."

"Alternative to what, commissario?" Magagna asked. "The Questore left no note. You're merely surmising."

"He's connected with Bassi's murder—and possibly Turellini's."

"Why?"

"No idea."

"Then how can you accuse him of murder?"

"The Questore didn't murder anybody with his own hands. Other than himself. But he was there at Bassi's place. Within a few hours of the body being found."

"He'd probably been informed."

"Of course he'd been informed. Magagna, the Questore was not a detective. I'd never seen him out on an inquiry. He'd have gotten his fine clothes dirty. Freezing his balls off in a stakeout?" Trotti shook his head. "There was something he wanted in Bassi's apartment. He was frightened Pisa and I had found it. He knew Pisa had taken the tape from the answering machine."

"What did he want the tape for?"

"It wasn't the tape. There was nothing on it apart from some message, probably from Signora Viscontini, that had never been wiped off."

"What was the Questore looking for?"

"Something that could incriminate him."

"Commissario, a Questore's not a murderer. Not in the real world."

"Since when has Italy been the real world?" Trotti laughed but there was no amusement. "In the real world, politicians aren't on the take. There's no Tangentopoli in the real world. In the real world, there's no collusion between the secret services and the Mafia. Between the terrorists and the Freemasons and the politicians. In the real world, there are no Giulio Andreottis, there are no Bettino Craxis. But we're not in the real world." Trotti raised his glass. "Welcome to Italy, Magagna."

"There's no case against him."

"Of course there is."

"What?"

"Pisanelli and I were driven off the road after going down to see the journalist Maluccio in Alessandria."

"Organized crime." Magagna raised his shoulders. "Nothing to do with the Questore."

Trotti banged his hand against the Formica tabletop. "When are you going to understand that the Socialist Party *is* organized crime? The Socialists and the Christian Democrats—they've had this country sewn up the way the Cosa Nostra has Little Italy sewn up in New York. Only this isn't Little Italy. This isn't New York. It's Big Italy—and the politicians' cut is a damned sight higher."

Magagna leaned forward and took hold of the bottle. He raised it towards Anna Maria who simply shook her head without taking her eyes from her cousin.

"Look, Magagna. You're not stupid. Can't you see Maluccio was framed? Somebody wanted him out of the way—possibly because of the article in *Vissuto*."

"Who?"

A gesture of irritation. "I don't know who and I don't know why. The cocaine found in Maluccio's car was a setup. The man neither drinks nor smokes. A family man—and you're telling me that with two little girls and a loving wife at home he was suddenly going to get involved in the drug trade? In Alessandria? In a place that's been the private property of the Calabrians and the Pugliesi for the last decade?"

"Who framed Maluccio?"

"No idea. But I do know it's not easy to throw an innocent person into prison. Suppose you or I wanted some innocent bastard put away for a few weeks. Not easy, Gabriele."

"Gabriele?"

"It's your name, isn't it?"

"You've never used it before."

"I never called Pisa Pierangelo," Trotti said. He took another gulp of wine.

"Sangue di Giuda makes you maudlin, commissario."

Trotti clicked his tongue in irritation. "It stops me from screaming."

"Why scream?"

"Because Pisanelli's going to die and it's my fault."

"You didn't push him off the road."

Trotti said, "You know he intended to leave the police? Anna told me Pisa was thinking of going back to his medical studies."

"Then he can specialise in intensive care."

"You're an unfeeling bastard, Magagna."

Anna Maria stood up. "Goodnight, gentlemen." She carefully set her chair under the table and went towards the kitchen door. "I'm sleeping on a mattress on the floor. If Anna Ermagni comes, put her in the big bed. Tell her not to trip over me." She closed the door silently behind her.

"An old maid," Trotti whispered. "A sour old maid. She hates it when anybody starts to appreciate a good wine."

"Very kind to me."

"Her fiancé was killed by the Germans and she subsequently

married a man she never loved. A Dutchman." Trotti added, "When I was a boy, I thought she was the most beautiful girl I had ever seen."

"I prefer your Signora Scola."

The smile vanished. "You're a married man, Magagna."

"You can call me Gabriele."

"You're married. So is Signora Scola."

"That doesn't stop her from holding your arm, commissario."

"I'm a married man as well," Trotti said, and standing up went to the sink. He ran water on to his hands and then rinsed his face. His eyes burned. He felt tired, worn out, but he knew he would not be able to sleep.

Trotti filled a saucepan with water and set it on the rear burner. "But she's an interesting woman." The blue flame jumped to life.

"Your cousin?"

"Simona Scola's intelligent."

Magagna smiled. "Attractive, too."

"Got a degree in child psychology."

"Commissario, when you hear the word psychology, you pull out your gun."

"I'd heard about Scola from various people. At the time of the Barnardi child. Somebody told me to contact her and amazingly, she managed to get the little Alessio Barnardi to reveal who had been molesting him." Trotti took a jar of loose chamomile from the cupboard over the sink.

"That's no justification for holding her arm."

"With the Viscontini woman—she saw I was being aggressive and she spontaneously fell into the friendly, understanding big sister role. Sweet and sour. I swear, Magagna, it's a technique I've used with a thousand men. But it's the first time I've worked as a team with a woman. Instead of clamming up, the Viscontini woman told us what she knew about Bassi."

"What did she tell you?"

"It's a shame Simona's not a cop."

"You could always set up a detective agency together."

"FBI? Like Fabrizio Bassi?"

Together the two men began to laugh while the water started to boil and dance in the saucepan. "Christ!"

A pale face had appeared at the kitchen window, to the left of the sink. A pale face deformed by the mist of the glass.

A hand tapped lightly at the pane.

73: Prontuario

"DOES THE PRONTUARIO mean anything to you?"

"Is this *Lascia o raddoppia*? Another Mike Bongiorno quiz?"

"I was told you were difficult, commissario. Difficult but honest."

"I was told you were from the South."

Judge Abete laughed. "You don't expect Southerners to be honest?" There was hardly any light other than the green dials of the dashboard but Trotti caught the movement of white teeth.

"I don't expect Italians to be honest."

It was a Fiat Argenta. The engine ran quietly, keeping the car heating effective.

Trotti had no idea where they were. Probably fifteen kilometers out of the city. They had driven northwards. When he pulled back the curtains, there was an amber glow against the sky.

Milan. Moral capital of the Republic.

"You're lucky to be alive, Trotti."

"What Prontuario, Signor Giudice?"

The voice came out of the darkness. "Firstly, I must apologize. All this secrecy. Coming to fetch you in the middle of the night. But I feel it's the least I owe you. It's the least I owe Bassi."

"Bassi?"

"Not necessarily the most intelligent of men. But I suspect that like you he was honest."

"Or unimaginative."

Abete laughed in the dark. "You denigrate yourself. You should know in Milan there are people who have respect for you, Trotti. For you and the people like you who've worked away these last thirty years and more. Keeping their faith in a Republic that's a republic only in name." A slight movement on the rear seat beside Trotti. "That's what I was afraid of. Secrecy that allows collusion and connivance. Secrecy that's the bedfellow of the corrupt and the corruptible."

"I'm not sure I understand what you're talking about."

Again the laugh. "I'm a lawyer by training."

"You astound me, Signor Giudice."

"I've taken a certain risk in coming to see you. Not for myself. Personal risk's something you try to put out of your head. Anyway, Milan isn't Palermo and I'm not Falcone. Just a second-rate judge buried away on the third floor of the Palazzo di Giustizia."

"What risk?"

"The inquiry."

"The inquiry into Turellini's murder?"

"I can't frighten you off, Trotti, in the same way I did Bassi. You do realize there never was an injunction. That was simply an act of bile on Bassi's part—or perhaps *Vissuto* hoped to increase their readership by denigrating the Palazzo di Giustizia. No injunction—but it's true I had to frighten Bassi."

"You want to frighten me?"

"You're a professional. I hope you're more intelligent."

"Everybody keeps telling me Bassi was a fool."

"He got himself killed, didn't he?"

"Falcone and Borsellino in Sicily were fools?"

"They were fools if they wanted to live out their lives and die in their slippers." Abete paused. "Fools die young."

"At least they achieve something."

"Let me tell you a little anecdote, Trotti. It might help you understand what I'm up against. What di Pietro and the other judges both in and out of the investigative pool at Mani Pulite are up against."

"You wouldn't have a sweet, by any chance?"

"Trotti's rhubarb? No, I'm afraid not. But perhaps my driver has some chewing gum." Silently, without seeming to move, the driver handed a packet over his shoulder—Trotti saw his hand against the light of the dashboard. Trotti took it and the movement of his arm set off the pain in his shoulder. Brooklyn chewing gum, banana-flavored.

"A couple of months ago I was in my office with a Calabrian. A Calabrian like me—but who'd landed up on the other side of the bars at San Vittore. A career within the 'Ndrangheta and one of the first people to opt for the government witness program. Un pentito. An intelligent man, but scarcely repentant. A man who, with a different background, could have gone far. Shrewd, with a sense of humor and a good understanding of human nature."

"Why San Vittore?"

"The man's already doing seven years for kidnapping. At the same time, he was on appeal against a life sentence for murder. I won't bore you with the details. Suffice it to say that although we're different, he and I, in other ways we could be Siamese twins. We are, I believe, all of us, victims of destiny."

"Some of us are more victims than others."

"This Calabrian was in my office and he seemed in a particularly good mood. I asked him why. He leaned forward and speaking in dialect—he's from Brancaleone—'You'll see, Dr. Abete,' he told me in his hoarse whisper, 'my appeal will be upheld. Somebody's already had a word with the judges.' I of course laughed. There was absolutely no possibility of the man's winning the appeal."

"And?"

"Two weeks later the appeal went before the court. My fellow Calabrian got off."

"How?"

"People seem to think our Palazzo di Giustizia's hermetically sealed so that we can get on as we please. That's not the point."

"What's the point?"

"We can't afford the leaks, Trotti. We can't afford having fellow magistrates being suborned. After all these years, at last we're getting the support we should've had when this First Republic was created."

"After forty years of sitting on your hands?"

"Little choice, Trotti. You know that."

"I know nothing."

Judge Abete sighed before continuing. "Things are changing, thank God. That's why I've come to see you like a thief in the night. That's why I had to scare Bassi off. That's why we told the Carabinieri at Segrate we were temporarily shelving the Turellini dossier."

"Why?"

"Does the Prontuario farmaceutico mean anything to you?"

"We're still playing at double or quits, Signor Giudice? Another quiz program for Berlusconi?"

74: Karaoke

"WE'RE ITALIANS—THE EASY victims of our own rhetoric. If we say something often enough, we begin to believe it."

"What do we believe?"

"Go into a court throughout this country. The law is equal for all. Written in big letters for everyone to see. For everyone to believe. And it's true we do have good laws, Trotti. Just, equitable laws. In many ways, ours could be such a civilized country. Capital punishment we gave up years ago, while the Americans, who have no doubts concerning their moral superiority, still fry their compatriots—preferably the black ones and the poor ones—to death in the electric chair. Or with a syringe."

"The Americans are no less victims of rhetoric than us?"

"There's a big difference between them and us. When an American court decrees you'll serve time in prison, no matter who you are, no matter how much you spend on your lawyer, that decision will be enforced."

"And?"

"Without enforcement, there's no law. Or rather, without enforcement, the law—so equitable in concept—exists not for your benefit but for the benefit of those who are more powerful than you, who can apply that law when it suits them. And who can forget about it when it ceases to serve their own interests." Again the laugh and Trotti could feel Abete changing his position on the seat. "Let me give you an example."

"Thanks."

"Trotti, you only play at being the dull policeman."

"By dint of having played it for such a long time, I've taken myself in. Forgive me if I don't like philosophical treatises. I even have difficulty with Costanzo's talk show on Berlusconi."

"You prefer Fiorello in karaoke?"

"At least I understand the words—when they come up on the screen."

Abete waited. "Then I'll try to speak slowly."

"Very thoughtful."

"The law in a democracy's there to protect everybody. Clearly Italy's not a democracy. Power is in the hands of an oligarchy. The nature of that oligarchy can change. Since the creation of the Republic, the oligarchy's been those members of the political parties who've carved up the juicy pie. Lottizzazione, Piero Trotti. Sharing the common wealth for their private benefit. And nowhere is this process more evident than in the pharmaceutical sector."

Trotti ran his tongue along his lips. His bruised shoulder was now throbbing uncomfortably.

"Medicine is, by definition, to help people get better. Consequently, it's only normal that a civilized country, a country that cares for the feeble, for the unwell, should ensure the drugs being administered have the effect their manufacturers claim. No point in taking a pill for a headache if in the process it destroys your nervous system. Do I make myself clear?"

"Very clear."

"Health's a multibillion-lire business—in any country. But in Italy, it is more than that. It's King Midas's gold."

"And who's King Midas?"

"Dr. Quarenghi is not King Midas—merely a very wealthy prince. The prince of the CIP."

"CIP?"

"There's a man in Rome who's probably richer in liquid assets than Agnelli or Berlusconi. His wealth isn't held down in capital he can't get his hands on. His wealth's in the Swiss banks. Or in the works of art—Picasso, Matisse, Modigliani—at his villa at the Eur in Rome."

"Who?"

"You'll find out, Trotti, but you mustn't be impatient. You must give me time. This is the most sensitive inquiry of my career—and it could destroy me."

"Not Dr. Quarenghi?"

There was a long pause.

Trotti pulled back the thick pleat of the curtain. Looking through the window, he could make out what he thought was a distant truck moving towards the glow of Milan. There were too many lights and he realized it must be a slow train heading to Porto Garibaldi or Lambrate.

The real world.

"People like to think di Pietro was responsible for Mani Pulite. In many ways, that's true. But he wasn't alone. The writing was already on the wall. Or rather, the wall had started to crumble. When the wall came down in Berlin, the Communists suddenly ceased to be the enemy western civilization had had to defend itself against for so long. Just as suddenly, the Christian Democrats and the Socialists could no longer count on the blind support of our dear NATO allies. On our good friends the French and, above all, the Americans. Suddenly our political masters, such staunch allies of NATO and the West, were being dropped in the shit. We, the judges, were the first to realize it."

"Congratulations."

"What had been going on at Sanità—we'd known about it for years. But what could a few motivated judges in Milan do? Against the might of Rome? What could we do about an entire edifice of corruption—in which everybody was implicated? Despite your sarcasm, commissario, I know you've found yourself in a similar situation. You know wrong's been done, you know who the wrongdoer is—and there's absolutely nothing you can do simply because the wrongdoer's a politician. A Christian Democrat, a Socialist, a Liberal. He's untouchable precisely because he's a politician—or the friend of a politician. Or the friend of a friend of a politician."

"I now work with sex abuse victims."

"Because you don't have any alternative, Commissario Trotti. As I said, Italy's a country with good laws. And over these last eighteen months, that's been the power of us magistrates. Trotti, when I was given the Turellini affair, I had no idea I'd be barricading myself into the Palazzo di Giustizia. That I'd be putting my private life on hold. A straightforward killing in Segrate? What appeared to be an ordinary murder—possibly a *crime passionnel*."

"*Cherchez la femme?*"

Again, Giudice Abete laughed. "In a manner of speaking."

There was a movement and suddenly the roof light came on.

Trotti blinked. The light was not strong, but his pupils were unprepared for it.

A clicking of metal on glass.

Trotti had seen the judge's face in the newspapers but now, sitting beside him in a car somewhere between the Po and the stale lights of Milan, Abete seemed very young to Trotti. Young, earnest and desperately tired, with dark rings beneath his eyes.

"Perhaps you'd care for something to drink, Trotti?"

The young judge had taken a flask from his jacket pocket and was pouring amber liquid into the silver thimble which he then handed to Trotti. "Dewar's," he said, with a crooked smile.

Without removing the gum from his mouth, Trotti took one sip and returned the thimble.

As suddenly as it had come on, the light within the Fiat Argenta was extinguished.

75: Congo

"FROM WHAT I can gather, Turellini was honest. Everybody I've spoken to says he had a great nostalgia for Fascism—but he was by and large honest. I can believe that. What I find difficult to understand is how it could take him so long to realize what was happening at the clinic."

"The clinic on Lake Maggiore?"

A deep breath. "Turellini had an extremely lucrative private practice on Lake Maggiore—a clinic he'd created in 1979 with his associate, Dr. Quarenghi. Quarenghi had specialized in clinical medicine in Milan. If they were friends then, by the time of the murder, Turellini and Quarenghi were no longer on speaking terms."

"Why not, Signor Giudice?" It suddenly seemed strange to use an honorific title with somebody who was less than half his age.

"Because Turellini was angry, I suppose." Abete took another sip of whisky. "Listen, Trotti, I'm counting on your discretion."

"I don't really see what I'm supposed to be discreet about."

"I can understand your desire to identify Bassi's murderer. Bassi's murderer and Turellini's. Try to understand the case has ramifications that go beyond a mere *fait divers* in the streets of Milan. I have to tread carefully, Trotti. Like everything else at the end of the First Republic, this is a minefield. Quarenghi's powerful. But Quarenghi's just one of several people who, should they find out about my inquiries now, will do everything in their power to stop me reaching the truth." He lowered his voice and Trotti could feel the odor of Dewar's against his cheek. "I hope to throw the bastards in jail. For good."

"What truth, Signor Giudice?"

"The truth of the Prontuario. The truth of billions of lire, Trotti. Money from the taxpayer's pocket that's been disappearing into Swiss bank accounts for the last thirty years."

The sound of the cap being returned to the flask.

"I had the man from Galaxa Eurochem in my office recently. An English company. He was American, one of those who try to be more European and more cosmopolitan than us Europeans. He'd come up from Rome. He came to see me because he realized he needed me as much as I need him. They're not like us, the Americans—they seem to think everything functions in black and white. Who knows, perhaps it does in their country. Yet another reason for my not wanting to go there." Abete started to laugh. "Forgive me, commissario, I belong to the generation that came of age after 1968. A generation fed on Coca-Cola and blue jeans and hamburgers. They say familiarity breeds contempt. Which would explain why I consider the Americans to be children. Naive, unsophisticated and potentially dangerous."

"You ought to live in our city. The Lega town hall has outlawed the use of English on street billboards."

"This man from Galaxa explained how every time he needed to get a new product on to the market he went to see Quarenghi at the CIP."

"CIP?"

"Comitato interministeriale prezzi per i farmaci—the committee which sets the price on all medicines that are on sale in the country."

"The Prontuario?"

"Precisely." A private chuckle. "Quarenghi insisted upon donations for his Clinica Cisalpina on Lake Maggiore."

"How could he do that?"

"Power and business speak the same language, Trotti. You should know that. The language of money."

"He asked for money?" Trotti asked incredulously.

"The clinic has its own foundation. A research foundation which, as I understand it, consists of little more than half a dozen postgraduate students, normally still studying at the university. Quarenghi's method is to ask the pharmaceutical company for a voluntary donation towards the research."

"What research?"

"That's the question that Carlo Turellini must have eventually asked Quarenghi."

"He didn't know about the research?"

"Of course he knew. But Carlo Turellini left the running of the clinic largely to Quarenghi and their accountant. Money doesn't appear to have been Turellini's driving force. His prime concern—both Signora Coddrington and his ex-wife agree on this—was getting the professorship in clinical medicine at your city's university. For the kudos. He was very jealous of Quarenghi's job in Rome—even if he realized that as a Neofascist and a one-time member of the Destra Nazionale, his hopes of getting anywhere in the academic world were seriously limited. Turellini wanted glory and kudos. Not, apparently, money."

"His ex-wife told me nothing about a conflict with Quarenghi."

"I don't think she knew."

"How did you find out, Signor Giudice?"

"An anonymous letter."

"Another anonymous letter."

"Where would we be without our anonymous informants, Trotti?"

"Out of a job."

"Some four months after the murder. To be honest, I'd always thought it was the Quarenghi woman who'd killed him. She's fairly unhinged. And she had a motive. She'd always believed Turellini had divorced his wife for her sake—and instead he'd gone off with a younger woman. Signora Quarenghi's behavior after the murder—turning up at the scene of the crime and making accusations—all that made her a prime suspect."

"Except . . ."

"Except she had an alibi—as did the other potential murderesses, all the slighted lovers or mistresses." Giudice Abete snorted. "A lady's man, Turellini."

"You think Quarenghi murdered him?"

"Quarenghi didn't murder him. Not physically, at least, because he was in Rome on the day of the murder. But once I got wind of the kickbacks coming from the pharmaceutical companies, the real motive at last became apparent."

"Money?"

"There was no reason for any of his women to kill Turellini. His ex-wife had long been used to the idea of a separation—and, anyway, they saw eye-to-eye over the will. She's wealthier than he is. Turellini was a self-made man, whereas his ex-wife inherited all her wealth. Both Turellini and Signora Lucchi were concerned the daughter Carla should be provided for."

"And the Englishwoman?"

"She wanted a child. Why kill the man who would finally give her what she'd always wanted? We all lost too much time looking for a woman when the real motive's money. I don't know who actually pulled the trigger at Segrate as Turellini drove through the gates. I'm convinced, however, Quarenghi paid the gunman."

"Why kill Turellini? Quarenghi and Turellini had been associates for years. Nobody ever mentioned to me there was a problem between them."

"Because they hid their problems. Doctors are like lawyers—or policemen. They close ranks so that nobody will see what infighting is going on. Of course Quarenghi and Turellini loathed each other. Or do you think Quarenghi was amused by his wife's infidelity with his close associate?"

"That's no reason to have Turellini murdered."

"Turellini had at last got wind of what was happening at the clinic. Perhaps he knew before—but I don't think so. That kind of easy wealth could only have done him a disservice in his attempts to get the professorship. For heaven's sake, he'd even given up his membership of the Neofascists for the sake of that professorship . . ."

"That's still no reason for murder."

"Most probably Turellini was threatening to blow the whistle. So he left Quarenghi with little choice."

"Nothing to stop Quarenghi from buying out Turellini's share in the clinic."

"Why should Turellini sell out? He possibly needed the regular income. I don't know, Trotti. Your guess is as good as mine. I doubt if we'll find out."

"You could ask Quarenghi."

"Not yet."

"Not yet?"

"Trotti, you forget this is the beginning of the end of the First Republic."

"Do I care?"

"It's not yet the end of the end of the First Republic. No magistrate—not me and not anybody else at the Palazzo di Giustizia wants to be thrown to the wolves."

"So you want me to wait for the end of the end of the First Republic? Is that it?"

"Elections are in March, commissario." Abete paused. "D'you realize the enormity of what Quarenghi and his friends have been doing?"

"You tell me Quarenghi murdered Turellini."

"Worse than murder, Trotti—a damn sight worse. These people have been fixing the price and the dosage on our medicines. Civil servants who, instead of defending society from the depredations of the pharmaceutical companies, are actively colluding with those companies. Civil servants using as their criteria nothing other than their own personal gain. Medicines that you or I, that your daughter or mine, take to get better when we fall ill—the dosages, the price, the use, all this—the medical Prontuario for the fifth richest nation in the world—placed in the hands of a few charlatans and quacks whose only concern is to get rich."

"So I can't arrest Quarenghi?"

"Worse than in Africa, Trotti. In Africa they're dying of AIDS. But in Africa the disease is not being positively propagated by doctors who see pharmaceutical intervention as a way to line their own pockets. The Third World is not the Congo. It's Rome."

"And Quarenghi?"

"Forget Quarenghi, Trotti. Forget about him. Look what happened to Bassi—when finally he got elbowed into the right line of inquiry. For the time being, just forget about him. Forget the whole damn affair."

"And if I can't, Abete?"

"If you can't wait for the elections, Trotti, you'll be putting my inquiry on the line. My inquiry—and inevitably the ensuing trial."

There was a long pause. Finally, Trotti said, "I'd be grateful if you could run me home."

"Have faith, Trotti."

"I gave up having faith a long time ago. Having faith's the best way to be exploited, manipulated and discarded. A lesson the Church taught me when I was an adolescent."

"If you can't have faith in human justice—sooner or later Quarenghi and the others at the CIP will face trial, God willing. That I promise you."

"Your promises don't satisfy me."

"Just supposing our frail, crippled justice never reaches Dr.

Quarenghi—just supposing that my colleagues and I never get him into court."

"Supposing?"

"You don't think Quarenghi will have all eternity to regret his wickedness?"

76: Favors

"YOU'RE COMING TO the funeral?"

"I want to catch the eleven twenty to Milan." Trotti dropped the packet of sweets on to the desk. "Funeral?"

"In the cathedral—a memorial service because the Bishop won't accept a funeral. Not for a suicide." Maiocchi leaned against the door jamb. "You can't postpone your trip to Milan? Your presence would be appreciated. And politically wise."

"A woman I need to see. A woman who lied to me."

"The Bassi thing?"

Trotti now stood up. "That's right."

"I don't understand why you bother so much."

"Bassi worked for me."

"Let Reparto Omicidi get on with it."

"Merenda wanted me to help."

"As if you could give a shit about Merenda."

"I don't give a shit about anybody or anything at the moment. Other than Pisa."

"How is he?"

"No change," Trotti said and looked away.

A silence.

Pushing away from the door, Maiocchi entered Trotti's small, uncomfortable office. "You know, Trotti, you ought to do something about the radiators."

"Help me by closing that door."

"It's freezing in here."

"The winter's nearly over—my last winter."

"Another four months, you mean. That Barbour's not going to keep you warm."

"That what?"

"Your English jacket. Very fashionable a couple of years ago. It's not going to keep you warm enough. You need a quilted anorak."

"Perhaps my daughter will find me something for Christmas. American shoes, English jacket. Perhaps she'll get me a Spanish sweater. She knows all about these things."

"Of course you could come to Venezuela."

Trotti started rummaging in one of the grey filing cabinets.

"What about Venezuela, commissario?"

"What about it, Maiocchi?"

"If you want, there's a third ticket. I'm sure Signora Scola could come with us."

"Come with you, Maiocchi." Trotti turned and smiled over his shoulder. The movement caused him to wince with pain. "Why don't you ask her?"

"I thought you had."

"Why should I invite Signora Scola to Venezuela? I told you what I want to do over the next few weeks. Tidy up this office and then get down to Bologna to be with my daughter and my granddaughter."

"And the Pavesi inquiry, Trotti? The missing parents?"

"That's your baby." Trotti added, "I didn't get the opportunity to thank you for helping Signora Scola yesterday. With the little Priscilla. You were good."

Maiocchi grinned. "As an agente?"

"You know, she was very grateful."

For a moment the young face brightened. "I like her."

"And your daughters?"

Maiocchi's features clouded. "Still no news."

"You want to go off to Venezuela on a wild goose chase? Why not spend Christmas with your children?"

"I want to get away from here, commissario. I haven't taken any holidays for sixteen months because of the wretched state exams. I know I haven't been much fun to live with. I don't hold anything against my wife or the girls. It's just that my existence has been too complicated lately. I'm tired and I need to rest."

"You could start by giving up that foul-smelling pipe."

"I was thinking we could go to Venezuela. Santa Margarita." He shrugged. "Looking for Pavesi shouldn't take up all that much time."

"We?"

"You, me and perhaps Signora Scola."

"If she accepted the offer to go."

Maiocchi shrugged. "Even if it's a false trail, even if Pavesi's dead and is floating down the Po, it'd still mean my getting out of here. Getting time to think. Getting my life in perspective."

"Ask Scola. Maybe she needs to get her life in perspective, too."

"I doubt if she'd accept without you."

"You can always ask her."

"Perhaps you could ask her for me, Piero."

"And then have you reproaching me for making your existence even more complicated?"

"You'd be doing me a favor."

"I don't do favors, Maiocchi."

"Never?"

Trotti rubbed his chin. "If I do, I do them for my friends."

"What friends?"

"Precisely," Trotti said.

77: MILAN

THE TRAIN STOPPED and Trotti looked up from the *Provincia Padana* that he held open on his knees. He looked out of the window at the backs of humdrum houses, at minute gardens and, wedged between two brick walls, at a bowling alley, now empty beneath the dull, grey sky.

Then the train started to move again and a few minutes later, it pulled into the suffused light of the station. Magagna was at the end of the platform standing beside a service truck. He looked up through his sunglasses and smiled as he caught sight of Trotti.

For once Magagna was well-shaved. "What news of Pisa?"

On the locomotive, an alligator had been painted on to the vast casing. The animal appeared to be running in the wrong direction, as if it were in a hurry to return to Genoa, Savona, Ventimiglia and the warmth of the Ligurian coast. As if it wanted to escape the cold and the damp of Milan.

"No developments."

There was disappointment behind the sunglasses. "What do the doctors think?"

"Very little. Anna Ermagni hasn't left Pisanelli's side."

"True love."

Together they pushed through the crowds—there were always crowds at the Stazione Centrale—and took the escalator.

"You think it's my fault, Magagna?"

"What?"

The car was parked on the forecourt, among the yellow taxis. The right wheels of the Alfa were up on the curb. Two taxi drivers were standing on the pavement, peering peevishly at the plates.

Magagna gave them a toothy, vulpine grin and flashed his ID. Trotti climbed into the car.

"Pisanelli's known you for years, commissario. He knew what he was letting himself in for."

Neither man spoke.

While Magagna drove along the Corso Buenos Aires, Trotti looked at the city, deadened under the winter sky. The snow had disappeared, melting before a warmer front from the south. Milan appeared shabby.

"Over there, commissario. You can get out. I'll find somewhere to park."

Trotti climbed out of the car at Porta Nuova. He banged his bruised arm against the door frame and gently swore as he crossed the road.

The London School was on the sixth floor of a nondescript building in via Manzoni. Trotti took the lift and stepped out into the vestibule. A woman looked up when he buzzed. She pressed a button and he stepped through the revolving glass doors.

"Commissario Trotti for Signora Coddrington."

"I'm afraid Signora Coddrington is not here."

"Signora Coddrington is expecting me."

The woman seemed surprised. With an embarrassed smile she gestured for Trotti to sit down on the sofa. With the other hand, she punched numbers on her telephone.

"Pisanelli was sulking."

"I beg your pardon."

Trotti looked up at the woman. "I'm sorry." He smiled sheepishly. "I was talking to myself."

She nodded understandingly. "Signora Coddrington will be along in a few minutes. Perhaps you'd like to wait for her in her classroom. This way." Moving briskly away from her desk and telephone, she led Trotti down a corridor that smelt of paint and into a small classroom.

The same classroom Pisanelli and he had visited on Friday.

There were no windows. The room was well lit by concealed overhead lighting. Trotti lowered himself on to one of the classroom seats.

"You'd care for a cup of tea?"

Trotti nodded. "And if you have any of that ginger cake . . ."

Trotti waited for over five minutes.

For somebody who gave little importance to the niceties of legal parking, Magagna was taking his time.

"Ah!" Mary Coddrington exclaimed as she bustled into the room. With a theatrical sigh she set down the pile of books that she was carrying. She shook Trotti's hand and slid on to the desk in front of the blackboard. "I hope I haven't kept you waiting." She was wearing jeans.

Trotti shook his head.

The English teacher was pretty, despite the wrinkles of fatigue at the corner of her eyes. Pleasant, even features. The face had managed to keep a childish innocence. Innocence and a strange buoyancy.

Trotti said, "You should never have lied to me, signora."

78: Shakespeare

"Everybody lies."

"A wretched, medieval country. That's what you called Italy, signora."

She smiled sardonically. "I didn't realize you were so sensitive. So patriotic."

"Can I suppose, signora, you don't lie in your own country?"

"It all depends." She made a gesture of exasperation. "I lie when I need something. Or when I'm scared."

"I don't see what you needed from me."

"Absolutely nothing."

"I certainly find it difficult to believe I scare you—a pretty, intelligent woman like you."

"What lie are you talking about, commissario?"

"You loved Turellini. It's what you said and I was quite happy to believe you."

"I didn't lie. Not about Carlo." Her face softened and the corners of her lips were pulled by regret. "I loved Carlo—I loved him more than life itself." She added, "I still do, if it's of any interest to you."

"How do you explain your lies?"

She shook her head in incomprehension. The blonde hair—the rain-washed mousy blonde hair of the English, strangely beautiful in the way it set off Mary Coddrington's features—danced with the sudden movement.

"That last night with Turellini. You remember?"

"Of course I remember."

"You never slept with him. That was a lie, signora. You merely ruffled the sheets for the benefit of the Carabinieri at Segrate. All very moving, of course. Romeo and Juliet, May and September. But you didn't fool anybody."

"Other than myself." The Englishwoman made a brief gesture. "I didn't lie. I couldn't lie about Carlo because his memory's too precious. May and September but for us both it was like June. It was like—"

"Why the pretence? And why couldn't you sleep in the same bed as the man you supposedly loved?"

"We quarrelled."

"That night?"

"Every night—and most of the time we were together. Those last three months, Carlo and I weren't together very much. The quarreling became unbearable."

"That doesn't sound quite like Romeo and Juliet."

The smile was sorrowful. "Unless I'm mistaken, it was a compatriot of mine who wrote Romeo and Juliet. A compatriot who knew all about love." She then said something in English.

Trotti frowned unhappily.

"I think, commissario, you should enroll in one of our courses. A knowledge of the language of Shakespeare could be profitable. Even for a policeman."

"Why did you quarrel with the one man you loved? Can Shakespeare explain that?"

She gave him a sad glance and then tapped her belly. "The pharmaceutical companies should be able to tell you."

"What pharmaceutical companies?"

"I told you—endometriosis."

"What's that?"

"I've aways had problems—from the moment my body started changing."

"And?"

"There'd been another man. A man that I loved almost a much as I loved Carlo. When I was a lot younger, when I thought I had all the time in the world. But in the end, it was no good. You see, a child's the cement that keeps the bricks of a marriage together. Do you have children, commissario?"

He allowed himself a brief, proud smile. "My daughter's expecting her second some time in the spring."

The Englishwoman nodded approvingly. "For Carlo's sake, just as much as mine, I knew there had to be children."

"That's why you didn't sleep with him?"

"I was taking a certain drug for my problem."

"I don't speak the language of Shakespeare."

"I'd tried almost everything else, commissario. There was a time when I spent more time in doctors' waiting rooms or flat on my back, with my knees apart, in their hospital surgeries, than I spent at home. It's true, I did say Italy's a medieval country—but after all these years of a pregnancy that refused to come, it was an Italian doctor who finally identified my problem as endometriosis. It was he who put me on the drug treatment."

"Carlo Turellini?"

She shook her head. "A gynecologist near Rho."

"You still haven't told me why you didn't sleep with Carlo Turellini the night before he was murdered. You lied to the Carabinieri and you lied to me."

"I was afraid."

"Of what?"

"To an outsider, it might've appeared our affair was on the rocks. I'm surprised the maid didn't say anything." A soft smile. "What a sweet girl. I don't think I was very pleasant to her, either. In all fairness, there's a lot that can be said about this country."

Trotti nodded and speaking in English, said, "Big Italy."

"Not least the warmth of the people. It's true I come from a country where the police are unarmed, where people stand in queues and where nobody'll hoot at you if you take time in crossing the road. But in Italy, I have found something very special."

"Good coffee?"

"Something unique and for which I'll always remain grateful. In your country—"

"Medieval country."

"In your country I've found the warmth of the Italian people. Even in this cold, foggy city of Milan—colder and foggier than London could ever be and a hundred times more polluted—there's a warmth that's very special. A smile at the baker's, a welcoming "buondì" in the bar where nobody's ever seen you before. The gentle hand of the lady beside you in the tram—and that resigned, cynical love of life so common to you all. You Italians are realistic—but affectionate. Can't you understand why I needed to have a child in your country?"

"Not sleeping in the same bed couldn't have been particularly conducive to reproduction."

"You understand fast, commissario—but that was the whole point. As a human being, I was unbearable. I was unpleasant with my colleagues and my pupils. I was unpleasant with everybody. Even with the maid, bless her heart. But for poor Carlo, it was a thousand times worse. He was there all the time and I couldn't stand him. Neither the sight nor the smell. I knew it was the drug—it's a synthetic male hormone and I could feel it transforming my body."

"Why?"

Mary Coddrington gave a girlish giggle. "Why? Because by temporarily changing my sex, by putting my uterus to sleep, the drugs allowed my body to heal. The growths on the uterus wall—the growths that had already provoked two miscarriages—they could now heal. Heal and disappear. Of course, there was a price to pay. I became a monster. I don't think I'm an aggressive person by nature, but with the drug I became—for the space of several months—a man." A snort of amusement. "A man or a monster—it's probably the same thing."

"That's why you lied?"

"For the previous ten days, we'd done nothing but quarrel. There were times when I was violent, quite hysterical. I was supposed to tell those Carabinieri that?"

"The truth shouldn't hurt."

"In this backward, medieval country? Even Carlo, who knew what I was taking, didn't really understand. Even Carlo thought I'd genuinely changed, that I didn't love him anymore. If he'd gone with another woman at that time, I would have forgiven him. I was loathsome." The Englishwoman paused, looking around the classroom as if seeing it for the first time. "You know what?"

"Tell me, signora."

"At the time of sweet Carlo's death, the sight of him slumped in the seat of that Mercedes—it's a horrible thing to say, but I swear inside me there was a voice telling me it was better that way. A man's voice, the deep voice of the testosterone coursing through my blood." She looked at Trotti. "I stopped the drug that day. Not much point anymore. As I recovered my femininity, I realized I'd lost my one hope in life. Carlo, sweet Carlo, for whom I'd been preparing my body—he was dead, murdered by that evil old woman."

79: London

"AND BASSI?"

"What about him?"

"Another lie, signora."

She gave an amused, girlish laugh. "I lied?"

Magagna had finally arrived, entering the classroom at the same time as the secretary with a pot of tea. He now sat like a dutiful pupil at one of the desks, dipping the slice of ginger cake into the cup of tea and milk.

"The night Bassi was murdered, people came to his apartment and they were looking for something. They turned everything upside down. They were looking for something that could be slid between the sheets of a paper or behind a photograph. Or between the pages of a book."

The Englishwoman looked at him in silence. She held the saucer in one hand and Trotti had the impression that the hand trembled.

"Something that these people assumed Bassi had in his possession. And they wanted it back. They wanted it back so badly that they had to silence him for good. With a bullet through the head."

"What's that got to do with me?"

"Absolutely nothing, signora. Except that you called Bassi after his departure."

"I called him?"

"You left a message on the answering machine. A message reminding Bassi he had a rendezvous with you."

There was silence in the room. Silence other than the sound of Magagna placing the soggy cake in his mouth. He shifted his glasses up on to the top of his head, no doubt to prevent their misting in the steam of the hot tea.

"Well?"

"Well what, commissario?"

"I believe Bassi was not quite the fool everyone took him to be. I believe he suspected Turellini's murder was the result of professional jealousies."

"Carlo didn't talk about that sort of thing."

"I don't believe you, signora. Everybody talks. There comes a time when we all have to let off some pressure. And I'm sure even before you ever took your hormone treatment, Turellini had mentioned his problems to you. After all, his problems would be your problems."

The woman said nothing.

"I believe Bassi realized you knew a lot more than you pretended. I also believe he'd found out about your strange behavior. Bassi had worked for me. He had a lot of failings—he accepted criticism badly and he was unsure of himself. His lack of self-assurance was one of the reasons for his always having a hand up some woman's skirt. But Bassi never struck me as being a complete fool. Like me, he's a peasant. But whereas I'm from the hills, he's from the plain. You know, it's not because you don't straighten your tie and because you wear a suit that you're a city dweller. In some ways Bassi was slow. But he had the peasant's cunning. And he had enough time to find out about you."

She said nothing.

"You gave him something."

"What?"

"I don't know. But it was you who gave it to him and it was because of the document and the knowledge it contained that Bassi was murdered."

She had begun to shake her head and the brown-blonde hair.

"I suspect it was a copy of the accounts of the Cisalpina Foundation. Perhaps it was that—probably something that Carlo Turellini had left in his safe."

"Why should I give anything to Bassi?" Her voice was querulous.

"Because Bassi threatened to tell the Carabinieri about how things had been between you and Turellini for the weeks preceding his murder. You really think the maid didn't talk? You really think a detective like Bassi, with little else to do with his time—you think he didn't know about that?"

Silence.

"Bassi's mistake was to privilege his *cherchez la femme*. Perhaps mistake's not the right word. Whatever. He wasted a lot of time barking up an entire series of wrong trees. But no sooner had he changed the focus of his inquiry than suddenly everything changed. All hell was let loose. The Palazzo di Giustizia warned him off the case. People started making oblique threats and in frustration he went to *Vissuto*. Which was as wise as signing his own death certificate."

The trembling of the pale hand had ceased but it now occurred to Trotti that she was not the beautiful woman that he had seen before him only a few minutes before. She was frail, a woman fast approaching middle age and aware of her own failures and frailty.

It was her smile that made her appear young and now Mary Coddrington was no longer smiling.

"No, signora, you have nothing to worry about. You didn't kill Fabrizio Bassi. I'm not accusing you of that. You gave him a document that was in all probability the direct cause of his death. But even without it, he'd've gotten himself killed. Sooner or later, Bassi'd've got himself killed because he wouldn't listen to the people warning him off."

She took a deep breath. "I have a class in an hour. I would like to go to lunch." With a white hand on the edge of the desk, she slipped into a standing position.

"You didn't kill anybody. But you lied to me, signora."

She said nothing. She scrutinized Trotti's face while almost imperceptibly she shook her head. It was as if she were searching for something that she could not find. She looked weary. Then she turned away and faced the blackboard.

Trotti spoke to her back. "If you'd told me the truth, perhaps my young colleague wouldn't have been driven off the road by the same people who murdered Fabrizio Bassi. Perhaps my young colleague wouldn't now be lying in a hospital bed in a deep coma, with only a cardiograph to prove that he's still in this world."

Somebody had written the word *London* on the blackboard.

She was staring at the word, no doubt wishing that she was there. Wishing that she was anywhere except in Milan on a cold winter's morning.

80: Track Record

SHE CAME TO the door of the apartment. Her nervous glance went from Trotti to Magagna. She was wearing the same necklace as before over the top of a black cardigan.

"Polizia di Stato," Magagna announced, smiling while briefly showing his identification.

She nodded unhappily. She took a step backwards. "You'd better come in."

Trotti and Magagna followed her into the large living room.

"Please be seated." Signora Lucchi added, "I do hope you're not going to be long. I'm expecting some friends over."

Trotti glanced briefly at the modern paintings in their old-fashioned frames.

Signora Lucchi made a movement of her hand to her necklace. "What do you want this time? Commissario Trotti, isn't it? I thought you'd seen my lawyer."

"Avvocato Regni offered me employment with you." Trotti smiled.

"So he informed me." A corroborating nod of the small, birdlike head. The woman pulled at a long sash and immediately the Filipino majordomo appeared. "Coffee for these gentlemen please, Pablo," she said, without turning to look at the small man. "You can bring me a glass of Fiuggi mineral water."

The butler left the room.

"Then you've decided to help us identify my ex-husband's murderer?"

"Why did you engage Signor Bassi, signora?" Trotti asked.

There was a tightening of the lines around her mouth. "You think Signor Bassi's unfortunate death is in some way connected with the inquiries he'd been carrying out into my ex-husband's death?"

"Why did you engage him?"

"Avvocato Regni knew the man. Regni seemed to think he was efficient."

"Very strange, signora. Most people seem to think Bassi was a fool. A womanizer and a fool, best left to divorce work. Far too slow for an important murder inquiry. You yourself told me he was incompetent. Like something in one of those awful American series on *ReteQuattro*."

She placed one hand on the knee of her pleated skirt. "I see you are entrusted with a murder inquiry."

Trotti brushed away the sarcasm with a gesture of his hand. "Bassi worked for me. I don't like seeing colleagues being murdered."

"I believe he was thrown out of the Polizia di Stato long before he was killed."

"Yet you employed him." Trotti gestured with outspread fingers. "Instead of going to one of the agencies here in Milan, you chose a provincial private detective with an inglorious track record."

"You must consult Avvocato Regni. He makes all these decisions."

"You're sure?"

She nodded.

"Regni came to my office a few days ago, signora. He was hoping I could help you in a private capacity. Avvocato Regni assured me it was you who wanted to employ me."

"Really?"

"You employed Bassi because you had no choice. It was your sister-in-law, Carlo Turellini's sister, who insisted on a parallel inquiry. The police seemed to be getting nowhere and she wanted to know who killed her brother."

"Understandably."

"Unfortunately for her, she decided to share the expense of a private detective with you. And you chose Bassi."

"Why, commissario?"

"You knew about Bassi. Indirectly, most probably, through your husband who was for a long time a friend of Dr. Quarenghi's. You knew about Bassi's affair with the Viscontini woman. Mayor

Viscontini and Quarenghi are brothers-in-law. Employing Bassi let you off the hook."

A quizzical frown. "I don't think I understand."

"You didn't want any inquiry. Why should you? But your sister-in-law insisted and since you were paying your share, you chose somebody incompetent. Incompetent whom you hoped to buy off."

"Incompetent in what way?"

"Incompetent in that he never asked himself the first question any self-respecting private detective should always ask."

Her head moved sideways. "Which question?"

"Bassi never wondered why you employed him. He never questioned your motives. Or if indeed he did, he allowed himself to be influenced by the easy money. Good, easy money."

"Are you accusing me of wanting to influence Signor Bassi's inquiry? At a time when I was paying his fees?" She gave a chirping laugh. "Is that what you're saying?"

Trotti looked at her.

"Well?"

"Quite simply I'm saying you murdered Carlo Turellini, Signora Lucchi. You murdered your ex-husband."

"An interesting theory."

"Since his sister insisted upon employing a private detective—you had no call to be very frightened by the Carabinieri's inquiry—you helped her choose the man least likely ever to get to the truth. Of course, you were quite right."

"Right?" she echoed.

"By the time Bassi was murdered, a bullet through his head, it'd never occurred to him Dr. Turellini had been murdered by his ex-wife. By the very woman who was paying Bassi's fees." Trotti glanced at Magagna. "Bassi died as ignorant as he'd lived."

Signora Lucchi laughed and the butler entered with two cups of coffee, a bottle of mineral water and a plate of biscuits on a silver tray.

81: Surly

THE BUTLER BOWED and left but before he closed the door, the cat entered the room, walking prudently, one paw in front of the other, its surly glance appraising Signora Lucchi's visitors.

"Bassi spent valuable time looking for a slighted lover. It never occurred to him the slighted lover was the woman employing him."

"Me?" Signora Lucchi hid a slight shudder. "Mere hypothesis, commissario."

"After a year of wasting good money on an inquiry you obviously never wanted, you needed to be rid of Bassi. You wanted to put the whole thing behind you. Your sister-in-law couldn't complain you hadn't done your best. At last you could decently dismiss Bassi. Which is precisely why the man started worrying."

Signora Lucchi shook her head. "You're merely surmising."

"Bassi saw you were going to turn off the tap and he went into overdrive. Afraid of having to go back to doing divorces. He'd always seen himself as an American detective. He'd hoped this case would make him rich and famous. Famous for succeeding where the police had failed. And rich because you'd offered him good money to find Carlo Turellini's killer. But with the threat of your dropping him, Bassi started looking into the possibility not of a *crime passionnel* but a murder among the medical community."

She nodded authoritatively. "I once believed my husband was killed because of professional jealousies."

Trotti laughed sardonically. "It was Bassi—not Carlo Turellini—who was killed because of the professional jealousies between your husband and Quarenghi."

She said nothing.

"Finally Bassi reached the same conclusion as the Carabinieri. It was precisely because Quarenghi believed Bassi was on to him that Bassi was murdered. Murdered with a bullet through the head, signora."

"A professional killing," she nodded.

"Bassi's was a professional killing. Turellini was murdered by a woman."

"What makes you say that?"

"Signora, you killed your ex-husband."

"What on earth makes you say a thing like that?" She turned, seeking moral support from Magagna who sat in silence, watching her from behind his dark glasses.

"A professional gunman would never use a piece of equipment dating from the war in Spain."

"You really believe I shot Carlo Turellini, commissario?"

"You'd grown up together. You'd had a daughter together, and although Turellini had divorced you, you weren't particularly upset. Divorced, but Turellini still loved you in his way. There was still something between you. You told me he'd ring you regularly whenever there was a problem. It was always to you he'd turn in time of need. He made you feel wanted. Appreciated."

Her voice was unexpectedly soft with reminiscence. "We should never've broken up. It was his fault. Carlo just didn't know how to be happy with the present."

"You loved him?"

"Of course I loved him. I still do."

"As long as Turellini was with Signora Quarenghi, you weren't apprehensive. The friendship between you and your ex-husband remained. Even when Turellini started living with the English-woman, you weren't particularly concerned. A younger body than yours. As you wittily observed, Mary Coddrington wouldn't know how to heat water. She wouldn't even know how to shit straight. You felt she couldn't give him what you'd always been able to give him."

"Why on earth then should I kill the only man I'd ever loved?"

The cat suddenly leaped on to Magagna's lap. Magagna sat back in surprise, then started stroking the animal. The cat purred with gratification. Magagna asked, "You saw your ex-husband just before his death?"

Signora Lucchi glanced at Magagna before turning back to
Trotti. "Tell me why I should want to harm the one man I loved."

"She was going to be pregnant."

"She?"

Trotti said, "Your ex-husband was always in such a hurry.
Always running after things."

"So?"

"Suddenly he was learning to slow down. I don't suppose he'd
been much of a father to your daughter Carla. At the time I imagine
he was concerned about his career. That's the way we men are. But
here, nearly twenty years later, he was going to have another child.
And that you couldn't bear."

"What proof can you possibly have?" She tilted her head as she
looked at Commissario Trotti.

"What was it you'd always told him? Something about seizing
the day. For once he was following your advice. Carlo Turellini was
learning to enjoy life. The simple pleasures of the family."

"What makes you think I'd be jealous of that silly Englishwoman?"

"There was also the question of money."

"Commissario, I have enough money."

"Money for Carla until she was twenty-one. But she'd soon be
twenty-one and with a child on the way, you realized there'd be a
new will. No reason for your husband not to change his will now
he was starting a new life."

Signora Lucchi hesitated before shaking her head. "Carlo married me because of my money. I didn't need anything from him."

"Signora Lucchi, you told me it was important Carla should get
her fair share of Turellini's wealth."

"I said that? You must have an amazing memory."

"Didn't you tell me it was for your daughter Carla's sake you
decided to hire Signor Bassi?"

A wry smile moved the narrow lips. "You're trying to suggest I
was responsible for Carlo's murder?"

"You killed him, signora. It was premeditated. You got up early
one morning and you went to his place at Segrate. You waited for
him to drive through the gates of his villa. I imagine when he saw
you, Carlo Turellini was surprised. He stopped and you shot him.
The first bullet jammed. The second went wide. Then you forced
yourself to concentrate on his cowardice—and how he was doing
your daughter out of her inheritance. The third bullet killed him."

"I did that?"

It was suddenly very silent in the house in the via Montenapoleone. Just the gentle purring of the cat.

Trotti looked at her sharply. "Of course you killed him. And Bassi was either too incompetent or too greedy ever to consider you as the culprit."

"You can't possibly have any proof."

"I don't need proof."

A hesitation. "You don't want to send me to prison?"

"Not necessarily. It all depends upon you."

Signora Lucchi looked at Trotti carefully. Magagna was also looking at him.

"I imagine you have watertight alibis, Signora Lucchi."

"I was with Avvocato Regni the morning my ex-husband was shot down."

"Of course. An interesting man, Avvocato Regni."

"You really think I was jealous of the Englishwoman to the point of killing Carlo? A blonde idiot and that's why my husband lived with her. Carlo needed to be surrounded by young and beautiful and worshipping women. By pretty idiots." She gave a brief cackle. "And now you want to arrest me for murdering the man I loved?"

The cat jumped from Magagna's lap to the floor.

"Well, commissario?"

"I'm sure we could come to an agreement, Signora Lucchi. Some form of compromise. We are both reasonable people."

82: Mani Pulite

SIGNORA LUCCHI GOT up and went to the window, then she turned to look at Trotti. "An agreement, commissario?" Amusement hovered along the thin lips.

For a few moments Trotti and the rich woman stared at each other without speaking.

(The old, moneyed class of Milan, more bourgeois than aristo-cratic. And very rich.)

She turned back to the window and stared down at the silent traffic and the crowds in via Montenapoleone. (Impervious to Mani Pulite.)

"You met Tenente Pisanelli, signora. He was with me when I first came to see you."

"A charming man."

"He's now in a deep coma."

"Ah."

"A coma from which he may never awake."

"I'm truly sorry to hear that." Signora Luciana Lucchi faced Trotti. She placed her hands behind her back and leaned against the sill. "He didn't behave like other policemen."

"I really don't know how other policemen behave."

"He certainly seemed charming."

Trotti said nothing.

She coughed. "An agreement, commissario?" She hesitated, then, taking a step forward, she said, "I haven't been totally honest with you."

"You haven't been at all honest."

"It's true I asked Avvocato Regni to contact you. Which he did. He consequently informed me you're intending to retire."

A nod. "In September."

"He also informed me you may be having difficulties with a house you share in the OltrePò."

"Avvocato Regni's very well-informed."

"I was wondering whether I could in any way be of aid to you."

"Pierangelo Pisanelli's a friend. As much a friend as a commissario in the Polizia di Stato can hope to have friends. We've known each other, Pisa and I, for a long time. We've done some useful work together. His fiancée is my goddaughter. We know each other well. Our respective qualities as much as our failings."

"I got the impression he understood women."

"The evening Tenente Pisanelli and I were driven off the road—that very evening he took me to task. He couldn't understand why I was allowing myself to get involved with Bassi. With Bassi and his inquiry into your ex-husband's death." Trotti replaced the cup back on its thin saucer and slipped a licorice sweet into his mouth. "He seemed to think I was attracted by your money."

Signora Luciana Lucchi returned to the seat. "I have money," she said simply. "That's a fact of life I learned to live with a long time ago. A fact of life that can have both positive and negative aspects. Now tell me, commissario. In what way can I be of use?"

"I was surprised by Pisanelli's attitude." There was no amusement in the brief laughter. "Surprised and hurt. I can remember blushing in his cold little French car. At that moment, I felt I was losing an old friend. Or even a son. The accusation . . ." Trotti glanced at Magagna. "Silly, isn't it? Pisanelli's lying in the hospital now in Rianimazione. I'm not sure I'll ever be able to speak to him again. Not sure I'll be able to tell him he was one of the best. That he'd come to be a surrogate son to me. That's why I was so often harsh and demanding. Because in so many ways Pisa's just like me."

Magagna was smiling as he mechanically stroked the cat. He had taken his sunglasses off and his eyes were on Trotti's face. "Self-doubt, commissario?"

"The way Pisanelli judged me on Saturday night as we were driving back from Alessandria in the snow, the way he attributed the motives to me was like a knife in the back."

There was an uneasy silence. Signora Lucchi turned away and again stared down on to the street.

The cat purred beneath Magagna's strokes.

"Tell me how I can help you, commissario."

"We all like to think we're above money, that we have values other than those of wealth. But once you've got used to a comfortable existence—it's hard to return to the bad old days."

"What precisely is it you want?"

Trotti took a deep breath. "Dr. Turellini was a specialist in clinical medicine?"

She frowned. "Why do you ask?"

"You didn't answer my question."

"Carlo Turellini held his specialty in obstetrics from your university. Dr. Quarenghi's the specialist in clinical medicine. Tell me, Commissario Trotti, what do you want?"

"There'd be no point in helping them in Rianimazione. The big pharmaceutical companies and the people who manufacture the scanners and the ECGS have already sponsored those places. High profile and that's the way Tangentopoli's always worked. A meretricious society based on the meretricious values of advertising and public relations. A Berlusconi society."

"I don't think I understand."

Trotti folded his arms. He sucked at the sweet. "I see no reason for your going to prison."

"I'm glad to hear it." The woman gave a chuckle but her eyes remained watchful, not leaving Trotti's face.

"Prison's not going to bring back anybody. Not Turellini and not Fabrizio Bassi. If for one moment I felt it would help Pisanelli, I'd happily throw you into prison. Or into the polluted Lambro where Bassi died. But Pisanelli's being on a bed with pipes running in and out of him has got little to do with you. More to do with my peasant stubbornness."

Magagna glanced sharply at Trotti.

Trotti continued. "You tell me your ex-husband wasn't a broad-minded man. I'd like to think he was a good man."

"A very good man."

"A good man who was above corruption. A good man who resisted the siren calls of Tangentopoli, of our partitocrazia, of this hobbling First Republic."

"You understand Carlo Turellini."

"Pisa's fiancee is with him at the hospital, Signora Lucchi. Thanks no doubt to the generosity of the pharmaceutical companies, there's a bedroom where she can sleep. She's there at his bedside, holding his hand. Praying and hoping. She's always loved Pisa—ever since she was a little girl and Pisanelli was new to the police."

"I'm sure your young man will pull through."

"Modern medicine's holistic—I believe that's the right word. Excuse me, I'm an ignorant old man from the hills." A gesture of modesty. "Doctors now say that the battle has to be won emotionally. The battle has to be won in the the patient's head, with his desire to survive. By being surrounded by people who love and care for him."

"That was my husband's first concern. Carlo was a marvelous doctor. A man who cared. Which explains the tremendous success of the Clinica Cisalpina."

"What better legacy, signora, than a gift of this sort?"

She frowned.

"Not a legacy to the high-profile university clinics. Your husband was of humble origins. I can imagine nothing more befitting his humility and his devotion to the alleviation of human suffering than a gift to our Pediatria."

The birdlike mouth had fallen open.

"At last a decent place for all the victims of child abuse. All those hurt children who without the intervention of doctors and the caring professions are doomed to carry their suffering on their backs. Like snails carrying their shells. I can't imagine a better, more worthy homage to your husband than the Turellini Child Abuse Institute. With a couple of bedrooms for the mothers and families to stay close by the children."

83: Grison

IT WAS ALREADY getting dark by the time they reached the Questura.

The place seemed empty.

Magagna and Trotti got into the lift and stepped out on the third floor.

The blonde woman raised her head. She gave a perfunctory smile of her thick red lips.

"News of Pisanelli?"

She shook her head. "Everybody's at the memorial service. I thought you'd gone too, Commissario Trotti." She took a large envelope from under the telephone console. "Commissario Maiocchi left you this. Said he'd be back by six at the latest."

The two men went down the corridor into Trotti's office.

It was strangely quiet. A fog was slowly rising from the river, beyond the window.

"In a way I regret not going to the service, Magagna."

"It would have been the decent thing to do."

"I imagine they're all there. Our Lega Lombarda mayor and his councillors. And of course the ex-mayor. And all Viscontini's Socialist friends."

"You're bitter, commissario."

"I'll be going to the hospital on my way home."

"Why are you so bitter?"

"About the Questore?"

"About Viscontini."

"I would have enjoyed seeing Viscontini and his friends bowing

and scraping and crossing themselves. They must be shitting themselves. They're scared out of their wits."

"Dr. Quarenghi's scared. Why the others?"

"I doubt if Quarenghi's been able to skim all that money for
himself. Most of it was going to the politicians, I imagine."

"What politicians?"

"To the Socialist party."

"Why?"

"That's the only explanation to the Questore's suicide. He was
compromised and he saw no alternative."

"There's always an alternative to death."

"Perhaps the Questore wanted to think of himself as an hon-
orable man. Goodness knows why. He's as much responsible for
Pisanelli's coma as if he'd been driving the Volvo himself."

"That's why he killed himself with a plastic bag?"

"Goodness knows what drove him to kill himself. Who can know
what's going on in somebody else's head? He realized he'd soon be
facing charges of gross misconduct. Once the socialists get kicked
out of power in the new elections."

"You really think he was responsible for Pisanelli?"

Trotti took a deep breath. "It was because slush funds were being
recycled for the Socialist party that the Questore had to intervene.
That's why he had Maluccio thrown into jail in Alessandria."

"Why?"

"Why what?"

"What need would Quarenghi have to distribute his money? Why
not keep it for himself?"

"Of course Quarenghi kept a lot of it for himself. As much as
he could. All the siphoning of money to the political parties passes
through various private pockets. Lining those private pockets."

"Why give the money to Viscontini and the city's socialists?"

"Not all the money, Magagna." Trotti sat back in the canvas
armchair. It was cold in the small room and mist rose from his
mouth as he spoke.

"Why give any?"

Trotti laughed. "You think he wanted to lose his position on the
CIP? If he'd been given the job in Rome, it was because Quarenghi
was in the odor of sanctity with the Socialists. Or rather, odor of
Mafia. Not just with the local Socialists but also the Socialists in
Rome. He had to pay them back. That was the tacit deal." Trotti put

his head back. "Tangentopoli, Magagna. Your problem is, you're dealing with Brazilian transvestites and whores. You know all about nipples and nothing about the seamier aspects of human nature."

"The greed's the same." Magagna lit a cigarette. "Just the manifestations that are different."

"Ah! Enjoy the memorial service?"

Magagna turned in the greasy armchair.

Maiocchi had entered the office. Beneath the overcoat, he was wearing a dark suit and a black tie. For once his unruly hair had been neatly brushed. Out of his habitual corduroys, Maiocchi looked a lot older, less like the perennial student.

"You saw the photos, commissario?"

Trotti gestured him to take the free armchair. "Photos?"

Stepping forward, Maiocchi placed a friendly hand on Magagna's shoulder. The unlit pipe was clenched between his teeth. He picked up the large envelope. "Take a look."

Trotti undid the clip and removed three large photographs.

Glossy black-and-white photographs.

The first was of a car wedged against a tree. Trotti could not recognize the make of the car because it had burned. There were no tires, no paint, no windows. The doors had been knocked inwards. The steering wheel appeared bent.

The second photograph was of a carbonized corpse. Or rather, part of a carbonized corpse.

"Who?" Trotti asked, repressing a shudder and raising his eyes to Maiocchi.

Maiocchi shook his head and pointed to the third photograph.

A human hand, partially burned but with a wedding ring encircling the scorched skin of a finger.

"Who's this, Maiocchi?"

"A woman's hand. A woman's wedding ring."

"Pavesi?"

Maiocchi nodded. He appeared tired. "A hiker found the car yesterday. In Switzerland. In the regional park near Pontresina."

"This is Pavesi?"

"Signora Pavesi," Maiocchi corrected him. "No autopsy as yet, but it looks as if the car had been there for ten days at least. Italian plates, probably stolen."

"Signora Pavesi? What was she doing in Switzerland? In a stolen car?"

"She was in the boot. Probably dead before the car was driven from the track thirty meters up the slope." He shrugged. "The lid of the boot opened as the car crashed against the trees."

"And Signor Pavesi?"

"I was hoping you could tell me that."

"Me?" Trotti tapped his chest.

Maiocchi said slowly, "Hoping you'd be accompanying me to Venezuela the day after tomorrow."

"Venezuela?"

"The daughter's already identified the wedding ring. No fingerprints but the Swiss've asked for Signora Pavesi's dental records."

"You think I can really be of use to you, Maiocchi, in Venezuela?"

Maiocchi's face broke into an unexpected grin. "What need do you have for cloudless skies, sunny beaches and palm trees, commissario? I imagine you enjoy the fogs of the Po valley too much."

With the stem of his pipe, he gestured to the thickening darkness outside the empty Questura.

84: Snail

SIGNORA SCOLA HAD left a message asking him to ring her, but a china was what Trotti most needed now.

A china before supper, he told himself, and then the walk to San Matteo. Trotti, who loathed hospitals, told himself it was time he went and sat with Pisanelli. He had been avoiding his duty for too long. He had scarcely spoken to Anna Ermagni other than over the telephone. He needed to tell her that she was always welcome to stay with him and Anna Maria in via Milano.

He needed to tell Pisanelli so many things.

Trotti came out of the main entrance of the Questura.

"You don't want to come to the hospital?"

"Another time, commissario."

"A drink?"

"I'm driving back to Milan. I've got to get home before the children go to bed. They like me to read them their bedtime stories. Or tell them about Pescara."

"Get a posting here, Magagna. I'll be out of your hair after September."

"That's what frightens me."

"Leave Milan before you start falling in love with all your South American transvestites."

They shook hands. "Love to Giovanna, Magagna. Tell her I'll be up to see you all in the new year. And take care. I don't want you being driven off the road."

A debonair wave of his hand. "Unlike Pisa, I drive an Italian car—not a French can of sardines." The burly policeman saluted briskly. "Buona sera, Signor Commissario," Magagna said, and went down the granite steps of the Questura and disappeared into the night.

"Ciao!"

Trotti pulled on the zip of his English jacket and turned into Strada Nuova.

It was dark and the overhead lamps cast their tinted light into the foggy Street. Trotti pulled his scarf up to his chin and headed towards the Po.

His last winter in the Polizia di Stato.

He softly whistled to himself. "Un bel dì di maggio."

Rush hour and the municipal buses rumbled past, heavy with their load of passengers and misted glass. Passengers going home to minestra, Berlusconi and bed.

The Questore was dead.

(*"Piero, Piero—I honestly think I've never met a man like you to take offence. And bear grudges."*)

Trotti took the turning right and heard the voice of a woman.

"Commissario!"

He stopped and turned.

She came towards him, small in her overcoat, the sound of her heels dulled by the wet cobblestones. "You didn't get my message?"

"What message?"

"I was hoping to see you at the service, Piero."

"Other things to do."

Bianca Poveri, the youngest female prison director in Italy, slipped her arm through his and fell into step beside him. "You never could stand the man."

"I'm not a politician. They didn't need me at the service."

The fog dulled every sound, dulled Trotti's voice, dulled the fall of their shoes as they walked, almost in step.

"Your cousin eventually arrived at Linate?"

"Anna Maria took a different plane. She came via Zurich."

"And your cousin Sandro?"

"Anna Maria came for the funeral."

"Another funeral?"

"Sandro's dead," Trotti said flatly. He could feel the damp fog working into his trousers and he longed for the dry cold of the hills.

Perhaps there could be no dry cold of the hills for Trotti, after all.

"Dead? You told me Sandro was your age."

"Sandro died," Trotti said, not wishing to elaborate.

"I'm so sorry."

They turned into Piazza Vittoria and along the empty, echoing porticoes.

Bianca asked, "What about your place in Santa Maria? Weren't you going to retire in the hills with Sandro?"

"Gone."

"What's gone?"

"Sandro incurred a lot of debts," Trotti replied. "More of a gambler than I ever realized."

The door of the Bar Duomo was misted and twinkled with the light beyond. Trotti pushed the brass handle and opened the door for Bianca Poveri to step past him. He noted her musky perfume but it was immediately lost to the other, familiar smells of the bar.

"Accompanied tonight, commissario?" the barman asked cheerfully, catching sight of Trotti through the crowd. "A beautiful lady, I see."

The mirror behind the bar threw back Trotti's smiling image.

A couple of heads nodded an evening salutation as Trotti and Bianca Poveri went to the far table where nobody was sitting.

On the pink cloth of the table lay a discarded copy of the morning's local paper, stiffened by a wooden rod. SUICIDE IN THE QUESTURA. Even without his glasses Trotti could recognize the now-famous photograph of the Questore shaking Bettino Craxi's hand, at the time of the prime minister's visit to the small, hardworking provincial town.

"A drink, Signora Direttrice?"

"Don't you dare call me that." She was wearing pearl earrings and beneath the coat, a black woolen dress that accentuated the youth of her face.

Trotti offered to help her remove the coat but Bianca Poveri shook her head.

Trotti lifted two fingers and mouthed the word two for the waiter.

"I can't stay. Got to get back to Anna Giulia."

"And Alcibiade," Trotti added as he unzipped his jacket. He rubbed his hands, the warmth quickly returning.

"What are you going to do, Piero? About your retirement."

He shrugged. "It's not important."

"And your chickens and your goats?"

"My cousin's staying with me. Last time Anna Maria and I lived together was over fifty years ago when she was a young fiancée, waiting for her man to come back from the wars."

"What are you going to do about your place in Santa Maria? The animals? The rustic life you keep talking about?"

"Don't worry about me. Anyway, September's still a long way off."

"You'll live here in the city?"

"I won't be lonely, that's sure. Anna Maria says she might stay on in Italy after all. She's a widow now. In Holland she rarely sees her grandchildren. I've got my daughter I can see in Bologna. And, as long as I remain married, there's always Agnese's villa on Lake Garda."

"That's what I wanted to see you about."

"About Lake Garda?"

Silent and discreet, the barman had moved from behind the bar and was now transferring a saucer of cashew nuts and two glasses of steaming Elisir di China from a steel tray on to the table. A slice of lemon had been clipped to the rim of each glass.

Bianca Poveri looked at the glass of china and smiled gratefully at Trotti. "Better than a funeral."

The waiter turned on the wall light. "Anything else you need, commissario?"

Trotti shook his head.

"And the lovely lady?"

"I need to get home to my family."

The waiter smiled philosophically, shrugged and picked up an overflowing ashtray. He went away with the crumpled *Provincia Padana* beneath his arm.

"I've been getting a lot of faxes from Trieste, Piero."

"Why?"

"Your Uruguayan friend thinks you can help her."

"I don't think l can help anybody at the moment."

"She's sent a couple more letters."

"I tried to help Eva once. In the end, I had to change all the locks in via Milano."

"They're going to send her back to Uruguay. I gather she was counting on you. She seems to think you can get her a residency permit."

"You were right, Bianca. Like snails and they carry their shells on their backs for the rest of their lives. There's not much that you or I can do about that." He sipped the hot china. "Not much I can do for Eva. Anyway, there's another woman in my life now."

Bianca could not hide her surprise. "A woman? After all these years."

He said nothing.

"A woman, Piero?"

"The longer Anna Maria stays the better. She's a battle axe but she's kind. Proud and stubborn, like all mountain people."

Bianca laughed. "Can I presume to think, Piero Trotti, now you no longer have a place in the hills, now the Questore's left for that other Questura in the sky, and now that your cousin's helping you rediscover all the charms of family life—can I hope you're going to stay on in the Questura?"

"Presume whatever you want."

Bianca Poveri seemed to catch her breath. "They need you, Piero."

"Nobody needs me. Nobody's indispensable."

"Before it's too late. Before the shell grows on their backs and there's nothing you or I or anybody else can do to help them."

Trotti was about to speak.

Bianca was leaning forward. Her face was gentle and attentive, despite the hard lines of her perm. "Stay on, Piero."

Trotti glanced up.

"Mind if I sit down?"

She was standing beside him, her hand placed possessively on his shoulder. Simona Scola smiled as she bent over and lightly kissed Trotti on the cheek. "I do hope you're not flirting with another woman, Piero," she said laughingly. There was no amusement in the glance that she gave the other woman.

Trotti could not contain his smile. His hand stroked her fingers.

Other Titles in the Soho Crime Series